A GOOD NIGHT FOR KILLING

About an hour after dark, the Rebel team began to gather.

Ben had two 9mm Beretta pistols on his web belt and was carrying a Colt 9mm carbine, select fire. Cooper was carrying a Stoner 63 — a 5.56mm belt-fed machine-gun with a 150-round magazine. Jersey carried a CAR-15, select fire. Linda carried a Street-Sweeper, drum-type sawed-off 12-gauge shotgun that was truly awesome in any type of close-in combat. Corrie was carrying a very light packback radio and a CAR-15.

"You know where to go and what to do," Ben said, and jacked a round into his CAR-15. "Move out!"

The Rebels began walking silently toward the darkened town. Only the faint outlines of the buildings were visible in the mist and fog of this quiet Irish night . . . that was about to turn deadly and bloody.

TERROR IN THE ASHES

WILLIAM W. JOHNSTONE

ZEBRA BOOKS
KENSINGTON PUBLISHING CORP.

This novel is a work of fiction. Names, characters, places, and incidents are either products of the author's imagination or are used fictitiously, and any resemblance to actual persons, living or dead, events, or locales is entirely coincidental.

Dedicated to John Cole.

ZEBRA BOOKS

are published by

Kensington Publishing Corp.
475 Park Avenue South
New York, NY 10016

First printing: May, 1992

Printed in the United States of America

Book One

We are so outnumbered there is only one thing to do. We must attack.

Sir Andrew Browne Cunningham

Prologue

Beginning in the last few years of the past millennium, a few months after the entire world was shaken and very nearly destroyed by germ warfare and limited nuclear war, one man rose out of the ashes of despair and with a few others of like mind began building a new society. This man was a walking contradiction. He was a visionary, a warrior, a philosopher, a teacher. He was so controversial that his own brother tried to kill him.

When a new government of the United States was hastily thrown together, the leaders declared this man an enemy and put a bounty on his head. The government destroyed the society he had built and thought they had killed him.

They were wrong.

Again this man rose out of the ashes and again he started building his army to fight the central government of the United States, now so corrupt and dictatorial some were comparing it to Hitler's reign of terror decades past.

The central government called the freedom fighters scum and traitors and malcontents. Those who supported the efforts of the breakaways called them Rebels.

The Rebels wrested the power from those who had turned what had once been the greatest country in the world into no more than a prison camp. Then the sickness struck the land. No one knew where it came from or how to fight it. The sickness spread world-wide, and that was the last blow for an already reeling earth. When the tide of death had run its course, there was not one stable government left on earth.

Chaos was the order of the day. Robbery and rape and murder and enslavement and assault became commonplace. Outlaws and warlords took control. The world was suddenly plunged back into medieval thinking.

Except for a few hundred men and women called Rebels who had kept their heads down and their wits about them and who followed the teachings of one man.

The Rebels then began the job of clearing the nation of human crud and crap and restoring order. It would take them years to accomplish that. But accomplish it they did. They fought the Russian Striganov until he joined the Rebels. They fought the mercenary forces of a man called West until he, too, realized he was on the wrong side and joined the Rebels. The Rebels fought mutants and wackos, religious nuts and gangs that numbered in the thousands. Still the Rebels grew and conquered, taking back the land from the thugs and returning it to men and women who wanted to live in peace.

The Rebels fought Sister Voleta and her forces of evil and destroyed them all. They fought the international terrorist Khamsin and ground him and his thousands of troops under the heel of democracy. The Rebels fought the cannibalistic sect

8

known as the Night People and wiped them from the face of America.

The Rebels cleared the countryside, then turned their massive war machine toward the great cities that still remained in the land of the free and the home of the brave that had once been called America.

Slowly but surely, in one bloody battle after another, the Rebels reclaimed the land. They systematically destroyed the decaying cities and the lawless gangs that occupied them. The greatest terrorist and mercenary the world had ever known, Lan Vilar, joined in the efforts to kill the dream of the Rebels. The Rebels hunted him down, along with Kenny Parr and Ashley and Khamsin, and destroyed them in Alaska.

The leader of the Rebels — which now numbered fifteen battalions strong — established outposts around the battered and bloody nation. Bastions of hope and freedom. There were a half a dozen outposts in every state, towns that had running water and sewerage systems that worked and street lights and schools and churches and libraries. Places where crime was nonexistent. The Rebels did not allow crime. It was not tolerated. Neither was bigotry. But acceptance in the Rebel way was not a right. It had to be earned. If you contributed nothing, nothing was what you got.

If you were able to work, you worked. There was no free ride in the Rebel system. No police officer had to read anyone his rights; an individual's rights were taught in public schools. From kindergarten on up. Public schools taught much more than readin', writin', and 'rithmetic. Young people were taught to respect the rights of others, they were taught to respect the land and the critters that lived in the woods and forests. Kids were taught the basics — such as, when one encountered a No Trespassing sign, you stopped.

Right there. What few written laws the Rebels had on the books were not there to be broken, they were there to be obeyed.

The Rebels took the complications out of society and brought it all back to the basics. It did not take a newcomer long to understand that life in any Rebel-held town was easy and fulfilling and good . . . as long as you obeyed the rules. Disobeying the rules could get a person quickly hurt or seriously dead. And there was no legal recourse. Lawsuits were practically unheard of. The Rebels frowned on lawsuits.

From the outset, way back before the central government put a bounty on the leader's head, way back when the Tri-States were formed and running smoothly, the Rebels' system of government was called a commonsense form of living together. Right away, a lot of people knew they could never live under Rebel rule.

Any Rebel society was based on order and justice. Not law and order—order and justice. Take a life through carelessness, contempt, disregard for the basic rights of others, lawlessness, or drunkenness, and you paid for it with a life. Yours.

Medical care was free in a Rebel society. So was education from kindergarten through college. Kindergarten through high school was mandatory. College was not. The Rebels understood that some people are just not mentally cut out for college. So vo-tech training was offered for them.

Physical education was stressed in any Rebel society. Every student received ten hours of supervised exercise a week. All sorts of games were allowed, but with this warning: "It is only a game. Play it, do your best, then forget about it. Anybody who would fight over the outcome of a game is a fool."

Life in the outposts settled down once the states

were, for the most part, cleared of any who had even the slightest leanings toward lawlessness. The man who was in charge of the Rebels and who wrote the laws the Rebels lived by was a hard man. That was quickly learned by the criminal element.

The Rebels lived in a society that had almost totally eradicated crime within their towns and communities. Criminals either stopped their lawless ways, allowing themselves to be educated and retrained, or the Rebels killed them. It was just that simple. Strict, but extremely effective.

The Rebel army was made up of everybody who lived in a Rebel society. Everybody over the age of sixteen was in the Army. Period. You either joined the Army, or were kicked out from under the umbrella of Rebel protection and put out on your own, your I.D. cards destroyed. And with that action, you could not receive medical aid or buy supplies from any outpost. When the towns came under attack, and they occasionally did, every person living there was expected to take part in the defense of that outpost.

There were many thousands of people who lived in what used to be called America and refused to be a part of the Rebel system of government. No one was forced to join. More people lived outside the Rebel-controlled towns than in them. But that was slowly changing as those outside received absolutely no help whatsoever from the Rebels. Life was difficult enough inside the Rebel-held zones; outside the cleared zones it was dangerous and extremely chancy.

So in dribbles and handfuls and sometimes entire communities, citizens would contact the Rebels, saying, "Okay. We can't make it out here without you people. What do we do?"

And the answer was always the same. "Obey the rules and understand that they are there for every-

11

body. When it comes to the administration of justice, the mayor receives no better treatment than the shoe repair person. You'll find it's really very simple."

And they usually did.

The members of the regular Rebel army were, to a person, a bold and daring bunch of men and women. They were trained to the cutting edge, honed down to hard muscle, gristle, and bone. And they liked a good fight. They went out of their way to hunt one.

There was General Ike McGowan, an ex-Navy SEAL. General Georgi Striganov, a former Spetsnaz commander. General Cecil Jefferys, now in charge of all Rebel zones in North America. There was Colonel West and his battalion of mercenaries. Colonels Rebet and Danjou and their Russian and French-Canadian and Canadian battalions. Colonel Dan Gray, a former British SAS leader and his battalion. Tina Raines and her battalion. The hippie-turned-warrior who was called Thermopolis and his battalion. There was Buddy Raines and his wild bunch called the Rat Pack. There were the outlaw motorcyclists called the Wolf Pack. People from all walks of life made up the many fighting battalions of the Rebels. The Rebels were the most feared fighters in all the world. They gave an enemy one chance to surrender. Only one. After that they rarely took prisoners.

The commanding general's orders.

And the man who had seen his dreams turn into reality, the man who had pulled a battered nation out of the ashes and set it once more on the road to productivity, the man who had drawn up the plans to clear the nearly ruined nation of gangs and warlords and lawlessness?

His name is Ben Raines.

When the country known as the United States was finally declared effectively clear of human crud, Ben took his Rebels and sailed for Europe. Might as well see what mischief they could get into over there.

First stop: Ireland.

One

It was late spring when the Rebels pushed inland from Galway, Ireland. General Jack Hunt had shifted his mercenary army around and also made a pact with the creepies. The Rebels would save the cities for last.

The Rebels had also learned that approximately ten battalions of European mercenaries had sailed across the Irish Sea from England to link up with Hunt and his people. And other warlords and gang leaders were sending troops. The lawless element meant to destroy Ben Raines and his Rebels once and for all.

But Ben and his people had been fighting unbelievable odds ever since the day the Rebels were formed. Being outnumbered fifty-to-one was something they had grown to expect.

"Big deal," the tiny Jersey said, when she heard the news. Jersey was one of Ben's personal team and his self-appointed bodyguard. "When ain't we been outnumbered?"

"We have nine full battalions and one short battalion," Cooper, Ben's driver, reminded her. "Hunt now has thirty-three battalions. And they're at least semi-professional fighters."

"Yeah," Jersey agreed, reassembling her M-16. "But

we got something goin' for us that those on the other side don't."

"What's that?"

"We're right and they're wrong."

Ben smiled as he listened to the exchange. His personal team, with the exception of Linda Parsons, who had joined them about a year back, had been with him for a long time. They worked together like a well-oiled machine.

His radio operator, Corrie, called from across the room. "Ike on the horn, General."

Ben took the mic. "Go, Ike."

"Everyone is in place, Ben."

Ben looked at his watch. It was seven o'clock in the morning. The Rebels almost always launched a campaign well before dawn, but not this time. This time they were in unfamiliar territory and facing thousands of well-equipped and reasonably well-trained troops.

The Free Irish, newly armed and raring to go, were to secure County Clare, then join with Ben's battalion.

Other Free Irish were being trained, but they were not yet ready to go into battle against what Jack Hunt had to throw at them.

Ben and his First Battalion were to drive straight across Ireland, stopping on the outskirts of Dublin. Ike's Two Battalion was heading first to Limerick, then pushing on to Kerry and the sea, then cutting east and taking Cork. Dan Gray commanded Three Battalion and would push south. Four Battalion, headed by West, was to secure County Mayo, then join Striganov's Five Battalion and push up through Roscommon and Sligo, securing that area. The objective of Rebet's Six Battalion was Tipperary and Waterford. Danjou's Seven Battalion was to stay north of Ben, pacing his movements, while Thermopolis' Eight Battalion stayed just to the south. Tina and her Nine Battalion would strike south through Offaly, Laois, and Kilkenny. The Outlaw Battalions, Ten, Eleven, and Twelve, were split up and used to beef up other short battalions. Everyone would secure, then some would link up, turn, and push east, toward the coast of the Irish Sea. Beerbelly and his Wolf Pack would roam about, wreaking havoc and all sorts of bloody mayhem as they went. And that group was very good at doing that.

"Well, it looked good in theory," Ben muttered. "Let's see how well it's going to work." He lifted the mic. "This is Eagle to all units. Strike!"

From locations all around and in Galway, the Rebels surged forward, while men and women and children stood on the sidewalks and by the side of the roads and in the meadows and pastures and waved them on. Most of the men and women were middle-aged, for the outlaws and warlords had taken the younger men and women to use as slaves, or to swap them to the creepies in the cities, for breeding or to fatten them for food.

"Scouts report that we'll hit the first resistance on the Suck," Corrie told Ben, once they were under way in the big nine passenger wagon, armor-plated and with bulletproof glass all the way around.

"On the what?" Cooper asked, behind the wheel.

"Don't think, Cooper," Jersey told him. "Just drive. Thinking strains you too much."

"It's a river, Coop," Ben told him. "About thirty miles up the road. Chances are we'll be hung up there for a day or two. Jack's people will surely blow the bridge."

"Scouts report the bridge is wired to blow," Corrie said. "Engineers are to the rear of this column."

"I love this country," Linda said. "It's so beautiful."

17

A bullet whanged off the side of the wagon, causing everyone to cringe just a bit. "Five miles out of town and they're shootin' at us already," Cooper bitched, bringing the wagon to a halt by the side of the road.

They all bailed out the left side of the wagon as Scouts pulled up in hummers, officially known as high-mobility, multipurpose wheeled vehicles, the hummers were outfitted with .50 caliber machine guns. Ben's husky, Smoot, stayed in the wagon as she'd been trained to do.

The fire, now coming from a machine gun, picked up and everybody ducked. But Ben had already pinpointed the location of the hostiles.

"The fire's coming from that stone hut right over there," Ben called to Scout. "Get a couple of tanks up here and drop some calling cards in on them."

The Scout grinned. "Like a Valentine's Day card, General?"

"Yeah," Ben returned the grin. "Sort of let them know we're here."

"Right, sir."

Two main battle tanks lumbered up, swiveled around on the roadbed, and lowered the muzzles of their main guns while the enemy machine guns rattled, the slugs bouncing off the heavy armor-plate. A booming heartbeat later, there was nothing left of the stone hut.

"Check it out," Ben ordered.

Scouts raced across the meadow. Moments later, Corrie's radio crackled. "Scouts report all enemy dead, sir. Do we bury them?"

"No," Ben replied. "The people living around here will take care of that. Move out."

Back on the road, moving slowly due to the badly deteriorated highway, Ben again picked up a map. "The town Athenry is supposed to be deserted. But I have my doubts about that. I suspect Jack has moved in troops over the past couple of weeks. I've told the Free Irish that we wouldn't destroy on a wholesale basis; but I also told them that I wouldn't give up a Rebel life to save a building. They understand that."

"It's so green and lovely," Jersey said, looking out the side window. "And so peaceful-appearing."

"Scouts report the crossroads up ahead is clear, General," " Corrie said.

"Stay on the road to Athenry, Coop," Ben said. "Corrie, have Scouts check out the southern route down to Loughrea. Advise them not to get themselves in a bind. We've got plenty of time and equipment to do this right."

"Yes, sir."

"Have the Scouts check it out and if they hit trouble, back off immediately and call in. Make that a direct order."

"Yes, sir."

Ben had vowed that this operation was to be done slowly and cautiously, keeping loss of Rebel life to a minimum. Dr. Chase, the Chief of Medicine, had hit the ceiling when he'd learned the Rebels would be fighting on so many fronts. But Ben was used to Chase's bitching and yelling.

"How in the goddamn hell do you expect me to provide quality medicine on six or seven fronts, Raines?" he had roared.

"I have complete faith in your ability to do the impossible, Lamar."

"Raines," Lamar said, in slightly less than a roar, "this country is approximately the size of *Maine,* for Christ's sake. The roads are in horrible shape, it's going to be a very slow campaign, the people are malnourished, we have our hands full just trying to keep these poor children alive, there are creepies all over the

19

damn place, it rains all the time . . ."

"It does not rain all the time, Lamar. Just . . . more often than we are accustomed to, that's all."

"Don't interrupt me. And I want you to finally realize, get it through that thick, hard head of yours, that your place is in the rear, directing operations from behind a desk, you overage Huckleberry Finn."

"Go suck an egg, Lamar."

"Damn it, Ben . . ."

"I lead troops into battle, Lamar. The Rebels expect that of me. Now is there anything else you want?"

"About a hundred more doctors would be delightful, Raines. And nurses, too."

"Canvass the people, Lamar. I'm sure Ireland had plenty of very fine doctors and nurses before the Great War."

"Oh, thank you so much, great and noble leader. Goddamn, Raines, I've already done that in this area. I can't very well go wandering out into the fine green hills of Ireland looking for more until you start clearing zones. Right?"

Ben grinned and pinched Lamar on the chin. "You're so cute when you get angry—you know that?"

The Rebel encampment was startled to see the chief of medicine, with a very large surgical knife in his hand, chasing the commanding general through the tents and vehicles. Lamar was cursing and shouting out exactly what parts of the general's anatomy he planned to cut off.

Luckily, Ben was younger and had longer legs.

Ben halted his battalion just outside of the town of Athenry and got out to study the village with his binoculars.

His son, Buddy, and part of his Rat Pack had joined

20

him on this run . . . at Colonel Dan Gray's insistence. "The name means 'Town of the King's Ford,' " Buddy told his father.

Ben looked at his ruggedly handsome son, heavily muscled, with a mop of dark hair, always with a bandana tied around his forehead. "I didn't know you were a student of Ireland."

Buddy grinned and held up an old tourist brochure he'd found back in Galway. "It was founded in the thirteenth century and much of the medieval town wall and keep of the castle still survives. Population of about fourteen hundred before the Great War. What is a keep, Father?"

"The strongest or innermost part or a central tower of a castle." Ben returned to his inspection of the supposedly deserted town.

"Thank you, Father," Buddy said with a mischievous grin on his lips. "You are a veritable well of information. Of course, when I reach your advanced age, I plan on being just as intelligent. However, that's well in the future."

Ben groaned and shook his head.

Jersey said, "You may outrank me, Buddy-boy, but watch your smart mouth around the general."

Ben grinned at the expression on his son's face. Buddy could have jerked Jersey up and broken her in two without much effort. "Yes, ma'am," he said.

Ben chuckled. "You have anything else to add, boy?"

"No, sir." He looked at the diminutive and dark-eyed Jersey, staring smack at him without one ounce of backup in her. "At least, not with her around."

"Fine. Never bad-mouth the general when the general's bodyguard is around."

"She's *always* around!"

"That's right," Ben said cheerfully and handed the

field glasses to his son. "Take a look at that village and tell me your first gut hunch."

"I was only kidding, Jersey."

"The town, boy. The town!"

Ben looked at Jersey and she winked at him. Jersey's jokes could sometimes be a little grim. But most soldier humor is.

Buddy studied the town for a moment, then slowly lowered the glasses. "It's a trap."

"Why?" his father pressed.

Buddy pointed to some tiny birds that were flitting along a row of wild roses. The birds paid them no attention. "Wild roses down there, Father. But no birds."

"Maybe they got tired of those roses," Ben said with a smile.

"And just maybe some of General Jack Hunt's people got careless and drove right through a mud puddle this morning," his son said, returning the smile and pointed to the town. "Leaving vehicle tracks that lead right up to that closed garage door down there in the village."

Ben nodded his head. "You're good, boy. You're in command. Take the town."

Buddy's mouth dropped open. "What?"

"You heard me!" Ben said sharply. "I said you're in command. Take the damn town. You don't expect me to live forever, do you? I could catch a bullet any moment. I could step on a mine. I'm a middle-aged man, son. Not some strutting rooster like you." He turned to Corrie. "Advise the battalion that Buddy is in command for this operation." He looked back at his son. "It's your show, boy. Do it."

Buddy gathered the CCs and PLs around him, while Ben leaned up against a fender and rolled a cigarette. Dr. Chase, whose MASH unit was attached to

22

Ben's command, walked up and gave the cigarette a disgusted look. "Damn things are going to kill you, Raines. What's this about Buddy taking command?"

"Time he stopped running around like a wild heathen and began taking some responsibility." Ben lit up and inhaled.

Chase peered suspiciously at him. "Are you sick, Raines? Have you been smoking funny cigarettes? You are actually giving up command?"

"For an hour or two or three. He's got to learn how it feels to make mistakes. He's got to learn how it tears a man up inside when men and women die on his orders. I can't teach those sensations, Lamar. He's got to experience them on his own."

"There's more to this than you just told me."

"Yes. Lamar, should something happen to me, Buddy would have to take command. Now Ike or West or Georgi could stand behind him and keep him propped up, but a *Raines* has to lead. You know that as well as me."

"I."

"What?"

"Not me. I."

"Lamar . . ."

"Oh, forget it. He's just a boy, Ben."

"Damned if that's so. He's twenty-five years old, give or take a year or two."

Buddy walked up. "I'm taking one company in and some armor, Father."

Ben shrugged. "Don't tell me. Just do it."

Buddy hesitated for a second. Sighed. "And what if I'm wrong, Father?"

"Then you get people killed and possibly yourself along with them. The day isn't getting any younger, boy, and the road is long. Take the town."

Buddy wheeled about and walked off.

"You're a hard man, Ben Raines," Chase said.

Ben smiled.

"And don't tell me it's hard times! You say that and I'll stick a stethoscope up your nose."

Ben looked at Sergeant Major Adamson, standing nearby, and jerked his head toward the town. The former French Foreign Legionnaire smiled and nodded. He walked toward the company Buddy was leading into the village and joined the group.

"Buddy's led troops before, Ben," Linda said.

"But not with me so directly looking down his throat. Oh, hell, people. He'll be all right. Those Rebels won't let him make a mistake." I hope, Ben silently added.

TWO

Ben sat drinking coffee and occasionally lifting binoculars to his eyes to watch as his son and a company of Rebels took the village of Athenry. He smiled as he watched his son take the small town using textbook tactics. It was slow but highly effective, and it reduced Rebel losses to a bare minimum.

Buddy took it house by house, block by block, moving his people forward behind heavy armor, utilizing smoke and teargas to drive the enemy out of the buildings and destroy them in the streets.

"Very good," Ben said.

"A real chip off the old block," Chase said. "But that chip down there uses a lot more common sense than this old chip I'm sitting next to."

Ben sipped his coffee and said nothing in rebuttal. Ben's team sat on the ground by the wagon and listened to the exchange. Dr. Lamar Chase and Ben Raines had been arguing almost since the moment they'd met, years back.

"Buddy is offering them surrender terms, General," Corrie called.

"His option," Ben said.

The firing was much lighter now. The very faint

smell of teargas wafted to the halted battalion.

"It's just about over down there," Ben said. "Corrie, get me reports from the other battalions."

"The Free Irish are driving hard," she reported in a few moments. "They've encountered little resistance so far but expect stiff resistance when they reach Clare and Shannon Airport."

"It'll be filled with Creepies for sure," Ben muttered.

"General Ike reports no resistance of any kind, so far. West reports only light resistance. General Striganov says not a shot has been fired. No one is reporting any resistance, sir."

"That's great," Chase said.

"It's too easy," Ben countered. "Jack Hunt may be a murderous outlaw, but he's a fine military man. Give him his due for that. Corrie, order all units to halt forward progress and let's have a skull session using SLURP."

"Right, sir. I'll have communications set up the equipment."

SLURP is slang for a highly sophisticated method of communication using electronically coded burst transmissions. A three-minute conversation can be compressed into a four- or five-second burst, then decoded electronically on the receiving end.

Buddy returned, bringing with him a dozen prisoners.

"What do you intend to do with them?" Ben asked.

"Turn them over to the civilian authorities for trial."

Ben shrugged. "Personally, I'd shoot them. But this was your show."

26

The prisoners were scared and their faces showed that fear as Ben walked up and down in front of them. "No officers among them, son?"

"Not that I can tell."

Ben smiled very faintly as he stopped in front of one man. "This one is."

Buddy was at his side instantly. "How the hell do you know that?"

"Look at his collar, son. See the pinholes where the rank insignia was displayed? Take this one for interrogation." He stared hard at the man. "It can be easy or hard, partner. It's all up to you."

"My name is Bob Miller," the mercenary said. "Captain, Jack Hunt's Army of Liberation. I am required under terms of the Geneva Convention to give you no more than that."

The man actually backed up at Ben's smile. A very thin sheen of sweat broke out on his face. "Get these other prisoners out of here, Buddy. Leave the captain."

With the others gone, Ben turned to Miller. "Have you ever been interrogated using chemicals, Captain?"

"No, sir."

"I'm told it's a very . . . ah, trying experience. But the interrogation team is very good at what they do. They always succeed. Do you really want to undergo that treatment?"

"Not really, General."

"Well, I'll give you a few moments to think about it, Captain. You think hard on it. And enjoy your ruminations. Because if you experience those chemicals, you just might not be capable of ever doing any rational thinking again. And either way you choose to play it, easy or difficult, I'll still know what it is you have in your head. Because you see, Captain, I am not a game player. We don't play games during war. We just win. We *always* win." He turned to a Rebel. "Get him out of here."

"General Raines?" Captain Miller said.

"Yes, Captain."

"What is it you want to know?"

Ben smiled. "I knew you were a sensible fellow, Captain." Ben pulled out a long-bladed knife. "Turn around."

With a puzzled look on his face, the captive slowly turned around, not knowing what to expect.

Ben cut the ropes that lashed his wrists together. "Have you eaten today, Captain?"

Miller faced the general. "No, sir." He smiled. "At least, nothing to write home about."

"I do know that feeling. Where's home?"

"Originally, Kansas. Little town name of Arkansas City."

"I know where it is. It's deserted now."

"Yes. I know. I had just gotten out of the Marine Corps when the Great War struck. Then the federal police came to relocate me and my parents. We told them we didn't want to be relocated." He sighed. "The feds shot my dad. dead. Mother jumped at them and they killed her, too. I went crazy. Grabbed up a Mini-14 and just let it bang. Killed them all and went on the run. Hooked up with a bunch of military deserters and I've been running ever since."

"Let's go get some coffee and food and we'll talk."

Jersey watched Miller eat and said to Corrie, "He sure must be hungry. Anybody who'd eat two packets of that crap is either half-starved or crazy!"

"It's far better food than Jack provides," Miller said, leaning back in the camp chair and accepting the makin's from Ben. He rolled a cigarette and said, "Jack's lettin' you people come on without much resistance. To build up your confidence, you might say."

Miller accepted another cup of coffee from Corrie with thanks and said, "I'm not privy to his plans — Jack doesn't say a whole lot until he's sure a man is trustworthy — and I haven't been with him long enough to gain inner circle status. I just took over this command after you creamed us at Galway." He smiled with some satisfaction. "Jack was pissed about that. Really steamed."

"You act as though that pleases you."

"I don't like Jack Hunt, General. But I'm a soldier. That's all I know how to do. I was a soldier down in Mexico, then in Central America, then in South America, for one two-bit dictator or another. Then I heard about Jack's really professional army and came over on the first boat." He shook his head. "Boy, did I get suckered in that time."

"Miller, have you ever raped anyone?"

"No, sir. But I've been present when it was going on and didn't stop it."

"If you had tried to intervene, what would have happened to you?"

"They would have killed me."

"So you did the only sensible thing."

"The sensible thing would have been for me never to turn to mercenary work. But yes, you're right."

"Ever killed anyone in cold blood?"

"Yes, sir. But then, so have you. Probably many more times than I have."

Ben grunted. "I'm certain you're right about that.

29

Miller, you come across as a man with some education, some conscience, some moral value. Do you have any of those attributes?"

"Oh, I think so, sir. I once beat the shit out of a man who was abusing a poor starving dog."

Ben threw back his head and roared his laughter. Miller looked at the man, wondering what in the hell was going on. Ben wiped his eyes and called for Jersey.

"Right here, sir."

"Jersey, take Miller down to the medics for a physical. Then have him outfitted in proper Rebel dress and arm him. He just joined the Rebels." He turned his gaze to a very startled Bob Miller. "You get that done, then come on back here. We'll talk at length."

As Jersey was leading him away, Miller asked, "Does the general always make up his mind that fast?"

"Sometimes. You must be an animal lover."

"Oh, I am. Always have been. I was a member of the Doris Day Animal League while I was in the Corps."

"I heard of her. Miller? Don't ever try to fuck over the general."

"The man just gave me a second chance. I don't have any intention of screwing it up. But what would you do if I did?"

"Kill you stone dead as a hammer, Miller. Cold."

Miller smiled at the pretty little bodyguard with eyes that could become cold and unreadable in a heartbeat. "You really would, wouldn't you?"

"Fuckin' A."

* * *

30

"Hunt doesn't give a damn for this island, General," Miller told Ben. "He's just about squeezed everything he can out of it. But Hunt and his new partners—that's all the crud and crap in England—would like to contain the Rebels here, rather than have you go ashore on the Continent."

"So our intelligence is correct about the ten additional battalions that landed during the past week?"

"Yes, sir. But that may backfire on Jack and the others."

"Oh?"

"There is a strong resistance movement in England. They are not a large force, but they're a damned determined one. Pulling that many outlaws away and sending them over here is really going to weaken the outlaws' hold and give the resistance movement a hell of a lot more room to do damage."

"People are starving on this island," Ben said softly.

"Yes, sir. That's one of the reasons Jack initially linked up with the outlaws in England. That was done long before I joined this . . . mess."

"They plan on taking part of the Continent." Ben did not put it in question form.

"Yes, sir. France, Spain, Belgium, Germany, Italy. With Jack Hunt as president."

"Ireland, England, and those countries you just named had such restrictive gun laws that once the unthinkable really happened, it was easy for the outlaw element to take over."

"That's right. An unarmed population is an invitation for takeover."

"We certainly agree there. And you really don't have even an inkling of what Jack plans to do?"

"No, sir. But I think I could guess and be better than fifty-fifty correct."

"Go ahead."

"Jack is not going to hit you head-on again unless he outnumbers you twenty-to-one. He learned his lesson well at Galway. Jack's not a stupid man. He's cruel and vicious, but intelligent."

"As is often the case," Dr. Chase said. He had been sitting quietly with Buddy, drinking coffee and listening.

"Yes," Miller said. "If, or I should probably say *when,* Jack realizes that you're going to shove him off this island, he'll cut and run for England."

"Leaving all his heavy equipment behind?" Buddy asked.

Miller looked at the young man. "He doesn't need to take it. England is an armed camp. So is Europe. And once he's in place in England, you people will be forced to make your assault by sea, and he'll be set up and waiting." He looked at Ben. "It won't be another replay of Galway, General."

Ben nodded his silent agreement. "Then I guess we'd better deal with Mr. Jack Hunt properly and right here."

"It's going to be interesting to see how you do it," Miller said. He smiled. "Or rather, how *we* do it."

Some of Georgi Striganov's people came eyeball to eyeball with a group of pale-faced creepies, cannibals who were trying to hunt a hole to escape the Rebels. The fight was short, brutal, bloody, and final. Striganov's men took blood samples for Dr. Chase's lab people to test, then poured gasoline on the stinking bodies and set them blazing.

32

The Wolf Pack came roaring into a village on their Harleys just as a group of Jack Hunt's soldiers were trying to leave. The outlaw bikers went to work, in dirty hand-to-hand fighting. Beerbelly and his people and Wanda and her ladies suffered only one dead and two wounded. When they pulled out, they left almost fifty dead mercenaries littering the streets and sidewalks.

Those were the only two incidents of combat, other than the operation Buddy had commanded, reported that day. Then Ben gave the orders to halt and wait for further orders.

The Free Irish reported to Ben's CP by coded radio messages. "Our intelligence says that the initial reports of Jack pulling his people back are correct, sir. But sad to say, General, a number of our own people collaborated with that filth. They're not going to stand still and let us take them in for a hangin' without makin' a fight of it. And they're just as well armed as we are."

"Where are these people, Pat?"

"All about the damn place, General. And they've linked up with them mercenaries that got cut off from their units when the Beast ordered the pullout."

Jack Hunt was known as the Beast.

"Irishmen fighting Irishmen," Buddy muttered, standing by his father's side.

"They've been doing that in Northern Ireland for generations," Ben said.

"Why do they hate each other so?" Jersey asked.

"I doubt they even know after all these years," Ben replied. "Each side is trained to hate the other from birth." He keyed the mic. "Pat, I suppose that these small groups have infiltrated towns and vil-

33

lages and are holding the people as hostages?"

"You are correct, sir. It's going to be a series of very small and dirty battles among our own."

"With the larger battle looming at the end of the tunnel."

"Yes, sir. That's the way I see it."

"What is your position now?"

"Halted just outside of Crusheen. The village is occupied by a gang of hooligans sympathetic to the Beast."

"Ike?"

"We're holding just outside of Nenagh, Ben. The town's filled with women and kids and Jack Hunt's sympathizers, along with some of his regular troops. We can't use artillery or mortar fire on innocents. We're gonna have to take it house to house with small arms fire."

"Son of a *bitch!*" Ben cussed. He listened to his other commanders report in. All reported the same as Pat O'Shea and Ike. "Hunt did this deliberately," Ben said to his group, gathered around him. "He deliberately left those people of his behind, knowing that we'd have to take time to root them out hand to hand, giving him time to get his army in place and dug in for a long battle. And you can bet he's got ships ready to transport to England. He also figured out that we won't blow those ships because we're going to need them to cross the Irish Sea. Most of our vessels are sailing back to America for supplies. The man is no fool, believe that."

Ben walked outside of the communications truck and stood for a moment. He whirled around and faced the crowd of Rebels that had gathered. "Jack Hunt wants it dirty, people." His smile was not a cheerful one. "All right. If he wants it down and

34

dirty, that's the way we play it. Scouts out to Atty-mon. Now. Corrie, tell all commanders to move out toward the next town in their sectors and take it. House by house, street by street. Double the number of medics with each unit to aid in the wounded civilians. And we all know there will be some of those. Let's go, people, we've got a war to win."

Three

"Holy Mother of God!" one turncoat Irishman said, crossing himself as he felt the earth beneath his feet tremble as the big main battle tanks advanced toward the village.

"He's bluffin'," another man said, but from his tone, he wasn't ready to bet the farm on that remark.

"Get them hostages out here," one of Jack Hunt's regular soldiers said. "Fill the streets with 'em. If Raines gets us, he'll do slippin' and sloppin' in the blood of women and babies."

Old men and women, young women with babies, and younger men crippled fighting the troops of Jack Hunt were prodded out of their homes by the muzzles of guns.

"Bastards," Ben muttered, his voice savage as he watched the streets fill with civilians. He lowered the glasses and turned to Buddy. "You want to handle this one, boy?"

"I defer to the older and wiser head among us, Father. But thank you just the same."

"West reporting that hostages are lining the streets of a town in his section," Corrie called. "Same with Danjou, Rebet, and Tina."

"Tell all units to put a loose ring around their objectives and then stand down and rest until dark. We'll go in blackface," Ben ordered.

"We'll go in blackface?" Chase said, walking up to the group.

"That's what I said, Doctor."

"Raines, need I remind you that . . ."

"Set up your MASH tents, Dr. Chase. Get ready to receive wounded."

"If you get more lead in you, Raines, I promise you that I will personally operate on your hide."

"My God, what an incentive to stay healthy!"

Chase walked away, muttering to himself.

"Pick your people, son," Ben told him. "We shove off at full dark."

At mid-afternoon, the skies darkened and it began to rain, a very gentle falling of rain. "Perfect," Ben said with a smile. "I just hope it keeps up." About a hour before dark, he changed into dark clothing and began removing or securing with tape anything that might rattle. He smeared mud on his face and then pulled on tight-fitting leather gloves. He petted Smoot and was telling the husky to behave when Linda walked into the tent. She was dressed in dark jeans and dark jacket, her face painted camo for night work.

"Where the hell do you think you're going?" Ben asked.

"With you."

"No way."

"Then take it up with Dr. Chase. I work for him, remember?"

Ben shrugged his shoulders. The chief of medicine could ground even Ben if he really wanted to,

37

and Ben would be forced to obey.

Ben's team began to gather. Cooper whistled at Jersey's tight jeans and she gave him the bird. But she was smiling as she did so.

Ben had two 9mm Beretta pistols on his web belt and was carrying a Colt 9mm carbine, select fire. Helmets bump and make noise, so they all wore dark bandanas tied around their heads. Various types of grenades were hooked to their battle harnesses, and all carried plenty of filled clips for their weapons.

Cooper was carrying a Stoner 63, a 5.56mm belt-fed machine gun with a 150-round magazine. Jersey carried a CAR-15, select fire. Linda carried a Street-Sweeper, drum-type sawed-off 12-gauge shotgun, which was truly awesome in any type of close-in combat. She wore bandoleers of shells crisscrossing between her breasts. Corrie was carrying a very light packback radio and a CAR-15. All of them carried small walkie-talkies secured to their belts and all with clip-mics so each could keep at least one hand free.

"Check equipment and radios," Ben ordered.

Chase stepped into the tent. His face was serious and he did not immediately kid around. "We're all set up to receive wounded, Ben. Buddy has his people ready to go. Good hunting to you all." He winked at Linda. "Watch yourself with this bunch of wild people, Linda. But you know that by now."

She smiled at him and Chase stepped back into the rainy and foggy night, Ben and his team following. Smoot crawled under Ben's cot and went to sleep.

"A damn good night for killing," Ben said, and jacked a round into his CAR-15. He spotted Buddy's group and walked toward his son and his team. When he reached the silent gathering, he said, "You've all studied maps of the town. You know where to go and what to do. Noise discipline in effect from this point on. Move out."

The Rebels began moving out in teams of five, walking silently toward the darkened town. Only the faint outlines of the buildings were visible in the mist and fog of this quiet Irish night . . . that was about to turn deadly and bloody.

Ben and his team approached a line of houses just before entering the main street of the small town. He stopped there and checked the luminous hands of his watch. In two minutes the tank and mortar barrage would begin, and if the outlaws and turncoat Irish holding the town did as Ben hoped, it would make this job of work a lot easier.

"Please, no more," the woman's words drifted out of a boarded-up window. "I can't stand it anymore."

The ugly sound of a fist striking flesh followed the woman's pleadings. The woman cried out in pain and a man said, "Shut your mouth, bitch. And spread your legs."

Weeping followed that as the hunching slap of flesh against flesh came to the Rebels crouched just outside the house.

Ben looked at Linda. His eyes were very hard and bright in the misty night. Ben pointed a finger at her, then at himself, then at the house. She nodded her understanding. He pointed at Corrie, Cooper, and Jersey, then to the next house in line.

They nodded and moved out. All but Jersey. She silently shook her head. Ben grinned. There was no way that Little Jersey was going to leave his side.

The artillery barrage began on schedule, the shells whistling overhead to land harmlessly in the meadows and fields outside the town proper. The explosions shook the ground beneath the Rebels' boots.

"Get them people out in the streets!" a man shouted the orders. "Stay in the houses and keep them people under the gun. Any tries to run, shoot into the crowd."

"Bingo," Ben muttered. "Let's go."

Using the shattering noise of the incoming to cover any sound they might make, the infiltrating Rebels began slipping into the houses and shops of the town. With the citizens grouped in the wet streets, out of harm's way, the Rebels had a field day inside the homes and shops.

The man who had been raping the woman was just stumbling into his pants when Linda entered the room. She leveled the Street-Sweeper and gave him two rounds in his belly. Very low in his belly. He screamed and flopped on the floor, both hands to his bloody groin.

"I'm ruint!" he shrieked.

"For a fact," Linda told him, just as Ben opened up with his CAR-15 and stitched a line of 9mm's across four men who had whirled around in the living room, lifting weapons. The slugs caused them to do a nifty little dance step seconds before they collapsed on the floor.

Corrie and Cooper cleared their assigned house

of all living things and dragged the dead trash out the back door and tossed the bodies into the backyard. Jersey was squatting by the back door when several men came running around the side of the house. She leveled her weapon and held the trigger back as the outlaws jerked and yelled and died in the misty night.

A half a dozen civilians died from outlaw gunfire before one of Buddy's team could toss a grenade into the house, silencing the machine gun. The citizens dived for whatever cover they could find, many of them running into the now-cleared homes.

One company of Ben's battalion came charging into the west side of town, following several MBT's. The Rebels pulled the panicked citizens behind the tanks and calmed them. Ben and his team moved through the wet backyards of homes, silently stalking their prey.

A man with an AK-47 in his hands ran out a back door. Five weapons fired at once. The man was knocked off his boots and slammed into the side of a house. He left a huge bloodslick as he sank dead to the grass.

Ben saw a man wearing cammies and dragging an M-16 crawl under a shed. Ben dropped to his knees and put half a clip between ground and floor. The man thrashed around for a moment then lay still. Linda's shotgun roared a few yards away and a man was lifted off his boots and slung against a stone fence. He died with a very startled look on his face.

"The citizens are pretty much accounted for," Corrie yelled at Ben, after listening to her headset.

"Let's mop it up," Ben gave the orders.

When the outlaws tried to flee the village and found the area surrounded by Rebels, they tried to give up. But the Rebels were in no mood to play the surrender game. They had seen what the outlaws had done to women and young girls. They shot the outlaws on the spot.

"You're nothin' but filthy heathen!" one outlaw yelled. "They's rules to war and we're tryin' to give this one up, man."

"That man and several of his friends raped my ten-year-old boy," a woman with a bruised face told a Rebel.

The Rebel gave the outlaw a burst of 7.62 slugs in the belly.

"God bless you," the woman said.

"Where's your boy?" the Rebel asked.

"He died."

"Oh, God help me," the wounded outlaw said.

The Rebel looked at the woman, then pulled a knife from his harness and gave it to her. He walked on into the misty night. Seconds later the outlaw began screaming. The Rebel did not look back.

Ben and his team linked up with Buddy and the four Rebels with him. "Let's clear this block," Ben said. "Corrie, advise the others of our location."

A burst of machine gun fire sent them all face-down in the mud, the slugs hammering into a hut behind them.

"Anybody spot that?" Ben asked.

Buddy spat out grass and mud. "Behind that stone fence at two o'clock."

"Too far for grenades. We can't get a tank between these houses. A couple of you people work around and get close enough to chunk some fire-frags in that nest of snakes."

Two Rebels from Buddy's team backed out, on their bellies, and disappeared into the mist. Less than two minutes later, the machine nest behind the stone fence exploded in a smashing flash of blood and shattered flesh.

"We yield!" a man called frantically, the voice coming across the street from Ben's location. "Jesus God, boys, we give it up."

Several M-16's rattled and the voice spoke no more.

"Goddamn you, Ben Raines!" another man hollered. "You people ain't human!" A grenade bounced on the earth and came to rest about a foot from the man's boots. He screamed and turned to run. The grenade blew and sent him flying over a fence, one side of his body shredded and peppered with shrapnel.

Buddy rolled in through a back door and came to his boots facing a woman holding a weeping and bloody child close to her. The woman had been beaten savagely. "It's all right," he assured her. "We're American Rebels."

"My girl's been shot in the leg. She was raped over and over by them trash."

"Come on. We'll get help for you."

"I can't walk, soldier. Them trash took gun butts and broke my legs."

Unlike his father, Buddy was not a hard-cussing man. But he said a few choice words under his breath about Jack Hunt and members of his army. "Dad!" the young man called. "Over here."

43

"Your father is a Rebel, too?" the woman asked, her battered face white against the pain in her legs.

"My father is Gen. Ben Raines."

"Jesus, Mary, and Joseph!"

Ben filled the doorway. "What is it, boy?"

"You'd be please forgivin' a woman for not risin' in your presence, General," the woman said. "But them trash broke my legs. It's my wee one here that I'm concerned about."

"Get some medics and two litters in here, Buddy," Ben said, kneeling down beside the woman and the sobbing little girl. "And tell Linda to get in here with her kit."

"I've seen some goddamn terrible things in my long years," the voice of Dr. Chase rose over the gunfire. "But damned if this doesn't rate right up there with the worst."

"And tell that old goat to get in here, Buddy. Jesus, there's a war going on and he's out sightseeing."

"Oh, shut up, Raines," Chase said, stepping into the small house. He quickly assessed the situation and roared for medics. He knelt down beside the woman and hiked her dress up past her knees. "Tell me where it hurts," he said, as gently as possibly touching her battered flesh.

"It hurts just about everywhere, Doctor — you are a doctor, aren't you?"

"That's been debated on more than one occasion," Ben said, stepping aside to let the medics in.

"Oh, go fight a damn war, Raines," Chase told him, without looking up. "I haven't got time to listen to your lip now. Easy with that girl, people!"

Ben stepped back outside and joined his team.

44

Corrie said, "Our people are wrapping it up now, General. It's down to just a few more blocks near the center of town."

"Well, let's go check it out. We don't want somebody else to have all the fun."

They passed one elderly man who was busy building a noose at the end of a rope. He looked up at Ben. "Damned murderin', rapin', torturin' scum. 'Tis a rotten shame when Irish turn agin' Irish. By the Lord God there'll be justice this night." He returned to his noose building.

Ben walked on. "It's what the good citizens of America should have done back before the Great War. And I was approached to take part in the overthrow."

"Really, Ben?" Linda asked, after they hastily took cover from a nasty hail of bullets. The lead wasn't coming at them but in combat, reflex had better take over.

"Really." The machine gun opened up again and this time the lead flew all around Ben and his team. "Will somebody please neutralize that son of a bitch!" a Rebel hollered.

"They have hostages in there, sir!" a Rebel yelled.

Ben keyed his mic. "This is General Raines. I might suggest using smoke," he said dryly. "And go in under it."

"Right, sir!" came the quick respond.

"That's Willison," Buddy said. "Something must have happened to Lieutenant Matthews. Willison's never commanded a full platoon before. He's nervous and cautious."

"He'll get over it," Ben said.

Smoke grenades were tossed around all sides of the house and Rebels worked their way in, staying low, for the rain was preventing the smoke from rising as it should.

A few moments passed. The gunfire in the town was sporadic now. "All clear, sir," Willison shouted. "We . . ."

A single shot rang out. The sound of a body hitting damp earth was clear. "There he is!" a Rebel shouted, rage in his voice. M-16's began yammering and the sniper was literally shot to bloody rags. He fell from the roof of a store and landed on the sidewalk.

"Get me a report, Corrie," Ben said wearily, getting to his boots.

"Yes, sir," she said softly. She spoke and listened and stood up, standing beside Ben. "Willison took one in the throat. He's the only fatality so far. Four wounded. One seriously. The other three will be on light duty for just a few days."

Ben nodded his head. There had been no gunfire for several moments.

"The town's ours," Corrie said.

"House to house," Ben said. "We don't want to leave *even one* behind and alive."

"Yes, sir."

"Willison just got married, didn't he? Right before we pulled out?"

"Yes, sir," Jersey said. "She's back at Base Camp One."

"Buddy, secure quarters for me tonight," Ben said. "I have a letter to write."

Four

After breakfast, Ben walked back up the road
to where his command was bivouacked. He passed
earth-moving equipment that was gouging out a
hole in the ground for the enemy dead. They
were wrapped in blankets and lined up on the
grass. Willison would be buried properly in
the town's old cemetery. Ben looked in on Chase.
The man was grim-faced at his field desk.

"What's the matter, Lamar?" Ben asked, taking
a seat.

"The little girl who was raped?"

Ben nodded.

"She died."

"You blaming yourself?"

"How can I? We've got the finest medical
equipment and know-how in the world. God
damn it, she just died, that's all!"

"You want to yell at me, Lamar? Go ahead.
Get it out of your system."

"No, Ben, I don't want to yell at you." He
threw his pen on the desktop. "What the hell is
in the minds of grown men who rape *babies*?
When do they start to go wrong? No, don't try
to reply. Just listen. As a physician, I used to

47

scoff at those who subscribed to the bad seed theory—and that would have included you, had I known you at the time. But now I'm not so sure." He tapped a thick notebook that he had closed when Ben walked in.

"Over the past decade, Ben, I have kept a careful journal. I'll keep this in layman's terms. There just might be a gene somewhere that goes wrong. That's not proper medical terminology, but it'll do. I think the bad seed theory might not be just a theory. I think there's something to it. Chemical imbalance in the brain. Genes. Something is haywire at birth. You know why I think scientists never went after that theory very strongly? Think about it, Ben. Suppose that modern science could have proved the bad seed theory. Then what? It's ethics. What would society have the doctor do? Kill the infant at birth? Imprison the baby as soon as it's weened? You know what else I think? I think science *did* prove it. They proved it in a lab, but couldn't find a way to correct it, so they remained silent on it. Or the man or woman who discovered the truth destroyed the papers and kept his mouth shut about it. That's what I think happened."

"And you think society should do what, Lamar?"

"Hell, Ben, I don't know. What we're doing, I suppose. It won't help those that have already been subjected to rape and torture and murder, but it does ensure that the criminal will never repeat his acts."

Ben nodded his head. "We're pulling out just as

48

soon as we bury Willison. How about the Rebel who was seriously hurt?"

"He's already back in Galway, in the hospital. Had to amputate his left leg."

"See you on the road, Lamar."

The column rolled out and toward their next objective, the town of Kilconnell. But this town proved to be merely a roll-through, for the outlaws and turncoat Irish had pulled out during the night. The spokesman for the survivors met the column on the edge of town.

"They were in communication with the scum in Attymon, General. They left shortly after your attack. I wish I could tell you what their plans might be, but I just don't know."

"We'll stick around long enough to tend to any sick or wounded you might have."

"And that's a-plenty, sir," the man spoke the words grimly. "Jack Hunt's people savaged us, they did."

The Rebel doctors and medics worked grim-faced on the victims of the outlaws. The sexually abused children hit them the hardest, for many of the kids—boys as well as girls—were very young.

"Was there any among them with even a shred of decency?" Ben asked a group of townspeople.

"Not none that we ever saw," a woman told him. "I never saw even one act of kindness or compassion or mercy. Them trash is beyond redemption. I say it knowing that God will not look kindly upon me for those words."

The citizens were armed with the weapons taken from past engagements, and as always, with Ben's

49

now familiar words. "Don't ever let any man or government take your weapons. Not ever again."

The Rebels stayed that afternoon and night, and pulled out at dawn the next day.

"Scouts report a large force waiting in Ballinasloe," Corrie told Ben. "All bridges over the Suck appear to be wired to blow."

"Hostages?"

"Plenty of them."

"What's the word from the other battalions?"

"Tied up just like us. Taking it one town at a time and trying to keep the civilian casualty list low. They report bridges being blown all up and down the Shannon."

"We still have units trapped on the east side of the river?"

"Yes, sir."

"They have been advised to dig in and stay low?"

"Several times, General."

"Chopper a SEAL team in here, Corrie. Right now. We make no moves until they're suited up and in place to disarm those explosives on the bridge at Ballinasloe. If we have to, we'll take Bailey Bridge across. But I'd rather leave what existing bridges remain intact. Get Dan over here and tell Ike to get his fat butt moving."

"We were only a few miles from the city when the bridges went up," Ike said. "How many do we still have operating?"

"Ballinasloe and Banagher," Ben said, pointing

at the map. "Ballinasloe is yours, Ike. Dan, your people take the bridge at Banagher."

"We'll hit it come dark," Ike said.

"We?" Ben looked at him. "No. Not we, Ike. I need you here. Besides, you'd look like a whale in that river."

Ike was more stocky than fat, but he could stand to lose a few more pounds. He grinned at Ben. "I'll have you know I've lost fifteen pounds since we sailed."

"Good. Lose fifteen more."

"Lard-butt," Dan said.

Ike gave the Englishman the finger.

"Now listen, both of you," Ben said. "The Free Irish say that the east shore is heavily manned with machine guns. Ike, Dan, you're the experts on these matters, so this operation is in your hands. Get to it."

Ben left it to them and went outside, where a table had been set up. He sat down and began studying maps. With the blowing of the bridges—which had not come as any surprise; Ben would have done the same thing—it put the campaign on a whole new footing. The original plans would now be scrapped and the backup plans hauled out and dusted off.

Of course, Ben knew what Jack Hunt was doing. He was buying time. From Ballyshannon all the way south to Limerick those Rebels west of the rivers Suck and Shannon were halted dead still. Those units trapped on the east side were in danger of being discovered and attacked . . . should Jack want to risk that, and Ben doubted he did. Jack had discovered just how fiercely the Rebels fought, and for him to attack would mean that he would lose ten personnel to every one Rebel lost.

No, he would use this time to mine roads, set up defensive lines, and prepare ships to cross the Irish Sea to England. Ben couldn't use helicopter gunships to attack Dublin for fear of killing civilians and of destroying the ships the Rebels would need to cross the Irish Sea.

"Start-over time," Ben muttered, as Jersey brought him a mug of coffee.

Rebet's Six Battalion and Tina's Nine Battalion were trapped on the east side of the river.

The SEAL teams and Dan's Special Operations people moved out just after dark, the mission commanded by Dan Gray. Ike sat with Ben, drinking coffee and waiting for word.

Only one very short-burst transmission had come from Rebet and Tina. EVERYTHING OK. STAYING DOWN.

A few Free Irish were to meet the SEALs and the Special Operations people on the outskirts of Ballinasloe and Banagher and guide them in. The SEALs would take Ballinasloe, leaving Banagher for Dan and his SO team.

Ike's battalion was quietly and quickly being shifted up north. At the instant the bridges were cleared, they would pour across at Banagher, secure the town, and lay a defensive line out to provide a buffer zone for Tina and Rebet, while Ben's people would attack Ballinasloe.

But once that was done, the Rebels on the east side of the rivers would have to stretch out their forces and hold what they gained until everything west of the rivers was clean and clear. Ben and Ike could not get too far out in front of other support troops for fear of Jack pulling an end-around, cutting them off and sealing their fates.

"They're in the water, General," Corrie reported.

"Let's go," Ben said, standing up and reaching for his short-barreled 9mm spitter.

Everyone that was going was ready and standing by for word. They had blackened their faces and wore dark clothing. They would drive up to within a couple of miles of the objective, running without lights. From there they would walk to the shores of the river, several miles upriver from both towns. Members of the Free Irish resistance forces would have small boats ready for them to cross. The Rebels could not roar across the standing bridges in their vehicles for fear of enemy artillery bringing the bridges down or doing severe structural damage.

The trucks rolled out, running without lights. Chase and his medical people would follow once Ben and his teams made the river crossing and Ike and Dan had secured the bridges.

The teams crossing the river were carrying only light weapons and plenty of ammo. Once on shore, they were going to have to move very fast to secure their objective.

They dismounted at a signal from a Scout and headed northeast across country, with Ben setting

53

a steady but distance-eating route step. The operation on Ben's bad knee had proven to be one hundred percent effective. But he still carried with him—unbeknownst to everyone except Linda and his personal team—a good knee brace. Just in case.

At the river's edge, the Rebels looked with dismay at what appeared to be rowboats.

"Those are rowboats," Jersey said. "We're going to cross the river in those?"

"George Washington did," Ben said with a cheerfulness he really did not feel.

"I'm seasick already," Cooper bitched.

"Shut up and get in the damn boat, Coop," Jersey said.

"Quickly now, lads and ladies," a Free Irish guerrilla said. "Time's a-wastin'. The patrol boat just passed and it'll be fifteen minutes 'fore it returns. That is, if it stays on schedule."

"And if it doesn't?" Cooper asked.

The Irishman grinned. "Why, son, we'll all be dead and gone to Hay-ven, now, won't we?"

"Jesus!" Cooper said. "On top of being seasick, I got to worry about drowning."

"Cooper," Jersey warned him, "you barf on me and I swear I'll shove you over the side."

"I can't swim!"

"Then don't get sick, is all I got to say."

The crossing was made without the return of the patrol boat or Cooper getting sick. The small boats were pulled up on the bank and hidden, and the Free Irish joined the Rebels for the march to Ballinasloe.

"Clear on Dan's end," Corrie said, after receiving a bump from the Englishman.

"Any word from my people?" Ike asked.

"No, sir. Wait a sec. Yeah. Hang on, sir." She listened and smiled. "All clear for our objective. Both teams are waiting under the bridges for the action to start."

"All right!" Ike said.

"Down!" the point man said, just a second before machine-gun fire ripped him apart.

"God damn it!" Ben said. "Corrie, it's in the fire now. Tell our people under the bridges to go. Give us a diversion of some sort. Buddy, knock out that .50 over there."

Moments later a half dozen grenades sailed through the air and the machine-gun emplacement was blown out of action.

And the Rebels were not yet inside the town limits.

"Ike!" Ben yelled on the run. "Take C and D Companies and swing around that way. A and B Companies, come with me!"

"God bless you, boys!" an elderly woman yelled from the darkened window of her cottage.

"Get them dirty bastards!" her husband shouted from her side, his ill-fitting false teeth clacking. "You find that filthy Jack Hunt, stick the barrel of your weapon up his arse, and pull the trigger."

"Michael O'Finnelan!" his wife said. "You hush that kind of talk!"

Linda laughed as she jogged alongside of Ben. "The Irish will never change, Ben."

"I hope not," he panted.

They rounded a curve in the road and saw dozens of headlights bearing down on them a good half mile away.

"Both sides of the road and stagger. Ambush positions," Ben yelled. "Now!"

The road was suddenly empty as Rebels bellied down on the grass on both sides and waited.

The vehicles were coming fast, and they were trucks, the beds filled with armed men. Ben grinned. "Beautiful," he said to Jersey. "Corrie, tell everyone to put it on full rock-and-roll and let it sing. Have every fourth person toss grenades."

"That's ten-four, sir."

The men of Jack Hunt's army and the traitorous Irish among them rode smack into an ambush. M-16's, CAR-15's, Stoners, M-14's, and grenades turned the mounted column into a burning, smoking death trap. The Rebels took no prisoners, nor would they take any on this excursion, not after seeing what Jack Hunt's men did to the civilian population.

The SEALs and Special Operations people had raised hell with those guards at the foot of the bridges and were now moving into the towns, moving silently and swiftly and deadly.

"Blow the damn bridges!" the order was given.

Nothing happened.

"Do it!" the commanders of Jack Hunt's forces in Ballinasloe and Banagher screamed into their mics.

But the SEALs and SO teams had taken the charges from the bridges and deactivated them.

The silence from the bridges seemed loud in the night.

"We've lost contact with an entire company, sir," the radio operator told the commander in Ballinasloe. "They don't respond to my calls."

A brick thrown by a citizen smashed through the window of what used to be a store and was now the CP of the enemy forces. Everyone in the room hit the floor. The brick-thrower vanished into the darkened alleyways of the town.

"Guerrillas attacking at a dozen points in both towns," the commanders were informed.

"Well, how the hell did they get across?"

"I would imagine by boat, sir," the weary radio operator said.

That got him a very dirty look. "Fall back," the commander finally said. "Regroup at Athlone and Tullamore. Let's go."

But Ike and his two companies had swung wide around the town and were waiting at the crossroads. They turned the retreat into a slaughter.

"Will you be the American Rebels?" a boy asked Ben.

"That's right, son. Do you know where the headquarters of Hunt's army is?"

"Indeed I do, sir. Next block up on the left." He smiled. "It's got a fairly busted window from a brick."

Ben and his teams caught the commander and his staff attempting to leave by the back door. The Rebels turned the dark alleyway slick with blood and the old bricks pocked and scarred by bouncing lead.

The streets suddenly filled with angry citizens, armed with axes and hatchets and clubs and chains and shotguns and old pistols and whatever else the men and women and kids could get their hands on. Ben grabbed one boy—about eight or nine—and turned him around—very carefully The boy had a butcher knife in one hand.

"Whoa, son! Easy now, we're friends. Where are you going with that pig sticker?"

"I'm off to find the man who done them bad things to my sister," the boy solemnly informed Ben. "Now kindly turn me loose, sir."

"Why don't you let us do that?" Ben asked. "And you stay here. We've got hot chocolate all ready to fix."

"Real hot chocolate?"

"Real as can be."

Cooper began stoking up the stove and Jersey dug out a packet of hot chocolate mix from her pack.

"But I'll keep my knife, sir," the boy said.

"That's fine," Ben told him. "That knife is, ah, sharp, isn't it?"

"Very."

"Where are your parents?"

"Dead, sir."

"And your sister you spoke of?"

"Dead. After them men used her bad they killed her."

Linda knelt down. "Where are you staying?"

"Down by the docks. I fish and catch small game and sometimes rats."

"You *eat* rats?" Cooper asked.

58

"Sure. Lots of folks do that. Jack Hunt's men take all the food."

"Go on inside and get your chocolate," Ben said. "You'll not have to eat a rat again, boy. I promise you that."

The boy, dressed in ragged clothing, walked up the steps. His shoes were nothing more than two pieces of old tire rubber. "They's folks starvin' in this town, mister. Folks that's been hurt and can't get no medicine. Little babies dyin' more often than they live."

"We're here to help, son," Ben told him, as a group of citizens walked up.

"Is it really General Raines and the Rebels?" a man asked, leaning on a cane.

"Big as life, Mayor," the boy said. "And he's brung food and medicine, too. They got hot chocolate in yonder."

"Lord love us!" an elderly woman spoke up. "I ain't tasted hot chocolate in years."

" 'Tis a fine evenin' for Ireland," the man said. "Welcome to Ballinasloe, General."

Cooper took the only packet of rations he'd brought with him out of his pack and stepped forward, handing it to the woman. He had suddenly lost his appetite. "This'll tide you over 'til the ration trucks get here, ma'am."

"With yer permission, lad, I'll take it to my granddaughter. She's ill with the fever and needs food more than me."

"Just as soon as the town is clear," Ben said, "they'll be doctors in. Is your hospital building intact?"

"Yes, sir," the Mayor said. "It's in fine shape. But nobody exceptin' Hunt's men could use it. His people vacated the buildin' when the first shot was fired this evenin'."

Ben looked around him and found Buddy giving his food packet to a little girl. "Buddy. Take a team and go with this gentlemen here. Secure the hospital and get it ready to receive patients."

"Yes, Father."

"Ike reports the town is ninety percent clean," Corrie called. "And Dan says he has neutralized Bangher."

"Get the people across the bridges," Ben ordered. "Start trucking in supplies from the harbor." He looked at the ever-growing crowd of ragged and hungry people; ragged and hungry, but with no defeat in their proud Irish eyes. "It's going to be a long night."

Five

At dawn, the Rebels had completed their flushing out of members of Hunt's army who had taken refuge in basements and sheds and abandoned houses. At Ben's orders, any taken alive were turned over to the townspeople. Trials were held and justice was handed down very quickly at the end of a rope. The dead troops of Hunt's army were buried in a unmarked, mass grave on the outskirts of town.

Ben slept for a few hours, checked in with all his people, and then began an inspection of the town. Ike had rejoined his battalion, and Rebet and Tina's people were safe and being repositioned. All the other battalions west of the river were resuming their search-and-destroy missions against Jack Hunt's army and the turncoat sympathizers who stayed with them.

There were some among them who wanted to give it up. But the Irish people have long memories, and the atrocities that had been committed against them were neither easily forgotten nor forgiven. The ranks of the Free Irish troops began to swell, taking some of the pressure off the Rebels, and putting a hell of a lot more pressure on Jack Hunt's people. Those of Hunt's army who were trapped west of the rivers soon realized they had only one thing to look forward to: a grave.

With each town or hamlet or village liberated by the Rebels, the citizens were organized, armed, and given a stock of ammunition. From the reports sent back to Ben, he doubted that any government would ever disarm these people again.

"Lord help anyone who even tries," Ben remarked.

And Irish doctors and nurses began surfacing. They had been forced to practice their profession underground, so to speak, for not a one of them wanted to work on any of Hunt's people. Chase put them to work immediately.

For a couple of weeks, the drive east was halted along the rivers while the Rebels moved equipment and supplies across the only remaining bridges and engineers worked to build temporary bridges across the rivers. At the end of two weeks, it was reported to Ben that the Counties of Clare, Galway, Mayo, and Roscommon and most of Sligo could now be declared effectively neutralized.

"We push on in the morning," Ben ordered.

"It's crazy, Jack!" one of his commanders said. "You can't stand and slug it out with these people. That's been proved true time and time again."

Jack shook his head. "No, Vernon, no. We've got basically the same equipment he's got—except for the gunships. But we've got three times the troops. Why drag this all the way over to England when we can settle it here?"

"I agree with Jack," another commander said.

"Raines got lucky on his sneak attack. But wars aren't won on luck."

"Thank you, Frankie. Anything else?"

"Yes." The man stood up. "You're forgetting the Free Irish that Raines is arming."

"What about them?"

"Don't sell them short. He probably has better than a thousand of them right now."

"I doubt it. More like five or six hundred, tops. So what. We've still got Raines outnumbered. I say we hit him hard and keep hitting him."

"You mean for us to go to him?" another battalion commander questioned.

"No. Let him come to us."

"Why that way?" another asked.

"Because I've learned that Raines is not going to destroy all this ancient shit on the island. That's the deal he made with the Free Irish."

"So?"

"So when we set up our lines, we set them up in old churches, around prized statues and all that crap. Raines will not, repeat, will not, destroy all that old shit. That means we can put fire out, but he's not going to return it. He'll be depending on his ground troops alone."

"You got that information firm?"

"Firm, Harris. That Free Irish asshole held out for hours, but we finally got it out of him."

"Well, now," Vernon said. "That makes me feel better. All right!"

Jack moved to a huge map of Ireland. "Artillery is in place here, at Tullnally Castle, and down here, at Durrow Abbey. Men are right now being set up in every castle, every church, and every ruins from

Ballyhaise to Castle Gardens. If we have to fall back, I've ordered equipment, food, and ammo to be placed in those ruins and churches and castles behind the new lines. Every time Raines has to stop for one of these old broken-down pieces of shit, we hammer them. Maybe use the people for shields around the old dumps and churches and the like . . ." He paused as a messenger came in and handed him a sheet of paper. "Scouts report that it looks like Raines is about to pull out come the morning. Let's get cracking, boys. It's gonna be a long night."

Ben read the message and said a few very choice words about Jack Hunt and men like him. He poured him two fingers of good Irish whiskey that a man had presented him in deepest gratitude — which Ben had accepted in even deeper gratitude — and drank it down neat. Then he calmed himself and rolled a cigarette. With a sigh, he said, "Corrie, advise all commanders that Hunt has put heavy artillery and heavy machine gun emplacements in all abbeys, monasteries, churches, castles, historical houses, and ruins. The son of a bitch."

Corrie paused for a moment, staring at Ben.

He nodded his head. "Yes, Corrie. You know what it means as well as I do. It bothered us all to destroy two- and three-hundred-year-old points of interest in America. Now we're talking about places a thousand years old . . . and older. Some, five thousand years old. What will be left for those who come after us?"

Chase had entered the room to stand in the door-

64

way, listening. "How about leaving them a world filled with law and justice and decent people, Ben? How about leaving them a new respect for others and all the creatures that inhabit this planet? How about leaving them democracy and order and books and learned men and women to teach them? And how about pouring me a shot of that Irish whiskey while you're at it?"

"I can't see myself destroying those places, Lamar," Ben said, pouring a generous slug in a coffee cup. A very faint smile creased his lips.

"What are you plotting in that devious brain of yours, Raines?" Chase asked, after a taste of Emerald Isle.

"It would be chancy," Ben replied. "And something I would have to work out with all the other commanders. But it just might work. It really just might work."

"What, Ben?" Linda asked.

Ben rose from the chair and paced the room. "Corrie, cancel those orders to move out in the morning. Tell all commanders I want to see them here at 0700, and that includes the commander of the Free Irish battalion."

"What the hell are you plotting, Father?" Buddy asked, looking up from the chess game he was playing against Jersey, who was beating him soundly.

"Unconventional warfare."

Beth, the last member of his team, had just rejoined them after spraining her ankle badly in Galway during the invasion. She looked over at him. "I didn't know that the Rebels ever did anything conventional."

65

"Sometimes, Beth," Ben said with a smile. "Sometimes. But not this time."

Georgi Striganov, the Russian, roared with laughter after Ben had laid out his plans. "I love it, Ben!" he shouted. "I by God, love it!"

Rebet and Danjou looked at each other and chuckled. It was a wild plan, but it might work.

Ike clapped his big hands and said, "What was it that Ali used to say? Yeah. 'Float like a butterfly, sting like a bee.' That's us, Ben."

West and Tina Raines both nodded in agreement.

Colonel Gray's eyes were bright with excitement. Now here was something to his liking. "I'm for it," the Englishman said.

Buddy and Beerbelly both laughed and said, "All right!"

Pat O'Shea, the commander of the Free Irish said, "It's a wee bit loony, General, but I think it'll work."

Chase shook his head. "Raines, you're crazy. But God love me, I like it."

"Supplies will be the problem. But once an objective is taken, and we'll have to be closely coordinated at all times to make sure we don't get too far ahead of each section, the supplies can roll in."

"We'll have Jack's army spread out from Donegal to Cork," Beerbelly said, looking at a map of Ireland. "We'll have them so confused they won't be able to find their asses with both hands and a huntin' dog."

"It's chancy, people," Ben dampened their enthusiasm. "And it could backfire on us. I want us all

66

to sleep on this plan. I want you all to think about it and offer suggestions in the morning. We've never done anything like this, not on this grand a scale. And once we're committed, there is no turning back. That is why I want our armored personnel in reserve and ready to roll, and three battalions in reserve in case we have to holler for help. The three battalions will be chosen by drawing numbers. Lowest three numbers stay in reserve. Now, wander around the rest of the day, give this some thought, and we'll meet again in the morning. That's it."

Twenty-four hours later, no one had changed his mind and no one had any suggestions to offer that would enhance what Ben had laid out previously.

"All right, let's do it," Ben said. He dropped slips of paper into a helmet, each slip with a number on it between one and nine. Each commander drew. The three battalions to stay behind were Striganov's Five Battalion, Thermopolis' Eight Battalion, and Tina's Nine Battalion.

"Shit!" Ben's daughter said, disgust in her voice.

"Breaks of the game, kid," Ben said.

Of the commanders in the room, seven knew that Ben had rigged the slips of paper. Only three of the slips had numbers on them. One, two, and three. Thermopolis' battalion, because he and his people had the least experience in guerrilla tactics; Striganov's battalion, because Ben needed someone with a lot of experience to stay behind and run the operations' board; and Tina's battalion, to help ferry supplies to the forward troops. Georgi Striganov had agreed in advance to his part in the rigged game; he was a career soldier who knew his duty and did it without any static.

Thermopolis and Tina might have suspected that Ben had rigged the numbers, but neither of them would question him about it . . . for the moment, at least. Thermopolis would question a stump, but for now he left it alone.

"Rebet," Ben said, picking up a pointer and slapping the map with it, "take your people north to Leitrim and Longford and split them up. Draw supplies and move out. I'll take Westmeath and Offaly. Ike, you'll have a heavy load in Laois and Waterford. West, start in Tipperary. Dan, Limerick and Kerry. Danjou, that leaves Cork for you. It's going to take us several days to get in place. Pick your teams now. We travel in full battalion columns and don't split up until we're in our objectives. Once there, start moving out at night. We're going to terrorize these people, gang. We're going to make them so scared they'll shit their drawers at the slightest noise. If this works, the men that Jack spread around the castles and abbeys and churches and ruins are going to be so demoralized they'll finally run back to Hunt like frightened children. And Jack won't know where to strike, because we'll be all over the country. This operation will either be an enormous success or the Rebel Army will be whipped for the first time since our inception."

Ben let those words sink in for a moment. "You three battalions in reserve, stay loose. We're counting on you. If someone hollers, come in hard. If armor and artillery has to destroy a church or other historical place to save Rebel lives, so be it. But I'm hoping we can pull this off without that happening. We'll damn sure know in a few days. Move out, people . . . and good luck."

* * *

"What the hell is he doing?" Jack tossed the question out as he stood before a huge wall map. "It doesn't make any sense. It appears that he's drawing very thin battle lines north and south of his present location." He shook his head. "No. No. Raines is too good a soldier for that. He knows that would never work. We'd bust through his lines and box him in. He's pulling something, but damned if I know what it is." He wheeled about to face an aide. "All our people in place?"

"In place and dug in tight. Food and ammo enough for weeks."

Jack Hunt nodded and turned back to the map. "Goddamn you, Raines. You sneaky bastard. Just what are you trying to pull now?"

Six

Three days later, Jack Hunt and his other battalion commanders were still scratching their heads and wondering what was going on when the Rebels just seemed to disappear into the air and the mist of Ireland. The mystery was about to deepen as an aide told Jack a forward recon leader was on the horn.

"What the hell do you mean, you don't know where they are?" Jack screamed into a mic, his face reddening and his blood pressure soaring. "Trucks and Jeeps and five thousand goddamn people just don't fucking disappear!"

"Well, they have!" the scout said, not knowing that the Rebels had carefully and as quietly as possible hidden their vehicles in barns and abandoned homes and camouflaged them carefully in woods and thickets and shady glens.

"Well, find them!" Jack screamed. He tossed the mic to the table.

Butch Smathers, a thug from London who had brought a mob across the Irish Sea to help Jack, sat in a chair and grew thoughtful. He liked none of this. He didn't like Ireland or the Irish. But he disliked Ben Raines even more. Butch and the other

70

warlords who had carved up London and the English countryside like a pie had been expecting Ben and his Rebels for several years. They were ready for him in England. But this operation was beginning to smell. Jack simply wasn't as smart as Raines, and that ignorance just might get them all killed.

"I'm pullin' my people back to Dublin," Butch said abruptly, standing up.

Jack turned on him. "What?"

"You heard me. Somethin' is a-fixin' to pop in this country. Somethin' nasty and mean and bloody. Raines is outfoxin' you, Jack. And I ain't gonna be caught asleep inside the henhouse when he slips in."

"Butch, stay with me. I'm sure we can contain him here!" Jack pounded a table.

"Contain him?" Butch said. "Hell, you can't even *find* him, man. Come on, Jack. Pull your people out and come back to England. Raines don't stand a chance against us over there. You stay here, and you're done."

"You said you were going to Dublin, not England."

"That's right. But I want my back to those ships we come over on when Raines starts raisin' bloody hell. And he's just a heartbeat away from doin' that, Jack. I can feel it; I can sense it."

"You liked my plan originally," Jack said sullenly.

"Yeah, I did. But now I think Raines has come up with one better, that's all. Come on, Jack. Let him have the damn island. We've used it up and wore it out. There ain't a decent-lookin'

71

woman left around here."

"They're all in hiding. We find them now and then."

"Well, Jack, you feel like lookin' for some now? No? I thought not. And with Raines out there— and he's out there, brother, bet on that—it ain't gonna do nothin' except get worse. I'm headin' back to the city. Bein' around them stinkin' damn Believers is better than sittin' here waitin' for Ben Raines to show up."

After he had gone, Jack looked at the other warlords who had come from England to join him. "How about you people?"

"We'll stick around," a warlord called Poole said. "I don't believe half of what people say about Ben Raines. Personally, I think he's a pussy. Don't you think so, Raft?"

"Yeah," the warlord said. "I do. I think the bloke is a lot of hot air and not much else. That's what I think. I'll stick around, Jack."

Another warlord called Mack nodded his head. "Yeah. Me, too. Me and my boys ain't had a good fight in a long time. Not since we took over Blackpool from Scotty and run his ass back up to Glasgow. Ben Raines ain't shit. Ain't that right, Johnnie?"

"You got it," Johnnie said. "Me and my boys'll stay."

"I'm in," a punk from Liverpool said. He went by the name of Morelund.

"Yeah, I'm game for the show," a London punk tossed in his bravado-filled words.

"Good for you, Eakes," a leather-clad outlaw called Acey said. He fancied himself quite a biker, as did all those who followed him, and they numbered about five hundred.

"Yeah," a cammie-clad and beret-wearing warlord called Duane said. He wore two pearl-handed six-shooters. "We'll show the Yanks a thing or two. How 'bout it, King?"

The remaining warlord nodded his head. "Right-O, me boy. We'll run them bloody bastards back into the ocean, I'm thinkin' we will."

"Damn right!" Jack Hunt said. An aide came in and handed him a note, then turned to leave. "Wait a minute. What is this?" Jack demanded. "Maybe them at 23 stepped out to take a piss. This doesn't mean anything is wrong."

"Dick says he's been trying to reach them for an hour. There is no response."

Jack moved to the big map and put a finger on position 23. That was the cathedral at Ballyhaise, just south of the Annalee River. And that was a damned important post.

"Tell him to keep trying. Maybe their radio is out. Yeah. That's probably it."

The radio at post 23 worked just fine. It was the personnel that were out of commission. Permanently. Rebet's people had taken a slight detour and did a little throat cutting. Now the were sitting around drinking coffee and listening to the calls from Hunt's CP at Nass, in County Kildare.

"Fellow is getting a bit testy, isn't he?" a Scout asked.

"Oh, quite," a Rebel said, slicing off a piece of cheese and chewing contentedly.

The Rebels grinned at each other. They enjoyed this brand of fighting.

"You have our objective cased out, boy?" Ben asked Buddy.

"Yes, sir. It's a real old home about two miles from here. Kind of a mansion, I guess you'd call it. And it's filled with Hunt's men. They seem to be doing a lot of partying with ladies."

"Ladies?" Beth asked. *"Ladies?"*

"Women," Buddy said.

"Thank you," Jersey told him.

"How many?" Ben asked.

"Women?" Buddy replied with a straight face, but with a twinkle in his eyes.

Linda had to struggle to stifle a laugh at the expression on Ben's face.

"No, boy," Ben told his son. "Rats in the keep. How many of Hunt's men?"

"Approximately twenty. We will be outnumbered probably two to one."

Ben checked the sky. About an hour of daylight left. "Let's get into position."

Leaving two behind to guard their meager supplies and to radio in for help should something go wrong, the team of ten Rebels moved to within a few hundred meters of the eighteenth-century home. Since little work had been done on the grounds in more than a decade, the grass was tall and a lot of brush had grown up. That made the advance of the Rebels almost easy.

"They should have cleared away all this brush," a Rebel remarked.

74

"That would have been a dead giveaway," Ben told the young man. "You'll learn."

The young man silently cursed himself for being so stupid, and vowed not to open his mouth again unless he knew for sure he wouldn't stick his boot in it.

"Don't be afraid to ask questions or offer opinions," Ben then told him, softening that with a smile and not taking his eyes off the mansion. "It's the only way you'll learn. Believe me, I speak from experience. Wind down just a little, people. We'll hit them at dusk."

Music from a tape player drifted out the open windows of the mansion. A woman's shrill laughter came faintly to the Rebs hidden in the thick brush of the old garden in the rear of the once elegant home.

With all the technology we once had, Ben thought, lying on his belly in the brush, it's all returned now to the stealthy game of cowboys and Indians. He wondered why cowboys always came first in the phrase.

Shadows began lengthening around the land and the pools and pockets of darkness grew larger. A very gentle rain, not much more than a heavy mist, began falling. "Go," Ben said, and Buddy and two Rebels moved out, Ben and his team right behind them.

When they reached the two-story house, the Rebels flattened themselves against the stones of the back wall and listened.

"Post four," the words spewed metallically out of a speaker. "Come in, post four."

"Post four," the radio operator responded.

"How's it looking?"

"Quiet as a church. No sign of the Rebels."

"That's ten-four. Stay alert."

"Ten-four, base."

Ben peeked through the dirty window. A man was sitting with his back to the rear of the house, radio equipment on a table in front of him. Ben pointed a finger at Buddy, held a finger to his lips, and then pointed to the radio operator. Buddy nodded his understanding of the silent kill. He pulled a knife from his belt and slipped into the house.

Seconds later, the radio operator's throat was cut wide and the body lowered to the floor. Ben and the others moved silently and swiftly into the house. Ben switched the radio to Off and then stepped into the hall, moving toward the sounds of music and laughter. Jersey was right behind him, followed by Buddy and the others.

At the foot of the stairs, Ben pointed to Buddy and then to the ceiling. His son nodded. Taking two with him, he moved up the stairs, staying close to the wall to avoid any squeaking. When Buddy reached the top of the stairs, Ben stepped into the living room of the old mansion, the others quickly following. Lanterns sputtered out light and showed a very relaxed group of Hunt's soldiers and a few women, all in various stages of undress.

"Can we join the party?" Ben asked, then pulled the trigger on his CAR-15.

Hunt's men yelled and leaped for their weapons. They didn't make it.

Ten seconds later, the mansion fell silent, both levels of the old home thick with gunsmoke and the smell of death.

"Take their weapons and hide them outside," Ben ordered. "The Free Irish will pick them up later."

"What about us?" one of the surviving women squalled. "Sweet Baby Jesus, are you goin' to kill us, too?"

"That is a problem," Ben told her. "You probably deserve a bullet, but I won't do that. We'll just tie you up and notify the Free Irish of your location."

"But they'll *hang* us!" another women yelled. "They've branded us as collaborators."

"And you're not?" Beth asked, no pity in her voice.

The woman cursed her and then fell silent.

The dead were dragged outside and piled unceremoniously in a ramshackle old hut behind the mansion. The three women left alive were tied securely, and Corrie got the CP on the horn and told them to inform the local resistance about the weapons, the bodies, and the women.

"O'Rourke's right here with me now," the operator said. "He says to shoot the whores."

Ben took the mic. "Tell O'Rourke he can do his own shooting. Eagle out." He looked at his group. "Let's get this pigpen cleaned up and have some dinner."

The Rebels were just finishing their meal when O'Rourke and a dozen resistance members showed up, appearing silently and deadly out of the fog and mist. The women started sobbing at the sight of the Irish guerrillas.

"Mickey," one of the women sobbed, "don't do this to me. I'm beggin' you, don't do it."

"Shut up, bitch," Mickey told her. "I don't want to hear nothin' from your whorin' mouth. Too

77

many good decent men has gone to the grave because of you and them like you."

"But it's near over now, Mickey," she pleaded. "The general here and his troops will soon set us free. He ain't holdin' no rancor in his heart for me. Time'll heal it all, Mickey. You'll see."

"Time'll do nothin' for you 'ceptin' rot your bones in the cold grave," Mickey's words were as hard as the time. "Get her on her feet and take her down to the forest."

"No!" the woman screamed.

The words of Dylan Thomas came to Ben: "Do not go gentle into that good night."

"For God's sake, Mickey," the woman screamed at him. "Let me see a priest."

Mickey stared at her. "Which one, me fair beauty? Father O'Florry? Oh! But you'll not be seein' that one, now, will you? 'Cause you torned him in for helpin' us in the resistance, and Jack Hunt and them rabble of his tortured and hanged the poor blessed man. Father Sheehan, perhaps you'd be wontin' to see? But you can't see him, neither, colleen, 'cause you led him into an ambush, now, didn't you?" He stepped forward and spat in the woman's face. He looked at his people, both men and women all heavily armed. "I'll be down in the forest, fixin' a rope. Drag her along."

The woman turned panicked eyes to Ben. "For the love of God, General, help me. It's said that you're Irish on your mommy's side. A McHugh, folks is sayin'. I can't stand pain, General. Jack and his men tortured me something awful. They whipped me with horsewhips and beat me near unconscious many times until they broke me down.

You can't blame me for what I done. You just can't."

"Every person has their limit. But I'm not here to make the law. I'm just here to help liberate your country. You say the soldiers beat you?"

"Something fierce, General. It was horrible."

"Back and buttocks, huh?"

"Yes, sir. I just couldn't stand no more of the pain."

Ben walked to her, taking long strides, and ripped the dress from her, tossing it to one side, leaving her clad only in bra and panties. He stood for a few seconds, looking at her nearly naked body. There was not a single mark or scar on her body. Finally, he nodded his head and sighed audibly. "Yes," Ben said dryly. "I can see where you've endured many a savage beating."

The woman slumped to the floor, sprawling out on her belly and weeping. "God damn you to hell, Ben Raines. God damn all of you to the hellfire!" she screamed, tears streaming down her face. She beat her fists raw on the old floor. "I had to eat. I had to survive. I'm sorry people died because of me. But they threatened to beat me and torture me. They threatened to give me to them damn Believers in the cities for breeding. I had to do it. I didn't have no choice in the matter."

Jersey found her rag of a dress and threw it over the woman. "Cover yourself, bitch. You ain't no turn-on for nobody here."

"What about me?" the other woman screamed.

"We got a rope for you, too, Tessie O'Baire," one of the resistance women said.

Tessie cursed them all until she ran out of breath.

79

The women's hands were retied behind their backs and they were hauled to their feet, biting and kicking and shrieking obscenities at the men and women. They fought the resistance members all the way to the door and out into the backyard of the old mansion. They were still screaming as they were led down to the dark forests at the property's edge.

At the door, one of the men turned to look at Ben. "Don't think this ain't a hard thing for Mickey, General. 'Cause I can tell you it is."

"Oh?"

"Yes, sir. You see, that fair beauty he was givin' what-for to? . . . That's his sister."

Seven

Five more of Jack Hunt's outposts fell before midnight, and by dawn he had lost ten more before he finally figured out what was happening. He had lost all his personnel at Tullynally, Annaghmore, Carrowmore, Ballymote, Clonalis, and Durrow Abbey, and nearly half a dozen more sites had fallen to the Rebels.

Jack was livid with rage when he finally pieced together all the puzzle. He screamed out the same words that outlaws and scum had been shrieking to the heavens for years. "God *damn* Ben Raines."

"Let's attack the bastards, Jack," Duane suggested, fingering the pearl-handled butts of his pistols.

"Sure," Jack said sarcastically. "Then Ben Raines would swing half of his people north and south and box us in. You got any more brilliant ideas?"

Duane shut up. He was not much of a tactician and had sense enough to know it.

"Jack, they're jamming our transmissions."

Jack looked up at the man. "That's impossible!"

"No, it isn't. Raines has got the finest electronic gear in the known world, and the best engineers. They're doin' it."

"You can't jam hundreds of frequencies, God damn it!"

"That's right. But they've got scanners. As soon as we start on another, they block it. Low or high band, it don't make no difference. They must have two, three hundred people, just doin' nothin' but monitorin' us."

Jack cursed savagely and looked to the west. "I hate you, Ben Raines."

The radio operator at Abbey Leix was alternately twisting the dial of his transmitter and cussing when he heard a slight sound from behind him. He turned to look into the smiling face of Ike. He would die with that face the last thing he ever saw.

"Hi, there, partner," Ike whispered, then shot the man between the eyes with a silenced .22 caliber Colt Woodsman.

Ike shoved the body out of the chair while the other members of his personal team went about neutralizing the rest of the enemy. Silently and effectively.

Ike grinned and set the frequency, knowing that his voice would not be jammed. The radio operator back at Nass almost fell out of his chair when Ike said, "Hi, there, buckaroos! This here is Ol' Ike McGowan talkin' to you from . . . well," he gave his best Mississippi drawl, "we don't have to get into that, now, do we? I just wanted to let you misguided scumbags and dick-heads that serve Jack Hunt know that us good ol' boys that work for General Ben Raines is a-comin' to kick your asses righteous-like, y'all hear me?"

"Where is he?" Jack demanded, his face flushed with anger.

"I don't know. But I'd say he's no more than forty miles away."

"Forty miles!"

"Yes, sir. The signal is very strong and he's broadcasting open. That means . . ."

"Jesus Christ, man, I know what it means. He's not transmitting on one of our preset frequencies."

"Yes, sir. That's why I can't pinpoint his location."

". . . Yes, sirrie," Ike was saying. "I just wrote me a name on a grenade. Jack Hunt, was what I wrote. If you're listenin', Jack, you better get you some lard and go to work, 'cause I'm gonna jam this pineapple up your ass and pull the pin just to see how far shit splatters."

Jack, tight-lipped and red-faced, listened to Ike drawl out his words. His men began backing away from the man called The Beast, knowing too well his explosive temper.

"Are you listenin', Jack?" Ike asked. "If so, just back your butt up to the mic and fart. 'Cause whether it comes out of your mouth or your ass, it's all the same."

That did it. Jack grabbed up the mic and began calling Ike every obscenity he could think of, in half a dozen languages. He spewed out invectives like a nest of spitting cobras. He cussed until he was breathless.

Jack waited for a reply. None came. Ike and his team had left the Abbey as silently as the dead that littered the old grounds.

* * *

Jack Hunt's troops manning the old historical spots in Ireland were now, as Ben had planned, so jumpy they were shooting at anything that moved and a lot times at things that didn't move—such as trees and bushes and very stationary stone fences— and firing at things that were there only in their jangled imaginations. One man was walking back from taking a dump in the woods and his own men shot him stone dead.

And Jack's grand plan had backfired. He could not pull his men back, because the teams of Rebels were working all over the place, turning the once peaceful green hills and glens of the countryside into a massive killing field. Jack Hunt had tanks pulled back and running on a line north from Monaghan down to Waterford. But he couldn't use them because Raines's Rebels had wired explosives to every damn bridge Jack would have to cross and had members of that damnable force called the Free Irish ready to hit the button or flip the switch.

"God damn it," Jack cursed. "The man doesn't fight textbook-style. He's writing his own textbook. He's using the most unconventional tactics I have ever encountered. Everytime you think he's going to do one thing, he does the opposite. Who in the hell would have thought he'd split up all his forces and send them out all over the country in five- and ten-man teams and fight like a bunch of damn red Indians?"

A grim-faced aide handed him a note. Jack read it, wadded it up, and threw it on the floor. "Tralee just fell to the Free Irish and the Rebels. The Rebels now are in control, or very nearly in control, in ten counties. Jesus Christ, we outnumber them twenty to one and so far all we've managed to do is get our butts kicked."

"Damn it, Jack," a weary battalion commander said. "How do you fight shadows? If we do spot a team and give chase, they lead our people straight into an ambush. They come out mostly at night and they've got our people so damn jumpy they're shooting at the slightest noise."

"Jack," Poole said. "Maybe Butch was right. Maybe we ought to just let him have this country. Hell, I've lost over a hundred people and I ain't never even *seen* a Rebel. I ain't never fought no bunch of people like this. Mack's lost almost a hundred, and he went back to Dublin. You ain't even got contact with almost two battalions, so you can figure they're dead. I say, take what we've got left, throw up a defensive position, say, from here in County Meath," he pointed to the map, "down to here in County Wicklow. There ain't no way in hell Raines will ever punch through those lines."

"And then do *what,* Poole? Defensive lines, defensive lines. That's all we've done since that goddamn Ben Raines landed. Defense, defense, never go on the offense. *I'm sick of it.* I planned for a head-on. But he won't fight that way. Why in the damn hell didn't my intelligence people let me know that Rebels are trained to fight both conventional and guerrilla? Nobody has an entire army where everyone is trained that way. Nobody." He picked up an ashtray and hurled it across the large room. It shattered against a wall. "Nobody except Ben Raines." He faced the gathering. "I'll tell you this, people. We're going to be the laughingstock of

Europe if we don't pull this off. Either here or in England. Preferably here. You better understand that. We're counting on our allies on the Continent to help us settle there. But they'll laugh in our faces if we don't stop Ben Raines and stop him cold, right here!"

"We could stop him better in England," King said.

"How? Why? There's more resistance groups in England than over here. Somebody better come up with a plan," Jack said, resignation in his voice. " 'Cause I damn sure don't have one. I hate Ben Raines."

The Rebels regrouped and began mapping out plans for a massive assault against the forces of Jack Hunt. The Rebels now had cleared almost two-thirds of Southern Ireland and were in control of fifteen counties and had lost only five people, with thirty-eight wounded, and only four of them serious.

Jack had also drawn his battle lines, stretching out his people from about the center of County Monaghan in the north, down to the mouth of the River Nore in County Wexford in the south. He had positioned tanks and artillery and was ready.

"We going to play it his way, Ben?" Ike asked.

"I don't know. We'll take a lot of casualties if we do." He looked at Pat O'Shea, the commander of the Free Irish. "It's your country, Pat. What do you say?"

"I say, get the scum out of this land. We can always rebuild, General. I've canvassed the people.

Ninety-nine percent of them say go for it."

Ben nodded his head. "Dan, have scouts start probing for weak spots. Pat, get me maps of the region, from north to south." The man turned to go. "And, Pat?" Ben's voice stopped him. "We don't take creepie prisoners. Dublin is very likely going to be destroyed."

"It will be a shame, General. But a man's life is worth more than a building. Your people have been very considerate of the landmarks and such. Now it's time to win the war. We have to do whatever is necessary to free Ireland. And then we'll accompany you to England for the bigger battle."

Ben shook the man's hand. "And we'll need your help. Pat? What about Northern Ireland?"

He shook his head. "I'll not interfere up there. As far as I'm concerned, they've all gone mad since the Great War. Them with any sense—and they was more than a few—made peace and headed down south. It ain't the folks out in the country—hell, most of them has lived in peace for years. It's them crazy people in Belfast and Londonderry. It's come down to gangs, now. When you look at it, it's senseless. There is no more England, or for that matter, Ireland or France or any nation in darkest Africa. Northern Ireland doesn't belong to England anymore. The fight is senseless. Let them fight until they kill each off, then we'll go in and scrape up the mess and bury what's left and it'll be dead and forgotten. I got no use for them people up there, Protestant or Catholic. It's all hate now. Stupid hate. To hell with them all."

Ben laughed. "You're a good man, Pat O'Shea."

Pat winked. "That's what me wife says."

87

* * *

The people left in the Irish countryside, and like the United States, there were more than met the eye at first glance, had never seen anything like the Rebel Army and its mighty machines of war. Helicopter gunships and attack choppers hammered the air as they moved into position. Huge tanks lumbered up and down the narrow and twisting roads, and where there were no bridges, Ben ordered his engineers to lay down metal scissors bridges. So with that done, Ben's armor pulled into positions that Jack Hunt's people could not possibly reach, for Hunt lacked the bridge-building equipment or the M60 AVLB's to launch the bridges.

"I ain't seen nothin' like this in fifteen years. We ain't got a prayer," one of Hunt's forward recon people said to his buddy.

"Shit, man! What are you talkin' about? We got them outnumbered twenty to one."

"That don't make no difference. We're fightin' for booty and pussy and slaves and the like. Them Rebel people is fightin' for a cause."

"So?"

"So if somebody come up to you and offered you better food, finer women, and nicer quarters to go and fight for them, would you?"

"Damn right!"

"Them Rebels wouldn't. You could offer them the world, they wouldn't leave the Rebel Army."

"Then they're fools."

"No. They're just right and they know it."

"You gonna quit Jack?"

"And go where and do what? Surrender and be

tried by the Irish? Not bloody likely. You know what they'd do to us. No. We're in this to the death, Jimmy-boy. Call in, Jimmy. Tell General Jack Hunt that Ben Raines is preparin' to throw everything he's got at us. And it's awesome."

Jack had moved his CP over to Dublin, into the old General Post Office building on O'Connell Street, and met with the leaders of the Believers. Butch Smathers had already taken his people back to England; he had seen that the Rebels were going to retake Ireland. It was going to be a hell of a fight, but they would eventually win. England, Butch felt, was going to be quite another matter.

Jack and the creepies agreed to fight together against the common enemy: Ben Raines and the Rebels.

Neither side liked the other—Jack Hunt despised the stinking cannibalistic Believers—but each knew their lives depended on them banding together. The Night People—the Rebels called them creepies—would fight out of sheer desperation, for they knew, having monitored the fighting in the United States, that the Rebels did not take any creepie prisoners. They were executed on the spot.

Inside the boundaries that Jack and the creepies were defending were the Believers' breeding and fattening farms, where men and women and children were kept alive for a constant source of food.

"Here and here," Ben said, pointing to the map. "North and south of the city, only a few miles from the coast. The breeding and fattening farms of the Night People. But I have my doubts that we'll be able to free those poor people. As soon as those defending the city sense that we're about to bust

through, they'll bug out for England, taking their
. . . food source with them." Ben always choked
when discussing that. Of all the perverted and de-
generative groups the Rebels had fought over the
long years, the creepies were the most hated.

"Commando-type raid?" Dan suggested. "From
the sea?"

"I thought of that and rejected it," Ben said.
"This area is strong creepie and Hunt territory. Intelligence states that coast watchers are all up and
down this area. They'd pick up any type of seaborne assault long before you could get ashore.
SEAL teams would be able to get in, but then
they'd be stuck with no way to get the prisoners
out." He shook his head. "Too risky. Getting people
in is no problem; getting them out with the prisoners is the rub."

He turned back to the map. "Rebet and West,
your battalions will be in the northernmost counties. My battalion, along with Ike's Two Battalion,
will punch through to Dublin. Directly south of us
will be Dan and Georgi, then Danjou and Tina,
then Thermopolis and the Free Irish. Those north
of Dublin will drive to the sea, neutralizing all sections, then cut south. Those south of Dublin will
punch through to the sea, then cut north. Dublin
County was just about a million population before
the Great War. It's not going to be a cakewalk. Our
Scouts report that Jack and his people are dug in
hard with heavily reenforced bunkers. A near hit is
not going to take them out. It's going to take a direct bump. He's laid down minefields and cut out
tank barricades. That's fine. We'll just lay back and
pound his ass with artillery. His long-range artillery

does not have the range nor the accuracy of ours. He has light mortars, we have heavy mortars. The heaviest mortars he has are the 60mm. Our 81's outrange him by a good fifteen hundred meters. I don't want a single Rebel sent in until an area has been pounded by artillery. Pat O'Shea and his Free Irish did a fantastic job of clearing the civilians out of that area. They didn't get them all—no one expected them to. So we'll have some collateral damage,* but that's something we'll have to live with. That about does it, gang. Any questions?"

The room was silent. No one needed to ask a thing. They had all done this many times in the past.

Ben smiled. "Let's rock and roll."

*A military term used to signify civilian deaths, among other things

Eight

Ben's heavy 203mm howitzers laid back some thirteen miles from the battle zone and began pounding Jack's positions along the front. The huge projectiles were high explosives, some antipersonnel warheads carrying up to one hundred and ninety-five grenades. When they struck, it sounded to Jack Hunt's mercenary soldiers like the end of the world, and for many of them it was.

Closer to the front, 81mm mortars, with a range of over three miles using some rounds, laid down a seemingly never-ending barrage of death, using Willie Peter and HE. Artillery is the most demoralizing of all warfare—there is no rest from it. Those receiving the incoming are constantly battered. Even if one is not physically wounded by it, the mental state it leaves is devastating.

And Ben kept it up day and night. He was relentless with the artillery assault. For a five-mile stretch, from the southernmost edge of Northern Ireland south to the sea, the ground never stopped trembling and shaking.

Most of the men in Jack's army were trained to some degree or another, and all had seen combat. But few had ever experienced anything like this.

The sight of bunkers taking a direct hit and body parts flying in bloody chunks for hundreds of feet caused many to bolt in fear and panic. Some lost their minds. Others became so numb from battle fatigue they were rendered useless as fighting men.

And still the mind-numbing barrage from the Rebels continued. Day and night. Never-ending. While Dublin had yet to receive even one Rebel round, it became a city that was rapidly filling with trembling, vacant-eyed men who had wandered in from the front lines, some of them reduced to weeping shells of their former selves.

Jack tried to attack. His people ran into some of the most hideous ambushes they had ever experienced. Hunt's men were learning—the lessons written in blood—that the Rebels played by no rulebook. They were the most vicious guerrilla fighters the world had ever known. They were trained and armed with most of the weapons the world's armament people had cooked up, and they did not hesitate to use them.

King took his men back across the Irish Sea to England, and Mack and Poole took their people on the next ship out. They tried to convince Jack and the others that they should do the same. But Jack was determined to fight until he was literally looking down the muzzles of the Rebels' guns.

"And that ain't gonna be that long off," the warlord Acey muttered. He wasn't about to get caught on this damn island. When things started going really bad, he and his boys were gonna haul their asses out.

Ben kept up the cold and unrelenting pressure on the troops of Jack Hunt. The first ships back from

America brought hundreds of tons of rifle and machine-gun rounds and artillery shells. A day behind them were ships carrying food and medical supplies. Behind that convoy were ships carrying grain for planting, clothing, and ewes and rams to replace the herds the mercenaries had eaten and very nearly wiped out. Bulls and cows were shipped to the Emerald Isle, as well as lumber and nails and sacks of concrete and hammers and saws and very human technicians to help the citizens of the battered land more easily put their lives back together.

Slowly the troops of Jack Hunt fell back. Rebet and West took their battalions to the seacoast town of Dundalk and then turned south just as the battalions of Ben and Ike were rolling into Kildare. Dan and Striganov pushed fifteen miles in and stopped at the town of Baltinglass, while just south of their position, Danjou and Tina set up outside of Bunclody. And to the south of them, Thermopolis advanced to about fifteen miles west of Wexford and halted.

Several of Jack's battalion commanders came to his CP and laid their feelings on the line. "Jack, we can't hold out much longer. And as far as we're concerned, it's stupid to try. We're holding on to just a tiny piece of this island and the Rebels are knocking on the door, Jack. And the door is splintering."

"This island was mine! I ran this island. I was a *king* here, and you men lived damned well."

"Yes, we did, Jack. And we can do the same over in England. But this time we can prepare for Raines' invasion. That'll be our kind of fighting over there, Jack. That's what we all do best: house

94

to house. We'll have time to boobytrap and mine and get set. There is nothing left for us here, Jack. We've had it. All we'll do here is be destroyed."

But Jack was not convinced. "God damn it, people, we can hold him outside Dublin. *I know we can.*"

"Jack," Frankie told him. "We *can't* hold. Some of the men are already deserting. That ain't thunder out there, Jack. That's artillery, and Raines is damn near in striking distance of this city. Hell, there's six to eight thousand of them stinkin' damn Believers here in the city. Let them see if they can get lucky with the Rebels. Jack, we were goin' to leave anyway."

"Yes. But with honor."

"*Honor!* Jesus Christ, Jack! Honor? We're a pack of thieves and murderers and rapists and God only knows what else. You want to stay here and have someone chisel the word 'honor' on your tombstone? Providin', of course, that anyone can find the body and take the time to bury it. Which I doubt they will. Look yourself in the mirror, man. You haven't shaved or taken a bath in two weeks. Two weeks, Jack. That's how long Raines has been hammering us. We all stink. We're scared and tired and a lot of the men have reached the breaking point. Now, you've still got a mighty army left. Probably twelve or thirteen battalions . . ."

"Twelve or thirteen?" Jack's voice was numb with disbelief. "But I had nearly twice that."

"They're dead, Jack!" Harris shouted. "Raines uncorked some high-tech shit and sent it in. Helicopter gunships that pop up out of nowhere and launch rockets and chain guns and Jesus Christ alone knows what else. Now listen to me, Jack. We'll hold on these conditions: you get our armor and artillery on board those damn ships in the harbor and get it the hell out of here and over to England. You have ships ready to receive us on a moments notice when it's time to bug out. Now that's it, Jack. I'm tellin' you what the men tell me. They've had it. They'll follow you, man, but not to their deaths when it can be prevented."

General Jack Hunt sat behind his desk for a silent moment. His unshaven face was ashen, and there were bags under his eyes. He sighed and shook his head. "Vernon, get the ships ready to load what equipment we're taking with us."

"Yes, sir."

Jack looked at the battalion commanders in his office. "But tell me this, gentlemen: what happens if we can't contain the Rebels in England? Do we retreat to France? And if he pursues us there, what then?"

Frankie smiled. "I got that figured out, too, Jack. We'll bug out all right, but we leave well ahead of Raines and he ain't gonna have no idea where we are."

"Where will we be?"

"Hawaii."

"General," Corrie called from her radio. "Forward people report that all of a sudden Jack's troops found some backbone and are putting up a stiff fight along a lot of fronts. They're really putting up a scrap."

"That's odd," Chase said.

"Not really," Ben told him, pouring a cup of coffee. "I've been expecting it. I'll make you a wager he's getting ready to bug out for England."

Conversation stopped in the big room. All eyes shifted to Ben. His son asked, "And you're going to let him go?"

"We've got a city full of creepies to deal with, Buddy. And we've got to wait for a few weeks after that to provision up for the assault against England. We'll be going up against a much larger force there than we met here. English resistance groups report as many as a hundred thousand hostiles on that island, all coming together to fight against us."

Lamar Chase whistled softly. "A hundred thousand, Ben?"

"Yes. And it's going to be a long, tough campaign. England is over fifty thousand square miles and before the Great War had a population of more than fifty million people. Its coastline alone is more than two thousand miles. We've got to have everything we need stockpiled here in Ireland before we jump off. It'll be probably mid- or late summer before we're ready to strike at Britain. We've got to set up training bases to refresh our paratroopers, because without them going in first to secure some territory and raise hell, those going in by sea would get the shit shot out of them before they established a beachhead. All I've got is tentative plans drawn up. Beth, put out the word for all jump-trained personnel to give their names to their company commanders and then forward that list to me."

"We're all jump trained, father," Buddy pointed out.

Ben smiled. "That's right, son. We sure are."

"Now, you wait just a damn minute, Raines!" Dr. Chase stood up.

"Oh, sit down, Lamar," Ben told him. "I didn't say I was going in first wave with the jumpers, did I?"

"Well . . . no."

"So relax. We've got Dublin to clean out first, and you all know firsthand how savagely the creepies fight. They'll give us a hell of a lot more of a scrap than Jack Hunt's people ever did. As far as letting Hunt's people go, I don't have much of a choice in the matter. We can't shell the docks because we'll need them intact for our own invasion." He smiled and let those in the room wonder about that . . . they'd find out in a few weeks. "We'll just have to take the chance that Jack won't destroy them. And in order to minimize that, we keep the pressure on, day and night. When he does bug out, and I'm thinking that moment is very close, we re going to be nipping at his heels. So we'll just keep up what we're doing now."

The Rebel artillery kept up its savage pounding on the lines of Jack Hunt's soldiers. When Hunt's people would fall back a mile, the Rebel lines would immediately close the gap.

Rebet and West took the town of Drogheda and then made a lightning-fast commando move against the breeding and storage farm of the creepies located just south of there, freeing hundreds of men and women and children the creepies were breeding and fattening for food. The creepie guards did not attempt much of a fight. Instead they fled to the city to prepare against the Rebel attack they knew was inevitable.

Dan and Striganov busted through the lines and took the second breeding camp of the Believers, located about fifteen miles south of the city. Danjou and Tina punched through to the coast just south of them, and Thermopolis and his battalion broke through to Wexford and secured the town and the harbor. Now it didn't make any difference if Hunt did blow the facilities at Dublin, the Rebels had a secondary jump-off point at Wexford.

With the entire Rebel Army and the men and women of the Free Irish less than five miles from Dublin, Jack Hunt was frantically loading his people and what equipment they would take on board ships.

And the Night People, those who called themselves Believers, whom the Rebels referred to as creepies, were digging in for a long and bitter fight of it. Jack was leaving behind tons of equipment, and the creepies would make use of every scrap of it in the fight against their most hated enemy: Ben Raines and the Rebels.

"Let them go." Ben gave the orders to advance no further until Jack and his people were clear of the city. "What do our recon planes report?"

"Near panic," Beth told him. "I can't believe you're just going to let them go, General."

Ben smiled mysteriously. "How many ships are now in the Irish Sea, Corrie?"

"Twelve, sir. All heavily loaded."

"And Thermopolis reported ships in good shape laying outside of Wexford?"

"Yes, sir. As soon as Dublin is clean, he's preparing to bring them up."

Ben chuckled. "Launch the Apaches with their antitank missiles. Tell the pilots to stay well back and out of range of the ships' guns. Let's see what these tank-killers can do against ships."

Everyone in the room smiled. To a person they had all held the belief that there was no way Ben was going to just sit back and let Jack and his people sail blissfully off to Merry Old England.

The Apaches' missiles have a range of almost four miles and they can penetrate any known tank armor. Each Apache carries sixteen antitank missiles, seventy-six 2.75 folding-fin aerial rockets, and three hundred and twenty rounds of 30mm ammunition. It is a deadly fighting machine.

"Jack's people probably need baths," Ben said, leaning back in his chair. "And I have a hunch that many of them are going to get wet this day. Those that don't go down with the ships, that is."

"Apaches airborne, sir," Corrie called.

"Have fun, boys and girls," Ben said.

"I hate Ben Raines," Jack said glumly, standing by the railing of the old cargo ship. Dublin was behind them and they were heading for the docks at Liverpool. "I hate that son of a bitch more than I ever hated any being in my entire life." He paused as his eyes picked up dots in the sky. "What the hell are those things?" He pointed.

"Helicopters!" a lookout called.

"Get the SAMs ready!" Jack hollered.

"They're staying well out of range of anything we got, Jack. No good."

"Jesus Christ!" the lookout yelled. "Those are tank-killers. Apaches. They've launched missiles."

The Hellfire travels very fast. The chilling words

had just left the lookout's mouth when the wheel-house exploded, killing all in there; the bow was shot off; five missiles struck midship, and Jack was knocked off his boots. He landed hard on his butt and for a moment was unable to move.

The engine room exploded in smoke and flame and the ship was dead in the water. The convoy was taking a terrible pounding from the missiles. No ships were sinking yet, but all were badly damaged and most were dead in the water.

Jack crawled to his boots, very conscious that the deck was warm and getting warmer from the increasing fires in the holds beneath his feet.

"Is this goddamn tub sinking?" he hollered.

"Not yet," one of his men said. "But we're on fire and dead in the water."

"He tricked me," Jack said. "The bastard tricked me. The low-life son of a bitch had this planned all along."

Another missile struck and the sixty-year-old former World War Two Liberty ship shuddered.

"She's breaking up!" Those words were screamed out just as Jack was watching a ship slowly roll over belly-up like some great dead prehistoric water creature and begin to sink into the cold depths of the Irish Sea.

"Lower the lifeboats," Jack said bitterly, knowing he was finished as any type of military commander. He'd been neatly suckered into this, and this would be his final command. Even if he made it to shore, he couldn't get a job washing dishes in a mess hall.

Jack Hunt was not concerned about the loss of equipment, for England was filled with war supplies. What he was worried about was staying alive in lifeboats, for he now knew for an ironclad fact that Ben Raines was a hard and ruthless man who would stop at nothing to destroy an enemy.

"All ships hit," Corrie called. "Two are sunk and two more are sinking. All of them are dead in the water. Pilots report crews are abandoning ship."

Pat O'Shea was watching Ben closely. He wanted to see if the rumors about him were true; he wanted to witness firsthand just how hard this legendary soldier was.

"Finish it," Ben said. "Tell the pilots to go in and strafe. It'll be that many less that we'll have to deal with in England. And it'll damn sure give those over there something to think about."

Pat O'Shea smiled a grim warrior's smile. Ben Raines was the hardest man he had ever met.

Nine

Butch Smathers was among dozens of other warlords from around England who had gathered in Liverpool after receiving the news of the attack to listen firsthand to the survivors' stories. Less than two hundred men had survived the attack on the ships. Butch and others had sent small boats out during the night to pick up the nearly hysterical men and bring them to shore.

Several of the older and wiser of the bunch quietly slipped away and vanished in the English countryside. They wanted no part of Ben Raines and his Rebels.

Butch had seen them leave and knew what they were doing was probably the wisest thing for them. But for the most part, the street punk/outlaw/to-hell-with-you mentality is formed early — perhaps even at birth — and Butch and those remaining really had no overwhelming inclination to do anything other than what they had been doing for a decade, and for most, for many years prior to that.

"We got to have a meet, boys," Butch said. "And I mean do it quick and get this thing settled."

"What you mean?" a punk called Joey asked.

"You all heard what happened in Los Angeles, over in America. All them gangs there operated independent of each other when Raines come. So I heard. They didn't have no central commander givin' the orders. They all died. We can't let that happen here."

"Nobody gives my boys orders but me," a young man said.

"Same here," another said.

"Jack didn't make it," one of the survivors said. "I seen him floatin' on a piece of wreckage, with half his head blowed off. Didn't none of the battalion commanders make it, neither. But Butch is right—you guys operate without a strong central leader, and you're dead meat."

"Hey, man!" a punk who called himself Maddy piped up. "We got tanks, guns, rocket launchers, explosives, mortars—everything them Rebels has got. We been operatin' just fine without no one man givin' orders."

"No, you ain't got everything the Rebels has got," the survivor told him. "You don't have training and experience. You don't have leadership. You don't have your moves down pat. And you don't have the drive or the spirit of the Rebels. And more important, you don't have someone like Ben Raines."

"Ben Raines ain't shit!" a punk sneered.

"Wrong," the voice came from the shadows of the cavernous room where the creepie had been standing silently.

The group fell silent. Although the various war-

104

lords and street punk leaders cooperated with the Night People, they did not like them and were just a bit scared of them. Too many of their kind had crossed the Believers and then just one day disappeared never to be seen again. Everyone knew where they had gone: into the bellies of the Night People.

The Believers almost never came out in the daylight, and many of them lived under ground, especially in London, in the bowels of the city. They were fierce fighters and backed up for no one. The punks provided them with live human beings in exchange for getting along with them.

The creepie said, "Ben Raines and his Rebels are the greatest guerrilla fighters and tacticians on the face of the earth. They can fight conventionally or nonconventionally. They have no equal, certainly not among the rabble I see before me now. You must make up your minds to fight them as a group, taking orders from one man, or the Rebels will chew you up and spit you out like meat from a grinder."

"I gotta see it to believe it," a punk said.

"You won't live that long," the Believer told him, then stepped out into the night and vanished.

Nearly a fourth of those who survived the missile attack and the strafing that followed were from Frankie's battalion. Frankie had not survived, but his plan lived on in the minds of those who did.

After the meeting had broken up into small groups of punks and warlords, each group arguing about who was to be the leader, the remnants of Frankie's command assembled outside the huge warehouse.

"This bunch will fight, but Raines will win," one man said.

"Yeah," another one agreed. "The Night People will give the Rebels the stiffest resistance. But what about us?"

"Let's check out the harbor and see what's floating. I got me a sudden yen to see hula girls and palm trees."

The men grinned and walked off.

The creepies in Dublin had not been surprised to hear and witness the demise of Jack Hunt's army at the hands of Ben Raines. They had been following Ben Raines — by shortwave radio — for years. No one had to tell them how ruthless the man could be. He had virtually wiped out their kind in America and if he had his way would do the same thing in Europe.

The creepies dug in and prepared themselves mentally for a fight to the death against the Rebels.

Outside the city, Ben and his commanders met for one last time before they began their assault against Dublin.

"This will be the toughest nut to crack," Ben told his people. "I've come up with and rejected a dozen plans. I thought about circling the city and starving them out. But we know the creeps hold hundreds of prisoners in there. They could last for years. Pat O'Shea says there are no civilians in the city who are there willingly. When the creepies surfaced, the citizens moved out. Those that learned of them in time, that is. I suspect the rest got eaten," he added.

To a person, those gathered around shuddered and grimaced. There was no way to express what the Rebels felt toward the Night People. Hate would be far too mild a word.

Ben's eyes swept the group. "I don't have to say this, but I will anyway. No prisoners. *None.* No compassion shown them. No pity, no mercy. Just a bullet. We're going to do this slow and do it right, with a minimum of casualties. Now we all know that even if we shelled the city down to rubble, we'd still have to go in and dig the creepies out of their underground homes. So we're going to take the city house by house, street by street. I want everyone in body armor and helmets. No berets, no bandanas. This campaign has pretty much been a picnic since Galway. Well, now the picnic has been invaded by fire ants, and the bastards are resistant to just about everything except being stepped on and squashed. So that's what we'll do. We're lucky in that Dublin, while once a major city, is a compact place and fairly easy to learn how to move about." Ben grinned. "It also once held over a thousand pubs."

"My kind of city," Rebet said.

"Yeah," Ike agreed. "Maybe we'll get lucky and find a warehouse full of Irish whiskey."

"Dream on," Ben told him. "All right, people, we hit the city at dawn tomorrow."

* * *

Ben shoved open the door to the home on the outskirts of town and looked inside. The place had been trashed, and trashed more than once. At first glance, no one had occupied this dwelling for a long time. But the Rebels had learned from hard and bitter lessons that that was the way the creepies liked to leave things. Ben stepped inside, his team moving in swiftly behind him and fanning out.

"Jesus, what a mess," Cooper said, looking around him. Then he stopped and sniffed the air. He cut his eyes to Ben.

Ben nodded his head. He, too, had caught the unmistakable odor of unwashed flesh, the telltale sign that Night People were close.

"Cellar," Ben said. "Find the door, inside and out. Coop, take your Stoner and cover the outside."

Beth found the inside door to the basement and sniffed at it. "Phew. Rotting flesh, General."

Ben slung his CAR-15 and took a fire-frag from his battle harness and pulled the pin, holding the spoon down. "Open the door."

Beth jerked open the door and Ben tossed the mini-Claymore into the rank darkness. The smell of rotting human flesh and the unwashed bodies of creepies struck them all as they stepped to one side.

The fire-frag blew and screaming began from the depths of the darkness. Coop's Stoner began howling as light filled the cellar and creeps threw open the outside exit and tried to run. One came charging up the steps, screaming hate at the Rebels, an AK-47 sputtering in his hands.

Beth slammed the door closed just as the creep reached the landing and ran into the door, the impact knocking him tumbling back down the steps.

"Nice touch, Beth," Ben said with a grin.

She opened the door and gave the basement a hosing with her M-16. There were no more sounds of life from the cellar. Just to make sure, Beth tossed another grenade into the stinking cellar and closed the door.

"First block cleared," Corrie said, after receiving reports.

"Only about five hundred to go," Ben said. All around them, the early morning air was filled with gunsmoke and the booming of grenades.

Thousands of Rebels, moving forward behind tanks and APCs, were starting on clearing the last major objective in Ireland.

"Corrie, have platoon leaders warn their people again about booby traps," Ben said. "If the creepies run true to form, the closer we get to the heart of the city, the more likely the chances of that."

By noon of the first day, the Rebels had cleared only a few blocks of the suburbs, but they had sustained no deaths or injuries, and Ben planned on keeping it that way. As they broke for lunch, Ben's eyes continually returned to a large, very stately home located on a corner.

"What's the matter, Ben?" Linda asked. "You're

not eating. You feel all right?"

"I feel fine. That mini-mansion over there bothers me. You people go on eating. Buddy, come with me, son. Let's check that place out."

Jersey rose and followed him, as did the rest of his team, munching on crackers as they walked. They all knew that Ben liked to lone-wolf it into mischief, and there was no way they were going to let him go it alone.

The home had once been a grand place, that was evident from half a block away. But what had bothered Ben were the dark drapes still hanging in place over not just a few of the windows, but all of them, top and bottom floors.

"What's up, General?" Jersey asked, walking between Ben and his son.

"That house there. It bothers me."

Jersey stared at the grand old home for a few seconds. "Yeah," she said. "You're right. It looks . . . spooky."

"Or creepie," Ben replied. "Spread out. Buddy, you take the back of the house in case we flush something. Wave a couple of your Rats over here to join you. Find the outside basement exit. I'm going in the front. Easy does it, now."

"*We're* going in the front," Jersey said.

Ben smiled. "Right you are, Jersey." He climbed the broad steps to the concrete-and-brick porch, his team to the left and right of him. Ben walked to the door and started to close his hand around the knob. Slowly he pulled his hand back.

"What's the matter, General?" Corrie asked.

"Order all troops back a full block from this

110

house, Corrie. Tell them to move right now."

"Yes, sir."

"Buddy!" Ben yelled.

"Here, sir."

"Back off. Get your people out of this area right now."

"Yes, sir. We're gone."

"Let's get out of here, gang," Ben said. "Like right now. Move."

With every Rebel at least one full block away from the silent yet strangely ominous old house, Ben called a Rebel with a rocket launcher over to him. "Put one right through the front door, soldier."

"Yes, sir."

When the rocket impacted with the front door, the blast that followed completely demolished houses on all sides of the small mansion, and virtually destroyed others within two hundred yards of the blast site. Flames leaped out of all sides of the home that was no more and started small fires all around the site. Debris rained down like shrapnel for hundreds of feet. The shock wave staggered Rebels who were standing a full block away and put some of the smaller and lighter ones on the ground.

"Jesus Christ!" Cooper said, looking around for his helmet, which had been knocked off by the blast. He found it and plopped it back on his head. "There must have been five thousand pounds of explosives in that house."

"At least," Ben said, digging a finger into first one ear and then the other. Everyone's hearing was temporarily impaired from the enormous explosion.

Ben looked around him. "Anybody hurt from falling debris?" he yelled.

A half dozen people had taken pretty fair licks on the head because they had not been wearing helmets. One had been knocked cold and would require some stitching.

"Put your goddamn helmets on your heads and don't take them off until your squad leader tells you to," Ben yelled. "Pass the word."

Pat O'Shea roared up in a pickup and hopped out. "Good Lord, General, what happened?"

"Booby trap, Pat. It's all part of it."

Ike and Dan were in the area right behind Pat. "We got to talk about this, Ben," Ike said. "We'd better lay down some ground rules."

Ben shook his head. "That's what they want us to do, Ike. They want us to become ultra-careful, to slow us down so they can dig in deeper and be harder to root out. From now on, fire a rifle-grenade into each home before troops enter. It won't destroy the dwelling—in most cases—but it'll damn sure set off any traps the creeps might have in place. We've never encountered any sophistication in their booby-trapping and I see no reason to suspect any now. Corrie, pass the word about entering buildings and tell CO's to provide plenty of grenades for everyone with a launcher."

Ben looked around at all the destruction caused by the enormous explosion. He shook his head and put out of his mind what might have happened had he not played his hunches. "Let's get back to work, people." He took a deep breath and yelled, "And God damn it, put your helmets on!"

Ten

The Rebels encountered no more booby traps to equal the one Ben had discovered, but they did find several much smaller ones planted in old homes in the suburbs of Dublin. They were very unsophisticated ones and all went off when the grenades blew, with no loss of Rebel life.

Ben had ordered gunboats to be on constant patrol just outside Dublin Harbor in case any creepies tried to flee in that direction. Then Ben ordered the noose to be tightened from all sides.

Rebels found a large pocket of creepies at Dublin Airport and called in that news to Ben. "Let's go see what we have," Ben said, adding, "I have never understood the creepies' fascination with airports. It never fails but what we find a large concentration of them there."

Ben stood on the edge of the battle zone and inspected the airport through binoculars. He turned to his daughter, Tina, whose battalion had discovered the creepies. Little by little, Ben was giving his son and daughter the temporary reins of command. "How would you handle it, Tina?"

"We can knock the buildings down with artillery and keep the runways intact," she said. "I think we can take it without losing a single Rebel life."

Ben smiled at her. "Exactly what I would do."

She returned the smile. "Yes. I know."

"Take it."

The Night People wanted the Rebels to come in after them so they could inflict heavy casualties on them during close-in fighting. They knew they were going to be destroyed and wanted to kill a lot of Rebels. But the creepies never quite figured out the Rebels' style of fighting, and again, they were disappointed.

"Snipers with .50's up," Tina told her radio operator. "Get artillery in place and stand by for my orders."

"Yes, ma'am," the young man said.

Ben sat down in a folding camp chair, rolled a cigarette, and accepted a cup of coffee. "Beats the hell out of being down there smelling those stinking creeps and having lead whistling all around you," Ben remarked. "Let it bang, kid."

Tina laughed at her father. "Right on, Pop!"

Ben sighed at the decades-old expression that was enjoying a revival among his troops.

"Tell artillery to fire when ready," Tina ordered.

"Yes, ma'am."

The terminal buildings began erupting in flame and shattered rubble as the 105's and 60- and 81mm mortars began howling and snarling, dropping in their deadly mail. Snipers firing the long-range .50 caliber rifles methodically and without emotion shot down the creepies as they tried to escape the devastating artillery rounds.

Ben sat in the shade provided by the bulk of a main battle tank and sipped his coffee and watched his people work. Totally professional, he thought; I'm watching the finest fighting force in the world.

"*Bor-ing*," Cooper remarked, stretched out on the grass, taking in the sun.

"It'll damn sure pick up when we enter the city, Coop," Ben told him. "Enjoy this while you can."

"General," Beth said, during a lull in the artillery barrage. "Are we wrong to be so . . . well, nonchalant about this? I mean, it's like we don't think any more of this than the folks back at Base Camp One, going to work in the hospital or the factories or the offices."

"Does the sight of abused and wounded and sick children still bother you, Beth?" Ben asked.

"Sure!"

"Do starving and hurt and crippled animals bother you, Jersey?"

"Yes, sir. I've bawled a lot of times at the sight. And I will again."

"Corrie, can you feel compassion for the good and decent people these outlaws and scum have abused and raped and tortured and enslaved?"

"Yes, sir. Everytime I witness it."

"Coop, do you feel outrage at the sight of wanton and senseless vandalism of priceless works of art and the enslavement of human beings?"

116

"I damn sure do, sir."

"Then you've all answered Beth's question, and you've all spoken for every Rebel in this army. Because that shit down there," he pointed to the bodies of creepies sprawled in death on the tarmac, "and all the other outlaw, trash, and scum we've scooped into mass graves over the years, if they had responded truthfully, would have answered no to every question I just asked. There is no reason for any of us to feel one iota of guilt or remorse about what we're doing. We're just doing a very distasteful job that needs to be done."

A man everyone assumed to be from the Free Irish Army had come up and had listened to Ben. He was dressed in military green, wore regulation boots that were bloused, and was quite definitely Irish. "You're quite the philosopher, General. You're an odd combination of things. Warrior, tactician, philosopher, and as cold as any English banker's heart when you have to be."

Ben waited until after another hard barrage of artillery had passed over. "Well," he said with a smile, "I used to be a pretty good writer, I think. But as far as those other things you mentioned . . . I never wanted to be any of them."

No one noticed as Ben slipped an over/under 410 derringer from behind his web belt.

"But you felt the call, seen your duty, and done it, ain't that right, General?" The man stepped closer.

"Cease fire," Tina ordered. "Mop-up teams in."

"That's certainly one way of putting it," Ben replied.

"Freshen up your coffee, General?" Cooper said, getting to his feet.

Ben gave him the cup. "Thanks, Coop. That'd be fine."

"Jersey?" Coop asked.

"No," she said shortly, never taking her eyes off the stranger with the strange smile. "Get out of the way, Coop."

"What's your problem?" Cooper muttered, heading for the ever-ready coffeepot in the mess tent.

Corrie was busy at her radio, Linda had gone off to help with any wounded that might straggle in to the MASH tent of Tina's battalion, and Beth was writing in her journal.

"You ready, Jersey?" Ben asked.

"Anytime, General," the petite bodyguard replied.

The stranger suddenly lifted a pistol and Ben and Jersey fired at the same time. The 410 round completely wiped off the man's face and Jersey's M-16 punched holes in his chest. The stranger was dead before he hit the grass.

The area was suddenly swarming with Rebels at a run.

"Are you all right, Dad?" Tina asked.

"Oh, yeah," Ben said, reloading the derringer. "Somebody fan the body for I.D."

"Nothing, sir," a Rebel said, after fanning the body. "Just this pistol. He's not dirty or smelly, so he couldn't be a creepie. I wonder who he is — was?"

Ben had a pretty good idea that the man was from one side or the other up in Northern Ireland. They didn't want Ben to bring his Rebels up there and put an end to their by now intensely personal war. They needn't have worried about it. Ben had no intention of getting involved in that mess.

"I don't know," Ben said, keeping his opinions to himself. For if the Rebels felt that a factor in the northern part of the country was putting death sentences out on their general, Ben would be hard pressed to contain his people, who would immediately want to set off on a mission to wipe out the whole lot of them.

"Bury with the creepies, sir?" Ben was asked.

Ben shook his head. Most of the Rebels gathered around looked strangely at Ben when he said softly, "No. Not with them. He deserves better than that. He's an Irishman. And I've a strong feeling he was not a collaborator. He was just fighting for a lost cause, that's all." Be looked all around him. "Bury him over there, on that rise. Close to that fence with the wild roses." Ben pointed. "Where he can feel the morning sun and maybe smell the sea every now and then."

As Ben and his team were pulling out about an hour later, Ben could see Sgt. Dempsey standing over the mound of earth, a harmonica to his mouth. Ben couldn't hear the tune, but he'd bet it was "Danny Boy."

* * *

The airport runways were functioning the next day and planes could now land, mostly old transport planes bringing in material from the docks at Galway.

The suburbs had been cleared of creepies and the few among Hunt's army who had been left behind in the hurried bugout, and a few Irish collaborators. Many of those who collaborated killed themselves rather than fall into the hands of the Free Irish.

Inside the silent city of Dublin, the creepies were dug in tight, as ready as they could be for the Rebel invasion. Flyovers showed that most of the bridges within the city had been destroyed by the creeps.

"The battalions who clean out this area," Ben said, pointing to a map, "are going to have to work slow and careful. All the bridges over the River Liffey and the Grand Canal have been destroyed. This spot will be the hottest, so I'll take my battalion and one other in, supported by light tanks."

"You get your butt cut off in there and you're in trouble, Ben," Ike pointed out.

"Yes. So here's the way it'll go. My One Battalion and Dan's Three Battalion will take the area between Liffey and the Grand Canal. Thermopolis and his Eight Battalion will be behind us to prevent any creepie swing around to box us. Ike's Two Battalion, West's Four Battalion, and Danjou's Seven will work the area north of the River Liffey, and Striganov's Five, Rebet's

120

Six, and Tina's Nine Battalion will take everything south of the Grand Canal. We'll link up at the Irish Sea. We'll call this Operation Clean Sweep. Any questions?"

The battalion commanders knew better than to attempt to dissuade Ben from taking the hot area, so none tried. He was going to go where the action was until the day he died and that was that.

Ben looked at Thermopolis, Emil Hite standing by his side in the big room of Ben's temporary CP. Emil, the little con artist who had worked most known scams both before and after the Great War, had proven to be a fine soldier. But on this campaign he had been unusually silent.

"Is he sick?" Ben asked Therm, pointing his finger at Emil.

"A psychiatrist would probably say yes," the hippie-turned-warrior replied.

"I feel fine, General," Emil said, drawing himself up to stand as tall as he could. The top of his head came to just about the center of Ben's chest. When he wasn't wearing cowboy boots and a turban. "This has been a very sobering experience for me. My mother's people came from this fair and green isle. Just being here has brought out the Irish in me. The misty breeze and the rolling hills, the scent of wild roses and the smell of freshly-turned earth have moved me so deeply I sometimes weep for joy at returning to the place of my ancestry. Why, just the other morning I removed my boots and socks and ran light-hearted and lithe through the dewy grass . . ."

121

"Emil . . ." Ben said wearly, now sorry he'd brought up the subject.

". . . A hundred Irish melodies filled my heart as an invisible choir, a children's choir, sang so pure and sweetly I could not contain my tears of joy . . ."

"Emil . . ." Ben was getting a headache.

Georgi Striganov had covered his ears with his hands. Ike was grinning at the expression on Ben's face. Lamar Chase was looking for a way out of the room.

". . . I felt as if I had finally come home." Emil was really getting into it now. "This ancient land where Vikings and Celts and Normans had trod was a part of me . . ."

"Jesus, Emil!" Ben said.

". . . No, He never got this far, but I'm sure He blessed this emerald isle. I threw all my cares and woes to the gentle breeze as I ran like a carefree and happy child. I . . ."

"Emil!" Ben roared.

"What, my General?"

"How'd you get that bruise on your face?"

"While I was racing willy-nilly through the dew, I stepped in a pile of sheep shit and busted my ass and knocked myself goofy for a time. When I regained my senses, a flock of sheep had gathered around, looking at me. Have you ever looked deeply into a sheep's eyes, General?"

Ben was laughing so hard he had to sit down. "No, Emil," he finally managed to say. "I've been spared that pleasure."

"They're lovely. I shall never eat mutton

122

again."

Ben wiped his eyes and said, "Everybody firm on what to do?"

Everybody was.

"Watch my back, Therm," Ben said.

"You may advance with not a worry nor a care about sneak attacks from behind, General," Emil said. "The fighting Eighth will cover you like a protective blanket on a cool night."

"Thank you, Emil," Ben said, trying to keep a straight face. "You just erased any worries I might have had."

"We shall fight in the hedgerows and in the streets. We shall fight until our enemies are vanquished from this land!" Emil shouted. "Neither rain, nor sleet, nor fog, nor gloom of night shall deter us from our duties . . ."

"Oh, God," Striganov said, looking around frantically. "He's going off his bean again."

"Come on, Emil," Thermopolis urged.

"Don't stop me now, baby!" Emil said. "I'm beginning to cook."

"That's what concerns me."

"No evil power on this earth can stop the Rebels when we get going!" Emil yelled.

Jersey had picked up a two-by-four and was moving menacingly toward Emil. Ben grabbed her by the back of her web belt just as she was preparing to conk Emil on the noggin.

Fortunately, he was wearing a helmet, so it probably wouldn't have done him much damage had she busted him one. But Ben preferred to keep his troops healthy.

123

"Easy, Jersey," he cautioned her, and held on firmly.

Beerbelly picked Thermopolis up like a sack of feed, tossed him over one shoulder, and carried him outside.

"Just think," Ben said, breaking the numb silence that always followed one of Emil's outbursts. "And I thought he was sick!"

Eleven

Ben launched the assault against Dublin at dawn. He hit the creepies hard from the north, the south, and the west. Dusters and MBTs spearheaded the drive; the MBTs were going to be too large to navigate many of the city's narrow, twisting streets. Scouts in LAVs—light armored vehicles—led the way in. Each Duster carried twice its usual complement of 40mm rounds, for once inside the zone, there was no way of telling how long it would be before they were resupplied, and there was always the possibility of getting cut off.

Ben had been expecting a tough fight from the creepies, and he and his people were certainly not disappointed. The creeps had thrown up roadblocks at every intersection, dragging in old cars and trucks, chaining them together and then chaining them to lampposts. Ben and his team were pinned down hard almost from the get-go.

"Where the hell are we?" Ben shouted, over the roar of machine guns and the rattle of smaller arms.

"Pinned down," Buddy said with a smile.

"Thank you, boy. I'll treasure that information

always. Smart-ass." Buddy laughed at him as his father crawled to the outside phone box of a Duster and told the commander, "See that saloon with the black and red trim about ten o'clock and that old boutique at two o'clock?"

"Yes, sir."

"Neutralize them. They've got fifties in there."

"Yes, sir."

The twin 40mm's were lowered and began hammering out HE. The Duster is capable of spitting out 240 rounds a minute. Within fifteen seconds there was nothing left of either the saloon or the boutique. Nothing left of the creepies inside them, either, except what one might wish to scrape off the walls.

An hour later, the Rebels of Ben's command had moved up two blocks, and they were hard-won blocks.

"Tell everyone to take a break and let's find out what the others are doing," Ben told Corrie.

She radioed the orders, and gradually the firing subsided all around them.

"All units are reporting slow going, sir," Corrie told him. "The creepies are really dug in tight. We're still twenty or more blocks away from St. Patrick's Cathedral."

"Get me Therm, Corrie. I heard some pretty heavy fighting back there just before we shut it down."

"You heard right, Eagle," Thermopolis radioed, using code names. "You figured it on the money. The creepies were trying to do an end-around and box you in. We're got it secured."

"That's ten-four, Hippie. Thanks for keeping

126

them off my ass. Eagle out."

"Eagle, this is Shark," Ike radioed. "We are bogged down hard and mired up to our knees. We are going to have to use the heavy stuff if we're to break through."

"Do it," the voice of Pat O'Shea came through. "It's a cryin' shame, but I can see that it has to be."

"Are you sure, Paddy?" Ben asked, using the code name the Irishman had chosen for himself.

"That's affirmative, Eagle. There's been too much blood spilled on this land as it is. I'll not have the blood of Yanks on my conscience over a bunch of damn buildin's."

"Bear to Eagle," Striganov radioed. "Go to burst transmission."

"Go, Bear."

"We can save the landmarks, or at least a large portion of them. We'll have to hand-flush the creepies out, but the churches and the libraries and museums can be saved."

"All right, boys and girls," Ben said. "Let's all catch our breath and start getting some heavy stuff up here. We'll kick this thing off in thirty minutes." He turned to Corrie. "Get teams with rocket launchers up here. Also we'll use MBTs on the larger and wider streets."

The Rebel engineers had taken the bazooka concept and improved on it, coming up with something very much like the Marine Corps's old SMAW— shoulder-launched, multipurpose assault weapon. But where the SMAW was limited to the types of rockets it could fire, the Rebel launchers could fire a variety of rockets.

A half a dozen huge main battle tanks lumbered

up to Ben's position. The behemoths dwarfed the Dusters, making the smaller tanks look almost petite.

"Everybody fall behind the tanks," Ben ordered, and the Rebels pulled back of the armor. Ben talked to the tank commanders. "At my orders, start putting rounds ground floor into every building you can see from this spot. Then cease fire and let us mop it up. Understood?"

"Yes, sir."

Ben checked his watch as the turrets whirred left and right and the main cannons were lowered. He watched the second hand of his watch move toward the mark. "Fire," he said softly.

Operation Clean Sweep kicked into high gear.

The ground floors of small shops and apartment buildings and old office buildings exploded in dust and rubble as the big guns roared. Over the sounds of falling bricks and rafters came the screaming of the Believers as they were caught in the crushing debris of the collapsing buildings. Many tried to run and were chopped down by the Rebels.

The tanks moved up a block, the treads of the sixty-three-ton tanks crushing out any life that might remain in those creeps shot down in the streets. The Rebels fanned out on either side to begin the mop-up.

Ben ran into what at one time had been a tobacco shop. The small shop, even after a decade of unuse, and after taking a hit from a 120mm tank round, still faintly held the aromatic smells of dozens of kinds of tobacco. And under those smells Ben could detect the stink of creepies.

Ben pointed to himself and then to a closed door

behind the dusty old counter, the door set in the only wall that was left undamaged. The west side of the shop was completely blown open. Beth and Corrie nodded their understanding and Jersey moved with Ben while Cooper maintained a vigil at the front of the shop.

Ben had laid aside his CAR-15 and was carrying his old M-14, the Thunder Lizard set on full auto with a thirty-round clip in its belly. The old .308 was tough to handle on full auto, but its capacity to deal out hideous wounds was three times better than that of the 9mm CAR.

Ben poured in half a clip through the door and blew it off its hinges while Jersey stood by with a grenade in her hand. When the door sagged, Jersey tossed the antipersonnel grenade into the stinking darkness and the team members flattened against a wall or hit the littered floor.

Blood splattered the counter an instant after the grenade exploded. The team grinned at each other and stepped outside to the sidewalk, moving to the next doorway.

It had been cleared by the tank round. The creepies had been bunched up in a storeroom and the HE round had not left many of them intact. Most of them were dripping from the walls and ceiling or splattered on the floor.

They moved on, staying on the same side of the street. During any mop-up, troops had to stay within the perimeters of their assigned sectors; moving away from them was a good way to get seriously dead from friendly fire.

Jersey found an unopened box and held up a blouse.

"Oh, that's cute," Corrie said.

"It looks like it might fit you, too," Beth said.

"Are we having a fashion show?" Buddy asked, stepping in through the rubble.

"If you find a sport coat, 44 extra long," Ben said, "I want it."

"This is a ladies shop, Ben," Linda said, holding up a pair of red panties. "I don't think these would fit you very well."

"I agree," Ben said.

They all hit the floor as a sniper opened up from the top floor of the building across the street. The lead tore into the walls and howled off the exposed bricks of the interior of the boutique.

"AK-47," Jersey said, listening to the rattle of the weapon. She folded the blouse and tucked it into a pocket of her BDUs.

A Duster spun in the street and lifted its twin cannon. Seconds later the section of the building housing the sniper no longer existed.

The Duster moved up the street and Ben and his team slipped into the next building. This one was three stories and virtually undamaged. The round had gone straight through the windowless front and right out the open back door, impacting against the building across the alley. Ben pointed at Buddy and several of his Pack and then pointed toward the stairs. They moved out to clear the top floors and Ben and his people concentrated on the ground floor.

It was difficult to tell just what the ground floor had once been. Looters had done their work many times. Ben picked up a yellowing sheet of paper and read, THE TIME IS HERE, REPENT NOW

AND YOUR SINS WILL BE FORGIVEN. THE BEAST HAS EMERGED AND THE END IS SOON.

"No kidding?" Ben muttered, and returned the paper to the floor just as M-16's rattled and .45 caliber slugs from Buddy's old Thompson hammered from the floor above him. Muffled and very short screams drifted to the team, followed by the sounds of bodies hitting the floor.

The ground floor was empty of hostiles. Ben sat down on an old bench and took a sip of water from his canteen, listening to the cannons of the tanks as they moved up the street.

"Corrie," Ben called. "Advise all tank commanders to hold what they've got. Don't get too far ahead of us. Also find out where Therm is. We don't want to get so far apart we stand a chance of being cut off. Advise all battalion commanders that the creepies are more than likely below us, underground, and remind them that the creepies do have a tendency to pop up from the most unexpected places."

"Yes, sir. General Ike reports that he's having combat engineers spot-weld manhole covers in place as blocks are secured."

"Good idea. Have all units do the same. Remember New York City?" The team nodded their heads. Only Linda had not been in that prolonged battle. It was there that the Rebels had really learned how to fight the Night People.

"Thermopolis is reporting heavy fighting, sir," Corrie called. "The creeps have surfaced out of the sewers all around him."

"Does he need help?"

131

"He says no. He pulled tanks in just before the attack."

Ben nodded just as Buddy and his people returned from clearing the building. "Buddy, round up your Rat Pack and get back to Therm's position, attack the creeps from the rear, and get some pressure off the Eighth. Corrie, advise Therm of this move."

Ben munched on a cracker and watched as Buddy yelled for his team, and the young hellions—male and female—who made up the Rat Pack began the run back to Therm's position. He smiled at Linda. "I was that young once, I seem to recall."

"Wish you could go back, Ben?"

"No way. Middle age suits me just fine."

"General, Striganov is reporting he's just beat back a suicide charge by the creeps. It was a very heavy attack. He took some damage and is holding until he can get his wounded evacuated back to a MASH."

"Get me reports on what's happening north of us, please. Start with Danjou's Seven Battalion."

"Danjou has found one of the creepie butcher shops," Corrie said with a grimace. "He says it's the most disgusting thing he's ever seen. Several of the newer Rebels got pretty sick at the sight."

Ben knew only too well what she was talking about. He hoped he would never see another of the Night People's butcher shops. Over the long years of fighting the creepies, many Rebels had become pure vegetarians.

"Those I've contacted are reporting only limited action," Corrie said. "And Buddy and his Rat Pack are attacking the creeps at Therm's position."

Ben consulted a map and marked their present position. The assault was going just about as well as he had anticipated. Dan was south of Ben's position, both battalions still in the area that had been known as the Liberties, so named because its streets once lay in the "free land" of the cathedral, just beyond the jurisdiction of the Lord Mayor of Dublin.

Those battalions pushing north and south against the city were gradually shoving the creepies against a wall from which there would be no escape.

Ben carefully folded the map and returned it to a pocket of his BDUs. He picked up his M-14. "All right, folks, let's catch up with the tanks."

The battalions moved on, two battalions stretched out north to south over a mile of shops and office buildings and twisting streets. And the Rebels had miles to go before they reached the harbor.

A bullet blew splinters into Ben's face and he hit the sidewalk, crouched down behind a rusted old truck. Corrie called for a Duster and the tank spun around and gave the top floor of the building a hundred rounds of 40mm shells. While those creeps in the building were taking punishment, Ben rolled into a store that had once sold hardware.

"Ace is the place," he muttered, knowing that of his team, only Linda would know what he was talking about. She caught his words and smiled at him.

Ben saw a flash of movement on the second floor of a building and gave the gray-clad figure half a clip. That brought more fire from the glassless windows across the street and above his position.

The Duster began really pouring rounds into the building until the second floor was virtually destroyed. Creepies poured out of the ground floor and ran into the littered streets, screaming hate and fury, running straight toward Ben's position. The Duster wheeled about and crushed one under the treads. Others climbed on and tried to breech the open gunner's compartment. Ben and his team shot them off just as a few creeps reached the old hardware store and flung themselves through the open storefront.

Linda whirled around and saw the rear of the store filled with wild-eyed Believers. She leveled her shotgun and held the trigger back, firing from the hip. The buckshot tore into flesh and threw the attackers back.

Ben emptied a clip and then reversed the M-14, using it as a club, beating in the head of a creep. He dropped the empty weapon, pulled out both 9mms, and let them both bang.

Cooper was lying on his belly, behind his Stoner, keeping the street clear while Corrie and Beth were trying to plug up a large hole in the wall made by a friendly tank round. Jersey gave Ben some relief and some time to slip in a fresh clip for his Thunder Lizard and full clips for his 9mms. Two Dusters backed up and blocked the storefront, allowing those inside to concentrate on the rear and the large hole to their north.

"We damn sure hit a pocket of them!" Jersey said, slamming home a full thirty-round clip.

"Where the hell are they coming from?" Linda yelled, locking into place a full drum of shotgun shells.

"Damn good question," Ben said, taking a fire-frag from his battle harness. "Everybody, chunk some oranges and apples into that store next to us."

A half a dozen antipersonnel grenades sailed through the hole in the bricks and blew dust and debris and various body parts all over the place. Wild shrieking followed the grenade attack, and one of the Dusters blocking the store front started pumping .50 caliber slugs into the mangled mess. The screaming faded off into silence. Before anyone could stop him, Ben was through the hole and into the store, his team scrambling frantically to catch him.

"God damn it, General!" Jersey cussed.

Ben paid her no attention as he stepped over dead creeps. "Look for a hole in the floor," he said. "I bet you a case of whiskey they've got holes leading to tunnels under the city. Corrie, radio all batt coms to stop advancing and look behind them for hidey-holes. There it is," he said, pointing. "Under that counter. Get some truckloads of explosives up here. We're going to have to backtrack and find these holes and blow them closed."

"That's going to take a lot of time," Cooper said.

"Better than waking up in bed with one of these creeps," Ben pointed out.

"Yekk!" Jersey grimaced.

Twelve

"You're right, Ben," Ike radioed from his position just north of the National Botanical Gardens. "The creeps have quite a network of holes and tunnels. Hell, they've had ten years or more to set it up."

"I've got explosives being flown in," Ben told them all. "We'll just hold what we've got for a day or two. And watch your backs. You can bet the creeps are going to counterattack from the rear. Buddy, stay with Therm's Eight Battalion. Dan, how's it with you?"

"We're spread pretty thin," the Englishman radioed. "But then, so is everybody. We took a creep alive, General. He confirmed that they have holding pens all over the city, underground."

"Fresh food whenever they want it," Cooper said. "Barf!" He looked at his packet of field rations and put it back into his pack.

The Rebels were settling down for the night, but no one was going to get much restful sleep, not with the knowledge that the Believers were all around them above ground and moving around under them.

Ben's CP for this night was the second floor of

an office building. He thought it ironic that he was using the offices of what had once belonged to an Irish defense attorney — according to the papers his people had found.

He wondered if the Believers had eaten him. He shook his head at the disgusting thought.

"We found the hole in this building," Beth told him, walking into the office. "It was in the back of a closet. We plugged it temporarily until we move out. Then we'll seal it tight."

"We've got to find every damn one of them," Ben said, opening a packet of field rations. "And plug them. If we miss just one, the creeps will pour out of it like rats." He looked at his rations and sighed. "I'd like to have an omelet. With chopped up onions and peppers and some Monterey Jack cheese."

"Chicken and dumplings," Cooper wished.

"Moo goo gai pan," Linda said.

"What the hell is that?" Jersey asked her.

"Chinese," Linda said gently, realizing that Jersey had been no more than a child when the Great War had struck the world. Many of the Rebels had only vague memories of baseball games, *The Golden Girls,* Sunday picnics . . . or peace.

"Sounds awful," Beth said. "But . . . seems like I remember something about it."

"We got something moving around out there," Corrie stuck her head into the room and announced. "All battalions are reporting movement."

The single lantern in the room was quickly extinguished and everybody grabbed weapons.

"The buildings across the street are secure," Ben said. "With Rebels on the roofs. So it's not going to come from that direction. We've got the hole plugged in this building, so that's out. They probably know that I'm using this building for a CP because of the heavy security all around it. Let's don't kid ourselves that they aren't watching us."

"Maybe we missed a hole," Linda said softly.

Those quiet spoken words chilled them all. Ben said, "Everybody on full alert. Make sure every closet door on the ground floor is securely locked . . . aw, to hell with it. We don't have time for that. Corrie, get everyone ready for a fight."

Jersey grinned at him in the darkness. "Hell, boss, we're *always* ready for that."

The Rebels waited in darkness, on full alert for several hours, with lookouts using heatseeking portable scopes detecting movement all around them. But nothing happened.

"Stand down to level two," Ben ordered. "Let's every other person get some sleep for a few hours, then wake the person next to them. The bastards are trying to exhaust us, keep us up all night so we'll be dull in the morning. Jersey, Corrie, and me will sleep for a few hours. Then we'll spell you others. Hit the sack, gang."

Ben's eyes popped open three hours later. He never slept for more than five hours anyway, so the loss of a couple of hours affected him little. Jersey and Corrie slept on, heads on their packs and using ponchos for blankets. Ben pointed to Linda, Beth, and Cooper, then pointed to the floor. They didn't need a second invitation.

He stood and stretched the kinks out of his muscles and joints and then picked up his M-14 and quietly slipped out of the room and made his way to the ground floor, being careful not to step on the sprawling Rebels asleep on the hall floor. He walked to the front of the building and looked outside.

"Same crap all night long, General," the guard told him. "Moving around just enough to make us think something big is about to pop."

"It'll probably pop at dawn."

Ben walked soundlessly to the rear of the building and spoke to the guards in the main hall, where a back door used to be. The opening had been secured with heavy timbers from the wreckage and behind that barrier was a heavy machine gun.

"Just a few minutes before dawn, get everybody up and let them get the kinks out and use the toilet," Ben told the sergeant in charge. "I think the creeps are going to come at us hard just about then."

Ben looked around at the sound of boots. Jersey and Corrie stood in the hall, glaring at him. He grinned at them. "Slipped away, didn't I?"

"You get lucky every now and then," Jersey conceded, an edge to her voice that silently stated he wouldn't do it again.

"Fresh coffee's ready, General," a Rebel said. "Third door on your right."

"Thanks. Where's the toilet area?"

"Porta-Pots up the hall and to your left."

Corrie and Jersey fell in step with him. "You're not going to the john with me," Ben told them.

"We'll wait outside," Jersey said.

A few moments later, Ben tapped on the closed door. "Coming in for coffee," he said, giving those inside time to cut down the lantern.

The three got their coffee and packets of rations

139

and sat down on the floor in the hall.

Ben checked the time. Four-thirty. He had noted that the night was cloudy and misting rain. A perfect setting for an attack from the Believers. He ate his breakfast rations, had a second cup of coffee, and waited with the others for the graying of dawn.

"They're massing out there, General," Ben received the word.

"Thanks. Get everybody up. Pass the word to all batt coms, Corrie. And if anyone finds an old can of Lysol, save it. I think the creepies are going to get pretty damn close this go-around."

"Yekk!" Jersey said.

The men and women of the Free Irish had been stationed at strategic spots all around the city, and other units of the Free Irish were still engaged in some fairly heavy mopping up all over their country. There was a lot of retribution killing going on against those who'd collaborated with the enemy, and Ben did not want his Rebels taking any part in that. Let the Irish deal with the Irish.

All the Rebels had drawn ammo and other replacement equipment before settling down for the night, so they were ready. Water and ration trucks had come and gone, so they were in good shape there. The tank crews—freshly resupplied—had crawled back into their armor and buttoned down tight. Now all the Rebels had to do was hold what they had taken.

A light but steady rain had begun, and that would work to the advantage of the Believers, covering the sounds of their furtive advance.

"It'll also wash some of the stink off of the bastards," Cooper pointed out.

"Sometimes, Cooper," Jersey said with a wicked little smile as she continued harassing her friend, "you do make sense."

"Thanks, Shorty," Cooper responded. "Did you take the vitamin in your ration packet? It'll help you grow up to be big and strong like me."

Ben chuckled. "He got you there, Jersey."

"I won't forget," she said.

Cooper moved a few more feet away from her.

Ben and his team had moved into an empty room that overlooked an intersection on the west side of the city proper. Ben figured the main thrust of the attack would come from the eastern section, the area that had not yet been cleared. The no-man's-land.

Ben laid clips for his old Thunder Lizard to his right and grenades to his left. "Helmets on and body armor checked, Corrie. Pass the word."

"Tell the Boss Eagle that all his little chickies are buttoned up nice and proper," Ike radioed.

"Tell Ike that the proper term is eaglets," Ben said.

Corrie did and then said, "I most certainly will *not* tell the general that, sir!"

Ben laughed and then caught movement in the gray mist across the street. "Heads up, people! Here they come."

A rocket fired by the creepies impacted against the outside of the ground floor wall and knocked a large hole in the building. Creepies began pouring in gray-clad hordes across the rain-slick street. By the time a few made it inside the building the street was even slicker with blood.

"Here we go, gang!" Beth shouted.

141

Rebels on the ground floor chopped the Believers down and tossed their stinking bodies back outside, then moved furniture and filing cabinets to cover the rocket-blasted hole in the wall.

"All units reporting extremely heavy fighting," Corrie shouted above the din of battle. "Everybody is holding."

Ben sighted in a running creep and cut him down. "Thermopolis and Buddy?"

"Completely cut off, sir. They have very heavy fighting on all sides."

"Shit!" Ben said. "Okay, Corrie. Have units of the Free Irish move in now and give them some relief from the west. That'll box in those creeps. When that's accomplished, have the Free Irish move north and south for a few blocks, then swing east in a pincher movement."

"Right, sir."

If it works, Ben thought, that will seal off those creeps in behind Therm's Eight Battalion, with the Free Irish to the north and south, Therm to the west, and us to the east.

If it works.

Ben put those thoughts out of his mind and returned to the battle that was raging on the streets below. The sky had brightened somewhat, even though the rain had picked up and was really driving down. Ben could see the creeps as they darted and worked their way closer to the intersection.

"Beth!" he shouted, making up his mind. "Tell the tank commanders to start demolishing the buildings on either side of the street east of this position. Tell them to use Willie Peter and HE. With this rain, the fires can be contained. I want to give

142

us some breathing room and knock out any places those creeps can use for hidey-holes. Pass those orders all up and down this battalion."

Ben used his walkie-talkie. "One and Three Battalion mortar crews, back up one block, set up, and drop them in directly in front of you. HE and WP. Don't drop any on my head, please."

Thirty minutes later, the tanks and mortars had set the area directly in front of the Rebels' long thin line blazing. Creepies ran from the rubble with their clothing on fire. The Rebels chopped them down as relentlessly as the cold rain fell.

"Where are the Free Irish?" Ben asked Corrie.

"Exactly where you planned on them being, sir. They have the creepies boxed, and Therm and Buddy are closing the lid now."

"Order second and fourth companies of this battalion to fall back and nail the coffin shut, please. First and third companies spread out and pick up the slack."

The firing from the creepie side had all but stopped. For two blocks up there was no place for them to hide, except in bombed-out and burning buildings.

Ben and his team picked up their brass from the floor and put them in a sack. Ben took a sip of water, then sat down on the floor and rolled a cigarette. He smoked for a moment, then said, "Ike and the others, Corrie?"

"The creepies are falling back, sir."

Ben nodded and slowly finished his cigarette. He rose to his boots and picked up his M-14. "Let's go see what we've got downstairs."

The Rebels on the ground floor were cleaning up

143

the mess caused by the battle. To a person their faces and hands were grimy from dust and gunsmoke. All expended brass would be picked up for reloading. One Rebel was wounded, and that was only a slight flesh wound in the arm. Several had fierce headaches caused by their helmets taking a round that bounced off, and a lot of them had chest bruises caused by enemy rounds impacting with body armor. But they were alive.

Upon sighting Ben, several Rebels moved toward open doors and blocked them. Ben hid a smile and said nothing about the obvious move. "Scouts out into the no-man's-land," he ordered. "Let's see how far the creeps are retreating."

"We're making fresh coffee now, sir," a young Rebel told him. "Be ready in about five minutes."

"Fine. Sounds good." Ben moved to what remained of a window and looked out at the smoking, burning no-man's-land. He checked his watch and was surprised to find it was still very early in the morning. He walked around the interior of the building, speaking to his Rebels. First platoon, Company A, was always assigned to Ben. They were ordered assigned to him by all the battalion commanders, and Ben accepted it as something he had no power to change. And there were few faces in the bunch that had not been with Ben for a long time. They were seasoned veterans of five hundred or more battles, and to a person, without hesitation, they would die to keep Ben Raines alive.

Ben took a snack pack from his kit and grimaced at the contents. It was some sort of high protein, high vitamin goop dreamed up by the lab boys and girls back at Base Camp One. And it tasted pretty much like he suspected camel shit would taste. But he ate it. Several of the Rebels laughed at the expression on their general's face. That was one of the things that drew people close to Ben like steel shavings to a magnet: Ben ate the same rations as anyone else. Many times Ben slept on the same cold bare floor as they did, or huddled under a poncho in a chilling, pouring rain. He drank the same lousy coffee they did, and insisted that all his commanders receive or demand no better treatment than those serving under them.

"Three battalion of Free Irish are in from clearing Cork," Corrie told him.

"Tell them to assume the stations that One and Two Battalions vacated on the outskirts of town, please. Have Pat and his people join us, and Bobby's Two Battalion to link up with Dan. We're going to shove these bastards right into the Irish Sea."

"Right on!" a Rebel yelled.

"I bet Thermopolis reintroduced that phrase," Ben muttered. "Just to bug me."

Thirteen

Scouts reported that the creepies had moved completely out of the Liberty District and had set up a defense line along Clanbrassil and New Streets.

"Those bastards," Ben said.

"What's the matter?" Linda asked.

"Saint Patrick's Cathedral is located on that street. So is Christ Church Cathedral, and Dublin Castle is right behind Saint Patrick's. They know damn well we won't destroy those places. So it's about to get low-down and dirty mean. Well, that's fine with me. That's the way I like to fight. Low-down and mad-dog mean. Are Danjou's people still holding the Grattan Bridge?"

"Yes, sir. As well as the O'Connell Bridge. Those are the only bridges intact north of us."

"Tell Danjou to beef up his people at the bridges. We've got to hold them. How about those bridges south of us?"

"Grand Canal and Lesson are still intact—so far as we know—but we have no way of getting to them."

"All right," Ben said, adjusting his battle harness. "Let's start the squeeze."

Two, Four, and Seven Battalions began putting

the pressure on from the north. Five, Six, and Nine Battalions began pushing from the south. Ben's One Battalion, Therm's Eight, and contingents of the Free Irish began the drive east.

With MBTs and Dusters spearheading, the Rebels moved through the district called the Liberties. They moved up to within one block of the creepies' heavily fortified battle lines. To the north and south, the creepies had tightened up, pulling back into Dublin proper. For now, it was a small arms battle, the heaviest weapons being used on the Rebel side, the big .50 caliber machine guns.

Not so for the Believers. They were using mortars and rocket launchers against their enemy.

Ben's patrol boats out in the harbor reported that no creeps had tried to leave by the sea. Believer leaders, called Judges, had certainly seen the armed patrol boats and had watched the airborne attack against the ships carrying Jack Hunt and his army and realized that to try to escape by the sea would be futile.

The stage was set for an all-out assault against the creeps; but Ben was hesitant to throw his people into what would surely be a nasty and bloody confrontation. To smash into the creepies without heavy artillery softening them up first would take a lot of Rebel lives. And even though he had the okay from the Free Irish to destroy the city, Ben did not want to do that. He had an idea, but wasn't sure if he could pull it off. He called for a meeting of all commanders.

"Check this out, all of you," Ben said. "I want your opinions on this plan. Therm, you and Emil and the ships' captains of the Free Irish get down to Wexford and get the big ships ready to sail. When you have them ready, we make a big show about pulling troops out from all sides. All kinds of trucks and big guns will be leaving the battle zone, all of them heading south, toward Wexford. While that is going on, Ike's SEAL teams, Dan's Special Ops people, and Striganov's Spetsnaz teams will be gearing up to make a night crossing of the canals leading into downtown Dublin . . ."

Ike, Dan, and Georgi Striganov started grinning.

". . . If the creeps behave as I think they will, they'll think we're about to attack from the sea and start pulling a lot of people back to defend the harbor. The harbor can be rebuilt. I want every type of heavy gun we can cram on the decks of those ships—81mm mortars, recoilless rifles, 40mm cannon. I want our helicopter gunships armed with everything they can fly with. When the special teams are in place—and you're going to have to carry it all with you, people, I won't have any way to resupply you—the ships' captains will make a big show of tossing rope ladders over the side and landing craft will start moving up to take on troops. If the creeps take the bait, many of their people will be in the harbor area, ready to defend and repel the enemy that isn't out there. That's when the gunships will strike very hard and very quickly, throwing everything they've got into the docks and warehouses. Then the guns on ships will take over. By that time, all the special teams will be striking from the rear, and we'll be hitting them from the front. There is it."

"I'll start getting the ships ready to sail," Therm said, standing up.

"We'll start getting our teams geared up," Ike said.

"And start laying out plans on where to place the special teams," Georgi said.

"Wait a minute!" Ben said. "Settle down. None of you have arguments?"

"Argue about what, Dad?" Tina asked him. "You've just outlined what the Rebels do best. Mean, sneaky, dirty, nasty, underhanded, unconventional tactics."

"I certainly am glad I took after my grandfather," Buddy said, an innocent look on his face. "I would never, ever, come up with such a vicious plan as that."

Amid the laughter, Ben picked up a helmet and threw it at his son.

The creepies were thoroughly confused. All attacks by the Rebels had ceased, except for some occasional and ineffective small arms fire, and towed artillery and trucks were pulling out. Then they began receiving reports from what few sympathizers they had left along the coast that ships were being readied for sail out of the port of Wexford.

"I was right all along," a Judge said smugly. "I told you all repeatedly that Ben Raines would not destroy the landmarks and churches. I told you he would finally launch an attack from the sea." He chuckled with dark satisfaction and stuffed his mouth full of freshly cut human flesh.

"It's a trick," another Judge said. "Ben Raines says one thing and does another. He follows no rulebook."

"I don't think it's a trick," a third Judge said. "I believe that Ben Raines has seen he cannot take the city without destroying landmarks, so he is going to launch troops from the sea, opening a fourth front. But this fourth front will be the largest. So we must shift people and do it quickly."

"Let's vote."

Five Judges in favor, one against.

"You're all making a very grave mistake," the lone dissenter said. "You're all forgetting that I came out of America last. I have much more experience in fighting the Rebels than any of you. Listen to me, please. Ben Raines is like a shadow in the night. Deceptive. He'll make you believe you're seeing something that isn't there. Anybody who can convince a hippie to take up arms in a fight for order and rules has a glib tongue indeed."

But the others were not to be swayed.

"Order the shifting of defenses," they decreed.

"They bought it," Ben said with a grin, after reading the reports from the lookouts stationed on high rooftops in Rebel-held territory. "The cannibalistic bastards fell for it."

"Thermopolis says some of those old rust-buckets down at Wexford will probably disintegrate ten seconds after the ruse is done," Buddy said. "But he says they're ready for sailing. How can a ship sail without sails?" he mused aloud.

"Take it up with Thermopolis," his father told him. "I know nothing about boats. I don't like boats."

"Ships," his son automatically corrected him.

"Ships, boats, whatever. They float on water and I don't trust them."

"Me neither," Cooper said.

"They're really shifting creepies around, General," Dan said, walking into the room, a clipboard in his hand. "These are the latest reports in; just got them handed me. The creeps are massing at the harbor."

"Start the loading tonight," Ben told Corrie. "No lights. Throw up a tight security screen around Wexford Harbor and at full dark, start playing those tape recordings we made of the troops when they pulled out of here." He smiled. The Rebels pulled out, all right—about ten miles inland. "Have everybody there load and unload about twenty times; make lots of noise."

Dan chuckled. "Sorry for finding all this commotion so amusing, General. But this is something that I always snickered at in the cinema."

"So did I, Dan," Ben admitted. "Are your people ready to go?"

"Oh, yes. Quite. Everyone is ready."

"You all will cross the canals tomorrow night. In thirty-six hours we'll all know how good this plan was."

"It'll work if none of the teams gets caught and talks."

Ben handed him a packet. Dan arched an eyebrow. "Cyanide pills, Dan. Compliments of Dr. Chase. Each team member gets one. They're in waterproof bags. You don't want to be taken alive by the creepies."

"Quite right," the Englishman said, putting the packet in a side pocket of his BDU jacket. "I'll see they are dispensed."

"Good."

Dan held out his hand and Ben shook it. "We'll be rather busy for the next twenty-four hours or so, General. So I shall see you at the link-up point, sir." He stepped back properly and gave Ben a very snappy salute, British-fashion.

Ben smiled and returned the salute—American fashion—and Dan executed an about-face and left the room.

Ben called his personal team together, including the lieutenant who commanded his personal platoon and the platoon sergeant and squad leaders. "I want to remind you all that there will be no radio traffic concerning this operation. None. Just to tell you how important silence is, every team member going across those canals has a cyanide pill in case he's captured, before or after the plan goes into operation. You know what creepies do to captured Rebels.

"When we go in, people, we are going to go in very fast. For the first few blocks, at a run. We'll be advancing behind the tanks. And make no mistake about this: I will be leading my battalion. We are going to push the creepies hard and take no prisoners. A lot of the time, some of us will be cut off from the others. Go light on food and heavy on ammo. Two canteens of water per person. Take only your ground sheets. Those will be used to carry out our wounded and to cover and carry out our dead . . . when we get the time.

"Everybody keep a very low profile until jump-off time. Tomorrow night, our people will start moving back in in small units. Our tanks will be moving up closer, but they won't really pour on the throttle until the bombardment starts just before dawn. The bombardment will cease at dawn, giving the gunships time to do their magic, then the bombardment will once again commence from the ships. By that time, we'll be running hard into creepie territory, and the creepies will know that they've been suckered.

"People, their backs will be against the wall, a wall of water. They have no place to go, they know we don't take creepie prisoners, so it's going to be one mother-humpin' fight." Ben eyeballed them all for a moment. "That's it."

Ben rested well that night and was up at his usual hour long before dawn. It was good that he did rest, for the day seemed to take three times its normal length to pass. That night Rebels began moving, returning to the area of their battalions, but staying well back of the front lines.

"Going to exclude my battalion from this assault, too, General?" Thermopolis' XO asked over coffee.

"You'll be bringing up the rear, but no, you damn sure won't be excluded this time. I want you and your people along here, taking and holding Christ Church and spreading out and opening the south end of Grattan bridge. And hold it, Captain. That bridge is vital."

"When did you change the plan, General?"

"About ten minutes before I called you to come up here. We're going to secure everything between the Liffey and the Grand Canal. And if possible, we're going to do it all tomorrow."

Fourteen

Ben was up before any of his team the morning of the assault. He took a spit-bath out of a pail of water and brushed his teeth, then carefully dressed. He put body armor on between his t-shirt and his cammie shirt, then slipped into his battle harness. By the time the rest of his team was up, he and Jersey were sitting and talking, having coffee.

Corrie checked with communications; it appeared that all the special ops teams had made it and were in place.

"One hour to jump off," Ben said. The stars were fading in the early morning sky.

Somewhere in the building, someone coughed nervously as Ben was putting a couple of high protein, vitamin-packed snack bars in his pocket and filling his canteens with fresh water from a drum.

Ben had laid aside his M-14 and once more returned to the 9mm Car-15, simply because he could carry twice the ammo and the weapon was lighter and easier to handle. This operation would be, for the most part, a short-range, house-to-house and face-to-face confrontation. He checked his Beretta 9mm sidearms and hooked a couple more grenades onto his harness.

Cooper was checking his Stoner and hooping bandoliers of ammo across his chest. Linda loaded her shotgun up full and, like Coop, wore bandoliers of magnum shotgun shells across her chest. Jersey was ready five minutes after she laced up her boots. She was sitting quietly, drinking coffee. Corrie was checking out her lightweight backpack radio. Satisfied, she slipped it on and checked her weapons. Beth was writing in her journal; she was the unofficial historian of the group.

Buddy walked in, loaded with weapons and ammo, a bandana around his head. Ben was seconds away from giving his son an ass-chewing when the young man grinned in the semidarkness of the hall and held up his helmet.

"Why'd you leave the Eighth?" Ben asked.

"General Ike told me to," Buddy responded. "Me and part of the Pack are to stay with you. Sorry," he shrugged. "I have to do what the ranking officers tell me. Right?"

Ben was sandbagged and knew it. "Right," he said. "Turn around."

Ben checked his son's battle harness, then turned to allow Buddy to check his.

"Ships are in the harbor, standing by," Corrie told Ben.

Ben looked at his watch. "Corrie, tell everyone to get into position, please."

She spoke a one-word code phrase, "Boots," and then repeated it.

"Laced," came the reply. It was repeated. Corrie looked at Ben.

"Outside to the line," Ben said.

155

The Rebels moved outside into the cool Irish morning.

"It's going to be a fine day," Ben said, looking up into the sky. "Clear and sunshiny. Certain tribes of plains Indians used to have a saying before a battle — 'It's a good day to die.'"

"Meaning, of course," Buddy said, "for the other fellow?"

"Not necessarily," his father told him, then walked away to chat for a moment with members of the Command Platoon.

"Jackie," Ben spoke to a squad leader. "How you feeling?"

"Rarin' to go, General," she said with a smile.

"Won't be long now." He walked on. "Lieutenant," he said.

The words had just left his mouth when the artillery on board ships began pounding the harbor area. Ben sensed someone standing just behind him and to his right. He did not have to turn around to know that it was Jersey.

"You ready, Little Bit?" he asked.

"Just about time to kick ass, General," she replied.

Chuckling, Ben walked on, speaking to Rebels as he approached them, Jersey right behind him, Corrie right behind her.

"Communications reports lots of creepie chatter," Corrie said. "They're getting awfully nervous about those rope ladders being heaved over the sides of the ships."

"Good. Tell our mortar crews to get ready with smoke."

"Yes, sir."

156

"Tell those tanks that are laying back to come on in as soon as the smoke is fired."

"Right, sir."

Ben pointed toward the ground. "Secure that boot lace, soldier," Ben said to a Rebel. "You'd look funny falling on your ass during a charge."

Embarrassed, the Rebel knelt down and quickly retied the lace.

Ben turned and walked back to his team. He was handed a fresh cup of coffee in a tin cup.

The harbor area was beginning to burn from the Willie Peter being dropped in on the old buildings. The eastern sky was glowing in the now gray of nearly dawn.

Ben adjusted the strap on his helmet, resettling his chin in the cup. "Won't be long now," he said to no one in particular. "The birds are up."

Gradually, the thundering bombardment from the ships began to abate. Soon, all could hear the whapping of the big blades of the helicopter gunships as they began their approach toward the targets, coming in at speeds of over a hundred miles an hour. The choppers began raining down death from the skies.

"Fire smoke," Ben ordered. "Special operations teams up."

Seconds later, the fluttering of mortars hummed overhead and the rockets exploded several hundred meters in front of the line, filling the air with smoke.

"Tanks in," Ben said, and the first tank sections roared up and past the battle line.

"Let's go!" Ben shouted, and charged into the swirling smoke of no-man's-land.

157

It did not take the Judges very long to realize that they'd been had by Ben Raines.

"There are no troops leaving those ships!" a radio operator screamed into his mic. "There appear to be no assault troops on them."

The Judge who had opposed the reshuffling of troops hung his head and slowly shook it. "I tried to warn you," he whispered. "I tried to tell you about Ben Raines. But none of you would listen to me. Now we pay the ultimate price."

"Troops back from the harbor," the Judges screamed.

"It's too late," the dissenting Judge said. "It's too late."

"Well, what the hell do you suggest?" one of his fellow Judges screamed.

"That we prepare ourselves to die as well as possible."

The attack from the Rebels came so quickly that many of the creepies manning the front lines were crushed to death under the tracks of the tanks before they could do more than scream at the 60-ton monsters roaring down on them out of the swirling smoke. The screams were crushed in their throats.

The First, Third, and Eighth Battalions charged across the no-man's-land and Eight Battalion swung north to cover the Grattan Bridge and Christ Church Cathedral. Ben dropped off a platoon to cover Saint Patrick's Cathedral and plowed straight ahead, while the Third Battalion dipped south and quickly secured four blocks of territory before the creepies threw up a defensive line and tried to hold.

But the special ops teams had surfaced all over the place and had been busy cutting throats and manning what were once creepie heavy machine gun and mortar positions. Now the creepies found themselves surrounded in their territory and fighting on all fronts.

The helicopter gunships had returned to base, rearmed, and now flew back to raise hell with those creepies trying to leave the harbor area and assist their fellow creeps in the city proper.

But the chopper pilots had other plans. They turned a three-block-long area into a searing inferno. Rebel engineers had altered the extra fuel pods and replaced them with napalm bombs. The napalm had to be dropped manually, and their accuracy wasn't worth a damn, but if they came within a block of their targets, the pilots were happy.

The creepies were very unhappy about the whole situation.

There were still thousands of the sect called Believers within the city, but they were cut off, confused, disoriented, and in many cases leaderless. Many elected to hole up right where they were and fight to the death.

When the chopper pilots had dropped their napalm loads, they went headhunting and went in low. They knew that anything moving between the center of the city and the Irish Sea was a bogey, and when they ran out of ammo and had to return to base, a lot of those who were moving before the helicopters came were no longer moving when the gunships left. The 30mm rockets make a terrible mess out of a human body.

The older helicopters were armed with .50 caliber machine guns and M-60's—called Pigs—manned by door gunners. They, too, had a field day chopping up creepies before they were forced to return to base.

Ben and his people hit their first real snag only a few blocks east of St. Pat's Cathedral when a heavy machine gun opened up and killed two Rebels. The body armor the Rebels wore was good, but it wasn't good enough to stop a .50 caliber round.

Two Dusters rolled up and put an end to that nest, but other creepies were setting up a line and the Rebels' advance was momentarily halted.

The Rebels were ready for a halt. They had been running very nearly all-out for ten blocks and Ben and some of the older Rebels thought they was going to die very soon if they didn't stop.

"Jesus!" Ben said, when he had caught enough breath to risk speaking. He looked at his son. The young man had broken into a sweat, but that was about it.

"Feeling all right, Father?" Buddy said with a wide grin.

"I'm not sure I even *like* anybody under forty," Ben grumbled, but did so with a smile. "Do you even have a heart and lungs, boy?"

"Yes. And if you'd quit smoking those nasty cigarettes and gulping whiskey every night, you'd be in better shape."

"When I want a lecture, boy," Ben panted out the words, "I'll go find Lamar Chase. Corrie, get us some reports, please."

"I'm under forty," she said with a smile.

"Oh, I trust my team," Ben said. "It's Romeo

here," he jerked a thumb at Buddy, "I'm not sure about."

He waited while Corrie bumped all batt coms and compiled the information.

"Those units south of the Grand Canal have pushed up to within five blocks of the canal. Those north of the Liffey have pushed down approximately ten blocks. The harbor area is burning out of control, as is a three-block area just to the west of the harbor. Our special ops people have secured little pockets all over the city."

"All units between the river and the canal hold what they have until those spec ops teams have radioed in their positions," Ben ordered. "We don't want them killed by friendly fire. Also ask what they think their odds are of holding what they've taken. Let's get that done, Corrie."

Ben caught his breath and took a few sips of water while Corrie and Beth worked. Corrie called out the locations and Beth marked them on an old city map. Ben looked at the bodies of the two dead Rebels sprawled in the street and silently cussed. He knew both of them personally.

"General," Corrie said. "We now control both sides of all the remaining bridges. All spec ops teams report they can hold at least for several hours. The teams now have control—however precariously—of all major churches and landmarks. The creeps appear to be confused and leaderless. Many of them are setting up what seem to be last-ditch stands."

"Get as many of those locations as possible. How about hostages?"

She shook her head. "Negative, sir."

Ben tapped the brick of the street. "Underground, probably. Just like in New York City. All right, folks, let's start clearing the buildings. I intend to have the grounds of Trinity College cleared by this afternoon."

Grudgingly, the creepies backed up under the onslaught of the Rebels. Their small arms fire was no match for the awesome firepower of the Rebel tanks. They backed up, but they had precious little backing room left them. There were those who tried to use the sea to escape. Machine gun fire from Rebel patrol boats chopped them up and left them for shark bait.

Across the Irish Sea, in locations all over England, Wales, and Scotland, warlords and mercenaries and street punks and Believers listened to the frantic talk from the creepies on their shortwave radios. Ben Raines and his Rebels were grinding the Night People up like hamburger meat, efficiently, brutally, and mercilessly.

Many of the Irish collaborators still trapped in the city tried to give up. The commanders of the Free Irish Army ordered them shot on sight. The punk biker Maddy shuddered.

"Them blokes ain't takin' no prisoners, mates — Rebels nor Free Irish."

"Has anybody got a copy of the Geneva Convention?" Duane asked.

"Conventions," another gang leader corrected. "The Rebels don't pay no attention to that no way. Believe me. I was in Dallas/Fort Worth when the Rebels took them cities. Then I run up into Kansas and that was worse. I come over here with a bunch of other guys and damned if Ben Raines and them

Rebels didn't follow a few years later. That son of a bitch ain't content with cleanin' out America and Canada. He wants the whole goddamn world!"

A female gang leader called Lulu studied her purple-painted fingernails for a moment. "So what's it gonna be?" she finally asked. "Ever since Raines hit Ireland all we've done is sit about on our arses. We've made no plans, elected no leaders, formed up no battle lines . . . nothing. We'd better get crackin', people. We either step lively or we're dead."

"All right, Lulu," Butch Smathers said. "You got a plan, let's hear it."

"We set up teams of people who do nothing but monitor radio transmissions from the Rebels . . . twenty-four hours a day. Write down or tape everything. Ireland is about to fall. Oh, they'll be fightin' in Dublin for several weeks, doin' mop-up stuff, but that city is through. We're next. We've got to figure out where they're gonna land when they come over here after us. We got to start layin' in supplies and ammo. We got to assign people to do specific things. Butch, you was in the Army. You was a paratrooper. Can you run this operation?"

Butch sighed. "I was a corporal, Lulu, not a general. But you're right on everything you said. I figure we got a month 'fore the Yanks come over here. My bunch has been ready. We've trained for years for this. But my bunch don't make up but about five percent of all the gangs in England. If we all come together, I think we could maybe whip Raines."

"I'll take orders from you, Butch," Lulu said. "Count me and my gang in as part of yours."

163

"Okay," Poole said. "I'm in."

Slowly, the others in attendance agreed to take orders from Smathers. Butch pointed to one of Lulu's girls. "Lizzie, you was in the BBC when the shit went down. I'm puttin' you in charge of communications. You get in touch with all the gang leaders on this island. We got to meet and we got to get organized and we got to do it fast."

"I'll get right on it," Lizzie said.

"We got a lot to do and a short time to do it," Butch said. "Let's move, people."

The Rebels sensed victory now, and they pressed the now panicked enemy harder. The Judges and their most faithful followers had moved under the city.

Leaderless now, the creepies on the surface could do nothing but fight very fierce and very short battles with the Rebels. They had no place left to run.

"Street punks and creepies control Trinity College," Corrie reported that to Ben.

"Wonderful," Ben said. "I'm sure they've spent their time educating themselves." He checked his CAR-15. "Let's go give them their final exam."

Fifteen

The Rebels hit the grounds of Trinity College from all sides and turned the hallowed grounds into a killing field. They tossed grenades through long shattered windows, kicked in doors, and went in shooting. The creepies and street punks who had aligned with the Believers had never faced anything like the Rebels. For years they had given no mercy or pity to their slaves and the girls and boys and women they had raped and abused and tormented and then handed over to the cannibals.

Now they received no mercy or pity from the liberating Rebel Army.

Some tried to surrender. It was a futile gesture, for the Rebels had found some of the creepies' holding areas for their human food source.

The Rebels had already been fighting angry, now they were outraged, disgusted, and appalled, and the killing fever was high. It did not take them long to take the old college grounds. A few creepies and punks were still holed up in most of the buildings, but the grounds were in Rebel hands.

Ben and his team headed for the library in the Long Room.

"That's not secured, General!" a Rebel yelled.

"It will be in a few minutes," Ben told him, and kept on running.

A burst of automatic weapons fire sent the team scrambling to the ground. "Second floor, people," Ben called, as he lifted his CAR and gave the windowless frame a burst. Then he was on his feet and running. He reached the building and jumped in through the open doors, rolling on the floor, the rest of his team following, ducking left and right, seeking whatever cover they could find.

"Bastards," Ben said, his eyes sweeping the place. The floor was literally ankle-deep in priceless volumes. "That's what I was afraid of."

A Free Irish soldier who had gotten separated from his unit and had linked up with Ben's team hissed his hate at anyone who would do such a thing.

"They always do it," he said. "The terrible bastards always destroy the books."

"Destroy the books and you control the minds," Ben told him, as his eyes continued to sweep the seemingly deserted ground floor of the Long Room. "Take away the guns and you control the body."

"Second floor," Cooper whispered. "About one o'clock."

"For once you're right, Coop," Jersey told him.

Linda's shotgun roared and the street punk screamed as buckshot ripped into his chest. He staggered first backward, then forward, and pitched headfirst over the railing, falling to the floor below and landing on his belly.

"I hope he landed on books I never cared for," Ben said dryly.

Lead started chipping away at the railing just above their heads. A single shot from a Rebel sniper rifle cracked. Probably a 7mm magnum. A creepie stumbled on the second floor landing, and fell over, and his foot caught in the spokes of the railing. He dangled there. He wore nothing under his dirty gray robe.

"That's not exactly a turn-on," Beth remarked.

Rebels from Ben's personal platoon began appearing at either end of the Long Room. The firing outside on the campus grounds was growing lighter as Rebels began mopping up.

More Rebels entered the building and began fanning out, a dozen of them taking up positions around Ben and his team. Ben rose to one knee and looked at the mess, then looked at the Free Irish soldier.

"Get some of your people in here to care for these books," Ben told him. "Your entire history is trashed on the floor." He put a hand on the man's shoulder. "The punks and dickheads did the same in America, if that's any consolation."

"They'll never get the chance to do this again in Ireland," the man said, steel in his voice. "The first politician who stands up and announces he's in favor of gun control is very likely to get shot."

By the end of the day, what creepies and street punks and collaborators remained were all hemmed up in an area no more than six blocks wide and four blocks deep. But the Rebels had no way of knowing how many creepies had gone underground, how long their tunnels were, and how many escaped into the countryside.

"It'd be a safe bet to assume that several hundred, maybe several thousand, got away," Ben said. "But it's very difficult for them to live outside the cities. They do stand out," he added.

"In more than one way," Ike agreed. "You can smell the bastards a block away."

"I'd bet on several thousand escaping," Georgi Striganov said. "The taking of Dublin was just too easy."

"Yes," Ben said, looking at a map. "What they've probably done, or plan to do, is work their way north and try to cross over at the narrowest point of the North Channel into Scotland."

"We have conflicting reports about the creepies in Northern Ireland, General," Pat O'Shea said. "We just can't get an accurate fix on it."

"Maybe we could encourage them to stay in Northern Ireland," Bobby Flynn said, not at all kindly in his opinion of conditions in the north. "That would be one solution to the problem."

"Now, Bobby," Pat said with a laugh.

"Well, they left behind enough weapons to re-arm the entire population," Ben pointed out. "And enough ammo to keep you supplied for years. Once we get England cleaned out, your two countries can work together. It's never going to be the way it was before the Great War—at least, not in our lifetime. We'll help you restore power and water and get sewerage treatment plants back in operation. Where did Jack get his gasoline?"

"From the platforms in the North Sea," Bobby told him. "Several refineries are still operating in England. Punks and thieves and hooligans they might be, but they've enough smarts to keep those going."

"You know where they're located?"

"Oh, yes." He pointed to several locations on the big wall map. "Right there."

"And they're heavily guarded?" Dan questioned.

"Very tight security, sir," Pat said. "English resistance forces say you can't get within five miles of those places."

"Somehow, I think we'll manage to get a bit closer than that," Dan said with a smile.

"Oh, quite!" Ike mimicked.

"Blow it out your arse, tubby," the Englishman told him.

Ike grinned, then his grin faded as he watched Ben turn from the map and walk to a window, staring out over the old campus of Trinity College. Rebels had cleaned out the second floor of one of the buildings and Ben was using it for his CP.

"What's wrong, Ben?" Ike asked.

"Too easy," Ben replied. "They just rolled over and let us walk on them taking this city. They're up to something. I just don't know what it is."

"But we beat them, General!" Bobby Flynn said. "We whipped them proper, we did."

Ben was silent for a moment, still looking out the window. He slapped his hands together and finally said, "No. But I believe they wanted us to think we did." He shook his head. "Corrie, give the word for all Rebels except for One and Three Battalions to get the hell out of the downtown area. Spread them out all over the city and prepare for a hard counterattack." He turned to face his commanders. "Get tanks up here fast and tell all CO's

169

to dig in tight and right." He looked at Ike. "Get back to your commands, gentlemen. I think all hell is going to break loose come night. Move!"

While they were filing out, Ben said to Buddy, "Get down into the basement, take a team with you, double-check all suspected creepie holes, and boobytrap them solid." To Corrie, "Have supply round up every perimeter banger we have and get them out to all units. I want everyone resupplied with everything we might need, and I want it done like yesterday."

He picked up his 9mm spitter and checked it. "When you're finished, Corrie, we'll all take a little stroll around campus."

"Anything in particular we're looking for, Ben?" Linda asked.

"I don't know. I only know I'll recognize it when I see it."

They came to a manhole and Ben squatted down, inspecting the heavy cover. "There is no grit or trash between the lip and the cover," he said. "This thing was used not very long ago."

"Might be booby-trapped," Jersey said.

"Probably is," Ben said, standing up. "From the bottom side." He smiled.

"You think that's funny, Ben?" Linda asked.

"In a perverse sort of way, yes." He walked away and spoke to a Rebel sergeant for a moment. The sergeant grinned and nodded his head.

Ben returned to his team. "Corrie, have the welding of manhole covers stopped immediately."

"Yes, sir." She wasn't at all sure why the general would want that, but . . .

"Let's get back to the CP," Ben said. "I have a lot of radioing to do."

It was a quick afternoon, but to any creepie who might be watching, nothing really out of the ordinary. Just troops moving around, inspecting this and that. But while it looked innocent enough, the troops weren't dawdling; they were moving with a definite purpose. Ben had thought of some perfectly horrible ways in dealing with the creepies who might be coming out of those manholes during the night hours. Ben thought it was amusing. So did Jersey. Dr. Chase just shook his head.

"Sometimes I worry about you, Raines," the old doctor said. "I really do."

Ben had ordered M18 mines, called Claymores, to be readied. At dusk, every Claymore the Rebels had would be placed around as many manholes as possible, at fifty to seventy-five yards, four to a hole. Behind the mines, dug in and fortified, would be Rebels manning heavy machine guns, carefully placed for maximum crossfire. The Rebels would hold their fire until the creepies realized there were no more mines and again started their stinking way out of the ground.

"We've all seen how quickly they pour out of hidey-holes," Ben told his people by scramble-net. "Give them time enough to get a crowd above ground, then cut them down and don't stop firing until no one is moving. Tomorrow, we'll decide on pumping chemicals into the system and flushing them out. Now play along with me on this next bunch of bullshit."

Ben looked at Corrie. "Take me off scramble,

171

Corrie. Let's see if they buy this gambit." Corrie put him on an open frequency. "This is General Raines. I want to congratulate all of you for a job well done. You have soundly defeated an enemy who outnumbered you. I'm proud of you. Tonight, you all can go to low alert and relax. This city is now in Rebel hands!"

All around the city, Rebels cheered and clapped their hands and shouted right on cue. Ben looked at Linda and grinned. "What a bunch of hams."

"Whoopee!" his team shouted in unison.

The Rebels quietly began getting into position and laying out the mines. Then they sat back and waited.

From a window on the second floor of his CP, the room void of light, Ben watched the street, his team spread out left and right of his position. In selected areas of the city, Rebels partied and sang songs and danced for a time after dark, just enough of them hopefully to convince the creepies the entire contingent had relaxed their guard.

After a time, the Rebels began turning down their lamps and making a big production of getting ready for bed. They were being watched from a few well-chosen vantage points; there was no doubt in anyone's mind about that.

Slipping on a headset, Ben bumped Dan. "How's it look where you are, Dan?"

"Quiet as a church, General."

"Ike?"

"Nothing movin', Ben."

"Georgi?"

"Our sensors are picking up a lot of scurrying around under our feet, Ben."

172

"Same here, Dad," Tina reported. "West reports movement under the streets."

"General," Corrie said. "We have movement under the streets in our sector."

"Therm?"

"We have bogies under us, Ben."

"Danjou?"

"Definite movement in the sewers and tunnels, General. Rebet reports the same."

"All right, people," Ben radioed to his commanders. "They're about to open up this street dance. Let's make sure the band is all tuned up."

"Manhole covers are opening in all sectors," Corrie said calmly, monitoring the frequencies.

Ben clicked his M-14 off safety.

"Spotlights are ready," Corrie said.

Vehicles had been parked so the streets could be easily illuminated by headlights and spotlights.

"Creepies coming out, sir," Corrie said.

"Jesus, would you look at them," Cooper said, behind his Stoner. "They're like roaches."

"Well, we're about to step on them," Ben said. "Just about . . . *now!*"

Sixteen

The Claymores blew and thousands of steel fragments tore into creepie flesh. Those closest to the blast were literally ripped into shreds. But the creepies did not pause in their pouring out of the holes. They just kept right on coming, screaming out their wild hatred for Ben Raines and the Rebels.

The Rebels opened fire and the streets were suddenly filled with stinking dead and dying Believers. And still they continued to pour out of the underground of the city, screaming and racing toward death.

"Un-fucking-believable," Cooper muttered, holding back the trigger on his Stoner and letting the lead fly.

On the ground, the booming and sparking of grenades turned the night surreal.

It was, as was once the saying, like shooting ducks in a barrel. Rebel fire was so intense, few creepies could get out of the manhole area. They were forced to climb over the bodies of their own dead, which were now two and three deep, and once there, faced the harsh light from dozens of vehicle headlights and spotlights.

The Rebels shot them dead.

No one among the Rebels — including Ben

Raines—knew why the creepies behaved as they did. They could, on occasion, plan good, solid military moves. Then, as on this night, they behaved very irrationally, racing headlong into certain death.

The warm summer air became choked with gunsmoke, the odor of unwashed bodies, the crashing and roaring of grenades, the screaming of the badly wounded, and the stink of death. The hands and arms of Rebels became sore from the gripping of weapons, and shoulders ached from the pounding of recoil.

Still the creepies poured out of manholes all over the city, screaming their hate and rage. But they were far fewer in number now, and the Rebels were still unrelenting in their deadly hail of fire.

Gradually, the firing lessened in the city. "Tina reporting all firing has ceased in her section," Corrie called, her eyes smarting and tearing from the acrid bite of gunsmoke. "Rebet reporting no more live creepies in his T.O."

Ben stood up and rubbed a sore shoulder. The M-14 could punish a shooter. As his ears adjusted to the sounds of normalcy, he became aware that no more shooting was occurring in his section. He looked down from his second story vantage point at a scene that never becomes acceptable to the human mind: hundreds of torn and ripped bodies clogged the streets and sidewalks and weed-grown patches of ground.

"Un-fucking-believable," Cooper said again, as he stood up and stretched aching muscles.

"Get me casualty reports," Ben requested. Only faint pockets of gunfire now reached his ears.

"Prelim reports from all batt coms say no Rebel dead and only a very few wounded," Corrie said.

Their faces were grimy from gunsmoke and their eyes gritty from strain and smoke and stink.

"All personnel stay at their posts," Ben ordered. "But I think it's over in this city. We'll mop up commencing in the morning."

The sight was macabre and the odor was disgusting. Hundreds and hundreds of stiffening bodies sprawled in the streets.

"Dr. Chase is hollering about a health hazard," Corrie said to Ben.

"Tell that old fart we're moving as fast as we can," Ben replied. "We've only got so much equipment. God damn it, I can't work miracles."

Corrie's reply to Dr. Chase was put much more diplomatically.

The bodies of the dead creepies were being scooped up, loaded into the beds of trucks, and hauled off to be buried in a mass grave outside the city. The weapons of the dead were being collected, taken down, cleaned, and then given to the Free Irish.

The morning had turned very warm and Ben had ordered everybody working with the bodies to get into gas masks; the stench of the dead was very nearly overpowering. He stood on the sidewalk outside his CP. Reluctantly, for he hated the damn things, Ben slipped on his gas mask and told Corrie to issue the orders that everyone do the same.

"Corrie, order water trucks and generators up and start hosing down the streets. We've got to wash this slop off. When that's done, we'll hook up hoses to the exhaust systems of our vehicles and start pumping carbon monoxide into the tunnels to drive out the

176

remaining creepies."

Over the long years of fighting the creepies, the Rebels had learned that was the easiest way to force the Believers out of their holes.

"I want all battalions of the Free Irish to start house-to-house, building-to-building searches," Ben said. "Pat and Bobby have stated that it's their country, they should bear the brunt of finishing the fight."

"Yes, sir."

"Get me a damage report on all landmarks and historical sites, too."

"I got it just a few minutes ago from Communications," Beth said. She lifted a clipboard. "It's pretty bad. Of the six-thousand-plus paintings in the National Gallery of Ireland, less than half can be restored, so the experts say. Dublin Castle was trashed. Marsh's Library was vandalized and some of it burned. It's going to take a lot of work to restore St. Pat's Cathedral. None of the landmarks and historical sites went untouched."

"It could have been worse, I suppose," Ben said.

"Thermopolis reports finding a band of war protesters."

"He would," Ben muttered.

"He's doing his best to keep them away from you."

"He'd better."

"They're demanding a meeting with you, and they're demanding that you take your army and leave Ireland immediately."

"Make a note of that, Beth. We'll get to it in about a month and a half."

"They're going to have a concert tomorrow night. They'll circulate a petition declaring that war is unhealthy."

"I've heard that before."

"They're going to go among the troops to ask that as many as possible desert."

Ben smiled.

"You find that funny, Ben?" Linda asked.

"It'll give Dr. Chase's people something to do."

"What do you mean?"

"Stitching up busted heads and repairing the broken teeth that will surely happen when Rebel gun butts impact with heads and mouths."

"And you'll let that happen?"

"I surely will."

"You won't stop it?"

"I surely will not."

"It's their country, Ben."

"Then they can fight for it as the Free Irish have done and will continue to do."

"You are stifling legal dissent, Ben."

"No, I'm not. If they want to stand in the street and wave placards and sing songs and make speeches, that's fine with me. But the first time they get up in a Rebel's face and call them a baby-killer or some such shit as that, they're going to get hurt."

She stared at him for a moment. "I'll never understand or like this side of you, Ben."

"You want to stay here, don't you, Linda?"

The question rocked her back for a moment. "Why . . . I don't know, Ben. I have thought about it."

"Come on," he said, taking her arm. "Let's get to a car, roll up the windows, and turn on the air conditioning. We can get out of these damn masks and talk."

"Sure, Ben," she said with a smile. "I know you pretty well. You're going to try to slip away from your bodyguards. It'll never work."

"I bet I give it the old college try."

But before he had even left the campus, two Dusters were blocking his way. He looked behind him. Cooper was there with his team, and his platoon was behind the wagon, and behind the wagon were two MBTs.

"You just tell us where you want to go, Eagle," the Duster commander said, "and we'll damn sure get you there and back."

"Away from this smell."

"That's easy. Follow us, Eagle."

The Dusters led them back through the Liberties and to the edge of the city where supplies were being stored. This was a very secure area, and Ben drove until he found a good spot to park. He and Linda got out. The smell was there, but tolerable without the masks.

"Linda," Ben said. "We've had some good times together. I don't love you and you don't love me. But we do like each other. And that's probably more important in a relationship. You came along just in time for me. You got me over some very bad spots. And maybe I was just as good for you. I like to think so. You've turned into a good soldier, and I was proud to have you as part of my team. But this outfit is not for you, Linda. You've been kidding yourself for some months now. I've seen it, and so have the others. Chase and I have spoken of it."

"No hard feelings, Ben?"

"Oh, no, Linda. None. My God, I've got wars to fight and battles to win. You've got to set out to save the world from itself."

"Now you're being sarcastic."

"Just a little bit. We're opposites, Linda. We attract, but it's a dangerous attraction. And I think, if you want to stay here in Ireland, the people would

179

love to have you. They are in desperate need of qualified medical personnel. And Dublin is going to be a long time rebuilding."

"Will you ever settle down, Ben?"

"When I'm too old for the field."

"Ben, that'll be *years!*"

"That's right."

"I'll miss you, Ben."

"And I shall miss you. But at least we're parting friends. If this had gone on for months more, we would have been at each other's throats and it would have been a bad ending to a good relationship."

"How, ah, *do* we end it?"

"You gather up your gear and report to Dr. Chase. He's swamped with work and will welcome you. I'll make myself scarce until about noon so there won't be any bumping into each other, creating awkward moments."

She touched his arm. "Ben . . . take care of yourself."

"You, too, Linda." He waved at a Rebel. "Drive the lady back to my CP, please."

Ben walked back to his wagon and got in the front seat. "Corrie, tell those nursemaid tanks we are going to inspect the city. Drive, Coop."

"Yes, sir!"

"I guess I'm a lousy matchmaker, Raines," Chase said, sitting in Ben's office, his feet up on the desk. Both of them were having a taste of Irish whiskey. "Tell you the truth, though, you do look relieved."

"I am. It was going sour."

"Was it Jerre?" Chase asked softly.

"Oh, no, Lamar. Jerre is dead. She will always be a

part of me, but I've buried her. No . . . it just wasn't working. Linda is a fine lady, and somewhere out there," he waved his hand, "is a fine man waiting for her. It just isn't me."

Chase drained his glass and stood up. "Well, back to work for me, Ben. See you." He stalked out of the office, looking for some young Rebel to frighten half out of his wits by roaring at him, and then walk away, chuckling.

Ben looked out the window. The creepie bodies were gone, the streets hosed down. Ben had elected not to fill the tunnels with exhaust fumes. Sensors had shown there were so few Believers left they weren't worth fooling with. O'Shea had told Ben the Free Irish would take care of any left. The scent of death was still in the air, but it was fading. A good rain would clear it away forever, and that was what the meteorological people were predicting for the next couple of days.

Smoot came to him and rubbed against his leg. Ben played with the Husky for a few minutes until Ike came in and Smoot was then all over Ike.

"What's up, Ike?"

"The invasion of England."

"I certainly hope you have a plan, 'cause I damn sure haven't got one."

Ike looked at him and grinned. "One that you're happy with, you mean."

"Yeah. Where's the rest of the crew?"

"They're on the way." The news of Ben and Linda splitting the sheets had spread throughout the Rebel contingent like an unchecked brushfire. But Ike knew if Ben wanted to talk about it, he would bring it up.

"Any large-scale invasion is out," Ben said, toying with a pencil. "Small teams are going to have to cross, and that's going to have to be coordinated with airdrops. We have to assume that the punks and creeps in England have eyes and ears over here. So just as soon as we start refresher jumping, that news will be radioed to England. Not much is going to come as a surprise to the crap over there."

The rest of Ben's battalion commanders walked in and poured coffee and took chairs. Tina gave her father a strange look but said nothing about the split-up . . . for now.

Ben stood up and moved to a large map of England thumbtacked to the wall . . . compliments of the National Geographic Society. "The way I see it is like this: we've got to go in where they least expect us. Trying to put myself inside the enemy's heads, I'd think of attacking the larger ports and seizing them so we can off-load equipment from transport ships. So that's exactly what we're *not* going to do." He turned to face the group.

"We're going ashore in small groups. We take the countryside first, saving the larger towns and cities for last. Our first order of business is to secure a port. If we fail to do that, we're dead. But it's got to be a port that those defending the island feel would be too small or unimportant for us to take right off the bat. Or," Ben said with a smile, "one that is so large they would never dream we'd attempt to take first. We'll talk about that.

"Once the teams are in place, we'll start checking out drop zones for the jumpers. We're going to have to work closely with British Resistance Fighters on this. And we're also going to have to assume that many of their units have been compromised. Dan is taking a team and going in early to work with the BRF, ferreting out any who are suspect.

"When we decide on a port, the operation has to be timed letter perfect. We've got to have teams striking from inside the town and paratroopers coming in fast to beef them up. Ships are going to have to be standing by, but well off the coast, so as not to give away our landing site. Engineers are going to have to be ready to go in and repair the equipment on the docks that we need to off-load. All in all, it's either going to be a great success or a massive fuck-up that's going to get a lot of people killed for nothing. And it looks like it's going to be early fall before we can jump off."

"Don't forget securing a place for my medical teams, Ben," Chase spoke up.

"You wouldn't let me forget that, Lamar," Ben told him. "All right, people, loosen your battle harnesses and freshen your coffee. Tablets and pencils are on the conference table in the next room, and every map we could come up with is available. So come on, we've got a long skull session ahead of us."

Seventeen

The session wore on into evening, with dozens of plans tossed out and rejected. The air became thick with cigarette and pipe smoke. Chase finally gave all the smokers a good cussing and left the room, saying he'd be goddamned if he was going to die from secondhand smoke.

"There was a naval base at Plymouth," Ike said, his voice a little hoarse from all the talking and sometimes shouting. "Let's look at that a little closer. What do we have on it?"

"BRF says it's still in good shape, although much of the equipment hasn't been used in a long time," Beth said. "It had a population of about 225,000 before the Great War. The airport is still in good shape, although inhabited by creepies."

"Well, the other sites we've talked about are just too damn small," Ben said. "We're going to have to land a lot of equipment and do it fast." Ben stood up and looked at the large wall map for a moment. "What's this country north of the city like, Dan? It doesn't appear to be heavily populated."

"It isn't. That's the Dartmoor. A lot of good DZs there, General. And some good country to hide in."

"Splendid."

Dan rose and walked to the map. "Right here," he pointed a blunt finger, "is, or was, a national park. There is also one here, and here. Here is Savernake Forest, about two thousand acres or so of trees, huge oaks and beeches. There is quite a contingent of BRF operating not just out of these forests, but in timbered areas all over the country. And there are more forests in England than Yanks have been led to believe," he added with a smile.

"Good, Dan. Good." He looked at Pat O'Shea and Bobby Flynn. "Plymouth all right with you gentlemen?"

"Suits me, General," Bobby said with a smile. "Just as long as I don't have to do no jumpin' outta no damn airplane. I'll swim across if I have to, but I'll not fling my body outta no plane — unless it's parked on the runway. Patty, here, he was in the paratroopers. I always said he didn't have the sense God give a goose."

"You want to jump in, Pat?" Ben asked.

"Sure! But I'll have to brush up some. It's been many a year since I swung under the silk."

"The man is a fool just as sure as I'm a-sittin' here," Bobby said. "Absolutely daft, he is."

Rebels began prowling the now slowly being restored libraries in the city, looking for any book that could tell them something about England. Ben issued orders that any maps found be brought to his CP, inspected, and then copied many times. Every commander, from batt coms on down to squad leaders, had to have maps of every area of England, Scotland, and Wales.

Those who were jumping in began refresher

courses, including Pat and about a hundred of his Free Irish fighters. Ben was not jumping in, much to the relief of all concerned — which was everybody.

He had not seen Linda but heard that she was very happy with her work — helping tend to the needs of the hundreds of malnourished and abused Irish children at a clinic. Ben silently wished her well and tucked her away in the gallery of beautiful women he had known down through the years.

Then he settled down to pore over a mountain of work on his desk. And Ben despised paperwork nearly as much as he despised anything in the world.

Ben began working out the logistics of this operation. And its success hinged on establishing a solid hold in Plymouth. Ben felt he could not land paratroopers too many hours before the invasion. Even if the enemy did not see the jumpers, they would certainly hear the planes, and that would be a giveaway.

He issued orders to search Ireland and find any plane that would fly. Just before the invasion, he would send planes all over England, from north to south, to confuse the enemy as to the Rebels' real objective.

The ships carrying the Rebels in would leave many days before the invasion. They would sail out of Galway, then turn south and, once clear of the southernmost tip of the island, cut east through the Atlantic; then, once past the Isles of Scilly, turn toward Plymouth. While that was taking place, dozens of smaller boats would be crossing the Irish Sea and discharging teams of Rebels all up and down the west side of the English coast.

When the plans were as nearly perfect as Ben could make them, he dropped the news on his team. "We're going in first wave with the smaller craft," he told them matter-of-factly. "I'll be coordinating the invasion from the shore."

About sixty seconds later, his field phone started ringing. "Are you out of your goddamn mind?" Ike yelled in his ear. "We'll secure the port and *then* you can go in."

"Nope," Ben told him. "I go in first. And that's that."

"I forbid it!" the Russian, Striganov, growled. "I absolutely forbid it."

"Don't be a fool, General!" Dan told him.

"No!" Rebet said.

"Unthinkable!" Danjou snapped.

"Irresponsible!" the mercenary, West, said.

Thermopolis and Tina said nothing. Thermopolis had long given up trying to tell Ben anything, and Tina knew better than to argue with her father. Buddy just put a finer edge on his already razor-sharp knife and kept his mouth closed.

"Kick-ass time!" Jersey said.

The XO of Dan's Three Battalion, who would be leading the Third, since Dan would already be in England commanding the Special Ops teams, said nothing.

"That's the way it's going to be, people," Ben put an end to the arguments. "So just settle down and get your people ready to go."

Since Thermopolis would be in command of the ships, and Dan's XO would be in charge of the Third, they would be the last battalions into England.

"God damn it, Raines!" Dr. Chase roared at him. "Who the hell do you think you are, John Wayne?"

"Be quiet," Ben told him. "I can't think with all your bellering and snorting."

"Who's John Wayne?" a young Rebel asked.

The jump training was over, the supplies had been brought in and shifted from ship to ship, everyone had their orders and knew what to do. Dan and his special ops teams had left for England. Jump-off time for the invasion was only a few days away.

"I feel rather foolish commanding this armada," Therm told Ben. "Every ship's captain out there has more experience than I do."

"I know you, and I trust you," Ben replied. "So don't sweat it. When the ships are docked, you're back in command of your battalion and you'll wish you were back at sea."

"That is probably very true."

"How is Rosebud?" Therm's hippie wife.

"Rosebud is fine. Stop changing the subject. I'll only put this to you once, and that will be the end of it: You're really going in first wave?"

"That is correct." He looked at the slip of paper Therm had handed him. "This ETA is firm?"

"As firm as I can plot it. The sea is unpredictable, Ben. It's approaching fall, and it can get rough this time of year. I gave us some leeway, so I can promise you that we will be in position no later than the time and date I gave you. I personally checked out the trawler you and your people are using going in. It's a fine little vessel."

"*Little* vessel!" Cooper said. "I'm sick already."

"Shut up," Jersey told him.

"I got to go see the medics and get some seasick pills."

"Oh, hush up and sit down. It's all in your head," Jersey said. "And that's about all that's in your head."

"You're a cruel person, Jersey," Cooper said. "I don't see how your boyfriend puts up with you."

"True love makes the stormy seas calm," Thermopolis said with a smile.

"Shit!" Jersey said. "Love doesn't have anything to do with it. It takes the edge off, that's all."

"How crude!" Emil piped up, then beat a fast retreat out of the CP at one look from Jersey's dark eyes. No one knew exactly what Jersey's heritage was, but Ben would bet a hundred dollars she had some Apache in her.

Ben held out his hand and Therm shook it. "Let's start getting the people on board, Therm. The weather experts say it's going to start raining late tomorrow. I want as many as possible on board before that happens."

"See you in England, Ben."

Ben and his team began checking equipment, then double-checking. They would be taking only emergency rations, carrying extra ammo and grenades in place of bulky food packets. As Ben had expected, Buddy showed up.

"Don't holler at me, father," the young man spoke from the open doorway of Ben's CP in Galway.

"I know, I know," Ben replied. "Ike told you to cover me like a blanket."

"Ike did, Dan did, Rebet did, Danjou did, West did, Tina did, and Striganov did . . . all very forcefully. It was beginning to sound like a recording."

"How many of your Rat Team did you bring?"

"I brought two squads. It was difficult choosing the best because they're all very good at what they do. They all wanted to come, but I thought that would be defeating the purpose of this mission."

"You thought correctly. Have you seen the trawlers

189

we'll be going over on?"

"Yes. Aren't they rather small for the open seas?"

"They're workhorses, son. Tough as Jersey."

Buddy looked at the diminutive bodyguard. "Then we certainly have nothing to worry about," he said drily.

"Damn right," Jersey said, closing the bolt on her M-16.

"That was meant as a compliment," Buddy said.

Jersey smiled. "I know."

Ben spent a day driving from airport to airport checking out the planes that would fly diversion the night of the invasion. Some of them didn't look as though they could get off the ground, and he wasn't too sure about the men and women who would be piloting them.

"I didn't know you could fly, Lucy," Ben asked, looking at the dilapidated old cargo plane that looked suspiciously like the one he was in once while working for the Company, and flying Air America.

"I couldn't until about two weeks ago," she said with a grin.

Ben could see Ike's fine hand in all of this. "You've had only two . . . weeks' flight training?"

"Right, sir. I'm hell on taking off and flying this crate, but not so good on landing. So I've decided not to land."

"Ah . . . right!" Ben said. "Ah . . . Lucy, has somebody invented a new way to survive crashing?"

She laughed at the expression on his face. "No, sir. What me and my team are going to do is this: when we get near our DZ, I'll set this bird on auto and we'll jump. The plane will crash out in the North Sea."

Ben took off his beret, scratched his head for a moment, and then chuckled. "How many others are planning on doing likewise, Lucy?"

"Oh . . . 'bout fifteen teams, General."

Ben patted her on the shoulder. "Carry on, Lucy, carry on."

Ike's Two Battalion was loading when Ben reached the docks; Tina and Rebet's Battalions were waiting to load. Ben called Ike to one side.

"If something happens to me, Ike, you're in charge. Orders to that effect have been typed up and I've signed and dated them."

Ike nodded his head. "West and Danjou have sailed; they'll be landing right behind you and yours, Ben. Striganov and his bunch behind them. Then me and Tina and Rebet. Keep your head down."

"I plan to."

They shook hands and Ike joined his battalion.

Ben's Husky, Smoot, and Dan's mutt, Chester, were on the ship with Thermopolis, being taken very good care of by Rosebud and others of the Thermopolis clan.

Ben pointed to a row of trawlers. "That's us. Load your gear on board. Cooper, park the wagon over there and a cargo ship will hoist it on board."

"When are we leaving, General?" Cooper asked.

Ben smiled. "Tonight."

The trawlers caught up with and pulled ahead of the deliberately slow-moving bigger ships carrying West and Danjou. Striganov and West were right behind them. Chase's medical teams were scattered out on all ships. Ben lifted a hand of greeting and good luck in the darkness, knowing that West and Danjou were doing the same, although neither could see the other.

191

They had pulled out about five that afternoon in a driving rain, shortly after the skies had darkened down to near night. The skippers of the trawlers figured thirty to thirty-four hours to Plymouth — that was at twelve knots. The skipper of Ben's trawler had grinned and pointed to the engine compartment hatch.

"We all put in new engines, General. This old girl will give you eighteen knots if you ask her."

"Fourteen knots would put us in Plymouth harbor in thirty hours even," Beth said. "That would put us close at midnight."

"That's perfect," Ben said. "Can you do it, Skipper?"

"You bet I can. The seas are uncommonly smooth for this time of year and the stars they've come out a-twinkling. You people just settle down and enjoy the ride." He looked close at Ben. "What was all that pukin' a few hours ago?"

"Cooper," Ben said. "He gets sick very easily."

"Then he'd best pray we don't run into no bad weather. This old girl will give him a bad time of it."

"We'll just shoot him," Jersey said with a straight face.

The skipper took Ben to one side. "That young lady there who just spoke — is she as mean as she looks?"

"Meaner," Ben told him without cracking a smile.

"She looks like one of them wild red Indians I used to read about."

"She is. Cochise was her great-grandfather."

"You don't say!"

"Oh, yes. She takes scalps, too."

"Jesus, Mary, and Joseph!" He went back to the wheelhouse, muttering and giving Jersey some cautious looks.

"They're going to know we're coming," Buddy said to his father.

"Yes. But they won't know where we're going. At two o'clock tomorrow morning, at my signal, teams all over Britain are going to start raising hell from north to south, east to west. At 0230 the paratroopers will land north of Plymouth and start in our direction. And we'd better, by God, have a firm toehold on the docks."

"Yes, I'm sure that the sight of all eighty of us will strike terrible fear into the hearts of the defenders."

Ben chuckled in the night. "The BRF will be attacking the city hard from the east, the jumpers will be coming in from the north, we'll be attacking from the south, and with the sea to the remaining side—more or less—that pretty well boxes them in."

"All those crates you had put on board—inflatable boats and motors?"

"That's right."

"So these trawlers, they'll never actually enter Plymouth harbor, will they?"

"Right again. We'll motor most of the way and paddle the rest. Our skipper is cutting some time off by not skirting the Isles of Scilly; we'll go between them and Land's End."

"It's chancy, isn't it, Father?"

Ben looked at his son for a long moment before replying. "Very."

Book Two

Let us have faith that right makes might, and in that faith let us to the end dare to do our duty as we understand it.

Abraham Lincoln

One

Ben soon found himself reassessing the known enemy. They obviously did not have pilots to fly patrol; they did not have crews out working patrol boats. The skipper had told him that radar sites all along the coast had never been used since the Great War.

"Shit-headed street punks," Ben said, sitting under the shade of a stretched canvas over a part of the deck.

"Beg pardon?" Buddy asked, looking up from his chess game with Jersey—he was losing again.

"Street punks," his father repeated. "That's who we'll be fighting. And of course, the Believers."

Jersey moved a piece and looked up at Buddy, smiling victoriously. Buddy shook his head. "You've got a fine mind, Jersey. When the war is over, please attend college and put that mind to work."

"This war'll never be over, Buddy," she told him, stowing away her small chess set. "We'll be doin' this until the day we die. Tomorrow, next month, next year. You can bet that now that the Rebels have left America, there are thousands of mercenaries, warlords, punks, gangs, dictators, all over

197

the world, and all making plans to attack the United States. We'll finish up in England, and it won't take that long; probably 'til mid-winter, and then we'll go somewhere else to fight again. France, Hawaii." She shrugged her shoulders. "Who knows? But by that time, General Jefferys will have hard intell that someone is planning on attacking America and we'll sail back to do it all over again. We'll clean it up again, and then we'll sail off somewhere else to fight somebody else's battles for them. That's what Americans—and a precious damn few of her allies—have always done."

Buddy stared at her for a moment. "So you think we'll all be back in America by . . . when?"

"A year, tops."

Buddy looked at his father. Ben smiled. "She's probably right, son. Irish intell and the BRF told me that a few large ships pulled out of Irish and British waters before we arrived. Then after the invasion, more ships left. Right before we took Dublin, still more ships pulled out. One hit an old derelict mine and was sunk. The survivors told the BRF they'd been heading to Hawaii to link up with gangs there. So I imagine that Hawaii is our next stop."

"Palm trees, coconuts, and hula girls," Cooper said, having recovered from his seasickness. "Especially the hula girls. That's for me."

"Any hula girl that would take up with you would have to be mentally retarded," Jersey told him.

Cooper shot her the bird and she returned it, twice.

Ben glanced at his watch. "Eight hours to jump-off time, folks. Let's start inflating those boats and loading equipment."

The trawlers carrying Ben and his teams reached their destinations an hour and a half early. By ten-thirty the teams were in the landing craft and preparing to shove off. And it was a good thing they were early. The seas were picking up and it was going to rain just about the time the Rebels reached shore.

"You'll make it before it gets really rough, General," the skipper called from the railing. "Godspeed to you all."

"Everybody got their life vests on?" Ben shouted.

Everybody did. Cooper had two.

"Let's do it," Ben ordered.

The rubber boats roared off into the darkness, the rolling and swelling vastness of the sea all around them. Each boat towed a second filled with equipment that was lashed down tight. It cut their speed considerably, and they were forced to stop a half dozen times before they found the right towing length and could adjust to it. Then they were on their way.

Long before they reached the dark shoreline, the sounds of planes reached them, all flying in from the west.

"I hope one of those pilotless bastards don't crash on us," Beth remarked.

"That thought did cross my mind," Ben said.

Lights popped on in and around Plymouth and wild shooting could be faintly heard. But the shooting quickly died away as the planes flew on and disappeared into the darkness.

A light rain, no more than a drizzle, began to

fall. One by one, the lights on the shore blinked out as those in the small city felt the danger had passed.

"Idiots," Ben muttered. "Kill the engines," he called.

The night was suddenly very quiet.

"Paratroopers on the ground," Corrie said. "Special ops teams moving."

"Paddle," Ben ordered, unlashing a paddle.

It was hard work, especially since they were towing a craft, but the shoreline soon leaped into view.

"Rat Team ashore," Ben whispered. "Everybody else rest their muscles."

They bobbed on the water for a full fifteen minutes, easy targets should the docks be guarded and a flashlight be directed their way.

"There is no one on the docks, General," Corrie relayed the message from the Rat Team.

"What?"

"Nothing, sir," Corrie repeated. "The docks are deserted."

"My God, but we're a lucky bunch. Let's go, people," Ben said, picking up his paddle. "Hard now."

The rubber rafts were pulled ashore and the Rebels quickly unlashed their equipment and loaded up.

"The Colonists have arrived, Your Majesty. Just hang tough." Ben looked at his team. "Welcome to England, folks. Corrie, get me the paratroopers' position."

"The main force is about ten miles north of the airport," she said. "Pat and his contingent of Free Irish went wide of the DZ and landed right in the

200

middle of a small village. Scared the crap out of a bunch of folks. Pat went right through a thatched roof and landed in bed with a man and his wife. Almost gave them a heart attack."

Everyone around who could hear chuckled at that. Pat was a pretty good hand at cussing, and they all imagined he did some fancy swearing when he hit the bed.

"Dan and his team have taken over an old building that used to be a lunatic asylum about fifty klicks north and east of here. They've been there three days and nights and haven't spotted a thing."

"We heard shooting," Cooper remarked. "We know they're here. So where the hell is everybody?"

"Pulled back into the cities," Ben said. "But they've got to have patrols working—somewhere. They can't be this stupid." He stood up from his kneeling on the ground. "Let's secure the docks, folks."

The Rebels did not encounter a single person as they worked the dock area. Ben set up his thin lines and laid out Claymores. And did it all without firing a shot.

Ben knelt down in the hollow emptiness of a huge old warehouse and studied the map of the harbor and the area around it. He came to the conclusion—again—that there was no damn way a unit this size was going to hold the harbor for any length of time.

Ben tensed. He smelled the bastard coming up behind him. A stinking creepie. He threw himself to one side just as the creepie jumped for him, the knife flashing through the air. Ben rolled to his boots, stepped forward, and kicked the creep in the nuts. As the cannibal doubled over, his mouth open to scream out the pain from his busted balls, Ben rared back and socked him on the jaw. The smaller man dropped like a stone and Ben stepped back, rubbing his knuckles.

"What the hell, General?" Jersey said, running through the open door of the warehouse. She pulled up short at the sight of the creepie on the dirty and littered concrete floor, Beth, Corrie, and Cooper right behind her.

"So we do have people in the harbor area," Corrie said.

Outside, the wet night was shattered by gunfire and screaming.

"Corrie," Ben said. "Give the signal. All units attack, all units attack."

Buddy appeared in the open doorway. "If you don't mind, Father, would you and your team kindly step outside and give us a hand? We seem to be under attack by a rather large and hostile group of people."

"God damn it!" West roared through a bullhorn. "Get those boats over the side and get in them. Move, God damn it, move!"

It was a strange invasion by modern standards. The Rebels had only a few military-type landing craft, and those had already shoved off. The rest of the first two full battalions were getting to shore in rubber dinghies and anything else they could throw over the side and hook a motor to.

As Ben always said, "It was a hell of a way to run a war."

Thermopolis received a frantic message from Emil, who was captaining the ship carrying Rebet's Six Battalion. "The goddamn ship is dead in the water, Therm. We hit something. Probably a nearly submerged old tub. It bent the shaft and probably sheered the blades off the prop. We ain't goin' anywhere, brother."

"What is your location, Emil?" Ike broke in.

"Right off Lizard Point, General."

"Put your troops ashore there and tell them to fight their way north to Bodmin. Secure it."

"That's a ten-four, General."

Rebet's men began tossing dinghies over the side and scrambling down ladders.

"Lower the lifeboats!" Emil yelled to some of his people. "Abandon this tub. We're going ashore with Rebet."

"May God have mercy on my soul," Rebet muttered.

"Get that equipment over the side!" Striganov roared like an angry bear. "The general is under heavy attack." Striganov jumped over the side, holding onto the rope ladder. His boots missed the rung and he fell into the cold waters of the western edge of the English Channel. Luckily he was wearing a life vest and he popped to the surface, flailing his arms and cussing in Russian.

One of his men tossed him rope and pulled him in. The young soldier could not get the grin off his face. He tried, but he could not wipe it clean.

"You think it's funny?" Georgi roared.

"Yes, sir," the Russian Rebel said honestly, and

then burst out laughing.

"Well . . ." Georgi said, heaving himself into the boat. He lay on the deck of the lifeboat for a moment, then a grin cut his craggy features. "I guess it is, at that. Come on, son, we have a war to fight. Wet drawers and all," he laughed.

"Striganov just fell into the ocean," Corrie told Ben, during a slight lull in the fighting.

"Is he all right?"

"Oh, yes, sir."

Ben shook his head. "Anything else I need to know?"

"Emil's ship is dead in the water. Rebet is taking his battalion ashore at Lizard Point. Ike's orders."

"Who's picking up Emil and his bunch?"

"No one. Emil gave the orders to abandon ship and he's joining Rebet's battalion."

"God grant him the strength to maintain his sanity. You in contact with the jumpers?"

"Still north of the airport, traveling as fast as they can. Some of them have commandeered bicycles and are pedaling their way in."

Ben ducked his head and laughed. The idea of heavily armed paratroopers riding into combat on a bicycle was funny to him.

"They're trying an end-around," a Rebel called from Ben's right. "Between warehouses at two o'clock."

"They're in trouble," Ben said.

The words had just left his mouth when the Claymores blew and parts of street punks were slammed against the old wet walls of both warehouses.

"This way!" the voice was barely audible over the

screaming and moaning of the wounded. "Watch them mines. The rest of you, follow me."

He tripped a wire and one side of a warehouse blew up in a flash of fire and debris. Ben looked at Buddy.

"I found a bag of fertilizer and several drums of gasoline," his son explained. "I thought the fertilizer might be too old to work. I was wrong."

"How much gas was in those drums, boy?"

"Fifty-five gallons in each, I suppose. They were full."

The old wood of the warehouse was burning brightly now, and the Rebels could clearly see dozens of bodies lying in unnaturally twisted positions.

A dozen street punks rushed Ben's position. An M-60 started belching out lead. The punks folded up and went down like dominoes.

"Fall back!" someone shouted. "It's the invasion. Jesus Christ, look at all them people in the bay. Back to the city, back to the city."

Ben turned around. Rebels from Four and Seven Battalions were storming ashore, climbing over old rusting cars and trucks and machinery.

"God must be on our side," Ben muttered. "Either that, or we're dealing with the dumbest bunch of bastards on the face of the earth."

"The first of Rebet's troops have landed and not a shot has been fired," Corrie said. "They have encountered no resistance whatsoever. Dan's teams are now engaged in a firefight with an unknown group."

West and Danjou came panting up to Ben's position. "Where is all the resistance?" West asked, catching his breath.

"It came and went," Ben told him. "Corrie, advise our people to disarm all remaining Claymores they set. Danjou, West, have your men stay to this side until that is done, please. Buddy, take your Rat Team and Scouts and see what's up ahead of us. And somebody clear out a building and make some coffee. We've got a toehold in England, people. But it's a big damn island."

Two

By morning, the entire dock area and several blocks all around it on all sides had been cleared. Not that there had been all that much to clear out. The only shot fired was when a very large rat — about the size of a well-fed housecat — ran across a Rebel's boot in a dark, cobwebby, and musty warehouse and scared the crap out of him. The rat got shot.

"I wonder how it got so large?" the Rebel questioned.

"Probably by eating body parts thrown away by those damn creepies," his buddy told him.

"Barf!"

The paratroopers had reached the edge of town and were setting up positions. And the street punks in Plymouth who had not thrown in with Butch and the others were scared.

"Corrie," Ben asked, "have you found the frequencies of the punks in this city?"

"Yes, sir. Several of them. They're a real smart bunch." She said that with the sarcasm dripping. "With the most advanced communications equipment in the world at their fingertips, they're using CB's."

Ben grunted. He looked at the BRF commander who had joined them during the night, coming into the harbor by motor launch. He and his men were all tough-looking and handled their weapons in the seemingly casual way an expert does. "This is the way we do it, Drake," Ben told him. "You might not like it, and I don't particularly care whether you do or not. It works for us. We usually give the enemy one chance to surrender. After that, we don't take prisoners. There have been exceptions, but not many. How do you want to play this?"

The Englishman stared at Ben, knowing then that all the rumors about him were true. Ben Raines was a hard man. "It's your show, General. If you can live with it, so can I."

Ben nodded his head. "Corrie, use your, ah, CB and contact whoever is in charge of the gangs."

"Standing by, sir," she said, after only half a minute.

Ben took the mic. "This is General Ben Raines. To whom am I speaking?"

"My, my, ain't you the proper one, now," the jeering voice came out of the speaker. "To *whom* is I talkin', huh? Well, you talkin' to Ace. What's on your mind, Mister Big-Shit General?"

"I'm talking about whether you live or die, punk. And this is your only chance to surrender. Lay your guns on the floor, on the sidewalks, in the street, wherever you may be, and come walking out with your hands in the air. This is the only chance you are getting."

There were several moments of silence from the city. Ace finally came back on the air. "You gonna kill us all, General?"

208

"Every goddamn one of you," Ben said, enough ice in his voice to cause Drake to take a step back away from him.

"Supposin' we fight you and see that we can't whip you, General? Can't we pack it in then? I mean, we soldiers just like you, man."

Several Rebels laughed at that.

"No, you're not," Ben told him. "You're a bunch of no-good murderers, thieves, rapists, and God only knows what else. I have absolutely no use for any of you. I shouldn't even offer you surrender terms. But I will, one time. And this is that time. Take it or leave it, punk."

"I ain't no punk!" Ace screamed. "But I do run this city. So fuck you, Raines. Just fuck you, man. Fuck you!"

"Fellow seems to have a rather limited vocabulary," Buddy remarked.

"He won't have it long," Ben replied. "Corrie, give the orders to take the city."

The gangs in the city were well armed, but they had no real knowledge of warfare, guerrilla, urban, or conventional. Ben Raines' Rebels smashed into the city. Tanks rolled in first, with the Rebels following. The street gangs who controlled Plymouth took one look at what they faced and were horrified.

"Jesus Christ, Ace!" a gang member yelled. "That's a real fuckin' army."

"So is we," Ace replied. "We stand and fight." He looked around him. "But not here. Fall back to the center of town."

Ace had just exited the building near the harbor area when an MBT, cannon lowered,

209

blew the old home apart with HE.

The creepies were the only ones to put up much of a fight. But there were few of them remaining in Plymouth. Most of them had slipped out hours before the invasion began, heading for London and Birmingham and other cities. They left their prisoners behind, after hosing them down with machine-gun fire. The members of the cannibalistic sect were the most vicious and utterly worthless bunch of people the Rebels had ever fought. The Rebels had tried to rehabilitate some of them and had yet to find one who would respond to treatment.

Ben Raines had then given the orders: any creepie found would be shot on sight.

The taking of Plymouth was the easiest any Rebel could remember. By nightfall of the first day, most of the gang members had fled the city, using alleys and tunnels dug or enlarged by the Believers, or by using escape routes the smarter ones had mapped out long ago.

"They left their children behind," the news was reported to Ben. "Dozens of them. The bastards and bitches just deserted their own kids."

Ben had expected that. He'd seen it too many times back in America to be shocked. "As we secure the countryside, we'll find foster homes for them. Take them to that hospital Chase is cleaning out." He shook his head. "It's always the children and the old people that suffer the most in war. Seems like I'd be used to it by now."

By noon of the third day of the invasion, Plymouth was declared secure. "Incredible," Striganov said.

Ben's Rebels were reporting from all over the surrounding countryside that thugs and punks and other assorted human crud were surrendering in large numbers; the Rebels were taking so many prisoners it wasn't uncommon to see one Rebel, wearing an expression of disbelief, walking along behind two dozen prisoners with their hands on their heads.

Ben ordered all prisoners to be turned over to the British Resistance Forces.

"You try them," Ben told the commander of the BRF. "You do what you want to with them. But I tell you this much right now: The Rebels are arming the general public. And we're arming them well. Don't even entertain the thought that society will return to what it used to be here, or anywhere else the Rebels have been. We're not expending time and effort in building prisons, and I've a hunch the good people of England will follow our lead. I don't want to have to come back here in any other capacity except as a visitor seeing the sights."

"You don't believe in giving a person a second chance, General?" a woman asked.

"That depends on the crime, lady."

Rebels had secured several smaller coastline towns on the westernmost tip of Wales, and Ben shifted two battalions over to that section of the country, one of them Thermopolis and his Eight Battalion, now that he was no longer needed to captain the big ships.

If the hardworking and tough people of Wales had had access to firearms, the thugs and punks and creeps would never have taken that section of the country. But England had long had very restrictive guns laws — decades before the Great War — and its citizens never had a chance when the criminals made their move. Politicians never seemed to learn that criminals paid absolutely no attention to gun laws.

The Rebels in and around Plymouth began the awesome job of clearing out the countryside and pushing out of Cornwall and into Devon County.

"No stinking damn politician will ever take my guns again, General," an elderly farmer told Ben, after he had stopped to chat with the man. "By God, they'll have to kill me to do it."

"You can bet that when some order is restored, someone will sure try," Ben replied.

"They'll rot in the ground shortly after they do," the man said grimly.

"The next town up is infested with human vermin," the man's wife said. "Their behavior is disgusting."

"We have just the cure for lice, ma'am," Ben told her. "We've found they respond well to lead."

She laughed, gave him a piece of pie, and wished him luck.

"Says here," Beth said, reading from a tattered old tourist guide as they rolled up the road, "that the next town on this highway has good food and hospitality."

"Sounds delightful," Cooper said. "You suppose they'll roll out the red carpet for us, General?"

"Somehow, I rather doubt it."

"Buddy says hold the column and for us to come on up," Corrie said. "He's on the outskirts of the town now. The gang holding the town is going to fight."

"Why does he want me up there? Tell him to take the damn town."

Corrie relayed the order and listened for a moment. "The gang leader has marched the citizens out and is hiding behind them. People of all ages, including young children and babies."

Ben muttered a few highly uncomplimentary phrases about thugs in general. "Corrie, ask Buddy if there is a back door to this town."

"That's ten-four, sir. Rebels could work their way into the town through the woods and slip in that way."

"How far off this road?"

"Just off this road. Take a road running straight back west just after crossing a bridge. We'll see a stone fence running alongside for extra concealment."

Ben smiled. "Tell my son to keep these goons busy with conversation. Let's go, Coop. Corrie, tell my bodyguards to lag behind a good quarter mile. When we stop, they stop. No tanks. That's a direct order. I want to check out the woods and the stone fence."

They parked on the low side of a small hill and got out silently, being careful not to bang any doors. They squatted down behind some thick brush and inspected the scene. They could see no one posted at the rear of the town.

"Surely they wouldn't be that stupid," Ben muttered.

He carefully inspected the area through binoculars and could see no sign of life.

"Corrie, tell the platoon to come up on foot, fast and silent. Stay in the ditch, close to the brush."

213

Ballard, the platoon leader, was the first at Ben's side.

"Lieutenant, we're going in the back door," Ben told him. "Nice and quiet." He pointed a finger at him. "Your people, follow my people. Let's go, gang."

"I ain't gonna tell you this but one more time, dude," the thug in charge of the town told Buddy. "Carry your funky ass on away from here."

"You're not English, are you?" Buddy asked.

"No, I ain't. Now move, 'fore I start killin' these folks here. They belong to me, I can do what I want to with them."

"They're your slaves?"

"That's right. Now carry your ass like I told you, man."

Ben and his people had left the woods and were now in the town, working their way toward the pile-up of people near the junction. Many of the homes they passed had bullet-holes in them, windows gone and doors missing. This town had been the center of many battles over the years.

"Across the street," Ben whispered. "Just to the left of that stone cottage. See the two men?"

"I see them," Ballard said. He motioned for two Rebels to go.

The other Rebels waited while the pair worked their way across the street and got into position for a silent shoot or a throat cutting—whichever seemed more appropriate. The two Rebels Ballard had sent carried silenced pistols for close-in work.

A few moments passed before Corrie received the word. "It's all clear over there, General. They say

214

we can cross over now."

In teams of three and four, the Rebels crossed the littered street at a run. They passed by the bodies of the thugs, each with a tiny hole in his head from silenced .22 caliber auto-loading pistols.

"Hey, slick," the gang leader said to Buddy. "Are you retarded or something? I told you carry your ass on away from here. Are you nuts? You wanna die?"

"We all have to die sometime," Buddy told him. He was inwardly seething with rage at the sight of the ragged and bruised and starving children and old people. He kept his composure only with immense effort.

Buddy estimated about one hundred male gang members and probably fifty to seventy-five female members, all heavily armed. The women were some of the trashiest- and sluttiest-looking females Buddy had seen so far.

Buddy picked up movement far behind and on either side of the gang, all spread out on the road and on both sides of the junction. Rebels, silently working their way toward the crossroads, led, of course, by his father.

Buddy's Rat Team was spread out left and right of him.

"Man," the gang leader said. "I'm gettin' tired of jackin' around with you. I'm fixin' to start shootin' these slaves if you and them others don't carry your asses on away from here. You got ten seconds to move." He lifted his pistol and pointed it at the head of a weeping young girl.

"All right!" Buddy said. "We're backing off. Let's go, team."

As he spoke, Ben and his platoon were drawing closer.

"And I mean get totally out of sight and leave me and mine the hell alone in this town," the punk shouted.

"I assure you," Buddy said, "that in a few minutes, you will never be disturbed again. And that's a promise."

One of the female gang members grabbed at her crotch and hunched her hips at Buddy as she grinned an invitation.

"You have to be joking," Buddy muttered, as he and his team began slowly backing up.

Ben and his people were almost in position. If only one gang member cut his eyes left or right, or looked behind him, the ambush would be compromised and a lot of civilians would be dead. Even if they didn't, Buddy knew that several of the slaves would surely be cut down by gunfire, some even by friendly fire.

"You ain't movin' very fast," the gang leader said. "Shove off, prick."

"We're surrounded!" a punk yelled, whirling around and spotting the Rebels on all sides.

"Hit the ground!" Buddy yelled at the slaves, as a Rebel bullet punched a hole through the head of the gang leader.

The men and women dropped flat to the road, pulling their kids down with them as lead began whistling above their heads. The gang members panicked and tried to run. They didn't make it as Rebels — who had been silently working their way into position — popped up all around them.

It was over in a minute, and as always, the silence after combat was slightly unnerving. Corrie radioed for the medics to come up as Rebels began checking over the slaves. The enemy received medical attention last—Ben Raines' orders.

One elderly man had been killed and one woman received a slight flesh wound.

"It could have been a lot worse," Ballard said to Ben.

"Yes. We got lucky," Ben said, looking around him at all the human garbage lying in their own blood. Many were still alive. The medics ignored them until they had checked out the civilians and the Rebels.

"Bastards," the woman who had made the obscene gesture to Buddy said. "Heartless bastards."

"You're calling us heartless?" Jersey said to her. "Hey! I know you. We chased your ass out of Texas. Dallas/Fort Worth area. I remember your ugly face. You were ramrodding a gang of street punks over there. Yeah."

The woman had a hole in her side and was obviously in great pain. But her hatred for law and order and justice overrode her pain. She spat at Jersey. The spit fell short of Jersey's boot.

"You spit on me, bitch," Jersey warned her, "and I'll punch your ticket right now."

"What are you going to do with us?" a punk moaned from his position on the road. He had taken a 7.62 round in the leg and the leg was twisted and broken.

"Turn you over to the British Resistance Forces," Buddy told him. "They'll deal with you."

"Oh, man," another whimpered. "They's gone back to hangin' folks over here. We're all Ameri-

217

cans, just like you. Cut us some slack, man."

Buddy turned his back to the punk. He had an almost overwhelming urge to shoot the bastard.

"You're General Ben Raines," a punk said, looking up at Ben. "I seen you before, back in Colorado. How's about givin' us a break, boss?"

Ben turned away without replying and walked over to the group of abused civilians. They were a pitiful sight, but one that he'd witnessed more times than he cared to remember.

"You're all from this general area?" he asked.

They were.

"We'll patch you up," he told them. "And we'll supply you with food to eat and grain to plant. And we'll arm you. After that, it's up to you. It's doubtful that we'll be back. Don't ever let anyone take your guns again. No government, no politician, no punk. You all had the will to fight, you just didn't have anything to fight with. Don't let it happen again."

Members of the BRF showed up and gave the prisoners some very hard looks.

"Don't let them people have us, General!" a punk shouted. "They'll hang us. For God's sake, please don't."

"For *God*'s sake?" Ben said. "You, calling on God? He must be getting a good laugh out of this. And He probably needs one. Mount up, people, we have miles to go."

Three

Rebet and his battalion, aided by the BRF, quickly secured everything in the southern part of Cornwall and pushed on to reach Ben's One Battalion. Battalions were regrouping now, the small teams scattered all over England linking up with units of the BRF. The Rebels soon learned that the thugs and punks and human garbage had no stomach for a fight with the Rebels . . . at least, not in the country.

"They never seem to learn," Ben said, rubbing his eyes and leaning back in his chair. "They can't understand that cities are death traps for them."

"Yeah, Ben, but in this case, they don't have any choice in the matter," Ike said, at a staff meeting. "We thought we'd seen bad in Ireland. But, Christ, the punks and creepies have really raped this country . . . literally."

Ben nodded his agreement. The advancing Rebel army had found living conditions to be appalling in most areas. The thugs and assorted crapheads were literally starving the people to death, forcing them to work the gardens and fields, and then taking the food, leaving the citizens not quite enough to get by on.

The people told the Rebels that the creepies had a number of large breeding farms around the country, but none of them could tell the Rebels where they were located.

Dr. Chase had been livid with rage upon seeing the hundreds and hundreds of malnourished children. And he had laid it on the line to Ben.

"Don't bring any enemy wounded to my hospitals, Raines. None. I'll personally cut their stinking no-good throats with a dull scalpel."

"All right, Lamar. I'll give the orders. What have you seen that's set you off so?"

"I've seen *babies* who were raped and sodomized." Chase's words were filled with loathing. "Boys and girls. Every deviant sex act known to humankind . . . I've seen the aftermath of it here on this island in only the short time we've been here. I've seen battle-hardened doctors and nurses who have been with us since the beginning break down and weep at the stories from the mouths of children. I've personally witnessed hardened Rebel veterans with tears running down their cheeks as they carry in kids, or what is left of them, after being assaulted, tortured, maimed, mutilated, and left for dead. I have yet to hear one child, one adult, male or female, tell me of one single act of compassion from the disgusting, perverted . . . *filth* who have taken over this land. I've had my say. Goodnight. If you need me, I'll be at the main hospital in Torbay."

Ben issued the orders declaring the death sentence on any punk, thug, warlord, and the like who offered even the slightest resistance to the Rebels.

By this time, his communications people had

every frequency used by the enemy locked in. Ben went on the air and laid down the options available to the lawless. There were only two choices. "You will surrender now and take your chances in a court of law, or you will be hunted down by the Rebel Army, the British Resistance Forces, and the Free Irish Army, and you will be killed. We will stand down for twenty-four hours to give you time to make up your minds and seek out a Rebel, BRF unit, or Free Irish, and surrender. At the end of that time, no one will be taken prisoner. That is all."

"He's bluffing!" the warlords told their already spooked followers. "He ain't gonna just shoot us down like animals."

"No," London Lulu said, after hearing the same from some of her followers. "He ain't bluffin'. We've had it, mates."

"What do you mean?" one of the group asked.

"The British courts will hang us, or the Rebels will shoot us. It's just that simple."

"But England done away with the death penalty a long time ago."

"Don't try to think, Sammy," Lulu told him. "You ain't no good at it. This is a new order comin' out of the ashes, people. All them sobbin', hankie-stompin' folks that went easy on the likes of us is gone. There's gonna be law and order now. And the only way that's gonna happen is for them out yonder to get rid of us. You follow me now?"

"They ain't gonna take us in London," another said. "There ain't no way that's gonna happen. We know ever' alley and tunnel there."

"They took every major city in America," Lulu

221

reminded them all. "And they didn't even slow down doin' it. No," she said, shaking her head. "I got to get with Butch and we got to map out a retreat route."

"This is it," Butch told her. "I've got people out now gathering all the small boats they can find. We'll stash them all up and down the coast. When the end is looking at us—and it will, kid; we can't win this—we'll set out at night for France and link up with them over there. Raines is going to clear the countryside first, saving the cities for last."

"The cities is gettin' all clogged up, Butch. People are comin' in from the country by the hundreds."

"I know. Those coming into London are being spread out on a line from the city down to Brighton. They're blowing bridges and cutting up the roads west of their positions. As those who elect to fight protecting their turf fall back from Birmingham, Nottingham, Manchester, I'll position them north of the city on the east side of the river. I'm already blowing the bridges, leaving just a few of them open for retreat. Once them that's coming is across, those bridges will go."

"It'll buy us some time, for sure," Lulu said. "But what if Raines decides to launch another attack by sea?"

"Then we're fucked."

Lulu smiled at him. "Speaking of that . . ."

Butch patted her denim-covered butt. "Might as well."

"You're so romantic, Butch."

"They're going to try to retreat using the Chan-

222

nel," Ben said, after reading intell reports. "Probably using hundreds of small boats that would be impossible to intercept and destroy at night. Especially if it's foggy and they'll wait for that, bet on it. What do we have on this Butch Smathers fellow?"

"Not much," Georgi said. "But he's had some military training. He's making some smart moves."

"All the special units are back with their battalions," Ike said. "As well as those who jumped in. Thermopolis and his Eight Battalion have cleared the county of Dyfed in Wales and opened the ports there. He reports that resistance has been extremely light. His people found one of the creepie breeding and fattening farms," Ike said, the words leaving a bad taste in his mouth. "Physically, the people are fine. Mentally, they're in rough shape."

"What is the word on those in Bristol?" Ben asked.

"They're digging in for a fight," Tina told him. "My battalion is standing by just south of the city. We've cleared Bridgewater."

"That's the last town of any size in Devon," Ben said. "But Bristol is another matter. That's a good-sized city. Over half a million before the Great War."

"But a lot of the thugs ran like rabbits, General," the commander of the BRF pointed out. "Our people tell me that no more than thirty five hundred to four thousand hard-core criminals remain in the city."

"How about the general population?"

The man shook his head. "I have to say that those who chose to remain were slaughtered. Either

223

that, or traded to the Believers."

"The birthplace of America," Ben spoke the words softly. "A treasure-house of historical importance."

"Not anymore," the BRF commander said. "It's been trashed and looted and vandalized over the years. Take it down, General Raines."

"That's the consensus of the people, Commander Drake?"

"It is, sir."

"Out of the ashes," Ben muttered. "We'll try to save the more important landmarks. Where is the Methodist Chapel located, Commander Drake?"

The man smiled sadly. "It isn't, anymore, sir. The hoodlums burned it."

Ben sighed. When something like that occurred, the loss was deep, for history could never be replaced. "What else have the bastards destroyed?"

"Nearly everything that was priceless and precious to us," the man replied. "England will not be rebuilt in our lifetime. These thugs and hoodlums have done more damage than the Nazis did more than half a century ago."

"The university?" Ben asked.

"Trashed and vandalized. The books were all destroyed. They heaped them in piles and burned them. I have eyewitness accounts of that."

"What do your people say about the punks' armaments?"

"Light weapons. A few mortars and rocket launchers. The tanks and other modern equipment were simply too complicated for them to master. But the taking of Bristol will not be a walk-through."

"No," Ben agreed. "It never is. All right, we'll use three battalions, plus armor and artillery. My One Battalion, Dan's Three Battalion, and Georgi's Five Battalion. The rest of you, hold your lines. Commander Drake, your BRF people will continue the sweeping of the countryside down to the coast. All right, people." Ben smiled and looked over at Jersey, sitting in a chair by the door, her M-16 across her legs. "What do you say, Jersey?"

Her dark eyes twinkled. "Kick-ass time."

Those in Bristol who had chosen a life of crime and pitched their lot in with the Believers knew the sands of time had very nearly emptied the glass when the mist of dawn was abruptly shattered by incoming artillery rounds that rained down on their heads like some hideous storm.

Ben was throwing heavy artillery and mortar rounds at the center of the city while his Rebels smashed into the suburbs north and south of the river and caught those there by surprise. Those who tried to flee toward the east ran right into two battalions of Free Irish who cut them down with heavy machine gun fire. To the west lay the heavily patrolled Bristol Channel.

Ben ordered the thundering pounding to continue for an hour. Then he ordered tear gas to be dropped into the center of the city, canister after canister of it. For blocks in any direction, people were staggering around, unable to see. Then Ben ordered pepper gas to be dropped in, and that really caused the punks and crud and creepies some problems. The gas was by no means lethal, one simply felt that death would be a relief from the choking and stinging.

When the creeps and crud staggered into a free-fire area, the Rebels cut them down. Some of the Brits (but not many) with the BRF thought this to be a bit on the barbaric side, and certainly ungentlemanly, but they kept their mouths shut and maintained a stiff upper lip.

"This offend you?" Ben asked a newly arrived observer from the BRF.

"To be truthful, yes, it does. But nothing that I can't live with," he added dryly.

"Want to get a little closer?"

"I thought you would never ask, General," the distinguished-looking gentleman said.

Ben had tried to pinpoint the man's age, but it was hard to tell. He might be anywhere from sixty to eighty.

Ben and his team and the BRF observer moved to within a block of the battle lines, which made the frontline Rebels awfully nervous. Ben ordered body armor and helmet for the seemingly unflappable Mr. Carrington and made the much older man get into the protective gear. Carrington carried an old bolt-action rifle which looked to Ben to be about a hundred years old.

"Ah, Mr. Carrington," Ben asked, pointing to the rifle. "Will that thing shoot?"

"My heavens, yes. Certainly, it will. It functioned quite well at Dunkirk."

"*Dunkirk!* That was more than half a century ago! I wasn't even born then."

Carrington looked at Ben, a twinkle in his eyes. "Quite right," he said, then returned his attention to the battle lines up the street.

"Bastards!" a scream cut the morning's chill. "Dirty, rotten bastards and bitches, all of you!"

A man appeared out of the fading fog of tear gas and pepper gas carrying an M-16. Carrington lifted his rifle, sighted in the man, and cut him down.

"Good show," Ben said.

"Thank you, General," Carrington said, as he worked the bolt and rammed home a round. "I do like to pull my weight."

The streets suddenly filled with Rebels, all running back toward Ben's position. "Get the general out of here!" one yelled. "We're about to be overrun. They're trying a suicide attack."

Ben jumped out onto the sidewalk. "Stand your ground!" he yelled, stopping the Rebels. "Spread out left and right of me. Corrie, get Dusters up here."

"Yes, sir."

"Oh, jolly good, I say, General," Carrington said. "This is just the place for a to-do, I should think."

"Quite right," Ben said. The English manner of speaking is very contagious. "Corrie, call up gunships."

"Yes, sir. Calling up gunships."

"Here the buggers come, men!" Carrington said, then looked around him. Jersey was staring at him. She shook her head. "And, ah, ladies. Stand firm now for God and the King."

"Right," Cooper said, from behind his bi-podded Stoner. "And for Ben Raines and America."

"Quite right, lad," Carrington said, a flush to his cheeks.

They could hear the screaming and cursing mob quite plainly now.

"Hold your fire," Ben shouted. "Hold your fire until they're in the middle of the block. We'll take the first wave and the choppers can have the rest."

"Marvelous things, those helicopters." Carrington's voice could just be heard over the rantings of the thugs and creepies as they rounded the corner and began the charge up the last block to Ben's position. "Wish we'd had them during World War Two."

"Fire!" Ben shouted, and there was no more time for conversation that would have gone unheard anyway.

The ground floor of the old building reverberated with the sounds of weapons on full auto—all but one. Carrington was calmly working the bolt and making each shot count. "Damn!" he said. "I'm all out of ammunition. Drat!"

A Rebel medic couldn't hear his words, but saw his predicament. He crawled over and handed the man two .45's from his kit and a bag full of clips.

"Oh, good, lad! Thank you." And Carrington was back in business with a vengeance, blasting away with both hands full of autoloaders.

The mob was right on top of them when the Dusters clanked up, lowered their cannon, and went to work. Overhead, helicopter gunships were just arriving and cutting loose with everything they had.

Thugs and punks and creepies and other assorted street slime hurled themselves through the glassless windows and the fight was hand to hand, eyeball to eyeball.

Knowing he was much too old to engage in this

228

type of nonsense, Carrington backed up, loaded up both .45's, and began picking his targets in the gunsmoke-filled room. And he was deadly accurate.

Jersey kicked a thug in the balls and then shot him in the neck as he bent over, puking.

Beth had a Beretta 9mm in each hand and was holding her own in a corner of the room. Corrie had slipped off her backpack radio and was swinging her empty CAR-15 like a club, and doing some terrible damage to jaws and heads. Ben shot a creep in the belly and another one point blank in the face before a punk jumped on his back and rode him down to the dirty floor.

Ben flipped the man from him and Carrington blew the back of the punk's head off with a round.

"By God!" the Englishman said. "I haven't had this much fun since Mum got her dress tail caught in a revolving door and took her right down to her bloomers."

Ben got to his boots as he realized the room was empty of live creeps and crap. "Load up," he ordered.

Corrie found her radio under the body of a dead punk and looked at it. "Busted," she said. "Took a round straight through."

"We're cut off, General," a Duster commander yelled through a hole in the wall. "The street gangs did an end-around and we're going to be all alone for a time."

"Get on your radio and order constant patrol of this area by gunships," Ben told him. "How's your 40mm ammo?"

"We're in good shape, General."

"All right. Button down as tight as you can."

Ben looked around him. The floor was two and three deep in places with dead punks and creeps.

"We've got two dead and five wounded," Corrie told him. "One of the wounded is serious and needs surgery right now."

"Not anymore," one of the medics called.

"Three dead," Corrie said.

"Let's get these stinking dead crud out of here," Ben said. "Careful in handling them, now. Strip ammo and weapons from them and stack them in the next room."

"It's clouding up real fast," Lieutenant Ballard said. "Starting to sprinkle."

"If it comes a downpour, that'll work to the advantage of the crud," Buddy pointed out. "And severely limit visibility for the chopper pilots." He smiled through the grime on his face. "Of course, I'm pointing out the obvious."

Carrington had taken a dead Rebel's M-16 and another Rebel was showing him how to operate it. "Complicated piece of weaponry," he remarked.

"How are Dan and Georgi faring?" Ben asked Corrie.

"Heavy fighting, sir. But in small pockets all up and down the line. Everytime they shift, the crud shifts with them. A lot of small units are cut off, just like us."

"Pretty good," Ben said. "Someone on the other side is starting to think."

"Here comes the rain," a Rebel called.

"And with it will come the crud," Ben said, clicking his CAR off safety and moving to a empty window. "Get set, people. It's going to get real busy here in a moment."

"Drat," Carrington said, looking at his watch. "And they'll be interrupting our elevenses, too."

"Do what?" Jersey asked.

"Morning teatime," Ben said with a smile.

"Precisely," Carrington said. "Terribly boorish of them, what?"

"Oh, yes," Ben agreed. "They have no appreciation of the finer things in life."

"Quite right," Carrington said. "For an American, General Raines . . . you'll do. You'll do."

Four

"If they'd played their cards right," Ben said after the attack, "they could have done some damage to us. They had years to learn tactics, but they blew the time away."

The creeps and street crud had charged out of the rain screaming and cursing the Rebels in small pockets all over the city. They ran right into the guns of the Rebels. The Rebels stood their ground and gave the enemy everything they had at their disposal, and that was plenty. It broke the backs of the creeps and thugs in Bristol.

The remainder of Ben's battalion punched through to his position just after noon and took the pressure off. Ben set up a CP on the second floor of what had once been a department store and the Rebels began mopping up.

Mr. Carrington took a Tommy-burner out of his kit and began heating water for his tea.

Rebels began collecting the bodies of the dead crud and creeps and tossing them into the beds of trucks. They would be taken out into the countryside and buried in a deep mass grave.

"Three thousand enemy dead in this city, General," Beth informed Ben. "So far."

"Tell the other batt coms to attack their targets commencing at dawn tomorrow. We'll catch our breath here for a couple of days and then move on."

"Yes, sir."

"Gloucester had a population of about seventy thousand or so before the Great War. So there's sure to be some nasties waiting for us. Send Buddy and his Rats on down to check it out. No heroics on his part, Corrie. Those are my orders. Just check it out and report."

"Right, sir."

Mr. Carrington strolled in. "I've just met two of the most astonishing people I have ever encountered," he said. "A man named Emil and his keeper, a beatnik, I believe, called Thermopolis. This Emil fellow, is he mentally sound?"

Everyone in the room laughed. Ben said, "There are some who would argue the point. But yes, he's stable . . . most of the time, that is."

"Tell me about this Thermopolis."

"He's a hippie. And he'll go back to being a fulltime hippie when the wars are won."

"I see. I think. I would have stayed to chat longer with him but that horrible music that was playing in the background rather jangled my nerves. What is that incomprehensible throbbing called? It sounded like fourteen cats fighting over a ball of yarn."

"It's rock and roll, sort of. But not the rock and roll that I grew up with."

"If one could somehow contain that wailing and blithering and caterwauling and ship it to the enemy, the war could be won without firing another shot."

Thermopolis and Emil came in and Carrington skirted them carefully and went outside.

"That's a strange man," Emil said, jerking a thumb toward Carrington. "Talks funny, too."

Carrington beat it back inside the CP. "We're being invaded by a band of leather-jacketed hooligans on motorbikes," he announced.

Ben chuckled. "No. They're part of this outfit. That's Axehandle and his boys and girls."

Carrington shook his head. "You have a very strange army, General. Very odd indeed."

Ben enjoyed a laugh at that. "You'll get no argument from me on that, Mr. Carrington. But you'll have to admit, we get the job done."

The old man smiled. "That you do, General. That you do."

Ben toured the devastated city. It was evident that his artillery had destroyed a lot of buildings, but what was even more evident was that the creeps and crud had done a lot more damage over the years. It was vandalism for the sake of vandalism, without reason.

All the churches were gone. Every last one of them, from once magnificent cathedrals to small chapels . . . the street punks and creeps had destroyed them all. In museums and art galleries and curio shops, it was the same. Paintings and valuable books had been ripped and slashed and burned. Statuary had been toppled and smashed.

Now only occasional gunshots could be heard; the Rebels had just about concluded the mopping up of Bristol. No prisoners taken.

"He's saving us for last," Butch told a gathering of warlords and self-styled mercenaries and street punks. "Just like I figured he would."

"All them people that was in Bristol," one warlord said, "and no more'un a couple of hundred got out alive. Scares me. It really does."

"It ought to, mate," Butch said. "And you stay scared, too. It might help keep you alive. You keep this in your mind: the Rebels ain't taking no prisoners. None. The deadline is past. Those are hard people out there, being commanded by a hard man. And don't think you can surrender to no English man or woman, neither. 'Cause most of them, more'un likely, will kill you just as fast as a Rebel. They ain't likely to forget what-all we done over the years. Everywhere the Rebels go, they're arming the people. They're settin' up what they done in America. Them outpost things."

"Butch, I got me an idea," Morelund said. "Let's let Raines and his Rebels have the island. Hell, man, we've ruint it anyways. We'll go to Hawaii."

The roomful of punks all began talking at once. Finally Butch shouted them into silence. "That's a great idea, Morelund. Now maybe you'll tell me how we're gonna get there."

"By ship!" Morelund said, exasperation in his voice.

"Do you know how to run one?" Butch challenged.

"Well . . . no. But, hell, they can't be that hard."

"Does *anybody* here know how to run one of those great ships?" Butch asked.

No one did.

"Well, folks," Butch said, eyeballing the motley-looking group. "I guess that means we fight right here on English soil."

"I guess that means a lot of us will die right here on English soil," another said in a quiet voice.

"That's right," Butch said. "When civilization broke down, we all had a choice. Didn't nobody force us into doing what we did."

"But we had to eat," a street punk said. "There wasn't no jobs or nothin'. There wasn't no law to make us behave. They wasn't nothin'."

Butch leaned his elbows on the lectern and chuckled. "Eakes, that is the biggest pile of horse-shit I've heard in a long time. There ain't no excuse for what we done. There ain't any. We're criminals because that's what we want to be. We've had a long run. More'un ten years. Now it's time to pay the price for that decision."

"Killin' us is a goddam high price to pay," Eakes said sullenly.

"And how many people have you killed over the years?" Butch asked, a smile on his cruel mouth. "Fifty, a hundred, a thousand? More than that? Probably. How do you excuse that?"

"We ain't axin' for no prizes for what we done," a burly warlord called Santo said, standing up. "But now that we's about to be caught or killed, why can't the law treat us like they used to? I mean, give us some jail time and rehabilitate us and turn us loose?"

Butch laughed. "They really did a splendid job of rehabbing us, didn't they? Aren't we a bunch of model citizens? We've really worked to restore law and order to England, haven't we?" He slammed a

236

fist onto the lectern. "God damn it, people!" Butch shouted. "We're criminals. We're rapists. We're kidnappers. We're slavers. We're murderers and street punks and thieves and everything that's mean and rotten and no good in this world. And we became that because we *wanted* it. Stop lying to yourselves. Make up your minds that we've got to contain Raines and the Rebels, giving us time to get across the Channel, or we're going to die. All of us."

"We're gonna die anyway you cut it up," a street punk said. "We can't beat the Rebs. I'd as soon you just shot me now and got it over with."

"All right," Butch said. He jerked out a .44 magnum and blew half the punk's head off. The street punk's feet flew out from under him as his brains splattered those closest to him. He hit the floor, dead cooling meat.

"Anybody else?" Butch challenged.

The roomful of crap was silent for a moment. "Jesus, Butch!" Eakes finally said.

"Don't Jesus me." Butch's voice was as hard as the lead that had punched through the punk's head. "I ain't your lord. But I just might turn out to be your savior. You've all got to listen to me and do what I fucking tell you to do! A long time ago there was some Yank that said we either hang together or hang separately. Well, that fits us nicely. If we don't hang together, we shall certainly hang one by one."

"All right. All right!" Duane said, getting to his feet. "I vote we make Butch the supreme commander of this army. We all follow his orders and do it without question."

"I second that," Mack said.

The vote was taken and it was unanimous.

"All I can say is, I'll do my best," Butch said solemnly. "Now somebody drag Jakes out of here before he starts to stink. We got a lot of planning to do."

Ben and his battalions headed for Birmingham, which was not going to be nearly as easily taken as Bristol.

Birmingham was the second largest city in England before the Great War, with a population of over a million. While many of the gangs that had occupied the city had fled to London, several thousand hard-core gang members still remained.

The Rebels rolled through quiet little English villages on their way to the city, many of the villages ravaged and empty, homes and shops looted dozens of times and then burned or vandalized. The Rebels had extra food trucks with each battalion, and stopped often, handing out food to people who had been beaten and enslaved, and were gaunt and starving.

Ben recalled that piece of pie the elderly woman had given him days back and wondered if she'd used the last bit of food in the cottage to make it. Ben got more and more depressed as the miles rolled by.

"All right," Ben finally said, still many miles away from Birmingham. "Hold up here." He gathered Dan and Georgi around him and then got all the batt coms on the horn. "We've got to assist the British people in putting their lives back in order. It isn't enough that we roll through victorious and

238

hand out food and clothing and then we're off again. We're going to have to stop and linger; study what each village and town needs, and then do it. We've chased the creeps and the punks into the cities. Fine. Let them stay there. We'll get to them in due time. First, let's help the good citizens of this country."

"General," Corrie said, "Buddy reporting a town just up ahead where the warlord didn't leave. He and about fifty of his thugs are still in the town."

"Well, tell Buddy to take the town."

"By force?"

"Corrie, that's usually the way we do it."

"Buddy says you'd better come up there, General."

"Give me that headset, Corrie. Eagle to Rat. What's your problem?" Ben listened for a moment. "Ten? Ten what, boy?" He listened for a few seconds. "Are you saying that the warlord is ten or twelve years old? Are you putting me on? Fine. The same to you, too. Good. I'll just do that." He handed the set back to Corrie. "Mount up."

The long columns of Rebels and their mighty machines of war rumbled forward, stopping at the edge of the town. Ben got out and walked to his son's side. Buddy handed him binoculars and Ben focused them, then refocused them. He sighed and returned the binoculars.

"Those are children down there, boy."

"That's what I told you, Father. Eight, nine, ten years old."

"Well-armed children."

"I believe I said that, too."

"That's a goddamn fifty-caliber machine gun

239

they've got set up on the edge of town."

"I know, Father. It took four of them to carry it over there and set it up."

"Well, how do you plan on taking the town, boy?"

"Me? I'm not running this show. You are. You take the town."

"Corrie," Ben said, stalling for time, "do we have communications with the, uh, enemy down there?"

"Yes, sir," she said with a smile.

"You think this is funny, Corrie?"

"Yes, sir." Then she doubled over laughing.

Dan strolled up and assessed the situation. He took a bullhorn and walked to the head of the column. "You children down there!" he called, his voice booming over the quiet landscape. "This is Colonel Dan Gray. Formerly of the Queen's Special Air Service. Now you've all had your fun playing at war. It's time to settle down and get back to school and games and things like that. War is serious business. Very serious business. You children could easily be hurt playing with those dangerous weapons. Come on out now and we'll have some tea and cakes and assist in finding proper homes for you. I . . ."

The big fifty started yowling, the slugs clanking off tanks and coming dangerously close to Dan. "Son of a bitch!" the usually unflappable Englishman yelled, and dived head-first into a water-filled ditch.

The Rebels close in hit the ground and hugged tanks for cover. Dan lifted his head out of the water and yelled, "I'll whale the tar out of you children! They'll be some sore butts this evening, I promise you that."

The fifty hammered again, the slugs knocking chunks out of the stone wall above Dan's head.

"Blow it out your arse!" a child's voice came over the speaker. "This is General Bennie Mays. This town is ours. Move on with you."

Buddy, lying on the road, turned his head to stare at his father, who was also on his belly, on the road. "Suggestions, Father?"

"At the moment, son, no."

Five

The column backed up and Dan sent a few of his Scouts in to grab a kid. "And try not to hurt any of them," Dan added. "I want that pleasure when I lay a belt across their butts."

The Scouts brought back two, a girl, ten years old, and a boy, nine. The Scouts were bleeding from being bitten and kicked, numerous times.

"Get those bite wounds tended to promptly," Dan told his people.

The kids were brought before Ben. They were defiant, but scared as well. Ben looked at the weapons the Scouts had taken from them, then stared down at the raggedy and obviously malnourished boy and girl. "All right, now, children. What's your story?"

The boy and girl exchanged glances and remained silent. Ben pointed to a camp table and chairs that had been set up. "Sit," he told them.

While the Scouts had been gone, Ben had ordered hot food prepared. Two heaping plates of food were set before the kids and two tall glasses of cold milk.

"Damn me eyes," the girl said. "Wouldya just look at them vittles."

"Help yourselves," Ben told them. "There's plenty more where that came from."

"This real milk?" the boy asked.

"Honest-to-God, from a cow."

Ben watched them dig in. They had never been taught table manners — or had forgotten them, ignoring the fork and grasping the spoon like a shovel. Their clothing was nothing more than rags, their faces and hands grimy with dirt, and both of them had fleas. Ben resisted an urge to scratch.

"Do you suppose your friends down in the town would like something to eat?" Ben asked, sitting down at the table with a cup of coffee.

"I 'magine," the girl said. "They ain't nothin' to eat on in the town. Them people's poorer than us."

"Yeah," the boy said. "All they got is some bread, and not much of that."

Ben was silent for a time, watching the hungry kids wolf down their food. They were just kids; they both had milk mustaches.

When they had slowed in chowing down, Ben asked, "You been in the outlaw business long, kids?"

"We been survivin' ever since I can remember," the boy said. "Runnin' from slavers, runnin' from them cannibals, runnin' from men who want to do bad things to us. All the time runnin'. Finally we come up on Bennie. Then we found some more kids and hooked up with them. Then the Yanks invaded and there was guns everyplace. We pick 'em up when we find 'em. You're General Ben Raines, ain't you?"

"Yes. I am."

"You gonna kill us?" the girl asked.

"Of course not," Ben said with a smile. "I'm not

243

here to hurt innocent people. Only bad people."

"Well, you found an island with a shitpot full of 'em," the boy said.

Dan had changed into dry clothing and walked up. The girl spotted him first. "Uh-oh," she said. "I think we're in trouble, Jackie."

"No, you're not," Dan said, smiling at them. "Not unless you were behind that machine gun, shooting at me."

"Oh, no. That wasn't us. We're not big enough to handle it," the girl said.

"What are your names?" Ben asked.

"He's Jackie," the girl said, jerking a thumb at the boy. "I'm Lacy."

"No last names?" Dan asked, taking a seat.

Lacy shrugged her slender shoulders. "We don't know them if we have any."

"Dear God," Dan said.

"God?" Jackie spat out the word. "There ain't no God, mister. All that talk is nothin' but sheep-shit."

"We can talk about that later," Ben said, noting the shocked look on Dan's face at the boy's outburst. "Lacy, tell me something, please. And tell me the truth."

"You want to know if we hurt anybody down in that town, right?"

"You're very quick. Yes. That's part of what I'd like to know."

"Naw. We didn't hurt nobody. We ain't never hurt no good people. We wasn't even gonna take their food, 'cause they had so little of it. Bennie's scared of you and your soldiers, though. He's . . . well, he's about half crazy. He's the oldest. He's about . . . oh, twelve, I guess. The cannibals, they eat his

244

parents. Him and his sister escaped and the gangs caught them. They done bad things to both Bennie and his sister. They left him in a ditch thinkin' he was about dead. He ain't never seen his sister since then. What they done to him, I guess it messed up his head. He don't trust no full-growed person. I asked him once what he was gonna do when he growed up. He went crazy, sort of. Screamin' and hollerin' and jumpin' up and down. Then he just fell down on the ground and went to jerkin' and foamin' at the mouth and then got stiff as a board. Then pretty soon he just got up and went on about his business."

"He's sick, Lacy," Ben said. "He probably has what is known as epilepsy. We have medication for that. But how would we get it to him?"

"No. He ain't got that neither. What he's got is a big knot on the side of his head. And it gets bigger ever' month. Right here." She pointed to her temple.

"Tumor," Dan said. "He's probably epileptic as well."

Ben nodded his agreement. Jackie was busy working on his second plate of food. Lacy said, "Stop that, Jackie. You'll get sick and you know it." When he continued gobbling down the food, she jerked the plate from him just as Buddy walked up and whispered in his father's ear.

"All right," Ben said. "Do it."

Buddy walked away.

Ben smiled at Lacy. Her hair was so dirty he couldn't tell what color it was. "How would you kids like a hot bath and clean clothing?"

Lacy narrowed her eyes. "Let me tell you something, General. I ain't no whoor and I ain't suckin' dicks for food or clothin', neither."

"Good Lord!" Dan said, jumping up from the chair.

"Hey," Lacy said, cocking her head and staring strangely at Dan. "Where are you people from, anyways? How do you figure a lot of kids stay alive 'ceptin' by usin' their bodies? But I tell you what: I can write my name and read some words. I taught myself that."

A lot of Rebels had gathered around, silently listening to the words of the kids.

"That's good, Lacy," Ben said, his voice husky. He cleared his throat. "Lacy, no one here is going to molest you or make any kind of sexual suggestion to you or to Jackie or to any child, for that matter. We no longer tolerate that kind of behavior in America. People who molest children don't live very long in the new society. All I asked was if you would like a hot bath and some clean clothing."

"I sure would," Jackie said. "I got fleas on me and I stink."

Lacy stared at Ben through wise eyes. "You're not a devil."

Ben laughed. "Well, now, some people might disagree with you on that. But who told you I was a devil?"

"Bennie."

"Well, Bennie is an awfully sick boy. And if he'll let us, we'll help him."

"He won't," Jackie said. He reached for the plate of food that Lacy had taken from him and she slapped his hand away. "I'm still hungry!" he protested.

246

"Save it for later. They'll be a lot more hungry times, boy-o."

"No, there won't," Dan said, his voice surprisingly gentle. "Your hungry days are over."

Jersey smiled at Lacy and the girl returned the smile.

Jersey stood up, walked around the table, and held out her hand. "Come on, let's get you cleaned up."

Dan held out his hand to Jackie. "Come on, lad. It's bath time for you."

Both kids stood up and turned to go. Lacy paused and looked back at Ben. "You sent that handsome young man off to take the town, didn't you?"

"He's my son, Lacy. And yes, I did. But it will be done without anyone being hurt. I promise you that."

"I don't know why I believe you, but I do." She and Jersey strolled off toward a hot bath.

Jackie jerked away from Dan and made another grab for the plate of food and Ben snatched it away just in time. "You'll have plenty of food later on, Jackie. You, and all your friends down in the town. That's a promise."

"We ain't the only ones hungry in this land," the boy replied.

"I know."

When Ben again saw Jackie, about an hour later, he at first didn't recognize him as the boy walked hand in hand with Dan.

Rebels began bringing snatched and gagged kids

247

out of the town, some of them kicking and biting and scratching, most of them coming along peacefully as they realized the Rebels, who had slipped up on them like ghosts, were not going to hurt them. They were first fed, then deloused and bathed, then they received haircuts and clean, fresh clothing. Clothing for the kids was beginning to be a problem because of their size, so Rebels took out needle and scissors and thread and began altering spare uniforms and what civilian clothing they had with them.

When the young General Bennie Mays began an inspection of the town he thought was his, he was shocked to find that the only territory he now controlled comprised about one block on the edge of the village and his troops now numbered seven. Behind him lay a solid line of Rebels. He was so frustrated he put his swollen head down on a stone and wept.

"Come on, Bennie," a girl's voice reached him through amplification. "These people ain't gonna hurt nobody. They're real nice folks. They done give us food and clothes and treated us right. Give it up, Bennie. They got doctors who say they'll help your head."

"Turn the machine gun around and kill them Rebels who slipped up behind us," Bennie ordered through his tears.

But his troops refused. "We're givin' it up, Bennie," an older boy said. "All of us. Chuck just jammed the big gun. It ain't gonna work no more. It's busted."

"You try to walk away from me and I'll kill you!" Bennie raged through his aching head.

248

"Then you ain't no better than the people who's been chasin' us all this time," another boy said.

"I didn't mean it," Bennie said, laying his pistol on the ground. "I didn't mean it. I'm scared."

They argued for a few moments, not paying any attention to their surroundings. When they looked up again, they were completely ringed by Rebels.

"Steady now, boys," Buddy said. "Keep your guns on the ground and stand up slow. We have hot food, clean clothing, and baths waiting for you. You're safe now. Everything is *all right*. I promise you." He waved another contingent of Rebels forward.

The boys had never seen so many soldiers. It seemed to them they were looking at thousands. Actually, it was only about twenty-four hundred making up the three battalions. But to the kids it was much more than that.

They surrendered without incident. Even Bennie was awed by the Rebels. The Rebel doctors checked Bennie and after a bath, sent him back to the main hospital after alerting a neurosurgery team. They gave him a tablet that soon put him to sleep so the helicopter ride would not frighten him to death.

Ben rode into the small town and talked with the people there. They were in very bad shape, with no food, and until the Rebels arrived, no hope of finding any. It was late fall in England; the winds were cold, and soon snows would fly. The punks and crud had taken everything the villagers had grown that summer, leaving them nothing.

Ben sent the kids to the rear, left a team behind in the town to assist the villagers, and pushed on.

All over England, Rebels were finding the most

appalling of conditions among the survivors. It was not that the people did not have the will to fight, for they certainly did, they just didn't have anything to fight with. When the world fell apart a decade back, those of a criminal nature sought out and found guns by raiding military armories and police stations, or just killing those who had guns and taking them.

The governments of America, Canada, England, France, Germany, and many other countries had banned the personal ownership of firearms, so when the Great War came, the law-abiding citizens of those countries got what they always got from big governments: fucked.

And the lawless took over.

"Corrie," Ben said. "Order every ship that can sail to put to sea and bring back food and clothing and blankets and fuel. We'll divert some of the materials that were to go to Ireland over here. We're going to need massive shipments of medicines, including vitamins. We're going to need flour . . . oh, shit! We need everything."

In the cities, in now armed and fortified camps of the creeps and crud and human garbage, the warlords monitored the almost stalled advance of the Rebels. They knew that once the Rebels personally witnessed the terrible conditions in which the lawless had left the citizens, they would be fighting with deep rage in them. There would be no mercy, no pity, no compassion shown the lawless.

The thugs listened to their shortwave radios and cringed at the news: Pontypool, Wales. Hanged ten this day. Ross On Wye. Shot twelve. Tiverton. Executed nine.

"Where in the hell is the lawyers and appeals and such?" a thug questioned.

"I think they're keeping their heads down and their mouths shut," another punk answered. "I think Ben Raines would just as soon shoot a lawyer as he would us."

"When's he gonna come at us?" Butch Smathers was asked.

"We're last," Butch said. "Raines is gonna save us for last, knowin' that our food supply will be down to nothing in the dead of winter. We'll be cold and hungry, and our morale will be low. Oh, he's a smart one, he is. He's a black-hearted, ruthless man for sure, when it comes to dealin' with the likes of us. We got to start killin' dogs and cats and rats and smokin' and jerkin' the meat. Tell them in the countryside to start roundin' up all the cows and sheep and drivin' them close to the city for pasture. It's gonna be a cold winter, mates."

Ben was studying maps when Ike and West walked into his CP and poured coffee. A heavy mantle of frost had covered the land that morning, and Rebels were in winter clothes.

"It's gettin' plumb borin' out there, Ben," the Mississippi-born-and-reared Ike said. "Resistance is the lightest I've ever seen it. Went all day yesterday without firin' a shot."

"Yes," Ben said. "But we've still got about seventy percent of the nation to clean up. Look here. Our recon flights show a battle line stretching north to south from Burnham Market down to Brighton. I think Butch's plan is to have the people still occupying the larger cities to fall back as we take over, then they'll hold while London is evacuated by sea."

"And they'll do that under the blanket of the nastiest, foulest weather," Dan added, sipping a cup of tea. "Our gunships will be grounded and we don't have enough patrol boats yet to be very effective. Smathers is a thug and a killer, but he is anything but a fool."

"Reading between the lines, you've found something more about him."

"All of it unpleasant. He's ex-army. Paratroops. Went to a lot of special schools, most of them dealing with antiterrorist movements. He was in Northern Ireland. The military had to pull him out; he was too quick to shoot, and enjoyed inflicting pain on people. But the real reason they pulled him out was because he raped a thirteen-year-old girl. He claimed he was interrogating her; Army doctors confirmed she had been raped and sodomized. He was court-martialed and ordered cashiered out of the service. But before that could happen, the world blew up in everybody's face. There is more, if you wish to hear it."

"I've heard enough now to look for a corner to puke in," Ben said.

"Yes," West said. "What a delightful person. I've done some terrible things in my life, but I rather like to believe I conducted myself in an honorable fashion." He smiled. "Most of the time."

"Let me add just one more thing," Dan said. "The man has the I.Q. of a genuis."

"That's not surprising," Lamar Chase said. "Many criminals do. All kinds of theories about that—which I shall not go into at this time."

"Thank the Lord for small favors," Ike said.

Dr. Chase smiled sweetly at him. The smile resembled that of a weasel leaving a henhouse. "Isn't it about time for your annual hemorrhoid check, Ike?"

"That's your ass, Lamar!" Ike told him.

"No," Chase replied. "That *your* ass, sailor."

"I got to go," Ike said, standing up. "See you people."

He vacated the room to the sounds of Chase chuckling.

"You wouldn't really do that to Ike, would you, Lamar?" Ben asked.

Chase smiled again. Very sweetly.

"Yeah, you would," Ben muttered.

Six

Slowly the Rebels began working their way north and Thermopolis and his Eight Battalion joined with Ben and his command as they worked their way toward Birmingham. Wales was now a secure area. And a well-armed area. Ships were docking daily, bringing in much-needed food and clothing and medicines and blankets and fuel.

Ben had ordered the battalions of the Free Irish, along with Danjou's Seven, Rebet's Six, and two battalions of the BRF, to face off against those punks, crud, and crap who had strung out along Butch's battle lines north to south, and not to let anyone through from the west. He told the batt coms to heavily arm each village they cleared and to alert the people about what they were doing.

Ben had a hunch that the villagers would take care of any retreating punks long before they ever reached the Rebel positions.

That news did not surprise Butch Smathers. "Oh, that Raines is a sly one, love," he said to Lulu. "And low-down dirty mean, too."

"Let's get out, Butch," Lulu urged. "Just say to hell with it and leave."

Butch shook his head. "Raines is keeping his helicopters and spotter planes in the air over the channel twenty-four hours a day, baby. And he's taking his good time in getting to us. He's deliberately letting us sweat. That's a wicked man, Lulu."

Lulu was scared and made no attempt to hide it. Butch put an arm around her waist. "I've got a plan, baby. Some of us are going to make it. Not a great lot, but some of us. We'll get out. I promise you."

The thought of changing their lives and becoming law-abiding citizens never entered the mind of either of them.

The battalions of Rebels and the ever-growing numbers of the British Resistance Forces ringed the city of Birmingham. No one was getting out, and only the Rebels and the BRF wanted in. Coventry, Nuneaton, Dudley, and Walsall had fallen to the Rebels. South of them, punks and crud and creeps had fled east, toward London. But they found their way blocked by troops. They tried to overtake villages and towns and were shot to pieces by the townspeople. Those taken alive were hanged.

The citizens of England had endured too many years of abuse at the hands of the lawless to forget or forgive. Already, even before the land was cleared of the criminal element, people were rewriting the law books and electing officials and setting up police forces. But as Ben Raines had

255

done over in the Colonies, the laws would be few, they would be clearly understood, they would not be ponderous; and the police, for the most part, would be used to come in after the fact, gather up the bodies of those who could not or would not obey even the simplest of laws, and leave.

And as in America, there were those who did not agree with the new order and refused to adopt the harsh measures. That was their right and no one tried to stop them. No one helped them, either. They were cold stone alone in hard times. They received no aid from the Rebels: no food, no blankets, no grain, no medical aid for the adults, no nothing. The Rebels owned the bat, the ball, and the glove—you could either play the game their way, or go home.

On a cold, blustery late fall morning, Ben stood on the outskirts of Birminghan, lowered his binoculars, and gave the orders. "Commence shelling."

Everything from 203mm artillery to 87mm mortars began dropping their deadly payloads into the heart of the city. The barrage was a never-ending roll and crash of thunder and smoke and flames and destruction.

To those trapped in the city, it tore not only at flesh and muscle and bone, it ripped nerves raw. There was no place to run and hide and feel safe; one could not get away from the booming crash. The barrage went on all day, all night, all the next day, and all the next night. Then, silence.

From the center of the city, running for blocks in all directions, there was nothing but rubble and smoke and flames and death. Those left alive in the city staggered out into the streets and stood in fear and awe, gazing through glazed eyes at what Hell must look like.

"Tanks in," Ben ordered. "Let's go."

Resistance was almost nil. En masse, the survivors of the continuous forty-eight-hour bombardment stood in the rubble-strewn streets, their shaking hands in the air. Hoping that the Rebels would not shoot them on the spot. Weeping and trembling and pissing and stinking in their fear. And praying that Rebels would take them and not the BRF.

"Turn them over to the British," Ben ordered.

"Then kill me now!" one outlaw screamed in panic. "Them people will hang us."

"That's your problem," Ben told him in a cold voice. "And I don't want to hear a slopjar full of shit about your troubled childhood, or that the coach wouldn't let you play, or that the prettiest girl in class wouldn't give you the time of day."

"You'll rot in hell for what you're doin', General," a woman told him, standing with her hands in the air. "The Lord preached love."

"I'm not the Lord," Ben told her. "If you've got a complaint, take it up with the real article. You'll be face to face with Him soon."

The prisoners were taken away to be tried in a British court of law. Most would hang or be shot, some would be tossed in the jug for the rest of their lives. A few of the younger ones would be given a second chance.

The Rebels and the BRF began digging out the

creeps who had retreated to the bowels of the city. They pumped teargas and pepper gas and carbon monoxide into the sewers and tunnels and basements and shot the Believers as they staggered out. The Rebels had learned a long time back there was no point in trying to rehabilitate a creepie. It was a waste of time.

The Rebels found several locations where the creeps had kept their human food source. Most of the men and women and children had been reduced to babbling idiots or something very close to it. They were turned over to the British. There was very little anyone could do for them except institutionalize them and care for them as humanely as possible.

The troops pulled out of the city. It was dead.

"Let them in London sweat," Ben issued the orders. "We take Scotland next."

The Rebels and the BRF spread out west to east and began their slow march north.

"Looks like my ass is next," Glasgow Scotty radioed Butch.

"Looks like it," Butch replied.

"Paratroops into Aberdeen," Ben ordered. "Secure the seaport and the airport."

"Watch for paratroopers," Butch radioed. "Raines is a sneaky bastard. He'll send jumpers in to attack from your rear."

"Once the city is secure," Ben told Dan, who would be commanding the jumpers, "start securing everything north of the Grampian Mountains."

"I've pulled my people out of the north," Scotty said. "We're concentrated in and around Glasgow."

"You're making a mistake," Butch warned him. "Get the hell out while you still have time."

"And go where?" Scotty asked bitterly. "That son of a bitch who runs Edinburgh hates me as much as I hate Ben Raines. I can't head over there. We've done took everything worth takin' in the north. I sure as hell ain't going to North Ireland. So where does that leave me?"

"Fucked, I guess," Butch said.

"That just about sums it up," Scotty replied. "Glasgow Scotty out."

Butch clipped the mic and sighed. "Raines has got a lot of England to cover before he reaches Scotland. But reach it he will. I don't like you, Scotty. But I wouldn't wish Ben Raines and the Rebels on anybody."

"Butch! Butch!" an aide called. "Switch to our coastline frequency."

"Go ahead, coastwatcher."

"Raines has got a whole bunch of old rustbuckets runnin', Butch. He's stretchin' them out from just off the Suffolk coast all the way down to Kent. There must be a hundred of them. He's got them rigged for helicopter landin's. Got pads on them and everything. And they're all armed with heavy machine guns and mortars and stuff."

"The choppers?"

"No, God damn it, Butch! The *ships!* They're floating forts. He's taken what looks like turret guns off old British tanks and mounted them

259

suckers on the ships. And he's got twin 40mm Bofers on 'em, too. Butch, he's *trapped* us."

"Just calm down and hang tight, coastwatcher. Keep me informed. Butch out."

"Has he, Butch?" Lulu asked.

"Has he what?"

"Trapped us."

"He's put the lid on, Lulu. But he hasn't screwed it down tight. Not yet. He's got to be thin. Real thin. He's got troops all over the island, and now he's got them at sea."

"And that means what, Butch?"

"I don't know. Maybe we can punch through and scatter, get away that way. I don't know. I got to think on this, Lulu. Raines don't hardly make mistakes. But he may have made one this time."

Not really. The crews manning the ships were not Rebels. The blockade was Mr. Carrington's idea, and the average age of the crews on board ship and behind the guns was sixty-five. It turned out that Mr. Carrington was actually a retired British admiral. He'd been a young sixteen-year-old sailor stranded on shore and had picked up the first rifle he'd found and fought with the Army. Now, some sixty years later, he just rounded up a bunch of his cronies, from all branches of service, and put them to work. They all needed something to do anyway.

"Look lively on deck, boys!" Carrington shouted from the bridge. "Stop that dawdling about and get that equipment secured. Tight and right, now. Hop to it."

"Hop" was not the right choice of words, since some of the men had trouble walking. But they managed. They were British, after all.

Back in the 1960s, it was "The Russians are coming, the Russians are coming." Now it was, "The Rebels are coming, the Rebels are coming." The Rebels were rolling thirty and forty miles a day north, oftentimes without even firing a shot. When the punks and crud and crap heard the Rebels were in striking distance, their resolve broke wide open and they fled north, toward Scotland.

Ben called a halt when he discovered they were outdistancing their supplies. He halted the convoys and told Ike and Georgi and West to take their battalions and plenty of artillery and see about Liverpool, which from his position lay just about due west.

"And check out the tunnel that connects Liverpool with Birkenhead, if it's still intact. If it is, that's where you'll find some creepies."

"And the Beatles," Ike said with smile. His smile faded. "If the city's full of crud, Ben?"

"Take it down."

"Sherwood Forest is not far from here," Beth said. "That sure rings a bell with me. Why is that, General?"

Ben smiled. "Robin Hood and his Merry Men, Beth. Take some people and go look at it if you like."

She shook her head. "No. I'd rather keep it the

way my mother used to read it to me. I remember now. I think it was my mother."

Like a lot of people who were young when the Great War hit, Beth had blocked out a lot of her past. It was the kids who had just been born when the world collapsed who had the worst of it by far—like Lacy and Jackie and Bennie.

"Be a hell of a fight when we do hit Scotty's position," Thermopolis said that evening. He and Rosebud had come over to visit friends in Ben's One Battalion.

"It'll be a scrap for sure." He looked up as Corrie walked in.

"Dan and his jumpers have secured the airport and the seaport at Aberdeen, General. Resistance was practically nil. Planes will be leaving in the morning to resupply him, and the ships that you ordered out of port ahead of Dan are only a few hours away from Aberdeen." She hesitated and Ben caught it.

"What's wrong, Corrie?"

"We're getting a lot of traffic out of the Continent, General—none of it good. Dr. Chase says they may be facing another plague over there, one that could make the Black Death outbreak in the fourteenth century look like a case of chicken pox."

"What did he call it, Corrie?"

"Bubonic and pneumonic. He's ordered vaccines to be flown over here from the States, General."

"Flown?"

"Yes, sir. Another group just graduated flight school and they're rarin' to go."

"All right, Corrie, thank you. Oh, have Lamar crank up some labs in Ireland and start producing the vaccine . . . why are you smiling?"

"He did that yesterday. But he needs whatever is coming over on the planes. How do you treat this crap, anyway, General?"

"Hell, I don't know. With antibiotics, I suppose. And I'm sure that old goat will personally line up all the troops to see me get the first shot—in the butt."

"Drop your pants and bend over," Chase told Ben the following morning.

"Well, at least you didn't line up the troops and have them watch," Ben said.

"I thought about it."

"I'm sure you did."

Chase popped him and Ben straightened up. "What is that stuff, Lamar, antibiotics?"

"Antibiotics—with the exception of penicillin— are used to *treat* the plague, Ben. What I gave you is a vaccine to prevent you from getting the disease. I've got teams setting up now all over Ireland and England to give shots. Get this island secured quickly, Ben. And I mean fast. We've got to innoculate every decent man, woman, and child or we're going to lose thousands."

"And be at risk ourselves?" Ben added.

"Not really. It's controllable. What we've got to watch out for is the pneumonic strain. It's nearly always fatal."

"Why doesn't penicillin work? I thought that was the magic bullet."

Chase sighed. "Because it isn't broad enough. Do you know what I'm talking about?"

"No."

"Then stick to fighting wars and leave the medicine to me."

"Okay," Ben said with a smile.

"I've started a flea eradication program and while we're at it we'll give the dogs and cats their shots for rabies and other canine and feline diseases. And we'll start a rat eradication program."

"Good luck. That's been tried for centuries and so far as I know, nothing has worked yet."

"O ye of little faith," Chase told him, then left the CP to start giving shots to Ben's team.

Moments later Corrie came in, rubbing her butt. "That man has the touch of someone shoeing horses," she said, and Ben laughed at her.

Beth followed her in. "Doctors give lousy shots," she said, then lifted a clipboard. "Ike reports contact with creepies only in Liverpool. It seems that the street punks have fled north into Scotland. Ike says the city appears to have been trashed, much of it destroyed. He's going to start bringing it down."

"What's the word from Dan and his jumpers?"

"He's secured his objective and is moving out into the countryside."

"Corrie, advise all batt coms that as soon as the innoculation program is accomplished, we'll move out. Ike, Georgi, and West will work the coastline and we'll drive straight up from here. Tina, Thermopolis, the Wolf Pack, and the remainder of the BRF take the east side of the is-

264

land and work north. We'll all regroup just south of the Cheviot Hills for the assault on Scotland. And Corrie . . . advise Admiral Carrington and all others patrolling the English Channel by sea or air that no vessel is to be allowed through from the Continent. We can't risk it. Order any boats, ships, whatever, to turn around and head back. If they refuse, sink them."

"Yes, sir."

Ben sat alone in his office, staring out the window. That was a hard decision to have to make, for not all the people fleeing the Continent would be outlaws and creeps. But when you ran the show, there was no one left to hand the buck. You made the decision, and you lived with it.

"Shit!" Ben muttered.

Seven

Personal pets of the Rebels, and there were many, from chickens to gerbils, were carefully bathed and sent back to the rear for safekeeping in a flea-free and rodent-free area. Smoot and Chester were being looked after by the hospital staff at Chase's main unit, which had now been relocated in Ireland.

Ike had set back outside of Liverpool and let artillery and gunships devastate the city before moving his people in to mop it up. It had been a hard decision to make until he got word that the punks and creeps had destroyed the churches and twin cathedrals overlooking the Mersey, had burned all the libraries to the ground, and in general had left the city in a shambles. It was a much easier decision to make after that.

The Rebels knew they had not killed all the Believers in Liverpool; there would be a few still lurking deep in the bowels of the city, in dark, stinking pockets. But the back of the hideous movement had been broken, and when or if the Believers again surfaced, the English people would be ready, and more important, able to deal with them.

"Colonel Gray says it's very boring up at his location," Corrie told Ben. "He' says he's spending most of his time trying to see the Loch Ness monster."

"Tell him to take a picture of it when he spots it. And to stand easy, we're just about ready to move. Waiting on Ike to resupply."

On a cold, sleety morning, Ben crawled into his wagon and looked at Corrie. "Let's head for Scotland, Corrie."

She lifted her mic and the columns surged forward.

"Did you remember to pack the tire chains, Cooper?" Jersey asked.

"Of course I did. What do you think I am, an idiot?"

Jersey smiled. "I'll let that one just die a natural death. I'm feeling charitable this morning."

Ben looked at her. "Are you sick?"

"Feel great. I've decided to stop picking on Cooper."

"I think she's in love," Cooper said.

"I just decided to start picking on Cooper," Jersey said. "Will you stop tailgating the damn tank, Cooper?"

Ben smiled. Everything was back to normal with his team.

The columns moved through what before the war was a very heavily populated area. Now many of the towns were deserted, utterly void of human life.

"Eerie," Beth muttered.

Even Ben admitted to himself that the silent

267

villages and towns were working on his nerves.

In Bradford and Leeds, the Rebel Scouts finally found signs of life and radioed the news back to the columns. "It's a trap, Father," Buddy said, calling in from the outskirts of Bradford. "They want us to think they are solid citizen types. But they just don't fit the mold. It's a setup."

"Ten-four, son. Back out of there. We're rolling up."

The three Rebel battalions rolled forward, buttoned-up tanks spearheading, and stopped at the edge of town. Ben smiled at the huge banner that the people had stretched high above and completely across the highway.

WELCOME GENERAL RAINES AND THE REBELS.

"My, my," Cooper said. "I wonder if they have soft drinks and cookies, too."

"They must think we're fools," Jersey said.

The Rebels waited, advancing no further, watching the crowd of men and women at the edge of town, and watching until they got awfully nervous.

While Dan was north, commanding the jumpers, his battalion had linked with Ben's One. Ben also had a contingent of Free Irish and BRF people. Since he was light on infantry, Ben was heavy with armor and artillery.

Ben was amused as they played the cat-and-mouse game. But he quickly tired of it. He got out of the wagon and took a speaker mic. "Give it up, people. You haven't fired at us, so I'll give you the benefit of the doubt as to your intentions. Put your hands in the air and walk toward us. Issue orders to those in the town to do the same. Do it right now, or I'll level the town with artillery."

The fifty or so men and women — mostly men — standing under the welcome banner exchanged glances. Ben watched through binoculars as they spoke briefly, then slowly pulled pistols from under their coats and laid them on the pavement. All around them, in the weed-filled ditches and fields, men rose slowly from hidden ambush positions, their hands in the air, and walked slowly toward the line of tanks.

"Let me see the people in the town start coming out," Ben's voice boomed over the cold landscape.

"I got to reach under my jacket for a walkie-talkie!" a man yelled, the words just reaching the column. "Don't shoot."

"Go ahead," Ben told him.

"Same thing is happening in Leeds," Corrie informed him.

"Dan's XO reporting a mass surrender. Not a shot fired so far."

People began filing out of the town, hands in the air.

"Bring that man with the walkie-talkie to me," Ben said.

The two men faced each other. One was clear-eyed, clean-shaven, wearing clean BDUs. The other stank of old sweat and grime, his clothing filthy, his eyes red-rimmed, and his face showing the strain of years of crime and brutality.

"Children?" Ben asked him.

"We got some," the man said. "They're with the women. We didn't think it would work. But we didn't know what else to do. What happens now?"

"You will be turned over to British authorities."

"In other words, we're dead."

"Some of you."

"We had a good thing goin' 'til you popped in."

Ben looked at the man's slovenly appearance. "Yes. I can see that you have been living in the lap of luxury."

"Beats work," the outlaw admitted.

"Any sickness among you?" Ben asked, not putting any emphasis on his words.

The outlaw shook his head. "Some of the kids got colds, that's all. Nothin' major. What's the matter, General — and yeah, I know who you are — you afraid we'll contaminate your pure and precious do-gooder army?"

"Something like that." Ben turned and walked away. He leaned against a fender and sipped hot coffee, watching as BRF people tied the prisoners' hands behind their backs and tossed them into trucks for the long ride back to a prison in the south of the country where the slime and crud were being held, pending trial.

Buddy returned from his inspection of the town. "Filthy," he said. "These people lived like degenerates. We don't want to bivouac here."

"No. We'll roll on. Our eyes in the skies say there is a town just north of here that appears to be deserted. Check it out."

270

The town was void of human life and had been for some time. The Rebels found a huge mass grave on the edge of town and Ben ordered it opened. The bones of men and women and children and even family pets were uncovered.

"They appear to have been shot," a Rebel doctor said, after an examination of a few of the skeletons. "And judging from the size of this grave, there must be several hundred people buried here."

"Cover it up," Ben said. "We'll probably never know the why of it."

"General," Corrie said. "Our eyes in the skies say there is a mass retreat north. Highways are clogged with vehicles."

"Where are Tina and Therm?"

"They've pushed all the way up to Middlesbrough."

"We can't send gunships in to strafe those retreating because we don't know for sure who they are — even though we all have a good idea." Ben looked at a map. "There's an airport near there. Have planes pick them up and take them to Aberdeen. Also have planes pick up Georgi's people and set them down at this airstrip here." He pointed to a small town just north and somewhat west of the Grampian Mountains. "Tell them to carry all the supplies they can stagger with. And start supply planes moving now. When they are in position, have them move toward the south. Dan and Tina's battalions will secure Dundee and Perth. Therm's bunch will join Georgi and move down to here, on the west side of the mountain range. That will give us four battalions to hold from the north while we use troops, armor, and artillery to smash in from the south."

Troops began moving and shifting while the punks and creeps and crud in the cities listened and waited nervously.

"Raines is boxing them in," Butch said. "It won't be long now." He looked at a clipboard filled with dispatches from communications. "I wish I could figure out what is happening on the Continent. There appears to some type of mild panic going on over there. But I haven't the foggiest what it is. It's baffling."

"Whatever could it be?" Lulu questioned.

Butch shook his head. "I just don't know. But I got a feelin' in my guts that it's bad."

"Butch!" the radio operator called. "Two of them old tubs out in the Channel just sank a couple of boats trying to make it across."

"That don't make any sense. Why would anybody over *there* want to come over *here?*" He frowned, his brow furrowing. "Folks, this is gettin' weird."

Using a small two-engine plane, Ben crisscrossed the island south of the Cheviot Hills as his troops got into place. Jersey and Corrie sat in the rear seats.

"How come you picked this old baby to fly in, General," the pilot asked, "instead of a chopper? I mean, I'm flattered, but puzzled."

"I don't trust helicopters," Ben said. "Or boats. Helicopters fall out of the sky and boats sink.

272

One engine quits on this plane, you can fly it with the other one. Both engines fail, it glides and you can land it on a highway. Now you know."

The pilot, who was both fixed-wing- and chopper-qualified, laughed. "Well . . . I guess you got a point, sir. I never looked at it quite that way."

Ben smiled. "Look down there, Jersey, Corrie. That's highway A696. Pretty impressive from the air, isn't it?"

Rebel armor was rolling north, toward the Cheviot Hills. The tanks and artillery stretched for a long way. The road flashed under them as they headed for the coast highway. The pilot circled for a moment before he sat down on a grassy strip just south of Berwick Upon Tweed, the northernmost town in England before crossing the river into Scotland.

"See those white cattle down there?" the pilot said. "I read about them. They're wild. They're called the wild white cattle of Chillingham. They're led by a king bull and they're direct descendants of the cattle that lived in Britian thousands of years ago."

"You're puttin' me on!" Jersey said.

"No, I'm not. I read it in a tourist guide and talked to folks in this area when I flew in supplies. Even though these people were hungry, they wouldn't kill those cattle. That kind of makes you feel good about things, you know?"

"Yes. Then there is hope for humankind yet," Ben said. "Unselfish acts like that can lift the hearts of us all."

273

"That's pretty, General," Jersey said. "Did you ever write poetry?"

Ben laughed. "When I was young and in love, Jersey. It was really bad. Luckily, my father found it and burned it."

Jersey and Corrie exchanged glances. They wanted Ben off the subject of love. Both knew he was still in love with Jerre and probably would be until his death. They knew that Ben publicly said that she was behind him. They also knew—being females—that Ben was lying, and both of them hoped that someday some good man would love them as much as Ben loved Jerre.

Ben met with his daughter, Tina, commander of Nine Battalion, and Therm, who commanded Eight Battalion. They were only minutes from lifting off to the north.

"Everyone in your command's been inoculated?" Ben asked.

"That's ten-four, Dad. And so have Dan and his jumpers."

"That's it, then. Every one of our people is secure and most of the residents—that are not opposed to us, that is." He shook hands with Therm and kissed Tina. "You two be careful. Godspeed."

It was a bitterly cold day, and the winds were coming straight off the North Sea as Ben stood and watched the cargo planes take off, make their slow half circle, and turn north over the sea.

"Let's get back," Ben said. "Jumpoff time is looking us in the face."

* * *

"We play by the same rules," Ben told his people. "We take it slow and clear every town and village as we go. We make sure we don't have any hostiles behind us when we pull out. We crash through tomorrow at dawn and take Hawick and Dumfries before nightfall. We're not going to get ahead of our supply trucks this time. That's it."

They needn't have worried about hostiles at their backs. Dumfries and Hawick were void of unfriendlies. Each town had only a few hundred citizens left in it, all of them hungry and sick and cold.

"They left us several days ago, General," a man told Ben. "Took every scrap of food we had and fled north like frightened rabbits."

"I'm going to probably destroy your cities," Ben told the man, and the others who had crowded around. "I don't see the point of losing people to save a building."

"Then bring them down, General," a woman said. "They're as useless to us now as horns on a hen."

The medics checked out the people and the supply trucks dropped off food, blankets, clothing, and fuel.

"All units settled in for the night and reporting no contact with the enemy today," Corrie told Ben. "It's a milk run."

Buddy shook his head. "They do it everytime. They're as predictable as a good watch. They run to the cities. I don't understand it."

"They're punks, boy," his father told him.

"They feel safe with all that concrete and steel around them. Street punks are like rats. They've got to have a hole to run into and hide in. They're cowards — just like most bullies. Anyone who joins a gang is a punk. Have you ever seen a bully pick on anyone his own size? I haven't."

"But they must know by now that we're going to grind them down."

"I'm sure some of them do, son. But look how we fight. We don't leave them any holes to hide in. They don't have any place to run. They actually help us box them in."

A runner came in and handed Ben a note from Communications. Corrie was relaxing away from her radio . . . at Ben's orders.

"People are beginning to flee the Continent," Ben said, reading the note aloud by a hissing gas lantern. "Carrington's armada has sunk more than half a dozen ships in two days. It must really be getting bad over there."

"You had to give those orders to sink those ships, General," Jersey said. "You didn't have any choice in the matter. You had to contain that plague."

Ben smiled at her. "Thank you, Jersey. Keep reminding me of that, please."

A Scout came in and set her rifle down and shrugged out of a light pack. "It's clear for forty miles north up A74, General. Not one bogie to be found anywhere. The industrial belt must be filled up with punks."

"Yes," Ben agreed. "The area from Glasgow to Edinburgh is crawling with punks and other as-

276

sorted two-legged vermin. But it won't be for long."

Corrie returned and Ben looked up in surprise. "I thought I told you to relax."

"You did. I went over to Communications to visit with friends. It's jumping over there, General." She sat down behind a bank of radios that was set up for her nightly in Ben's CP—wherever that might be—and slipped on a head set.

"What's happening, Corrie?" Ben asked.

"All up and down the European coast, starting about an hour ago, there have been a series of explosions. No one can figure out what's happening."

A runner from Communications hustled in and pinned a map to a wall, then began placing tiny colored flags along the coastline. "These are the newest ones, Corrie," he said. "They're coming in fast now. These were received by radio. Not confirmed." He left the room.

Ben walked over and studied the map for a moment. "Those are ports. Get some birds up, Corrie. I want to know what the hell is going on."

"Right, sir."

Ben looked around the room. "The rest of you people get some sleep. We've still got a war to fight."

An hour later, they were all confirmed. All up and down the French coast, fires were burning out of control. Corrie received a communiqué and wrote it out, handing the paper to Ben.

He read it with his expression growing grimmer.

277

"What is it, General?" Jersey asked. She had paid no attention to Ben's order to go to bed.

"The French Resistance forces are blowing all the ships and ports along the coast. Same with other resistance forces in Europe. They're trying to contain the Black Death over there, keep infected people from leaving by sea."

"They're signing their own death warrants," she said softly.

"Yes," Ben's reply was just as softly given. "In order to save others. What next, Lord?" he asked. "What next?"

Eight

As usual, Dr. Lamar Chase had flown up and was ready to set up a mobile field hospital very close to the front lines. He was summoned and was now speaking through an interpreter to the commander of the Free French. Ben had coordinated drop zones for the vaccine and planes had already left the states. Ben had ordered vaccine flown in from the states, and had put the laboratories working around the clock.

He listened as Chase conferred with the Free French. "Save the vaccine for those who do not show any signs of the disease. It's useless for those already infected. Anyone showing signs of edema is gone. Pneumonic plague is a killer ninety-nine times out of a hundred. Save the vaccine for those showing no signs and save the other medicines we're dropping for the less severe cases of the infected. Isolate the patients. We're dropping you streptomycin, tetracyline, and sulfonamides to treat the infected. Spray yourselves with a flea repellent. Burn the dead. Burn down the houses. Clear out trash and garbage. Then pray," he signed off.

Chase turned to face Ben. "Don't let any ships

through, Ben. Not a one. We can't take the chance."

"I understand, Lamar. Do we have any reported cases here in England?"

"A few. None up here. And I don't think we will. But I have a strong suspicion that London is only a few days, a week at most, toward becoming a death city. Didn't you get reports before we sailed that troops from the Continent had come over to beef up London?"

"Yes. But how about those that we know pulled out by sea right after we landed?"

Chase spread his hands. "Who knows?"

"Wait a minute!" Corrie said, turning around in her chair. "That might account for the strange messages that Communications has been receiving. Or had, I should say. They stopped about ten days ago."

"What messages?" Ben asked.

"They were garbled and hysterical and no one could make any sense out of them. Communications pinpointed them as coming from south of Cape Horn."

"Can you recall anything else about them?" Chase asked.

She shrugged her shoulders. "The words were 'Sick, dying, alone.' Then, 'Ships wallowing. All dead. All dead.' That was the last we heard. No more transmissions."

"Ben, what do we have in South America?" Chase asked.

"Chaos. Wars. A total breakdown."

"No one you could radio to sink those ships?"

"Oh, no. Nothing."

"Right now, those ships are floating flea factories. The rats are eating off the dead. They'll be enough dead flesh to keep them alive for weeks, maybe months. Whatever inhabited land those ships bump into . . ." He shook his head. "God help the people who might live there."

"Can you imagine somebody boarding those ships?" Jersey said, then shuddered. *"Jesus!"*

Ben moved to a world map and studied it. "Hell, it's probably seven thousand miles from here to Cape Horn. Even if we had the ships to send, it'd be like that needle in a haystack. I guess we have to leave it in the hands of the Lord."

"Yes," Chase agreed. "But I have to conclude that He hasn't looked too favorably on Earth the past decade or so. Maybe this *is* Hell after all." He threw up his hands. "What do I know? I'm just a doctor trying to keep decent people alive in a world gone mad."

Ben smiled. "You hear your own words, Lamar? 'Keeping *decent* people alive.' You judge just as much as I do, and I'm not sure that either of us has that right."

Chase looked at him for a long moment. "Well, Ben, maybe I don't have the right, since I did take that oath when I became a doctor. Maybe you don't either. But in this crazy, gone-wild world, if mortal men don't make those decisions, we may as well all go back to the caves and paint ourselves blue."

Ben nodded. "Maybe you're right, Lamar. Maybe you're right."

"When do you kick off this next campaign?"

"Tomorrow morning."

281

* * *

But it was the shortest and least bloody campaign in anyone's memory. The news of the Black Death now sweeping Europe had reached those in the cities of Scotland. They didn't wish to die in some horrible fashion any more than anyone else, so it didn't take them long to decide which was the best way to go. Ninety percent of them elected to throw down their guns and walk out under a white flag of surrender, knowing they would be given the precious vaccine if for no other reason than to keep the disease off this island.

"Bastards!" Ben said. "Now we've got to give precious medicines to crap like that while withholding it from decent people. Goddamn sons of bitches."

Ben was so mad he stalked up and down the highway like some enraged panther, while his Rebels gave him a wide berth. Finally he calmed down long enough to study a map for a moment. Then he turned to Corrie. "What's up here in the Shetland Islands, Corrie?"

"I can answer that for you," Dan Gray said. "I had my pilots check it out. They are totally void of human life."

"Get ships readied, Corrie," Ben ordered. "We'll haul this human garbage up there and dump them. Buddy!"

"Sir!" Buddy jumped.

"Take two companies up to the Shetlands and either destroy or sail back everything that'll float. We're going to isolate these people up there and see if any develop the plague. I'll send ships up with food and other provisions for them. But, I'll be

God-*damned* if I'll waste vaccines and medicines on trash like this."

"Father, if just one of them has the Black Death, they all will die."

"Did you hear me, boy?"

"Yes, sir!"

"Then *move!*"

"Moving, Father. Like right now!"

"You black-hearted son of a bitch!" a motley-looking warlord screamed when he heard the news. "We demand our rights. You hear me, you bastard? We're prisoners of war."

Glasgow Scotty sat on an overturned bucket and kept his head down and his mouth shut. He'd been a convict before the Great War and quickly fell back into the con's role: you kept your mouth shut and didn't make waves. He felt they were getting a raw deal, but he was realist enough to see Ben's point in doing this.

"Shut up, cheese-dick," a Rebel guard whispered to the warlord. "You want to die right here and now?"

"Fuck you, pretty-boy," the warlord said. "Hey, Raines," he shouted. "You peckerhead. I'm talkin' to you."

But Ben was not going to be baited. "Split them up and house them in those old prisons you found, Dan."

"Right, sir. It's better treatment than they deserve, at that."

"Hey!" a street punk yelled. "I'm hungry, man."

"Eat shit," Jersey told him.

* * *

"They've packed it in," Butch told his commanders. "Scotty and the rest of them surrendered hoping to get vaccine for the plague and Raines refused to give it to them. He's sending them all to the Shetlands to isolate them."

"At least they're alive," a warlord pointed out.

"Sure. Until the British courts get hold of them," Butch said. "Then they're dead."

"I ain't gonna hand my ass over to Raines on no platter," Acey said. "I got too many marks against me to do that. They're gonna have to kill me."

"How say the rest of you?" Butch put the question to them.

It was unanimous. They voted to fight to the death.

"There are no trees," Buddy reported back to his father. Three days had passed. "And there are no people, either."

"How was the weather?"

"Cold, but not as bad as one would think. I did some reading on the Shetlands. It's very interesting." He took another look at his father's face and wisely decided this was not the time for a dissertation on the climate of the Shetland Islands. "Scalloway and Lerwick are ready to receive the, ah, guests. There is not a boat that will float anywhere. Will they be guarded, Father?"

"Not by us. The BRF has agreed to man patrol boats on a twenty-four-hour basis. Get the outlaw leaders in here, son, please."

Ben faced the group. "There are still a number of sheep and Shetland ponies where you will be going.

They damn well better be there when we decide to try you. If one hair on their bodies is harmed, I guarantee you all that I will strap parachutes on you and drop you in the middle of the most highly infected part of Europe."

Glasgow Scotty and the other leaders of crud and slime took Ben at his word. His face frightened them, his voice frightened them, and just being in his presence frightened them. Where they had at first been defiant, they were now humbled and awed by being around the highly professional Rebel army. They had witnessed people of all faiths, all colors, all nationalities, working together like smoothly running machinery. They had yet to hear one racial slur from anybody. It amazed them.

"We ain't gonna hurt no one up there, General," a woman said. "We're just hopin' you'll forget all about us."

"Lady," Ben said, "and I use that noun only because I don't know your name and don't want to know your name if I was in my own country, I'd shoot every goddamn one of you and be done with it. But you're the responsibility of the British now. And may God help them find the strength to deal with scum like you. Get this shit out of my office, Buddy."

The next day, Ben and the Rebels began the job of clearing the Scottish cities of the Believers.

It was easier this time, for the warlords and street punks had been eager to give their interrogators the locations of the creepies and all the ways in and out of their hiding places. The Rebels pumped tear-gas and pepper gas into the sewer tunnels and basements and all the dark and odious places where creeps lived their disgusting lives and practiced their cannibalism.

All along the once heavily populated and urbanized stretch from Greencock to Edinburgh, the air was heavy with the residues of teargas and pepper gas and the smell of death. The Believers would stagger out of their stinking holes and the Rebels would shoot them. Or the Rebels would fill the basements with fire from flame-throwers, seal the entrances and exits closed with heavy explosives, or blow up the buildings and turn the basements into sealed tombs.

In London, the street punks and gang leaders sweated it out, listening to Rebel chatter on their radios. The Rebels talked on open frequencies now, wanting Butch Smathers and the others to hear them. They talked about how many creepies they'd killed that morning or that afternoon or that night, and how they died. It was pure psychological warfare, and it was working. Many trapped in London were breaking under the strain; a half a dozen a day were sticking pistols in their mouths and ending it. Many others were right on the edge of insanity.

"Come on and get us, then, you son of a bitch!" the warlord Duane screamed into a microphone. "Goddamn you all to hell. We don't want to hear no more of your shit!"

Commander Drake of the BRF told several of his colleagues that Ben Raines was the hardest man he had ever known.

"He's what we need at this time," one Brit countered. "He's giving us a second time. And God forbid we repeat the mistakes of the past."

Butch's troops, facing the Rebels, the Free Irish,

and the British Resistance Forces along the line that stretched north to south, tried to goad the freedom-loving men and women into a fight. They screamed obscenities over the air to them. It didn't work. Ben's troops silently stared across the distance at the street punks and warlords and outlaws.

The skies grayed and began dumping snow over the land, adding to the outlaws' woes. It didn't bother the Rebels. They had fought for years in all sorts of weather, from the blistering heat of the desert to the frozen ground of Alaska. They had every piece of equipment necessary to stay as comfortable as possible, under the circumstances. They waited.

London Lulu lifted a glass of whiskey to her mouth. Her hands were shaking. She downed the whiskey neat and banged the shot glass to the table-top. "Why is he doing this?" she asked. "Why?"

"Take it easy, kid," Butch said. "Why? He's punishing us for past sins. I've gone back and read everything I could find about Ben Raines and some of the books he wrote back in the old days. He never believed in that sentimental slop from the mouths of social workers and liberals and do-gooders. Raines wrote that society should give a criminal at least one chance to redeem himself. After that, if he fucked up bad again, get rid of him. Raines wrote that values should be taught in school as well as in the home. He's a strange and complex man, Lulu. I wish he had been in power when I was growing up. I wish his views had been accepted and practiced."

"Would you have changed, Butch?"

"Sure." He smiled. "That's the beauty of the

Rebel philosophy, kid. One's options are very limited. Go straight or get dead."

"But he's not goin' to give us a chance to do that, is he, Butch?"

Butch shook his head. "He gave us that chance, kid. When he hit the island, he gave us surrender terms. We refused. What happened up in Glasgow was a fluke. That mass surrender took him by surprise. That won't happen here. When he attacks, it'll be from three directions: north, south, and west. When he gets close enough, he's going to give us about a week or so of heavy artillery. He's going to turn this city into a shambles, and our nerves will be in a shambles, too. Oh, he'll take prisoners. But no more than a couple hundred."

"Butch, let's appeal to the Brits out there. They'll cut us some slack. I'm sure of it."

"No good, kid. The BRF, they gave Raines carte blanche. This is his show. Raines is this island's lifeline, and they know it. They're not going to interfere. It would be suicide and they know it."

"It's funny, Butch. Not ha-ha funny, but strange. We're sittin' here talking about our deaths. And I don't want to die. I mean, man, when that big door is slammed, it's over. Jesus God, if they'd just give me another chance, I'd change."

Butch laughed and poured a drink of whiskey. The whiskey was running out. The food was running out. They had no medicine. "No, you wouldn't, Lulu. And neither would I. Oh, we'd go straight for a time; but not for very long. We'd see something that we wanted, that belonged to someone else, and we'd take it. Whether it was a car, or bike, or whatever. You see, Lulu, we didn't have those hard options comin' up. And people like you and me, and all the rest of this so-called army trapped in London, we got to have ultimatums. Ben Raines knows this. Ben Raines knows that you must have some hard and fast and permanent rules that cannot be broken or changed for anyone. That's the only way democracy can really work. And he's proved that time and time again."

"Fuck Ben Raines!" Lulu said, her voice hardening. "Them rules is too restrictive."

"Actually, Lulu, they're not. They're just rules that people like us couldn't, or wouldn't, live under. Anyway, it'll be over soon. Then we won't have to worry about it."

"Jesus, Butch!" She fumbled for the whiskey bottle. "How can you take it so matter-of-factly?"

"Because there is no other way to take it, Lulu. We're trapped. We can't go north, south, east, or west. Ben Raines is not going to accept our surrender. And you know why? He's smart." Butch tapped the side of his head. "There are two reasons for it. One: With the island in such bad shape, the survivors can't waste the time housing us, feeding us, guarding us, providing us with medical attention. Not after Raines leaves. Two—and this is what I believe is his main reason for isolating Scotty and the others, and for not accepting our surrender: Raines believes we have the plague among us. And so do I."

"Oh, no, Butch. I don't want to die that way. No!"

"We'll never know for sure, love, but Raines is giving us more of a break than he's giving Scotty and the others. He's going to kill us quick. Scotty and those others are going to die a slow and rather horrible death. I don't blame Raines for it. I'd have done the same thing. He had to get those people gone. Now, for us here in the city, we can't do anything except die honorably. And that is what I intend to do. For once in my life, I am going to do something honorable." He smiled. "Sort of."

She stared at him. "And what might that be, love?"

"I'm going to kill just as many Rebels as I possibly can, baby. We all are. We're going to make suicide charges and do all sorts of brave things once the Rebels enter the city. I am going to die like the soldier I once was."

"Butch!" the door flew open and one of his men stood there. "Raines is massing for attack, north and south. His people punched through the line and stormed Brighton this morning and took it. And they ain't takin' no prisoners."

"Well, love," Butch said, standing up and picking up his Uzi. "Let us go do something honorable."

The messenger couldn't understand why the two were laughing almost hysterically as they walked out into the snowy morning.

Nine

"Brighton is ours and almost half of Norfolk County is in Rebel hands," Corrie said to Ben.

"Commence the shelling," Ben said. He waited until that order had been given, then stood up. "Everything in the wagon, Coop?"

"All loaded."

"Let's go, gang."

Before they had driven the few miles to the front, Corrie received word that the lines of the enemy were crumbling.

"Tell our people to maintain their existing positions," Ben said. "Do not attempt to advance."

"Can I ask you a question, General?" Beth said.

"Sure."

"The ones we send to the Shetlands—you suspected they had the plague, didn't you?"

"Yes, Beth, I did. And I suspect it's reached London as well. Chase told me he suspected the same. That's why we isolated the first bunch as quickly as possible and got rid of them just as fast."

"And you think the BRF will find . . . what, when they finally dock there?"

"I think they know already that those quartered

291

there are dying. Another three or four days and it will be over."

"How will they enter then?" Coop asked.

"In contamination suits, Coop," Jersey said. "They burn the bodies while others start killing rats and fleas."

"But there were animals there," Corrie said. "You warned them about harming them."

"There were very few animals on the island where they were put ashore. Buddy and his team made sure of that. That talk I gave them was pure B.S. Corrie, what's the latest from Admiral Carrington?"

"No further ships or boats have attempted to cross the Channel from the Continent, General, and none have tried to leave the English coast."

"Butch and his people know by now that it would do them no good to sail to Europe."

"Why not advance our people now, General?" Cooper asked.

"You want to take a bunch of prisoners who are carrying the Black Death, Coop?" Jersey asked.

"Ah . . . right. I see your point, Jersey."

Ben said nothing. He made the decision, he alone had to live with it.

As they were walking up to what would be Ben's CP, a lovely old stone farmhouse the Rebels had checked out and cleaned up, a runner from Communications came up. "All enemy lines collapsing, sir. They're all beating it back toward the city as fast as they can travel."

"Corrie, issue cease-fire orders. I want them all in the city. Spotter planes up and flying high and fast."

"Yes, sir."

Ben sat down in a camp chair, accepted a cup of coffee, and studied a map for a moment. When Corrie was through issuing his first orders, he said, "Order all available gunships up north and south of London to strafe anything moving on the roads. North between Thetford and Braintree, south, all of Kent. Order our people at Brighton to keep their heads down and their asses in one place. We know the outlaws took all the transportation from the citizens, leaving them bicycles only. Don't strafe anyone pedaling along, please. As soon as the spotters tell us the retreating forces are in London, resume the shelling."

"Raines didn't stop the shelling for humanitarian reasons, you can bet on that," Butch told Lulu and a few dozen others, as they sat deep underground beneath the city. "That cunning bastard's always got some sneaky trick up his sleeve."

Somewhere close to where he sat, the darkness punctuated only by a few flickering pockets of candlelight, a man began to cry. A woman began singing "Nearer My God To Thee" in a quiet voice. Another man was praying.

Butch looked down at his grimy hands. His clothing, like everybody else's, was filthy. He felt eyes on him and turned his head. A man he knew only as Faro was staring at him.

"Something on your mind?" Butch asked.

Faro chuckled in the deadly silence. "We're really something, aren't we, Butch?"

"I don't know what you mean." Butch's reply was short and sharply given.

Faro smiled. "Sure, you do, Butch. I was watching you. We're really something, aren't we? Big-time outlaws, that's us. Big tough boys and girls, that's us. Yet here we sit, in the tunnels with the rats. Hear them scurrying about? We're dirty, ragged, cold, hungry, facing death. But, by God, we made our point, didn't we? We sure as hell weren't going to play the establishment's game, were we? And we didn't . . ."

"Aw, shut your trap, Faro!" a man said.

"No," a woman said. "Let him talk. Go on, Faro."

"Oh, there isn't that much left to say. I just see the dark humor in it, that's all."

"You think this is funny, man?" another outlaw questioned. "I think you're bonkers."

"Yeah," another street punk stuck in his opinion. "You ain't no better than the rest of us."

"Oh, I never said I was," Faro replied. "But I'm not sitting down here feeling sorry for myself, either. Whatever I get—and it will certainly be death—I know I deserve. I'm a big enough person to admit that."

"Hey, man, we had to survive," another popped. "We only done what we had to do."

Faro started laughing at that.

"Son of a bitch is crazy!" Lulu said.

"Make your point, Faro," Butch said. The sudden silence was beginning to unnerve him. "Then shut up."

"I made it, Butch. And you know it."

"Oh, preach to us, Holy One," a man jeered at him. "Pray for our sins and offer us salvation. Me, I'll take pussy anytime."

The gloom filled with derisive laughter. Faro only smiled.

Butch's walkie-talkie crackled. He lifted it and said, "Go ahead." He listened for a moment. He sighed heavily and said, "That's ten-four.

"Raines has got helicopter gunships working north and south of the city. They're choppin' up those units far out. Them furthest from the city can kiss their asses good-bye. Some of them run into an ambush: citizens armed with axes and pitchforks. They were hacked to death."

"If he'd just give us a chance to surrender," a woman sobbed, her voice breaking with fear. "I'd go straight. I'd go to church. I'd be good."

"The hell you would," Faro said, contempt thick in his words. "You were a goddamn thief before the Great War, and you'd be right back in business if Raines pardoned you. Good God, people, stop lying to yourselves."

"And what the hell were *you* before it all fell apart?" Lulu shouted at him. "Just who the hell do you think you are, moralizing to us?"

"I was a minister," Faro said, shocking them all into silence. "I spread the legs of every good-looking woman in my congregation and lifted a lot of money from the collection every Sunday. And you know what, people? I'd do it again. I wouldn't change a thing. Now, if asked, I would tell the Rebels quite the opposite; but I'd be lying to save my butt. That's the difference between us. I admit to being a scoundrel. And contrary to what you all might think, we are most definitely not going to visit Heaven."

"You lie!" a man said, jumping up. "My faith told me that if I confessed to my sins, I would be absolved of them."

Faro laughed and laughed, infuriating them all. He wiped his eyes with a dirty handkerchief and said, "Your religion is a very convenient one, isn't it? Ah, but you go right on believing that, if you wish. You'll believe it right up to the time the devil jams a hot pitchfork up your ass. No, my friend, your religion suckered you. God doesn't like to be played with. God doesn't demand that we be perfect; He just asks that we sincerely try. And I would have to say that none of us here . . . sincerely . . . tried."

"Who give you all the answers?" a man shouted, his voice hollow and echoing in the dank tunnel under the city. "Who made you some sort of goddamn expert?"

"Six years of hard study helped; but I'm no expert. But I am pretty good at reading between the lines. And when you read the Bible, you better read between the lines."

"I wish I had a Bible," a woman said. "It would be a comfort to me now."

"I'm sure it would," Faro said, his tone dry enough to make the world's most perfect martini . . . if he just had a little gin. "I used to have trouble preaching. I wanted to crack up with laughter when I looked down into the faces of hypocrisy all looking up at me. I saw people who, six and a half days out of the week, willingly and knowingly committed every one of the seven deadly sins: Pride, Avarice, Lechery, Anger, Gluttony, Envy, Sloth, and on Sunday morning they all dressed in their finest, politely ignored the sick and old and hungry and needy on their way to the House of the Lord, and lo and behold, they were Christians for a few hours. They were washed in the blood and their sins were swept away. Hallelujah, brothers and sisters, I'm such a good person. It made me want to puke. So I turned it into a game.

"And after church, that afternoon, what would these good Christians do, after they had feasted on a grand Sunday dinner, while half the world starved? They'd go out to the golf links and swill beer and cuss and whack away at a little white ball, telling filthy jokes and eyeballing the asses of the ladies, who dressed as provocatively as they could, knowing the men would lust after them, and wanting them to. Or they would plop down in front of the telly, spending the afternoon getting half-popped on beer, watching the most ridiculous of games, go to movies and watch half-naked, or totally naked, men and women engaging in the most vile and degenerate behavior . . . oh, hell, the list is endless. Depressingly so. I met a few good people while I ministered, but not many. Not many."

"Then why did you stay a minister?" Butch asked.

"For comic relief. I told you, it became a game with me. I wanted to see just how long people would actually continue this charade. Hell, they'd do it right up to death's door, and then call for a preacher to hold their hands. It was laughable."

"I think you're disgusting," a woman told him. "Pretendin' to be a minister of the Lord and liftin' ladies' skirts all the while."

Faro laughed at her. The earth above them began to tremble from the impacting of artillery shells.

"All them that was out is either dead, or they made it to the city," Butch said, as the intensity of the incoming rounds picked up. He looked at Faro. The man was smiling at him. "Insufferable ass," Butch muttered.

Ben kept the pressure on the besieged city, the rounds crashing in twenty-four hours a day, a never-ending thunder that tore and ripped open nerves of those outlaws in the city. Artillery crews were changed every half hour, to give them some relief from the bombardment and to preserve hearing, even though the Rebels wore ear-protectors.

The devastation inside London was enormous, comparable to the German blitz of the Second World War. But Commander Drake had given Ben the green light to bring the city down, and he had done so without hesitation.

After seventy-two hours of constant bombardment, Ben ordered the shelling stopped. The silence took a little getting used to after three days and nights of pounding.

Ben ordered planes to fly low over the city, dropping hundreds of thousands of rat poison pellets he'd had flown over from the packed Rebel warehouses located all over what was once called the United States. Rebels saved everything. If they discarded it, it was worthless. They used machinery until they wore it out, then they rebuilt it and used it again. They had billions of nails, millions of rounds of ammunition, ten million commodes and toilet seats, thousands of tons of brick and concrete blocks; they had located, hauled in, fixed up, and stored all the vehicles they could find, of all discriptions. They had stripped hundreds of warehouses of shingles and roofing felt and tar. On the orders of Ben Raines, if somebody, someday, might be able to use it, they took it and brought it to a depot. They had millions of miles of all sorts of wiring—name anything, anything at all, from pluto-nium to pantyhose, and the Rebels had it labeled and stored, somewhere.

Ben had moved his CP about halfway between London and Gatwick Airport, south of the city. Thousands of Rebels, Free Irish, and British Resis-tance Forces now ringed outer London on three sides, while heavily armed patrol boats kept watch in the Channel. No one was getting out, and every-one knew why Ben was not attacking. Those closest to the city could smell the stench of the dead. They could see the smoke from burning piles of bodies. It made good sense to the men and women of the Rebels.

Why risk Rebel lives when the Black Death could do their jobs for them?

Not that many of those trapped in the city had not tried to get out, for many had. Not one had made it to within five hundred meters of a Rebel position.

"What happens when the city is dead, Ben?" Georgi asked.

"We fumigate it, time and time again, until noth-ing could live in there, using a variety of chemicals so the fleas cannot develop immunity to it. Then teams go in wearing protective gear to assess the damage, then we seal it off and let it rot. That's my plan; the BRF may have something else in mind. It's their country."

The Russian studied the American for a moment.

"What is troubling you, my friend?"

"It is that obvious, Georgi?"

"Yes."

"We can't go back the way we came?"

Georgi blinked. "What on earth is preventing us from doing so, Ben? Or should I say, what on the *sea* is preventing us?"

"Pirates."

Georgi blinked a couple of times more. "Did you just say *pirates,* Ben?"

"Yes, Georgi. Pirates. As in, 'Ho, ho, ho, and a bottle of rum.' "

Georgi stared at him for a moment and then smiled. "You are having a joke with me, old friend."

"I wish. No, it's no joke. I'll tell you now, then go over it more fully when we have a briefing in a couple of days. Pirates are operating out of Cuba, the Bahamas, Puerto Rico, and those islands in the Lesser Antilles. You know why you haven't seen Ike and Therm and Emil for the past week?"

"I wondered about it."

"They're helping to get some smaller British warships ready for the trip back home. They'll serve as escorts. A lot of Brits and Irish who were serving on these ships are going back with us."

"The pirates are stealing people for slaves?"

"Yes, among other things. It's like we've been suddenly catapulted backward in time a couple of centuries. From what Cecil has been able to learn, their equipment is not fancy, but it can damn sure sink us. They have cannon and are able to launch torpedoes from the deck, and there are a lot of them raiding all along the coasts of Central Amer-

300

ica and the northern tip of South America. It's a damn miracle we slipped through the first time. The last supply ships that came through were attacked. None was sunk, but several were damaged. Now they're waiting for us. From now on, everything has got to sail north of the Sargasso Sea — well north of it. As for us, do you want to cross the upper part of the North Atlantic in the middle of winter?"

"Hell, no!"

"It's moot anyway. We're not going back home just yet."

"Oh?"

"No."

Georgi waited.

"We're going to Hawaii."

"Around Cape Horn?"

"Yes." Ben smiled. "With a few stops along the way just to sightsee."

"But of course," Georgi said dryly.

Ben smiled. "Relax, Georgi. It's only approximately twenty thousand miles away."

Ten

"With your permission, sir," Commander Drake said to Ben, "we'll wrap up this campaign."

"You certainly have my permission, Commander."

The British Resistance Forces now numbered over five thousand and growing.

Commander Drake saluted smartly and said, "I speak for all the people when I say thank you, General. We are forever grateful to you and your Rebels."

"Corrie," Ben said. "Have our people stand down. From now on, we act as observers and advisers only."

"Yes, sir!"

"Anticlimactic, Ben," Ike said. "We came in with a roar and leave with nary a whimper."

"That's the way I like it, Ike. Another part of the world is free and we suffered only minimal losses."

"My people want to sightsee, Ben."

"As long as they go armed and in squad-sized groups, it's fine with me. Tell them to have at it. But I know what they're off to do."

Ike smiled. "We're all Americans, Ben. It's the

American way to help a country once it's liberated."

Ben looked toward the city. Fires in London were burning out of control; even ten miles away the stench of death was in the air. Rebels, Free Irish, and the BRF had burned a half mile stretch of land on the west, north, and south side of the city, then literally doused it with pesticides. There wasn't an insect known to humankind that could cross that area and live. Most would be dead seconds after entering the zone.

"Thousands are dead on the Continent, Ben," Chase informed him at a staff meeting. "No one will ever know for sure how many died. But from the information my people have received, we believe the disease has run its course. We were awfully lucky, Ben. This could have turned into a disaster."

"You have adequate vaccines and medications for our voyage, Lamar?"

"Oh, yes. When do we shove off?"

"It'll be another month, even with people working around the clock. Those troop transports are going to be heavily armed in case we come under attack from . . . pirates," Ben said the last with a note of incredulity. Pirates in the twenty-first century was just a bit too much. "If those sea-going bandits attack this convoy, they're in for one hell of a surprise."

"The BRF have taken prisoners out of the city," Georgi said. "Amazingly, none of them are contagious. But they say things got real bad in there toward the end. Drake told them it was a pity they all didn't die. The English attitude toward crime and criminals has certainly toughened."

Ben moved to a wall map of the world and

picked up a pointer. "Tankers will be in the center of the convoy for protection. We won't try to break any speed records. This is our route, gang. Madeira Islands, Canary, Cape Verde. When we get clear of the northern part of South America, we'll pull in closer to the shore and see what we can see. We might send parties ashore; we'll play that by ear. When we get opposite the Gulf of San Jorge, we'll cut down to the Falklands, then around the Horn and up to Easter Island, over to Pitcairn, Tahiti, up to the Marquesas Islands, then on to Hawaii.

"From what our communications people have been able to pick up, we're going to have a very tough fight of it in the Hawaiian Islands. We can't pick up any sign of resistance forces battling the outlaw element.

"I don't know what we going to find on these smaller island chains we'll be visiting. If the criminal element has taken control, we'll kick them out. We now have proper landing craft — thanks to the British — and the ships to handle them. This will be the largest convoy to set sail since the Great War. A lot of Brits and Irish will be going with us. Without them we couldn't make this trip. Many have asked to join the Rebels. Of course I said yes. They understand the Rebel philosophy and agree with it.

"Now, people, we had a lot of help and a lot of luck taking Ireland and England. We're going to need a lot more taking the Hawaiian Islands, because we damn sure won't have much help. It's going to be a very long trip, and very tedious. The British have loaned us hundreds of books and we've scrounged a lot of old movies and projection equipment to help ease the boredom. We sail out of

Portsmouth. Start moving your people down there immediately. Our job here is done."

The Rebels left the smoking ruins of London behind them and started their move south to Portsmouth. So many Irish and English joined up that a new battalion was formed. Pat O'Shea now commanded Ten Battalion of the Rebels . . . complete with bagpipers puffing and honking and shrieking.

The tankers pulled out first, followed by the supply ships, then one by one the transports left the harbor to the sounds of bands playing and people waving. Several dozen Rebels had requested permission to stay, including Linda, and Ben granted them their wish.

If she was at dockside when the ships left, Ben did not see her.

Commander Drake of the British Resistance Forces and Mr. Carrington were at dockside when Ben's flagship was tugged out. They saluted him as the bands played, and he returned the salute. The armada put the coast of England behind them on a cold and snowy New Year's Day.

Ben watched the coastline slowly disappear into the mist. "We're off to see the wizard," he muttered. "But I'm afraid the yellow brick road is going to be stained with blood."

"Isn't it always?" Lamar Chase said, leaning on the railing beside Ben. "When hasn't it been? There is always somebody, leading some force, that rises out of the ashes of war. This time it was you."

"Us, Lamar."

"No, Ben," the old doctor said. "You."

"There is a camel walking along the beach," Buddy said, looking through binoculars at the shoreline of one of the islands in the Canary chain. "A camel, Father?"

"Yes. They used them for draft animals." Ben watched as the ladder was lowered and Ike scrambled up. He knew what Ike was going to say and held up his hand. "Easy, Ike. West speaks fluent Spanish. He's taking a party ashore. I'm not going."

"That's a relief. Ben, we've been laying off for more than an hour. I haven't seen any sign of life."

"Nor have we. These islands had a population of a million and a half before the war. Somebody's there. I'm sending West in after dark in dinghies, just in case of unfriendlies."

"Radio room has contact with the island, sir," Corrie said. "They are warning us away."

"Tell them we are not a hostile force. Tell them we wish to buy, or barter, for fresh fruit."

"They say to leave immediately or they will launch an attack."

"Repeat: we are not hostile. We wish to come ashore, a small party only, and gather fruit."

"Leave," Corrie said.

"Ask them if they would like for me to blow their goddamn island off the face of the earth," Ben said, his temper rising. They had come in peace, had broadcast repeatedly who they were and why they were here, and wished only fresh water and fruit.

When a giant offers you peace and friendship, only a fool becomes hostile.

"No response, sir," Corrie said.

"Let's assume they have artillery capable of reaching us," Ben said. "Tell the captain to get us out of range."

When the ships had pulled back well out of range, Ben called for all commanders to assemble on his ship. The Rebels had scoured Ireland and England for every map they could find prior to this voyage, and the commanders pored over them. "The city is Las Palmas," Ben told them. "Population over two hundred thousand before the war. We aren't going to soften it up with artillery because I don't want innocents hurt and killed—even though there might not be any innocents on the island. So we'll do it the hard way. Ike, send your SEALs in at dark. Dan, take your special operations teams in right behind them. West, your people will go in directly behind them. Once the docks are secured, I'm coming in. That's the way it is. No arguments. We'll be going in very fast and without a lot of knowledge of our objective. And they'll be ready for us—make no mistakes about that. Coordinate your operations and study the maps of the town carefully before you leave this ship."

Ben stood by the railing, watching the sun go down bubbling into the sea. He was dressed in full combat gear, including inflatable life jacket. Communications was scanning all frequencies and had not picked up any long-range messages from the island calling for help. What they had picked up was inner-island chatter.

A man who called himself Oso—the Bear—was in control of the islands. His army, and it was a fair-sized group of outlaws and malcontents and thugs of all nationalities, had enslaved the people and were using them as forced labor, forced prostitution, and forced everything else that was vile and inhuman. All that was about to change.

Orange and scarlet softly changed to hues of gray and black around the ships.

"No bogies anywhere on the water," Corrie said.

"What's over in that direction, General?" Cooper said, pointing.

"Morocco. We won't be going over there."

"SEAL teams over the side now," Corrie said softly. "Special Operations teams getting in place."

The island of Gran Canaria lay silent and without lights. A huge dark shape in the peaceful-appeared subtropical night. It was about to become anything but peaceful.

"Special Operations teams over the side and moving," Corrie said.

The moments ticked by. "West and his people seaborne, General." Corrie said.

"Just as soon as they are clear, order landing craft up to the ship. One Battalion, stand by the side," Ben said. "Let's go, people."

"SEAL teams reporting they have made contact with the enemy," Corrie said, as tiny flashes of light could be seen on the shoreline. "Fighting is intense."

"Come on, people, over the side," Ben shouted, climbing over the railing and grasping the rope ladder. His boots quickly touched the deck of the landing craft.

The flat-bottomed craft quickly filled and they were off, heading toward the sights and sounds of battle.

"SEALs and SP teams report they have a toe-hold, but just barely," Corrie shouted over the roar of the engine and the rush of water.

"Tell whoever is running this tub to put us ashore south of the battle," Ben shouted. "One Battalion will stretch out along the coastline highway. Advise West of the change in plans and tell him to stretch his people along and north of the docks."

As soon as she had relayed the orders, Ike started screaming in her ears. "General Ike is pissed, sir," she told Ben.

Ben grinned. "Naturally. Tell Ike to calm down and to watch his blood pressure."

"Machine-gun emplacements on the bluffs over-looking the coast," Corrie said.

"Put us south of there," Ben told her. "Split the company. First and second platoons with me, three and four go in behind the main force."

She relayed the orders to the coxswain and all felt the change in direction.

They hit the wide beach running toward the bluffs. The ruse worked, for all gunfire was concentrated about a half mile to the north of their LZ. Stopping at the crest to catch their breath, Ben motioned Buddy to his side. "Take your Rat Team and check down that road toward the city. Bring me back one alive, boy."

Buddy grinned at his father and was gone into the darkness of early evening.

Ben took that time to carefully look all around him. Those who had taken over the islands, or at least this island, had never really planned for any invasion, so when the Rebels came, they rushed everybody they could muster on short notice down to the docks.

Buddy was back in only a short time, bringing with him two utterly terrified bandits. *"De donde es ud?"* one asked, his voice breaking with fear.

Ben spoke enough border Spanish to get by. "America," he told him. "Do you want to live?"

"Sí, sí!" the man whispered.

"Do you speak English?"

"Sí. Yes, sir. A little bit."

"How many of you are there on this island?"

The man looked confused. "Only me, *señor.* I am but one man."

"No, damn it," Ben said. "How many others . . . how many soldiers in your army?"

"Ah! I don't know. Two, three thousand, I guess."

"I have twenty-five thousand waiting in ships out there." Ben told the men a blatant lie.

"Mother of God," the other man whispered. He put both hands up. "We surrender."

"You're already my prisoners," Ben reminded him.

"I surrender again. Sometimes battle is confusing and people forget."

"I have no intention of forgetting. Now, get up. You're going to lead us into the city."

"We are?" the first man asked.

"You are. Move!"

The Rebels began walking right down the center of the highway, toward the ever-louder sounds of battle.

"I have a wife and eight children," the second bandit said. "And my aged mother lives with us. How would they eat if I am dead?"

"You're a liar," Ben told him.

The man shrugged his shoulders in resignation. "Sometimes it works. It was worth a try."

Ben chuckled.

"Are you really the great American general Ben Raines?" the first bandit asked.

"Yes."

Both men made the sign of the cross and said a quick prayer. They knew all about Ben Raines and the Rebels.

"I have a great throbbing and much pain in my head," the second bandit said. "I think I am going to pass out."

"You're going to get a bullet in your ass if you don't shut up and move."

"Alfredo, we have fallen into the hands of savages."

"Evaristo . . . kindly shut up your mouth and perhaps we will not be killed."

"That is a very good suggestion, Evaristo," Ben told him. "Tell us when we are approaching any spot where your soldiers might be located."

"They are not *my* soldiers, General. I . . ." He shut up when Ben placed the muzzle of his CAR-15 against his cheek. "Sí, patron. I will tell you and that is a promise. It would be foolish of me not to do that, since I am leading the way and any bullets meant for you would surely hit me first."

Alfredo sighed audibly. "He is the burden I must bear, General. He is my first wife's cousin, and she made me promise on her deathbed to look after him. It was the most foolish promise I have ever made. Since he seems to have been struck mute, as well as stupid, I will tell you that just up ahead,

General, there is a machine-gun emplacement."

"When was that put there?" Evaristo asked.

"Yesterday. While you were drunk and in the company of whores."

"Left and right of the road, people," Ben ordered. "Take it out quietly, Buddy."

Lying on the ground by the road, Alfredo whispered, "That is a very formidable young man you sent ahead, General."

"He is my son."

"I should have guessed."

"You don't sound like a terrible bandit, Alfredo."

"Oh, I am a most reluctant one. I was a merchant seaman when the war broke out. We sailed for weeks, trying to find a safe port. We hit something in the night and a few of us made it to the lifeboats." He looked at his first wife's cousin. "Including this dodo. We landed here. Already, bandits had taken over most of the island. The bandits gave me a choice; actually, two choices. Join them, or die. I consider myself a sensible man. I elected to live."

Buddy returned, wiping his bloody knife on his trousers, the others in his team doing the same. "You may proceed now, Father."

Ben told the bandits, "Take the machine gun and several cans of ammo. You two just joined the Rebels."

"We did?" Evaristo asked.

"Be thankful, stupid," Alfredo said.

"Let me get this straight," Evaristo said. "We are now going to be fighting against the people we were fighting for yesterday?"

"That is correct."

"I am confused."

"You have always been confused, Evaristo. But you have the strength of a bull. Pick up the machine-gun and follow me. Be brave in battle now. For if we win, we can leave this wretched place and return to Mexico."

"I am excited about that."

"General," Jersey said. "If you had a choice between these two and Emil, which would you choose?"

Ben glanced at her. "Do you even have to ask?"

Eleven

Ike had landed his battalion at the same spot that Ben had put ashore, while Danjou and Rebet had put their battalions north of the main docks and begun a slow circling of the city. While other battalions poured ashore, Ben and his small contingent were walking down the main highway straight toward the docks.

"This is madness," Evaristo said. "General, we are heading toward a thousand or more men fighting at the docks."

"Yeah, I know," Ben told him. "Keep walking. Corrie, bump the SEALs and the Special Operations teams and tell them we're going to punch a hole on the south side of the docks. That'll give our people a path to the highway."

"Impossible!" Evaristo said. "We are much too small a force."

"Just carry the machine gun and try not to think," Alfredo told him. "There, General," he said, pointing below them. Below them, the battle for the docks raged. "But I do not know how you plan on us getting down there undetected."

"We walk down and set up directly behind them, in those warehouses," Ben said. "Let's go."

Evaristo made the sign of the cross and said, "Tonight I will meet the angels."

"You cavort with whores and drunkards one day and talk about angels the next," Alfredo admonished him. "We are not going to die. The General is not going to walk calmly toward his own death, idiot."

"I think this General is *un poco loco.*"

"You might be right, Evaristo," Ben told him. "Move. We're about to walk through enemy line, Alfredo. You handle the language. Bearing in mind that I do speak your language and if you screw up, I'll personally shoot you."

"*Sí, patron,*" Alfredo said, as they approached several dozen bandits. "I am taking these men and meeting the enemy on the other side of the warehouses," he told the bandits. It was so dark everyone looked the same; just a dark blob in the night.

"That is good, Alfredo," one of the bandits said. "You have much courage. The *jefe* will be pleased at your actions."

The Rebels walked on toward the warehouses. "Set up all along here," Ben said.

"I cannot believe we actually did this," Evaristo said.

"It ain't over yet," Jersey told him. "Just as soon as we open fire, we're gonna have bogies all over us."

"You really are a very lovely young lady," Evaristo told her.

"Shut up," Jersey told him. "And get down behind that machine gun."

"I never before in my life have encountered such savage women," Evaristo muttered, on his belly be-

315

hind the machine gun. Alfredo fed the belt into place and Evaristo jacked a round into the slot.

"Well, look at this," Ben said. "Here comes a whole company of bandits, running to join their *compadres*. When they get even with us, open fire."

"General," Alfredo said. "Evaristo and myself, we have never killed anyone in our lives. We always fired into the air."

"To kill is a great sin," Evaristo said.

"I have priests coming ashore very soon," Ben told them. "They'll hear your confessions and forgive your sins."

"Okay," Evaristo said. "When do I fire?"

"Right now," Ben said, and lobbed a grenade.

The attack from behind and almost within their own lines turned the dock area into chaos. The Rebels cut down the running bandits, knocking them spinning and screaming to the ground and confusing those who were facing the invaders from the sea.

Buddy and his team ran to the rear of the warehouse area and cut toward the sea, coming up behind a thin line of bandits who had several companies of Rebels pinned down with heavy machine gun fire. A half a dozen grenades and two dozen M-16's spitting death fixed that situation and the Rebels swarmed inland through the gap in the lines.

The bandits began running back toward the city, leaving their dead and wounded behind them.

"Secure the docks," Ben ordered. "No pursuit. They know the city and we don't. We'll finish it in the morning."

"They have gone into the hills, *patron,*" Alfredo

said. "That is very rugged country back there."

"Can we go home now?" Evaristo asked.

When dawn broke and the bandits saw just how many Rebels there were, and several battalions never left the ships, the fight went out of the majority. They began surrendering.

"What the hell are we going to do with them?" Ike asked.

"I don't know. We'll stick around until some form of government is set up and we distribute arms, then shove off."

A priest sought audience with Ben. "Alfredo and Evaristo," the priest said with a smile, "are basically good men. They have never harmed a soul. Evaristo is not, ah, well, he's slow, I suppose would be the kindest way of putting it."

"They won't be harmed by any of us," Ben assured him. "We want to turn the running of this place back over to the civilian population and shove off as quickly as possible. Tell me about the other islands."

"Much the same as this one. Bandits and thugs run parts of them. In other areas, the people have weapons and keep them at bay. Weapons are the key."

"We'll arm you with the weapons taken from the bandits. From what I can see, conditions are pretty grim here."

"Very bad, General. We have plenty of medical personnel, but no medicines. We've been cut off from the rest of the world for a decade."

"We cleared the British Isles, and I've been in

317

contact with them this morning. They're going to be sending ships down soon and trade can once more resume. Have you heard any news about conditions on the Azores? There was no sign of life on the Madeiras."

The priest shook his head. "We have heard nothing from them, General. But you are going to have a lot of trouble when you land on the Cape Verde Islands. Thugs and pirates control everything there."

Georgi stuck his head into the room. "We found the leader of the bandits, Ben. The townspeople just hanged him."

"Oso," the priest said. "So the Bear's reign of terror finally ends. He was an evil man. But he was a Catholic. So I must go. I will see you before you leave, General."

Georgi came in and poured a cup of coffee. "Our troops are working with the citizens of the island, Ben. They're tracking down the bandits and destroying them. Dr. Chase says we cannot leave until he and his medical people tend to the needs of the sick."

"I know. He told me the same thing. Medicines are on the way from the States, but God alone knows when they'll arrive. Well, we'll take this time to clean out the other islands. We'll take the big island tomorrow."

But those bandits on the island of Tenerife had fled the coastline and headed into the rugged interior. Ben ordered gunships off-loaded from the ships and the hunt-down began.

Ben hopscotched from island to island—Hierro Ferro, La Palma, Tenerife, Gran Canaria, Gomera, Fuerteventura, Lanzarote—as his troops, aided by locals, hunted down and destroyed or captured the fleeing bandits. As usual, wherever there had been outlaws and warlords for any length of time, the people they conquered were malnourished and sick. Among the adults, venereal disease was rampant— brought to the islands by the bandits, and spread as the bandits raped their way through the female (but not always) population, and certainly not always adult women. To see a ten-year-old girl or boy dying of syphilis was not something the Rebels were accustomed to witnessing. After seeing a few cases of that, the number of prisoners taken by the Rebels dropped dramatically.

The mopping up and clearing out of the bandits was slow, dirty, and dangerous work, for they were dealing with the hardcore now.

Ben intercepted a radio message from a team working in the rugged mountains of La Palma. "This is the Eagle. What do you have?"

"About a hundred bad ones, Eagle," a platoon leader radioed back. "And they're well-armed. I've got one Rebel dead, and half a dozen more hit pretty hard."

"You stay put. I'm coming in with the dustoffs." He glanced at his team and winked at Jersey as he picked up his M-14.

She returned the wink, picked up her M-16, and said, "Kick-ass time."

The bandits, including the man who was second-in-command before Oso got his neck stretched, were holed up in a large stone house with a magnificent view of the valleys all around. There was no way the Rebels were going to breech that near-fortress without taking a lot of dead and wounded.

As it was, the medivacs had to come in low and twisting around the base of the mountains to avoid being hit by bandit fire, and the wounded carried more than a mile to the dust-offs.

Ben studied the situation for a few moments. "All right. They're got .50's on three sides, but that south side is semiblind for them. Corrie, I want two Apaches in here, fully armed. Give the pilots our coordinates, and emphasize this grid here." He pointed to the map. "That's the mountains I want them to hover behind until I give the word. When I say so, lift up and give that minimansion up there every damn thing they've got."

He turned to the platoon leader. "Son, when those gunships open up, we've got to be in place to cream the survivors when they come out. So the instant the gunships fire, we're going to be running up that path over yonder with everything we've got to get into position. Pass the word."

"You, of course, will not be running up that path," Buddy said.

"Who the hell says I won't?"

"Merely wishful thinking, Father."

"Wish for Holly Hunter or Julia Roberts, why don't you?"

Buddy blinked and stared at his father for a moment. "What battalion are they in?"

Ben shook his head. "Son, your education is sadly lacking, I'm afraid."

Buddy nodded his head. "They are attractive women, I suppose."

320

"Very. Now go tell your team to get the kinks out of their legs. We've got about three hundred yards of exposed ground we'll be covering."

The Apaches came quickly and settled down just behind the crest of the mountain.

"We're going to be running when you fire," Ben told the chopper pilots. "So kindly make those birds fly hot, straight, and true."

"That's a roger, General. Will do."

"All right, gang," Ben said. "Everybody in place. Tell the pilots to rock and roll, Corrie."

As soon as the props were whining in lift, Ben and team leaped in front of the platoon leader and were running across the vacant expanse of ground.

"God damn it!" Buddy yelled, and took off after his father.

The Apaches opened up, and it was hell on the mountain for those bandits in and around the small mansion. One entire end of the house blew into thousands of pieces as rockets impacted and their chain guns opened up, hurling 30mm rounds into the house.

Ben did a little dance step as a bandit got his range and opened up with an automatic weapon, the slugs kicking up dust and dirt all around his boots. But firing downhill is tricky, and Ben made the rocks and timber without losing anything except breath, and that was only temporary.

Buddy and his team piled in behind him and laid down covering fire for the others.

"Head-rush," Ben said with a smile.

"Whatever that means," Buddy said. "I am not into the quaint colloquialisms of your youth, Father."

321

"Youth!" Ben laughed. "Hell, I was a grown man when that expression came around. It means, 'Wow, what a kick.'"

"Sometimes I worry about you," Buddy muttered.

"Come on, kid-of-mine," Ben said. "Let's go make bang-bang with the bad guys."

Buddy was still muttering as he followed his father up the now-protected slope toward the mini-mansion, which was smoking from the rocket attack.

Ben rounded a brush-covered curve in the path and came face to face with a bandit. His M-14 came up and roared. The bandit was knocked to one side, down and dead. "Left and right," Ben ordered. "They've got to come this way."

All could hear the sounds of running feet coming at them hard. Ben took a grenade and held it up so the others could see and follow suit. They pulled pins together and let them fly. The explosives were enormous, and the sounds of running feet was replaced by the moaning of badly wounded.

They waited until the others joined them. The platoon leader waved people forward. Seconds ticked past.

"That's it," a Rebel called. "We've got wounded bandits up here."

"See if Oso's second-in-command is among the dead," the platoon leader said. "What was his name?"

"Carlos," a Rebel told him.

A civilian who was the guide for this contingent of Rebels went forward and stared at the dead and wounded. "Carlos," he said, pointing to a bandit who had taken the blast of a grenade in his chest and stomach. He kicked the lifeless form, spat on the body, and walked on.

Ben had watched the reaction of the civilian guide. "Nothing like being loved and respected," he said.

While several battalions of Rebels hunted down and destroyed the ragged remnants of the bandits, other Rebels were turning volunteer citizens of the islands into a paramilitary force and seeing to it that free elections were held. Some degree of law ·and order and justice and stability would be in place before they left. Representives from Britian and Ireland sailed in and began talking trade between their nations.

Ben made preparations to leave.

"Cape Verde Islands, Father," Buddy asked.

Ben shook his head. "No. The British say they'll handle that group for us. In exchange, we'll check out the Falklands for them."

From years of practice, once the Rebels decided to pull out, they did so in a hurry, with very little wasted motion. The convoy, now laden with fresh beef in the lockers and various kinds of fresh fruit, sailed out and headed south When they had skirted the northeastern edge of South America, the ships pulled in close enough to that continent to enable Communications to monitor any traffic that might be bouncing around in the air. And there was plenty of it.

"Chaos in there, Ben," Ike radioed from his ship. "But so far the convoy's remained undetected.

Makes me sick that we can't help those people."

"Someday, Ike. Someday," Ben radioed. "I don't like it any better than you. All I can say is, we'll be back."

The days blended in, each passing day no different than the one behind them or the one ahead of them. Except for those working Communications and Intelligence. All along the coast of South America, those two departments of the Rebel Army stayed busy, recording and then analyzing each radio message received. They pinpointed, whenever possible, each trouble spot for future reference.

Before the convoy reached the Falkland Islands, Intelligence had the names of many of the warlord and bandit leaders, the self-styled generals and colonels, where they were, the size of their armies, and how much territory they controlled.

Standing by the railing, Ben could but mutter, "We'll be back, people. Someday."

Twelve

"The captain says he's made this run many times," Buddy said to his father. "He said we'll lay off Port Stanley while teams go in to check out the place. The islands cover over forty-seven hundred square miles, yet Stanley is the Falklands' only town. I find that amazing. Where do all the other people live?"

Ben smiled and handed his son an old copy of a travel magazine. "Read all about it, son. And then you'll know as much about it as I do. But you can take your time, we still have many, many miles to go."

Ben studied the young man's ruggedly handsome face. This trip had been a real adventure for him, and for many of the younger Rebels, who had never been out of the shattered remains of the United States.

Ben thought of the Rebels who lay in quiet graves in Ireland and England and hoped they had not died in vain, and of the ones who had been sent back to America minus hands and arms and legs and vision.

And he wondered for a moment how Linda was doing.

He stood by the railing, deep in thought, and others left him alone. What few reports they had monitored coming out of Hawaii had been growing increasingly grim. The islands were nothing more than a safe haven for bandits and assorted thugs who had enslaved virtually the entire island group. Military bases had been looted time and time again until now there was practically nothing left of value on any of the installations. The cities had been turned into cesspools, nothing more than criminal havens where torture and slavery and human degradation was so common no one paid any attention to it.

The islands were not going to be easy to take. The terrain was rugged. He had spent hours studying maps of the group and had warned his commanders not to think the upcoming invasion would be a milk run.

Chase joined him by the railing. "What are you getting out of the Falklands, Ben?"

"Not much, Lamar. There is some chatter, but Intelligence doesn't seem to think there is any trouble there. I hope that's true."

"The British and the Argentines finally settled their differences, I suppose. Even though it took a world war to accomplish that."

Jersey walked up, a puzzled look on her face. "We're not too many days away from the Falklands," she said. "I been studying some maps, and I thought the weather would be colder than this, as close as the Falklands are to the Antarctic. But it doesn't seem to be getting colder."

"It's spring, Jersey," Ben said. "It's winter back home, but spring here."

"Well, I'll be damned. Sure, I remember that from grade school geography." She grinned. "Now I'll go mess with Cooper's mind."

"Good luck in finding it," Chase called after her.

Rebel communications made contact with the Falklands and were advised that what population remained was in desperate need of medicines and doctors. Communications told them to hang on, the Rebels were on the way.

"How many still there?" Ben asked.

"They advised about four hundred men, women, and kids. They had twenty-three hundred on the Islands when the balloon went up. They didn't tell me what happened to the rest."

"We'll know soon enough."

"Ben," Lamar said, "they may want to leave. They're damned isolated."

"We have room. We'll see what they say."

They said no.

The Rebels sailed into Port Stanley and the medics and doctors went to work immediately upon getting their land-legs back under them. But the people of the Falklands did not wish to leave.

"We know you cleared out the thugs from Ireland and England, so we'll be getting supplies on a regular basis now," the spokesman for the group said. "So we'll be stayin'. It's our home, General—for many, the only home they've ever known."

"What happened to the others?"

"Some left in ships. We never heard from them again. Many died from lack of medicine. We're all suffering from far too few vegetables. We grow some in hothouses, but mainly we've lived on mutton and fish and squid. We've coped, General. We simply had no choice."

"No trouble from the mainland?"

"No. None. We monitor them closely. It's terrible over there, General Raines. It's just been a total breakdown of law and order and decency. At first, we prepared ourselves for an invasion. But it never came. We had troops stationed here, but when the war came, they sailed and flew out. We don't know what happened to them. What really saved us were the stores the military left behind. I think we would have died if it had not been for that. But the vitamins ran out years ago, along with the boxes of bully beef, and the medicines became outdated and dangerous to use. You people saved us, General. We can never thank you enough."

"I see you're all well armed," Ben said with a smile.

"Oh, yes. We have plenty of guns to go around, believe me. We're few in number, but any attacker will pay a dreadful price in the taking of the Falklands."

The Rebels repaired existing radio equipment and also installed more modern equipment. Now the people could communicate world-wide, and more important, with the Canaries and with England. The Rebels stayed on these lonely, barren islands for several weeks, giving the doctors time to thoroughly check and treat every resident, and some required extensive surgery. The lone doctor on the Falklands had zero supplies with which to treat the sick.

"What about Easter Island?" Ben asked.

The man shook his head. "We don't know. I don't know if anyone is even alive up there. Is that your next stop?"

"Yes."

"There is no natural harbor there. I suggest you anchor off the coast of Hanga-Roa, on the west side. And be careful. There was a leper colony there, and they've been without medicines for many years now." He shrugged his shoulders. "Who knows?"

Ben looked at Chase.

Chase nodded. "Oh, yes, Ben, we have the drugs to treat it. Sulfone and dapsone, primarily. And before you ask, no, medical science still does not know the mode of transmission of the disease. What we do know is that it usually takes prolonged and close physical contact to contract it. And many work near it all their lives and never contract it. It's a baffling disease, Ben."

The Rebels left some of their fruit and vegetables for the residents of the island—ships from England and the Canaries were already on the way—and prepared to shove off. There were lots of tears and many lumps in throats on both sides as the convoy steamed out of harbor. The residents had put together a band of sorts, and they were playing as the convoy sailed out of sight.

The trip to Easter Island from the Falklands was nearly five thousand miles. As highly trained as the Rebels were, and as sharply as their killing skills had been honed, had it not been for these stops along the way, there would have been some blood spilled among the troops due to the boredom.

The convoy rounded Cape Horn, staying well

away from land, and turned northwest into the South Pacific Ocean. Ben and his troops settled in for another long, boring trip.

It was a bored bunch of warriors who lined the rails just at dawn when Easter Island became a tiny dot in a vast moving sea. The convoy anchored outside the usual harboring area and the Rebels stood by the rails, many with binoculars, and tried to spot some sign of life. The island, only forty-five square miles of it, lay silent under the subtropical sun.

"Communications has been scanning all frequencies," Corrie told Ben. "Nothing."

"They may be hiding," Ben said. "But I've got a bad feeling about this place. Corrie, tell the chopper pilots to give it a fly-by."

It did not take the recon helicopters long to traverse the tiny island.

"No signs of human life, General," Corrie told Ben. "Cows, sheep, some horses. No sign of human habitation."

"Tell Dan to take his team in. Helicopters will circle until the small airport is secure and then land."

"Yes, sir."

"Oh, to hell with it, Corrie. Let's go exploring."

She grinned. "The team's all ready, General. We sort of felt that would happen."

Dan met him near the outskirts of a small village on the western side of the island. "The town is deserted, General—and has been for a long time."

Ben entered the first house he came to. He had experienced some eerie sensations in his life, but this scene hit him hard. There were plates on the

330

kitchen table, knifes and forks and spoons laid out properly. Hardened remnants of food lay in the charred bottoms of pots on the stove. House slippers were placed on the floor by the bed, and nightclothes lay untouched on the turned-back bed.

"Place gives me the heebie-jeebies," Cooper whispered.

"Why are you whispering?" Jersey asked.

"Why are *you* whispering?" Cooper countered.

Nearly every house in the villages was very much the same. Meals were in the process of being cooked when whatever happened happened. There were few signs of struggle or conflict, a few bullet holes, and some expended brass on the ground. The Rebels inspected the graveyards. No signs of any hurried mass digging. The last marker was dated 1989.

"That's years ago," Beth said, then felt slightly foolish for pointing out the obvious.

It did not take the landing parties long to scour the island and conclude that it was void of inhabitants.

"Tell the troops to start coming ashore so they can feel earth under their boots again," Ben ordered. "One battalion at a time. We'll spend several days here and try to determine what happened. But I doubt that we'll ever know."

One thing that did puzzle Ben was that the leper station had been destroyed by fire.

"They probably all died of natural causes and the islanders burned the place out of fear and ignorance," Chase told him, looking at the old, charred ruins.

"Almost two thousand people lived on this is--

land," Ben said. "What the hell happened to them?"

"What happened to the damn trees on this chunk of real estate?" Jersey questioned. "There are no trees."

"Historians and researchers say this place was a forest at one time," Ben replied. "But the islanders cut them down to build platforms to use in hauling those giant statues like that one over there." He pointed. "There are over a thousand of them scattered over the island."

"What are they?"

"That's a good question. No one really ever knew."

"And now, no one will ever know," Dr. Chase said.

"Big suckers," Coop said.

"Some of them over fifty tons and about seventy feet tall, if memory serves me correctly. Beth, have someone chisel on a boulder that the Rebels, a multinational force of soldiers home-based in America, landed on this island on this date and found it deserted, with no sign of human life."

"Yes, sir."

Ben walked around a small part of the island. He didn't want to off-load a lot of vehicles because without an adequate port, it was a pain in the ass. He stood before a row of tall and stately statues, their sightless eyes staring at . . . nothing, he assumed.

"You know what happened here," he said. "But you never give up your secrets, do you?"

Ben stared at the tall and mute statues for a moment, then turned and walked away. He was going back to his ship. Damn island depressed him.

Almost exactly one thousand miles to the west lay Pitcairn Island, where back in 1790 or so, Fletcher Christian and some of the crew of the HMS *Bounty* mutinied and made their way to this desolate two-square-mile island smack in the middle of nowhere. Ben and Rebels checked it out.

According to the latest figures the Rebels had, the population of Pitcairn Island, when the Great War struck, was sixty-one. At first glance it appeared to have changed little.

Since there was no port, the Rebels went ashore in motor launches. The man who met them was not unfriendly, but then, neither was he bubbling over with joy at the sight of the Rebels.

"We are not armed," a man said, a peculiar accent to his words. "We harm nobody and wish only to be left alone."

"Do you want our doctors to look over your kids?" Ben asked.

"No."

"Do you mind if we look around the island?"

"You have the guns."

"That's not what I asked."

"You have already frightened the young people."

"Do you want us to leave?"

"Would you?"

"It's your island."

The man turned around and walked off.

"Okay," Ben said. "Suits me. Back to the ship, people. Beth, log that we tried to help the inhabitants but they refused. We will not be back."

"Yes, sir."

"Wait, sir!" a man's voice called, turning the team around. A young man was walking down the boat ramp toward them. He reached them and held out his hand. Ben shook it.

"We are not all so rude," the young man said. "Frank forgot one of our tenets: Speak gently and with dignity. My name is Martin Christian. We do have sick people here, and I would very much appreciate your doctors checking them over."

"We'll bring them in by helicopter. It's safer than landing a launch here," Ben said dryly.

The ride in had been rough, ploughing through crashing surf to reach the tiny concrete jetty built by British Royal Navy Engineers at Bounty Bay.

A landing pad was cleared in Adamstown, the only town, and naturally, Chase was the first one off the chopper and immediately started bellering and hollering to his medical teams.

"His bark is worse than his bite," Ben told a group of Pitcairners who had gathered around him. He noticed that Frank—whoever the hell Frank was—was nowhere to be seen.

"What's your population now, Martin?"

"One hundred sixty-five. We can't support much more than that."

"Birth control?" a young Rebel doctor asked.

"It's voluntary, but it works. The people know that overpopulation would be the end for us all."

"Easter Island is void of human life," Ben told him. "Certainly open to resettlement. We'd help you."

"We know. They were wiped out by pirates heading from South America to Hawaii. Those who were not killed were taken as slaves, or for barter. Especially the women and girls. The pirates tried to come ashore here. After several of them drowned, they gave up and sailed on. Your destination is Hawaii, General?"

"Yes. I expect a pretty good fight awaits us there."

"You don't seem too worried about it."

Ben smiled. "We've been fighting for over a decade, Martin. We've got it down to a fine art, believe me."

"Oh, I believe you. Before we ran out of fuel, we used to track your movements all over the United States."

"We'll resupply you, set you up with new radios, and arm you, if you wish."

"Oh, I wish, sir. Oh, my, yes. We've been lucky over the years. Very lucky. But luck will run out someday. That's Frank's problem. He thinks because of our poor docking facilities here, we'll be left alone. He was shocked to see the helicopter. He is not . . . worldly."

Ben nodded his head. "Come on, let's start making a supply list."

"Oh, that's easy," Martin said with a smile. "We need everything."

Thirteen

Ben sent two ships back to where they had spotted a drifting tanker—about four days out from Pitcairn. They had checked it and its cargo was diesel.

Pitcairners are great scavengers, plucking from the sea whatever washes up, and that was plenty. Their homes are made from lumber thrown overboard from ships. Now they were in terrible need of repair. And they had 55-gallon drums that had washed up stacked all over the island.

"We'll use those to store the fuel in. But that will only be a small portion of what's on that tanker. I don't know what to tell you about the rest of it."

Then Ike came up with, "Hell, let's beach her on one of the uninhabited islands. We'll run her aground on the lee side and you folks can take what you need when you need it. We'll drain the forward compartment before we beach her."

"There you go," Ben said, as Martin and the others laughed and clapped their hands.

"That will be enough fuel oil to keep our generators and tractors going for the rest of our lives."

Then Ike sobered. "No, it won't work."

"Why?" Martin asked.

"If the old girl sprang a leak, you'd have an ecological disaster on your hands."

"Not necessarily," said a man who looked to be about as old as God. But he moved nimbly to a map of the islands. "Bring her in here, at this spot, at high tide. After you have blown out a deeper trough. This area is surrounded on three sides by high rock walls. Enough explosives here," he pointed, "and us working to build a sea wall, would ensure the ship would be virtually dry and aground for years and lessen the danger of a spill."

A Rebel engineer studied the location carefully and said it could be done.

"So do it," Ben ordered.

With Rebels swarming all over the island, repairs were done quickly and done well. Ben ordered a ship dispatched from the west coast with badly needed medicines and supplies, and a doctor and two medics agreed to stay on for a time.

One of the few things the residents could tell the Rebels about Tahiti was that like everywhere else, when the Great War struck, the outlaws took over.

"The French Foreign Legion had a small detachment of men there," Martin said. "But the hoodlum element quickly killed them all and began taking over. Pirates operate out of the two big islands, Tahiti and Mooréa. They roam all up and down the Tuamotu Archipelago. They might even try to attack your convoy. Although I think that would be a terrible mistake on their part."

"The people on the Marquesas?" Ben asked.

"That I don't know. We lost contact with them years ago. But if I had to guess, I'd say it was a pirate's haven."

The men shook hands. "Will we see you again, General?" Martin asked.

"I doubt it. But you'll be seeing American ships several times a year. That I can promise you."

"Godspeed, General."

The Rebel convoy put the tiny dot in the vast ocean behind them.

The convoy had not traveled three hundred miles from the tiny island when lookouts spotted three ships coming up on them fast. Ben lifted binoculars and had to smile, even though it was extremely dark humor.

"The bastards are actually flying the Jolly Roger," he said. "I cannot believe it. Battle stations," he ordered.

"All guns ready," Corrie reported.

"Helicopters up," Ben said.

"Yes, sir. General? The pirates are ordering us to heave to and prepare for boarding parties."

Ben chuckled. "Those simpleminded outlaw bastards. My God, can't they see the size of this armada?"

"They are going to open fire, sir."

"Tell them to strike their colors or die."

Corrie relayed his orders. Then listened intently. Ben looked at her. "Well?"

"Ah, sir, they say for you to fuck off."

A cannon shell whistled overhead and landed harmlessly in the sea.

"Blow them out of the water, Corrie."

Apaches launched missiles and the three pirate ships took hard hits. One went down fast, the other two were burning and taking on water.

"Prepare to launch boats to pick up the survivors," Ben ordered. "Apaches return home. When the pirates are cleaned up, patched up, and in dry clothing, bring the leaders to the stateroom, please."

"Some of them won't make it, sir," Corrie pointed out. "Sharks."

Ben could see fins slicing the calm waters. "They definitely have a real problem," he said, then walked away.

The first prisoner Ben and the others in the stateroom questioned was a big burly brute of a man with cruelty and savagery etched on his face and in his eyes. His head was shaved and he wore rings in both ears and in his nose. His huge arms were covered with tattoos, most of them highly obscene.

"Ye let them good men die to the sharks, mate," the man said. "Ye's a cold-hearted bastard."

"And you are a stupid-looking motherfucker," Ben replied. "You're about two heartbeats away from getting a slug right between your eyes. So you shut your mouth until I tell you to open it. Is that clear?"

The pirate was taken aback by that. He obviously was not used to being spoken to in such a manner. But before he could respond, Cooper stuck his head into the stateroom.

"We picked up a few of their prisoners, General. Mostly women. They've been treated bad, sir. Real bad."

The pirate laughed. "We like to see how much pain they can stand. It's a game. Some of them gets dragged over the side and et on by the sharks. It's a fun game."

Ben stared at the man for a moment. "You openly and freely admit to those disgusting practices?"

"Hell, yes!"

Ben was silent for a moment, studying the brute of a man standing grinning arrogantly before him. "Get him out of here," he finally said.

"What's the matter, big-shit General?" the ape sneered. "Does I frighten you?"

"You disgust me," Ben said, his voice low. Those Rebels in the room could feel the menace in Ben's voice.

"Well, la-tee-da," the pirate sneered. "Ain't we the dainty one, though? I sure am sorry that I dis-gust you. You want to kiss and make up?" He puckered up thick wet lips and made kissing sounds at Ben, leaning as close to him as his restraints would allow. "Maybe you could suck my dick, too."

Ben looked at Ike. "Take him out and hang him. Now."

The pirate stiffened in shock. His face paled under his heavy tan. He tried a smile. "Ah . . . with you bringing law and order back to the world, General, I kinda figured on a trial."

"You figured wrong."

"What about his body?" Ike asked.

"Throw it to the sharks."

"You cold-blooded son of a bitch!" the pirate said, the words exploding out of his mouth.

Ben smiled, his lips a thin line and his eyes void of emotion. "How do you like it, now that you've finally met someone as cold as you?"

The man was cussing and shouting out oaths as the Rebel guards dragged him to a makeshift gallows.

"We're turning out of the Archipelago, General," Beth told Ben. "Heading toward the Windward group of the Societies."

"Won't be long now," Ben said. "I'm surprised we haven't had more attempts to board."

"The ships that have seen us have turned tail and left," Coop said. "So you can bet they're waiting on us."

Ben walked to the communications room. "Anything?" he asked the woman on duty.

"Plenty, General. And none of it good. They're sure massing for us. I was just finishing typing it up for you." She handed him a clipboard.

Ben quickly scanned the pages. "Well, they're definitely waiting for us Get me an all-ship hookup with the batt coms, please."

Ben took the mic. "As you probably know by now, the crud is waiting for us on the islands. Go over our plans again, make sure you haven't missed anything. Start issuing supplies. Make sure everybody has water purification tablets and they take two canteens of water in with them. We all know the drill, so all I can add is, Good luck."

The outlaws on the islands that made up the Society chain watched with dismay as the large convoy of ships approached the big island of Tahiti and slowly began circling, well out of range of anything the outlaws had in the way of weapons. The island was only thirty-three miles long, and the convoy, made up of dozens of ships, appeared to the outlaws to be much larger.

"You got your passport ready, Ben?" Ike joked as they stood by the railing, looking through binoculars at the capital city of Papeete.

Ben lowered his binoculars. "All ready, Ike." He turned to Corrie. "What's the chatter about on the island?"

"They don't know what to do," she replied. "I'm getting chatter from a dozen different groups. Some want to surrender, some want to mix it up right now."

"Either way they want it is fine with me," Ben said.

They stood by the railing and waited.

"Here's one who wants to talk," Corrie said, handing Ben the headset.

Ben slipped on the headset. "This is General Raines. Say what's on your mind."

"We'd like to make a deal," the outlaw said.

"No deals," Ben told him. "You lay down your arms and surrender or you die. Those are the only two options that you have."

"You are not offering much, General. Suppose we choose to fight?"

"Your funeral," Ben said flatly.

"You have no right to come here and dictate terms to us," another voice spoke.

"I don't intend to argue about it," Ben said. "Make up your damn minds, one way or the other."

There was no reply.

Ben returned the headset to Corrie. "I think they're going to fight," he said to Ike. "The special teams will go in at midnight and raise a little hell. The rest of us will strike just before dawn." He looked at a map. "We'll save Papeete for the last. Take your battalion and go in here at Teahupoo, Dan's people go in up here at Tautira, both parties work toward this bottleneck here at Afaahiti. I'll take my people and go in here and secure the airport and the town of Faaa. Georgi will go in here at Mahina. Rebet will take Paea, Danjou's people will land here at Tiarei. Everyone else will stay in reserve. The convoy will pull back for several miles before beginning the shift. Give the orders, Corrie."

Rebels began gearing up for action, and they were ready for it. The weeks of inactivity had charged them up and they were spoiling for a fight. On the island, the outlaws watched and knew their years of terror were about to end.

Beaten, abused, enslaved, raped, and tortured islanders whispered among themselves. "The American Ben Raines and his Rebels are here."

"Here?" came the astonished whisper.

"Here. And now is the time for us to help them."

Those who had put up with a decade of abuse reached for their hidden machetes and axes and hatchets and homemade spears. They had long memories, and very sharp blades.

Fourteen

Ike and Dan sent their special operations people in under cover of darkness with orders to terrorize the outlaws and blow up a few things. The highly trained hellions grinned and waggled their thumbs in reply, then went over the side into rubber boats for silent approach.

"Let's get into position," Ben said.

The transports began moving into position, slowly encircling the island, getting ready for the Rebels to make their pre-dawn strike. On the island, in the towns and villages, the outlaws wiped the sweat out of their eyes, wiped sweaty palms on their shirts and pants, then gripped their guns. Many of them never dreamed that the Rebels would ever leave America, much less travel thousands of miles to these islands.

Now they were looking death in the face and not liking the sight at all.

The Rebels slept for a few hours, and most did not have to be awakened at 0400. They were that ready to go.

Corrie walked up to Ben's side. "Special operations report a lot of ships have pulled out of harbors, sir. They took a north by slightly east course."

"Heading for the Marquesas," Ben said. "They might convince those there to head for Hawaii. We're going to have our hands full, no doubt about that."

"Small craft approaching from the island," the captain's voice came over the loudspeakers. "Coming at us at high speed."

"Blow them out of the water," Ben said quietly.

All around the island, the big ships began unleashing their muscle. The small boats of the twenty-first-century pirates had no chance against the guns of the Rebels.

"Prepare to take prisoners," Ben gave the orders. He sipped at a mug of coffee.

When the few surviving pirates were hauled on deck, they lay looking up into the hard faces of the world's most highly trained and motivated soldiers, well-fed, groomed, eyes shining with good health.

"Mercy," one said.

"That's us," a Rebel told him. "Angels of mercy, for sure."

The pirates were jerked to their feet and shoved down passageways, to be inspected by doctors and then tossed in the brig. They would be tried by the island's civilians once the area was secured. And the Rebels had little doubt but what most, if not all of them, would hang.

Ben looked at his watch. "Prepare to jump off," he said to Corrie.

"Yes, sir. SP teams report the airport area is ringed with outlaws. They haven't been able to make much of a dent in their defenses."

"Tell them to hold what they've got and keep their heads down. We're on the way." Ben stepped over the railing onto the rope ladder. "Let's go."

Ben's battalion struck left and right of the airport and drove in hard, while only a very light force struck directly in, but producing enough firepower to make the outlaws think the main thrust was coming at them head on and right out of the sea. They threw everything they had at the smaller force. Ben closed the pincers, and the small force of Rebels withdrew to either side of the airport. By the time the outlaws realized what had happened, they had but one direction to run: straight into the sea.

They threw down their weapons and sat down on the ground, the concrete, the tarmac, and the floor, holding their hands high above their heads.

"Shit!" one Rebel bitched. "There ain't a good fight to be had anywhere."

The other battalions were experiencing the same lack of resistance. When the outlaws saw the massive numbers of troops coming straight at them, the fight went out of most of them and they threw down their weapons.

Those who tried to run back into the jungles fared much, much worse, as they ran into bands of Tahitians who hacked them to death with machetes and axes, beat their heads in with clubs and stones, or drove spears through them. The citizens were in no mood to strike any sort of bargain with those who had so tormented them over the long and painful years since the Great War rocked the earth and destroyed nearly all vestiges of civilization and order.

By noon of that day, Ben had assembled a dozen men and women who appeared to be respected by their other countrymen and -women and sat them down.

"We're not here as conquerors," he told them. "These are your islands. We'll stay until the outlaws are rounded up and tried—and how they are tried is entirely up to you people."

"They will be hanged," one woman said. "Promptly."

Ben shrugged. "That's up to you. We're leaving you all the captured weapons. I would suggest you familiarize yourselves with them and get some sort of organized resistance force together as quickly as possible. We might never be back."

That got them moving.

Ben drove over to the capital city, Papeete. It was nearly in ruin. The outlaws and pirates had looted and vandalized everything. Ben noticed the bodies hanging from lampposts and tree limbs and power poles and sturdy awnings. He made no mention of them.

Ben sent those battalions he'd held in reserve over to Mooréa and they found much the same as Ben and his people had on the bigger island—very light resistance and many, many prisoners. Ben ordered the prisoners be turned over to the Tahitians. Let them deal with the problem.

They did. Very expeditiously.

Ben set some of his people to training the police and the newly formed citizen-soldiers who would make up the Tahitian Army. Several hundred of the outlaws and pirates had made it back into the rugged interior of the two bigger islands.

"Do we clean them out?" Ike asked.

"No. Let these people do it. They know the country, and I think they'll do a good job of it." He handed Ike a thick folder. "Maps of Hawaii and many of the towns on the islands. Pass them around." He held up another folder. "Maps of the Marquesas. Only six of the islands were populated — at the time those maps were made, that is. And the entire population was about seven thousand. I don't have any idea what we're going to find over there, Ike."

Ike's sailor eyes quickly scanned the charts. "About seven hundred and fifty miles from here."

"Pretty good, Ike," Ben said with a smile. "It's seven hundred and forty. Communications have picked up a lot of chatter. We're going to have some resistance, but many of the pirates have set sail, or steamed, whatever, for Hawaii. Those islands are going to be a real humdinger." Ben looked at his closest friend. "You have something on your mind, Ike?"

"Not really. I just never did like Hawaii. And I always got the feeling that the true Hawaiians didn't like me, either."

Ben nodded his head. "You want to take your

battalion on back to the States, Ike?"

Ike looked startled, then laughed out loud. "Oh, hell, no, Ben. But you know me; you ask me a question, I'm going to tell you the truth. I just never could shake the knowledge that it was their ancestors who *ate* Captain Cook."

Ben laughed at his friend. "Now, Ike, history says they killed them. I don't whether they ate him or not. Anyway, our ancestors burned people at the stake as witches."

Ike tried his best to look hurt. He didn't make it. "Not mine, Ben. Mine just planted cotton down in Mississippi."

Order was very quickly restored on the islands. None of the new groups of citizen-soldiers brought back any prisoners from the interior, and Ben said nothing about it. Neither did he say anything when men and women who had collaborated with the outlaws and pirates were executed. The Tahitians had learned a hard lesson about justice when the criminal element had taken over, and Ben felt that episode would not be repeated.

Rebel engineers worked side by side with Tahitian engineers to restore power to the islands, and communications were established with Base Camp One in the States. Three weeks after the Rebels sailed in, they sailed out, heading for the Marquesas. Those islands would be their last stop before they launched their assault on the Hawaiian chain.

And Ben made it clear to his people that the

assault on the Hawaiian chain was going to be a piss-cutter. This time they could not stand back and punish the enemy with artillery fire. They were going to have to go in from the git-go and slug it out. The Rebels were going to take casualties, and they probably would be high.

Ben never lied to his people, so they knew that when he told them the battle was going to be a tough one, it would be.

The trip to the Marquesas was a short one, and the convoy approached the small islands and slowed to a crawl.

"The pirates are getting antsy, General," Corrie told him. "There is a lot of nervous chatter going on."

"I'd be nervous, too, if I was in their shoes," Ben said. "Corrie, tell communications to advise those outlaws on the islands I will give them one chance to surrender. If we have to come ashore fighting, there will be very few prisoners taken."

The sight must have been both awesome and terrifying to those on the small islands. The outlaws and pirates and thugs paled at the sight of the huge ships with thousands of Rebel troops on board.

Corrie listened for a moment, then smiled. "General . . . they have no stomach for a fight. They're packing it in."

"Well, *shit!*" Jersey said. "Are we ever going to see any action?"

Once again, the Rebels assumed the role of administrators and set about bringing order and justice back to the people of the small island chain. The only Rebel blood that was spilled came from the bite of a vicious little sand gnat called the nono fly. The bite is painless, but scratch it—and scratch it you will—several hours later, and the welt will burst, bleed, and become infected unless immediately treated.

"Irritating little bastards!" Ben muttered, mightily resisting the urge to scratch.

"I'd rather be fighting people," Cooper bitched. "At least you can *see* them."

Ben left the fate of the prisoners to the Marquesans. And as happened on Tahiti, the islanders dealt with them quickly. Ben did not ask what they did with the bodies. However, not all were hanged or shot, for the island's structures and roads needed rebuilding. Many prisoners were put to work, under heavy guard.

"These people also practiced cannibalism," Ike said, reading from a book. "Or their ancestors did, rather."

Ben smiled and slapped at a gnat. "Don't worry, Ike. There isn't a pot on this island big enough to put you in."

Dr. Chase stood by the railing beside Ben as the convoy began its last leg, toward Hawaii. "What will it be like here fifty years down the road, Ben?" His eyes were on the island, now rapidly fading from view.

"As isolated as they are, Lamar. God only

352

knows. They are the most remote islands on the face of the earth. But, with Tahiti once more with order and law, the old link will probably be restored. It's up to them, now."

Corrie walked up. "General, Communications says we have distress signals, in English, coming from American Samoa, and the same from the Fijis. The captain wants to know what course to set."

Chase laughed at the expression on Ben's face. "It's still part of America, Ben."

"Yeah. I know. All right, Corrie. Let's go see Pago Pago. How far is it, anyway?"

"A little over two thousand miles," Beth told him.

"Wonderful," Ben said dryly. "There is nothing like an ocean cruise to clear one's head. How's Cooper?"

"Down below," Jersey replied. "Puking."

The convoy turned west. But this time, unlike the long voyage around the Horn, they began seeing ship after ship, long dead in the water. Teams boarded the ships, inspecting them and returning with the logbooks.

Ben held the decade-old log of a freighter, turning it around and around in his hands. His thoughts were not of the logbook, however. They were of the old tourist pamphlet he'd read that morning. About American Samoa.

"Corrie, are we still receiving distress signals from Samoa and Fiji?"

"Yes, sir. Those people must really be taking a pasting to have held on this long."

Dr. Chase looked at him. "What's on your mind, Ben?"

"It's a trap," Ben said, tossing the log to a Rebel. "We're being set up."

"Those calls sound pretty damned sincere to me," Chase said.

"Oh, I'm sure they are. But from whom? Look, at the start of the Great War, the entire population of those islands was only about thirty-five thousand. Disease, pirates, outlaws, all those things would have taken a toll. These calls are coming from Pago Pago, right, Corrie?"

She nodded.

"A decade ago, three thousand population. Say it's still that, although doubtful. Five hundred would be men able to fight. Holding off hordes of invaders all these days we've been at sea, Lamar? Not likely."

"But how would they fool us long enough to get us ashore once we're there and have seen it?" Jersey asked.

"Mock battles, at first. Then, as soon as we storm ashore, the so-called enemy would retreat. We'd follow, and they'd have us in a trap. Corrie, I want Communications to press those beleaguered people for details. I want numbers, how many are defending, how many attacking. How long they've been under attack, wounded, food and ammo supplies left, where they want us to land, the whole nine yards."

"Right, sir."

354

"And get all the batt comms on this ship, pronto."

"Right, sir."

Ben smiled. But it was not a pleasant thing to witness. "They want to play deadly games? I can do that."

Fifteen

Ben read the reports and knew he'd been right. They were sailing into a trap. The answers to the questions Communications had asked were too pat, too quick, and too obviously a lie.

"Eyes in the skies," Ben ordered. "Turn them into flying gas tanks if you have to, but I want them ranging out as far as they can safely go. We're either being followed or closely tracked electronically, or they've got attack vessels tucked away behind some of these tiny islands. You can bet your bippy on that."

"Maintain course and speed?" the Captain asked.

"Right. Stay with it. Ike, you and Dan get your special ops people ready to go in. Use your minisubs and underwater delivery vehicles. Dan, your people go in silently and in blackface."

Both men nodded and left the room.

Ben lifted the reports and read them again. "Bastards," he muttered.

"We get some action this time, huh, General?" Jersey asked.

"You bet, Jersey. This will warm us up for Hawaii."

"This going to take long?"

"It might take longer than we think. But the big island is only about fifty square miles. Shouldn't take us too long."

"Are we going to this Fiji place?"

"I don't know, Jersey. I just don't know."

Corrie stuck her head inside the room. "Bingo, General. Choppers found some ships all tucked in nice." She moved to the wall map. "Around this little bit of an island here." She pointed. "Choppers veered off just as soon as the ships were sighted. The spotters were using powerful binoculars, so there is a good chance they weren't seen."

"Good. We'll keep monitoring their distress calls to see if there is any change in voice timbre." He looked up as Buddy and Rebet walked in. Ben pointed to the map. "When we get here, sometime late tomorrow, we'll slow speed down to dead slow or whatever it's called and launch our night attack from that point. We'll go in right behind the special ops people. One hour before dawn."

"Who will be leading the assault?" Buddy asked.

Ben looked at him and smiled.

The pirates later confessed that they were sure Ben and the Rebels would just sail right into Pago Pago's deep-sheltered harbor, which is guarded by a twenty-one-hundred-foot peak called Matafao. Once there, the pirates planned to use fast little torpedo boats to sink some of the Rebel ships and block the harbor. How they planned on

357

eventually removing the huge sunken transports was something to which they had not given any thought at all.

It was all moot anyway, as a pirate on guard turned to a friend in the darkness. It was an hour before dawn. "Cigarette, Marcel?" he asked.

Marcel did not reply. It would have been nothing short of a miracle had he said anything.

"You asleep, hey, *mon ami?*" the pirate asked. He touched his friend on the shoulder and the man fell over. The pirate dropped to his knees in the gloom and touched the man's neck, feeling for a pulse. What he found was stickiness. His friend's throat had been sliced. He jumped up and opened his mouth to yell. A wire was looped around his throat and jerked tight, cutting off the shout. He died a moment later as a knife was jammed into his stomach and ripped upward, cutting the heart. His body was lowered to the ground.

Two of Ike's SEALs smiled at each other and moved on.

All around the edges of the U-shaped harbor, dead pirates lay in their own blood, their throats sliced wide open.

Pirate commanders began to feel a chill as their radio operators could not contact guardposts. "Find out what's happening. Contact the lookouts on the bluffs above the harbor."

Silence greeted their calls. Dan's Scouts had moved through the town like wraiths, climbed the bluffs, and eased into position. Ten minutes before the assault boats carrying the Rebels were to hove off from the mother ships, they went about their deadly business.

Then both special ops teams began blocking roads. There is only fifty miles of paved highway on the island, and once the intersections were blocked, travel by vehicle was severely hampered.

Tension grew on the island and many pirates began to panic, looking wildly around them as the silence grew.

"Assault craft approaching the coast!" one of the few lookouts left shouted. "Jesus Christ, I never seen so many boats. They's thousands of troops."

His words were a prelude to dying as a special ops member tossed a fire-frag grenade into the room and ducked as the lookout was splattered on the walls.

Charges planted by the special ops teams were detonated, the explosions rocking the pre-dawn. Rebels stormed ashore and set about their deadly trade.

"Squad one here," Ben called. He pointed to a stone fence. "Set your machine gun there. You two put some rockets into that house right in front of us."

The house erupted in shattered wood and stone and body parts. Heavy machine gun fire hammered the cool darkness.

The pirate in charge, who was later identified as a thug named Leo, screamed out orders, trying to rally his forces. But his forces were demoralized and scared, and many of them were already dead as the Rebels' advance was sudden and mer-

ciless. They took very few prisoners. If anyon
greeted them with a gun in hand, they were dea
on the spot. There were a lot of dead in a ver
short time.

Ben's team was on the move, and his platoo
was having a hard time just keeping up with him
Ben grabbed up a pale and badly frightened littl
boy. The child trembled in his arms. "Where ar
your parents, boy?"

"Dead, sir," the child replied. "I'm the slave o
Leo. I jumped out the winder when the shootin
began."

"You're nobody's slave," Ben told him, the
handed the child to a medic. "Check him ove
and get him back to safe lines. Come on
people."

"God damn it, Father!" Buddy yelled from be
hind him. "Will you slow down and hunt a
hole?"

"No," Ben called over his shoulder. "You eithe
lead, follow, or get the hell out of the way."

"I'm *trying* to follow," his son yelled.

Everybody hit the ground as several heavy ma
chine guns opened up, the lead howling and whis
tling over their heads. Ben and his people rolle
for the safety of walls.

"Grenades on three," Ben called. "Pass th
word."

The count went down and two dozen grenade
blasted the grayness of dawning in the smal
town. The machine-guns fell silent. Moanin
drifted to the Rebels.

Ben was up and running for a grocery store—o

360

what had once been one. He ran through the empty doorframe, his CAR-15 rattling as shapes spun around in the gloom, weapons lifting. It was 9mm slugs that spun them around. Ben dropped to one knee, giving those behind him room to fire. The old store trembled as M-16's, M-60's, and Stoners roared and clattered. The rear wall of the store was slick with blood and pocked with bullet holes.

Ben ran up the short block and ducked into another store just as hostile fire opened up from the second floor of a building across the street. A dozen M203 grenade launchers thumped in the dawning and the entire second floor was blown apart.

"Ike reporting one of the canneries is ours and the second one is under hard attack by Rebet," Corrie said.

Buddy had rallied a full platoon and came running up to flop down beside his father, as the other Rebels fanned out around Ben's position.

"Where have you been, boy?" Ben asked, a smile on his lips. "Resting?"

"Very funny, Father. Quite amusing. What are your plans now? Other than playing the hero, that is."

Ben chuckled. "Taking the old hotel, one block over and just up the street."

"Now, if you have never before been here, as you said, just how do you know that?"

"I looked at a map, son. Let's go!" Ben was up and running, his team right behind him, Buddy and the platoon bringing up the rear, with

Buddy doing some pretty fancy cussing, all of it directed at his father.

A line of pirates tried to run across the street. Ben and his team cut them down and left them flopping as they jumped over the bodies and headed for the old Rainmaker Hotel. Every ground floor window suddenly bristled with guns and the Rebels hit the streets, rolling and ducking for cover.

"Launch the gunships," Ben spoke to Corrie. "Take the hotel down. All Rebels, back off a block. Now. Move!"

The Rebels pulled back as the choppers came hammering in, unleashing their terrible array of weaponry.

Within seconds, the old hotel was burning from the rocket attack and pirates were running outside for safety. Had they come out weaponless, they would have been taken alive. But they chose to come out shooting. That lapse in judgment got them Rebel bullets and very quickly dead. The choppers headed for the airport to give Striganov and his battalion a hand. Just over an hour later, Pago Pago was, for the most part, in Rebel hands.

By the end of that day, it was apparent that the pirates had killed a large part of the population of the island.

"They were very cruel people, General," a man introduced as Paale said. He had been in the House of Representatives before the Great War. "They tortured and raped and mutilated for the fun of it. When they wanted to have target practice, they used the old and the sick for targets."

"Western Samoa?" Ben asked.

"The same. It will not be so easy over there. Those are two big islands. Twenty times our size."

"We'll secure it," Ben assured the man.

"How about trials and punishment for those taken alive?"

"That's up to you people."

Paale smiled, excused himself, and went off to aid in the hunt for fugitive pirates. Ben had a hunch that justice was going to come down very quick and very final.

He turned to Corrie. "Have Thermopolis, West, Danjou, and Dan's battalions establish a beachhead on Upolu. We'll clean up here and join them in the assault on Savaii."

"Right, sir."

Within minutes, the big ships had ceased their slow circling and were heading for Western Samoa.

"That wasn't no fair court of law!" a pirate protested, his hands tied behind his back. "You can't just take me out and hang me."

"You want to bet?" a Samoan asked him, prodding him along with the muzzle of a rifle.

The pirate spotted Ben. "Hey! Soldier boy. You can't let them do this to me. I'm American. Just like you."

"There is nothing about you that is like me," Ben told the man. He looked at Jersey. "Now he's going to tell me he was abused as a child."

"Right," she said.

"I was abused as a child!" the pirate said. "Society made me do all them things I done."

"Poor fellow," Beth said. "My heart just goes out to him."

Buddy looked at her. "I can see that you are awfully upset about it."

Beth took a bite of sandwich and washed it down with water from her canteen. "Sure," she said.

The Rebels were ice-cold emotionally when it came to criminals. Whenever one of them wanted a good laugh, Ben always kept copies of books and newspapers and magazine articles for them to read. The books and articles were collected souvenirs from the 1970s, and '80s, all written by so-called experts on the subject of crime. The Rebels thought it hysterically funny when they read the theories about why people turn to a life of crime and do horrible things to other people. It cracked them up when they read that because a coach wouldn't let a kid play, the kid immediately went out and hacked his grandmother to death and then got off without serving any time, or at best, a few months or years. Hack your grandmother to death in any Rebel society and you might have time to pray (but do it quickly) before somebody slipped a noose around your neck and stretched it.

The Rebels knew for a fact, because it was a fact, that people who entered into a life of crime did so because they wanted to. Most of the Rebels now serving had been through the most traumatic experience that anyone could endure—the Great War and its hideous aftermath—and they didn't turn to a life of crime because of it. Most of them ignored the newly hanged bodies.

Ben toured what he could of the island with Paale and suggested that the two Samoas unite for more than just safety's sake.

"I think we most certainly will do that, General," Paale said. "We were talking about it when the pirates came. We just were not prepared for them."

"You will be when we leave," Ben assured him.

The assault on Tutuila had taken the fight out of the pirates who occupied the islands of Western Samoa. They put up a half-hearted resistance for a few hours and then gave it up before the Rebels could even get all their troops ashore. They were a sullen bunch as they were herded into groups and placed under guard, awaiting trial. Most of them knew what lay ahead for them, but this way, at least they would be alive for a few more hours or a few more days.

"What's at Fiji?" Ben asked Paale.

"More of the same as you found here," he was told. "Although not on such a grand scale. The pirates could not conquer such a large population. They control maybe ten of the one hundred inhabited islands. With us fighting with you, one of your battalions could easily retake the chain."

"We'll make it two battalions, just to be on the safe side," Ben told him.

Ike and West and their battalions, plus a contingent of Samoan men, sailed off the next morning, the Samoans using pirate vessels. The two battalions would link up with the convoy at the Phoenix Islands.

Ben and his people were one day away from sailing when Ike radioed. "All gone, Ben," he reported. "As soon as the pirates here got word of our sailing toward Tahiti, they split for Hawaii. They left a lot of gear behind and I've distributed that among the islanders. I'm sailing this evening. I'll check out the Wallis Islands while you're checking the Tokelau Islands. See you, Eagle. Shark out."

Ben had met with Paale and the other leaders of the island, including representatives from Western Samoa. Trade would once more resume between them and the United States mainland, for Ben and his people had been starved for tuna. Before the Great War, American Samoa had shipped nearly $300 million in tuna to America. Rebel engineers had worked side by side with islanders in helping to restore the old canneries and Ben was leaving Rebels behind to make damn sure no dolphins were caught and killed in the nets.

Paale had smiled at that. "You would kill a man in a heartbeat, General. But you are more concerned with a fish, hey?"

"I think you know that a dolphin isn't a fish, Paale."

The man nodded his head. "Oh, sure. You know what I mean."

"We have a chance to save this planet, Paale. Make up for the wrongs that were done to it. I intend to see that I do my part in it."

366

"You are a hard man, General."

Ben smiled. "Hard times, brother."

"There are no signs of life, Father," Buddy said, lowering his binoculars. They were anchored just off the small atolls that made up the Tokelau Islands.

"There were about fifteen hundred people here before the war Ben replied. "Get a landing party together, son. Let's go check this out. Parties to inspect all three atolls. It shouldn't take long," he added dryly. "All three islands make up only 3.9 square miles."

The Rebels inspected all the islands. They found no evidence of human inhabitation . . . there had been none for years. Most of the homes were intact. Hollowed-out coconut tree trunks, used for rain catchments, were overflowing. The schools and hospitals, on each island, were intact.

Dr. Chase had tagged along. "They were pretty nice hospitals, I'd say. At one time." He picked up a metal medical chart holder and opened it.

"All that scribbling tell you anything?" Ben asked.

He closed the metal folder and tossed it on the rat-chewed mattress. "Yeah. Fellow had a hernia."

Sixteen

The convoy became whole again after linking up with Ike and West at the uninhabited atolls that make up the Phoenix Islands. The convoy changed course and headed for Kiritimati Island, better known as Christmas Island, just about twelve hundred miles from the Hawaiian Islands. The island had an airfield, a good port, and before the Great War, a large government-owned copra plantation. Now it was deserted.

As had become their pattern, the Rebels went ashore and carefully inspected the island. Before the war, the island had had a population of just over a thousand. The Rebels could find no clues as to where the inhabitants had gone, or why. And as before, Ben ordered these words chiseled into stone: THIS ISLAND INSPECTED BY THE MULTINATIONAL FORCE KNOWN AS THE REBELS, THIS DATE, AND FOUND IT DESERTED AND VOID OF HUMAN LIFE.

"I suspect we'll find nothing at Johnston Island," Ben said. "But there were about four hundred souls there when the war broke out. Let's go take a look."

They found the skeletons of about a hundred

people, stacked in a large concrete block building with the doors locked. But the Rebels could find nothing to tell them why the bodies had been stacked there, or what had caused the people's deaths.

"This place was used as a chemical weapons dump," Ben told the landing party. "Makes me nervous. There is no telling what kind of crap is stacked and stored and buried around here. All in the name of peace, of course. Let's get the hell out of here. Corrie, advise all Batt Coms to gather on my ship. We're only seven hundred miles from Honolulu. We've got a lot of planning to do."

With the convoy under way and fresh coffee poured, the battalion commanders gathered. Ben stood up in front of a large wall map of the Hawaiian Islands. He held a pointer. "Our communications people had been hard at work. The big island of Hawaii is where the majority of all pirate and outlaw radio chatter is concentrated. Maui and Oahu hold the next concentration. Kauai and Lanai come next. We have received no, repeat, *no* chatter at all from Molokai. That tells me we have a landing site all ready to receive."

"Why has there been no radio traffic from this island, General?" Pat O'Shea asked, a puzzled look on his face.

"I can guess," Ben said with a smile. "But I would rather you people put it together." He lifted his coffee mug and took a sip.

Georgi Striganov grunted, then smiled. "When the pirates and outlaws and thugs first showed

369

up," he said, "I would guess the residents of Molokai played on their fears and put up signs warning that the island was quarantined due to an outbreak of Hansen's Disease. Leprosy. Molokai is where the large colony is."

Thermopolis said, "So the islanders played on the pirates' fear. They probably showed them grossly exaggerated photos of quote/unquote 'victims,' and that scared the shit out of the pirates."

"Precisely," Ben said. "Most intelligent people know there is little to fear from the disease. But you can bet the residents of Molokai played up the worst, probably put on an Academy Award winning performance and the pirates got the hell off that island and to this day leave them alone. We've got a number of native Hawaiians in our ranks. Find them and ask for volunteers to go ashore and check out the island. Get on that promptly. If what we think is correct, we'll land there, establish a command post, and begin launching assaults from all over the island. If our thoughts prove out incorrect, we'll just have to hit the bastards head on."

Ben looked at Ike. "Might be a problem getting them ashore."

The ex-SEAL smiled reassuringly. "No sweat, Ben. We have ways of delivering them."

Ben nodded and sat back down at the table. "Let's kick it around, people."

"If those people on Molokai pulled this off," Dr. Chase said, chuckling at the thought, "they've pulled off the greatest con since the Piltdown Man. For if memory serves me correctly, the col-

370

ony there closed down years before the war and became a National Historical Park, with guided tours and the whole bit. The people who remained on, calling it home, were no longer contagious and were free to leave. In addition to that, Father Damien, the Belgian priest who really got the colony off the ground and really cared for the patients, and restored dignity to those confined there, was, ironically, the only voluntary resident who ever contracted the disease."

"When was that, Lamar?" the mercenary, West, asked.

"Oh . . . back in the late 1800s."

"Back when Lamar was just a lad," Ben said. The crusty old doctor gave him the bird.

When the convoy drew within a hundred miles of the coast of the Hawaiian chain, the ships began a long, slow circling. They had seen no other vessels on the water, other than floating derelicts, which they always boarded, inspected, and then scuttled.

"They'll be expecting us from the south," Ben said. "So we'll fool them and come in from the northwest. I was thinking of running between these two islands here, Necker and Niihau, but if the pirates have any sense, they've got patrol boats working all up and down the southern coast. We'll swing wide and come in at night to put ashore our people. If anybody's got any objections, now is the time to voice them."

No one did.

Ben nodded at Corrie and she called the bridge, okaying the change in course.

"Are the Hawaiians briefed and ready to go?" Ben asked.

"Yeah," Ike said. "They're anxious to go home. Two lived on Molokai and have plenty of family there. The Hawaiians probably will not return to the States with us."

"That's fine. I intend to leave Rebels on the islands once we've cleared them. Only a few more days, people." He grinned at Jersey, knowing what she would say.

"Yeah," the little bodyguard said. "Kick-ass time!"

The convoy was not spotted after it changed course, and it gave the big island a wide berth, ran for half a day, then cut west. The Hawaiian Rebels and two special ops teams went over the side at full dark and disappeared into the Pacific night. The huge convoy backed off and began circling while they waited for work.

Ben was awakened at midnight. "You called it, Father," Buddy told him. "That's exactly what the residents of the island did. But the pirates have grown suspicious over the years and now the island is cut in half. The thugs and pirates control the western half, and the eastern half is the so-called confinement area of the sick. Of course, there are no sick."

Ben was instantly awake and dressing. "We start going in now, son. Have the special ops people found a harbor?"

"They haven't, but the people who live there know of one. I've got it marked out in the ward-room."

"Let's go. Get my battalion up and ready to move, son. Like right now. I'm sick of this damn tub."

Ike and the others yelled and bitched and kicked things and behaved predictably when they learned that Ben and his battalion were going in first. But it didn't do any good.

"Georgi and Thermopolis, your battalions come in right behind me, followed by Dan and West, Danjou and Rebet, Pat and Tina. Ike, your battalion stays behind and mans the guns of this convoy. You know the convoy is going to be at-tacked."

"All right, Ben." Once orders were given, Ike would not argue with them. Usually.

"The rest of you, get back to your ships." He looked at the captain of the flagship. "Get us in close, Captain," Ben ordered.

"You'll be there before you know it," the cap-tain said.

"Take one day's rations," Ben told his platoon leaders just before jump off time. "Food should be plentiful on the island. I'm not sure about the water, so take plenty of purification tablets. And all the ammo you can comfortably carry." The Rebels noticed that Ben was once more carrying his old Thunder Lizard, the big M-14.

Ben walked off to be alone for a few moments, while the landing craft were being readied.

"Landing craft are ready, sir," Corrie said.

"Let's go," Ben said, and stepped over the railing.

The captain had brought them in as close as he dared on this moonlit night. But the waters were calm and the ride in was smooth and uneventful. The special ops team signaled with a single strobe and the landing craft veered slightly, slowed, and crunched onto the sandy beach.

"Welcome to Hawaii, General," a burly man with a wide grin said, stepping forward and holding out a hand. "And, sir may I add that we are damn glad to see you."

Ben shook the hand and stepped out of the way, allowing his people room to exit the craft.

"Jim Peters is the name," the man said.

"What's the situation, Jim?"

"First thing the pirates did was collect every gun on every island. When we knew that our leprosy ruse wasn't going to protect us very much longer, a few of us, pitifully few, wrapped up our shotguns and rifles and buried them along with what little ammo we had. Outlaws are just like politicians, aren't they, General Raines? Take the guns and you control the people."

Ben chuckled and slapped the man on the back. "Jim, I think you're going to be a fine Rebel."

The men stood shoulder to shoulder, watching as Ben's One Battalion silently stormed the beach and formed up into columns. Jim would leave residents to meet each landing party and guide them to their assigned destinations.

"We've got a pretty good walk, General," he

old Ben, "but a safe one. This entire end of the island is void of thugs and pirates and their ilk. They're still frightened to death of Hansen's Disease, especially when they learned that we had no more medicines left to treat it."

"Do you have anyone with the disease?"

Jim laughed. "No, sir. Not a soul."

The Rebels made it ashore and then kept their heads down until all battalions and mounds of equipment had been safely off-loaded. Ike then took the convoy out to sea. The Rebels stayed low during the day and marched at night. Jim and friends came up with horses and mules and burros to bring in the tons of equipment that had been hidden in the lush vegetation along the beach. Quietly, the Rebels got into position on the east side of the highway that marked the boundaries. Ben told Jim to pass the word for the citizens to get ready to move west into the forbidden zone at a moment's notice.

"We can't possibly hope to get everybody out, and you'd better understand that you will take civilian dead and wounded."

"I understand," Jim said. "We all do."

"We've got to take this harbor here at Kaaupapa and also the airport for our attack choppers to land and refuel. These four towns, plus the harbor and the airport have to be taken simultaneously. Or within moments of each other. We're going to be moving very fast, Jim. And believe me, when the Rebels start to move, anyone with hostile intent who gets in our way is dead."

"I understand."

Ben looked at all the other leaders who had gathered in the house just off of highway 450 and just east of the town of Kaunakakai. "There is something else you'd all better understand. These are Rebels laying down their lives for you people. This is American soil. The Rebels run America. These islands will come under Rebel rule and Rebel law. There will be no ifs, ands, or buts about it. Does everybody understand that?"

"It's clear, General," an elderly man said. "Your way is harsh, but so are the times. Your laws and rules are not nearly as harsh as the men and the women who have enslaved our people, and murdered and raped and tortured for all these years. They have killed a full quarter of the population. They have desecrated the holiest of our places. They have raped tiny children. They have killed human beings for sport. But you know all this. You and your people have been fighting against these types for years. None of us will interfere in any way. You have my word on that."

The others nodded in agreement.

"Everyone is in place, General," Corrie said, walking into the den of the home. "Ike says the convoy has, miracle upon miracles, not been detected."

"Thank you, Corrie. Get some rest. Jim, tell your people to start making themselves scarce at dark. We're going in at midnight. By dawn, I intend to have two-thirds of this island in Rebel hands."

The others raised eyebrows at that. They muttered and mumbled and shook their heads at the statement. "But that is impossible, General," one said. "This island is fifty miles long and ten miles wide. And your people are *afoot!*"

"We won't be afoot long, I assure you all of that. Now get some rest. We're going to be needing your help tonight. And it's going to get real busy, real quick."

Ben walked the edge of the highway. He was only a mile from the town of Kaunakakai, on the bottom of the island. Dan and two other battalions were poised to strike at the harbor at the top of the island. Several other small villages had already been taken by the Rebels, silently and deadly. Buddy and his Rat Team had moved in, located the pirates and thugs, and taken them out with very sharp knives.

Ben glanced at his watch, then at Corrie. He nodded his head. "Give the orders, Corrie. Let's take this damn island!"

Seventeen

The town of Kaunakakai was the largest on the island, with a population of about twenty-five hundred before the war. Its business district was three blocks long. Jim and the others had pointed out the houses where pirates would be sleeping, and Buddy and his Rat Team had already pinpointed machine gun emplacements and where the heaviest concentration of pirates would be found.

The Rebels waited until the town had been blanketed with troops from one end to the other, then just kicked in doors and started shooting. Caught totally by surprise, the pirates and assorted thugs and no-goods were chopped up like liver.

Ben's M-14 covered a pirate who was reaching for a rifle. "No!" the man yelled, swinging the rifle around.

"Oh, yeah," Ben told him, then pulled the trigger.

The force of the slugs lifted the pirate off his knees and he staggered back, falling through a window.

Many of the pirates and slavers never had a chance to do much more than open their eyes before a machete, wielded by a man or woman who, for years, had been abused by them, neatly decapitated the thug. When the Rebels saw human heads sitting on the porch, eyes open in shock and lips pulled back in a macabre grin, they knew that house was clear. They saw a lot of houses with those bloody statements on the porch.

"Find all the vehicles that'll run and get them moving toward the edge of town," Ben told his people. "That way." He pointed to the west.

Jersey's M-16 rattled and two more pirates went down, kicking out their lives on the shoulder of the road.

The Rebels' taking of the town was swift, and by the old rulebooks of war, savage. Initially, they did not give the pirates a chance to surrender. Only when the mopping up began, by Rebels held back in reserve for just that purpose, would the slime be allowed to give it up.

Buddy kicked in a door just as a man was frantically calling on a radio. "The goddamn Rebels are here, I'm tellin' you. Can't you hear the damn shootin'? I . . ."

Buddy ended the transmission, the pirate's life, and the usefulness of the radio with .45 caliber slugs from his Thompson. He jerked a frightened woman off the soiled sheets of the bed and slung her toward the porch. Half a dozen citizens were waiting there, stony-faced and hard-eyed. It would not be a pleasant night for those who had chosen to collaborate with the criminal element on the island.

"They'll kill me!" the woman wailed.

"That's your problem," Buddy told her, then stepped off the porch and went trouble-hunting in the night.

There wasn't that much more trouble to be found in town. Most of the pirates who'd escaped the initial attack had fled into the night. And that was not terribly smart of them, for hundreds of islanders waited in the thick vegetation, machetes and axes in hand. The island would run red with criminal blood by the time the sun's light touched it several hours from now.

Calling in those Rebels left in reserve to secure the town and the harbor just a few miles from it, Ben and his battalion headed out in commandeered vehicles, racing up Highway 460 toward the Molokai airport on Mauna Loa Road.

All along the route, they saw islanders standing by the sides of the road, all of them smiling and waving, and many of them with bloody machetes and axes in their hands. Only a few held hunting rifles, pistols, or shotguns.

In less than one hour, the Rebels had seized control of the largest town on the island and two harbors, and with the taking of the big airport, they would be firmly entrenched on Molokai.

On the islands of Oahu, Kauai, Hawaii, and Maui and in isolated pockets on Molokai, the thugs and outlaws and pirates who more or less were in command screamed out orders and generally accomplished nothing—mainly because none of them really knew what the hell was going on.

There were thousands of criminals scattered all over the Hawaiian Islands, but they really had no plan of defense against an all-out attack from the sea. They had spent hundreds of hours, in small groups, discussing it, without ever coming up with anything.

Now they were facing the most highly trained, disciplined, and motivated army in the known world. There were others to match the Rebels in size and discipline and fighting ability, but they had not yet surfaced. But they would—soon.

"Where the hell did they come from?" a thug screamed into a mic. "Why in the hell didn't our lookouts spot them? Are these really Ben Raines' Rebels? God damn it, will somebody get off his ass and answer me?"

Everybody with a radio started talking at once, each profane and panicked signal walking all over the other. Consequently, the criminal element on the islands managed to accomplish nothing of substance in these crucial first hours of the battle. And that was exactly what Ben Raines was counting on.

"Northern and southern harbors secure, General," Corrie told Ben. "The airport on the Kalaupapa Peninsula is in Rebel hands and attack choppers are coming in from the ships."

"Very good," Ben said. He and his team were riding along in an old Cadillac stretch limo. Leave it to Cooper.

"Emil Hite thinks he might stay on this island," Corrie said with a smile, after listening to a transmission. "He just fell in love."

"I wouldn't wish Emil on anybody," Ben said. "Tell Thermopolis that I order Emil to fall out of love and get back to Rebel business."

Bullets pocked the windshield and nearly tore the steering wheel out of Cooper's hands. "Jesus Christ!" Cooper hollered. He managed to get the limo off to the side and it slid into a ditch, Ben and his team piling out into the dewy-wet vegetation.

"Someday, Coop," Jersey said. "I keep hoping you'll learn to drive."

"Are there snakes in Hawaii, General?" Cooper asked, looking around him.

"I don't think so, Coop. I don't believe reptiles ever made it here. Anybody spotted that machine gun?"

The machine gun opened up from across the road. A few of those Rebels who had been following Ben's limo chunked in grenades and the machine gun fell silent.

Buddy flopped down beside Ben. "Perhaps now, Father, you might realize that you are not invincible and allow someone else to take the point?"

Ben stared at him for a few seconds. "You know, son . . . nobody likes a smart-ass."

Then they both broke out in laughter.

Buddy took the point, leading the way to the airport.

All that night and into the next day, the Rebels fought and clawed their way to the airport and beyond, with more and more pirate reinforcements arriving from the other islands to beef up the badly demoralized thugs on Molokai. The pirates sent old and reworked torpedo boats and small armed cruisers out to try to sink the huge convoy. They couldn't even get close. The Rebels' attack helicopters creamed them almost before they got away from port. Even if the helicopters had not been able to fly, the huge guns that Ike had ordered placed on most of the ships would have knocked out the smaller craft long before they became a threat.

The pirates gave up that idea as a very bad one.

When the huge cargo and transport ships came in to off-load supplies, their escorts were Apache gunships and PT boats that Ike had ordered brought along from England. The PT boats had been reworked and refitted with the most up-to-date weaponry.

It had been a long and sometimes very rough ride for the skippers and crews of the patrol boats, but they'd made it and were now proving invaluable.

Finally, on the afternoon of the second day of the invasion of the Hawaiian Islands, the pirates stopped them, so they thought, and were jubilant about it. The pirates had pulled back to a line running north to south, about five miles west of the airport. What they didn't know was that Ben had stopped the attack for reasons of his own.

"All right," Ben told his commanders. "It's time to hit the other islands and start arming the citizens. I want special operations teams on every island, organizing resistance and pestering the crap out of these pirates. I want to make their lives a living hell. Everytime they turn around, I want something blowing up in their faces. Find out who the leaders are and start waging urban warfare against them. Pure terrorist tactics. Anything goes." The commanders all grinned at that. If the Rebels were better at one thing than another—and they were experts at all types of combat—it was guerilla warfare.

Ben looked at each batt comm. "At the conclusion of this meeting, I am going to take my battalion and Pat O'Shea's Free Irish, and we are going to go down to the lines the crud have withdrawn to and kick the shit out of them. We are going to run their asses right back into the sea. And then we are going to hoist the new American flag all over this island."

The flag displayed huge red and white and blue stripes, with an American bald eagle in the center. It had been designed by an elementary class back at Base Camp One . . . in honor of all the Rebels who had fallen in battle.

It took some getting used to, but Ben and the others had been so moved by the efforts of the kids, the flag had been adopted.

"And then, people," Ben said, "we are going to free these islands, and then we're going back home."

That brought a round of applause from the multinational commanders, who had all adopted what was left of America as their home.

Georgi Striganov, a big bear of a man, stood up. The Russian looked over at Jersey and smiled.

She returned the grin. "Yeah," she said. "Kick ass time!"